You cannot cr...
worked throug...
man.

That's not going to happen! He tried to ruin me!

Suddenly everything grew dark. The gold light disappeared. Rachel gasped, then coughed violently.

Someone was kneeling at her side, his hand gripping her shoulder. He was screaming for a medic.

She continued to gasp, forcing air into her lungs. No more smoke! She was alive!

Mind barely functioning, Rachel heard the man calling for help once again. He sounded desperate. Afraid for her. Then, as consciousness grew, Rachel felt a shock wave. The man at her side was Captain Tyler Hamilton. Tyler Hamilton, who hated her as much as she hated him.

Groaning, Rachel couldn't handle the emotional tsunami that rolled through her. She blacked out. The last thing she felt was his protective hand on her shoulder. He was the last man on earth that she ever wanted to touch her.

HIS DUTY
TO PROTECT

BY
LINDSAY McKENNA

First published in Great Britain 2012
by Mills & Boon, an imprint of Harlequin (UK) Limited,
Eton House, 18-24 Paradise Road, Richmond, Surrey TW9 1SR

© Lindsay McKenna 2012

ISBN: 978 0 263 89527 8
ebook ISBN: 978 1 408 97732 3

946-0512

Harlequin (UK) policy is to use papers that are natural, renewable and recyclable products and made from wood grown in sustainable forests. The logging and manufacturing processes conform to the legal environmental regulations of the country of origin.

Printed and bound in Spain
by Blackprint CPI, Barcelona

As a writer, **Lindsay McKenna** feels that telling a story is a way to share how she sees the world. Love is the greatest healer of all, and the books she creates are parables that underline this belief. Working with flower essences, another gentle healer, she devotes part of her life to the world of nature to help ease people's suffering. She knows that the right words can heal and that creation of a story can be catalytic to a person's life. And in some way she hopes that her books may educate and lift the reader in a positive manner. She can be reached at www.lindsaymckenna.com or www.medicinegarden.com.

On August 6, 2011, thirty brave men and a dog from the military were shot down while flying in a CH-47 in Afghanistan. I want to honor them and their courageous families. They are truly heroes and paid the ultimate sacrifice for our freedom. My prayers for each family who has lost so much. Bless them all.

Chapter 1

Captain Rachel Trayhern was five steps away from Bravo Base Operations and the control tower when the first Taliban grenade struck the tarmac.

The hot August sun beat down upon her, and their mission had just ended.

A sudden disruption made her flinch, and she whirled around at the hollow "thump" sound. Panic raced through her as she anticipated the fall. Lieutenant Susan Cameron, her copilot, had already gone inside to file their Apache gunship flight report. At least she might be safe.

The enemy grenade landed squarely on her helicopter. The ensuing explosion sent booming shock waves rippling across the landing area. Cheating death once more, the crew that was coming to hitch the Apache up with a motorized cart drove in the other direction. Fire flew toward the sky. Metal erupted and became deadly shrapnel in every direction. Thick, black smoke rolled outward and upward.

A second, third and fourth grenade popped into the sky. Rachel hit the asphalt hard, her helmet bag flying out of her hand. The August sky had been clear blue. Now, as the well-aimed grenade launchers hit the second Apache and a CH-47 Chinook that had landed a few minutes earlier, the whole airport was under siege. *Attack!*

Gasping, Rachel kept her hands over her head. Her helmet bag lay nearby but not close enough. The smoke was thick and choking. She heard the surprised cries of men as the attack continued. Return fire began. Bravo Base was one of the most forward CIA operations in Afghanistan, not more than fifteen miles from the line between this country and Pakistan. And it was always a target of the Taliban.

Crawling to try and find some kind of protection, Rachel heard another *thunk* and knew the enemy had launched yet another grenade. She was out in the open and completely vulnerable. A piece of shrapnel could kill her as easily as a grenade exploding nearby. More shock waves rolled across the air facility. Shrieks of wounded began to fill the air.

Oh, God, let me get out of this alive. The Apaches roared and burned, creating smoke so thick she couldn't see one foot in any direction. Rachel heard the pounding of feet across the tarmac. Orders were screamed above the devastating attack. She felt strangled, helpless. Her brown hair fell loose from its knot, and tears ran down her face as she continued to crawl blindly along the edge of the tarmac. So far, Ops wasn't hit, but she knew the Taliban would try and take it out. She was in real danger.

With return fire of heavy artillery in full force, thumping sounds filled the smoke-clogged air. Special Forces had to be heading for the edge of the base to engage the Taliban. Bravo was surrounded by two ten-foot tall walls with razor-blade sharp concertina wire on top. Somehow, the Taliban had gotten close enough to inflict major damage. The heavy chutter of machine gun fire began in an attempt to ward off the Taliban located at the end of the runway.

Hacking and choking, Rachel crawled swiftly away from the control tower. Her elbows and knees smarted with pain, the asphalt hard on them. Her mind spun with shock over the violent attack. Somehow, she managed to scramble off the tarmac and into the weeds and dirt. She was a good fifty feet away from the tower, which was an obvious target. She worried for her co-pilot, Susan, whom she hoped had escaped in time.

A hot, black cloud of smoke overtook her. Burying her head in the grass, Rachel could barely breathe. She felt as if she were going to die. As she continued to crawl, blind and constantly coughing, she knew her only way to live was to escape the attack. The roar of the burning helos, the return fire from heavy machine guns reverberated against her unshielded eardrums. Her strength began to dissolve. She was barely getting any oxygen, so she thrust her face down into the weeds, the only place with clean air. Fire sucked and ate up oxygen. Heat from the flames rose.

The wind shifted toward her, a bad sign. Pushing forward, her flight boots digging into the hard Afghan soil, Rachel felt the small rocks and stouter weeds poking into the chest and belly of her green flight suit. She thrust out her hand, fingers like claws digging into the resisting earth. It rarely rained in August at eight thousand feet. The land was hard and unyielding.

No! I can't die! Rachel gasped like a fish out of water, saliva drooled from her mouth as she tried to suck up the life-giving air. *Oh, God, don't let me die like this!* Her vision began to gray. More smoke rolled toward her, hot and stealing her oxygen. The breeze across the mountains where the base was located was constant. Now it blew toward where she tried to crawl.

Her senses dulled and tears ran down her face. Trying with all her might to escape the smoke, she began to sob. At thirty years old, she had her whole life ahead of her. And even though she'd been an Apache gunship pilot for the last five years, she'd never thought that she'd die crawling across the ground.

Weakened, she lay still for a moment, fighting to get her consciousness back. The smoke was an oxygen-sucking monster. The heavy *chut, chut, chut* of machine guns spitting out their bullets became distant. The flames and roaring fire sounds lessened, too. Her aching ears seemed filled with cotton, erasing all the noise that had pounded relentlessly seconds earlier. Rachel collapsed, her face pressed to the ground, small rocks biting into her cheekbone. Even that pain seemed to float away. She was losing consciousness because she couldn't get enough air into her lungs. No matter what she did, she no longer had the strength to pull herself forward. The last thought she had was that after the fires were put out, they'd find her body in the weeds.

It was an ignominious end, Rachel decided. She was a combat pilot. A damn good one. She'd battled through Apache flight school and nearly got kicked out thanks to Captain Tyler Hamilton, who hated her. And yet, she'd fought back and remained to graduate.

Shutting her eyes, Rachel thought of her family. Her father, Noah Trayhern, danced before her closed eyes, his smile making her feel better. And her mother, Kit, who was a police detective, had a sharp and alert gaze. Praying, her lips moving, Rachel didn't want her parents to hear from the Army that she'd died of smoke inhalation on a barren, godforsaken mountaintop in Afghanistan.

As her world grayed, her body went slack and consciousness receded. Darkness was complete.

And then Rachel felt someone standing at her side. She couldn't see who it was, but she felt love radiating from this being.

Welcome, Rachel, the being said to her. *You are all right now. You're here to review your life. Are you ready?*

This had to be a dream. There was no voice she could hear. But she could feel the words. Confused, afraid, she looked around. Everything was a bright white light, but not so bright as to make her squint. Finally, she said mentally, *I guess I am ready.…*

She began to see the moment when she was conceived. Her mother was very young, very beautiful. Her father was in the Coast Guard, a commander of a cruiser. The love they had for one another overwhelmed Rachel. Her heart opened powerfully.

You were brought into this world with love, a voice said.

Rachel felt hot tears come to her eyes. She loved her family so much! Her given name was Melody Sue Rachel Trayhern. She laughed when she saw herself as a ten-year-old girl talking to her mother, stubbornly telling her mother that she hated the name, Melody Sue. She wanted to be called Rachel, her middle name, because that was her grandmother's name. And Rachel fiercely loved the elder. She saw her mother smile and laugh. From that point on, everyone called her Rachel.

Everything moved swiftly for Rachel as she reviewed her life. She saw four more sisters born to her parents. She was the oldest. And they'd had a very happy childhood. Rachel, the pathfinder for the family, as her father referred to her, wanted to go into the military. She'd been allowed into West Point and had been one of the top ten officers to graduate from that military academy. Rachel's gut tightened as she saw her orders were for Fort Rucker, Alabama, the flight school. She had dreamed of being a pilot, of flying, all her life. Her father told her that flying was in the blood of the Trayherns. Rachel remembered her powerful reaction to that information.

Rachel felt her heart slam shut with pain. She saw her first days at the Apache flight school. Her anger rose as she saw her instructor, Captain Tyler Hamilton. He stood in front of her company, arrogant, a real bastard, who hated women on the same tarmac with him. And he'd singled out Rachel because she was doing better than the other men learning to fly the Apache helicopter. More rage rose as she watched Hamilton plot her demise. Sheer hatred, that's what flowed through her. This son of a bitch was going to flunk her out of school. The dream of flying was dying.

Rachel, the voice said gently. *Until you make peace with this man you cannot leave.*

Confused, Rachel looked around. She was surrounded in a white-and-gold glowing fog. How she wished again she could see who owned this voice.

That way she could explain face-to-face that she could never forgive Hamilton. He tried to ruin her.

He'd said the Trayhern family was always trying to get what they didn't deserve. Well, that wasn't true. She'd worked damned hard to get her wings at Fort Rucker. She was a good pilot. That bastard wouldn't take her dream away. The Trayhern family served its country with pride and honor. No way would she stand there and let him kick her out.

Because of your ongoing hatred, you must go back and work through this with him.

Before Rachel could say a thing, she felt a powerful, whirling sensation, as if she were in a funnel, spinning around and around. Then she fell and everything grew dark. The gold light disappeared, and the blanket of love dissolved. Suddenly, it was as if an anvil were sitting on her chest. She gasped and coughed violently.

Her eyes flew open. The sunlight nearly blinded her, and she found herself on her back in the dirt and grass. Someone was kneeling at her side, gripping her shoulder. He was looking into her eyes, panic in his. His mouth opened and he raised his head, screaming for a medic.

Rachel felt the strong touch of his hand, saw the care and fear in his blue eyes. Her mind refused to work properly. She continued to gasp, grabbing her chest as if to force air into her lungs. Weapons continued to fire in the distance, and she heard men and women calling out orders. The sky. Staring up at the blue sky, Rachel blinked as her chest heaved. No more smoke! The smoke had moved. She was alive. Alive!

Mind barely functioning, Rachel heard the man at her side calling for help once again. He sounded desperate. Afraid. For her? And then as her consciousness grew, Rachel felt a shock wave of another kind roll through her. This one took her breath away. The man at her side was Captain Tyler Hamilton, the instructor pilot who had almost gotten her flunked out of Apache flight school. What the *hell* was he doing on her base? Rachel's mind shorted out, and she struggled to make sense of what was happening. Was this a nightmare?

Groaning, Rachel couldn't handle the emotional tsunami, and she blacked out. The last thing she felt was his protective hand on her shoulder. He was the last man on earth who she ever wanted to touch her.

"Rachel? Rachel, wake up...."

A woman's urgent voice filtered through her gray consciousness. Rachel frowned. There was a hand on her other shoulder now, a woman's hand. She fought to wake.

"Hey, Cousin. It's Emma. You're all right. You're going to live. Come on, wake up."

Cousin? Her mind was frayed. Rachel tried hard to surface. The hand on her shoulder was gentle and soothing, as if to remind her she was alive. Was she? Emma? Yes, she knew Emma. Emma had just married Khalid Shaheen, an Afghan officer in the U.S. Army. He flew the Apache. Rachel clung to this bit of information. If she didn't, it would leave. Desperately, she forced herself to remember. In July, everyone had gotten leave to fly back to San Francisco. Emma and Khalid had been married there in Golden Gate Park. The whole Trayhern clan had attended, including patriarch Morgan and his beloved wife Laura, Noah and Kit, and Emma's parents, Alyssa and Clay, were there to celebrate the wedding.

"Rachel? You're doing fine, you're coming back," Emma whispered near her ear. "You're here at Bravo

Camp. You're in the dispensary. You're going to be okay...."

Emma's husky voice was like a beacon. She fiercely loved Emma. And Rachel had cried when the Army had released her cousin from duty. Emma had sustained nerve damage to her left hand after being captured by the Taliban. And without her feeling in that hand, she wasn't permitted by the U.S. Army to fly her beloved Apache. But Emma was strong, and her fiancé had given her a CH-47, which his family had bought, to fly instead. Emma had come back married, and still worked out of Bravo Base with Khalid. She flew nearly every day as a civilian contractor hired by Khalid's family to deliver books and educational supplies to villages along the Afghan border. Now, Emma was here with her. Emma!

Though it felt as if bricks were weighted upon her eyes, she forced them open. Rachel saw fuzziness at first. But Emma's red hair, her face and those dancing green eyes slowly came into focus in front of her.

Emma smiled and brushed some hair away from Rachel's scrunched brow. "Hey, Cuz, welcome back to the land of the living. How are you doing?"

Rachel lifted her hand and felt an oxygen mask over her nose and mouth. The air tasted wonderful! She tried to reorient. Emma continued to gently rub her shoulder as if to coax her back to full consciousness. As she closed her eyes, the attack on the base roared back at her. The noise, the danger, the carnage. Her Apache helo had been destroyed. The thick, black smoke rolling across her and cheating her of oxygen came next.

"Come on, open your eyes, Rachel."

She obeyed and saw Emma in her dark green flight suit standing beside her. She was smiling down at her, relief clearly written in her expression. "Hey, you had me scared there for a while."

Groaning, Rachel was now aware of the frantic activity in the dispensary. There were orderlies, nurses and doctors rushing everywhere. Of course, she thought, we're under attack...people are hurt...maybe dead....

Patting her shoulder, Emma gave a sigh of relief. "You're okay, Rachel. The dude who brought you in said you'd nearly suffocated in that smoke. Thanks to him, you're alive and not dead."

Mind spinning, Rachel took off the oxygen mask. Her strength had returned. She was no longer weakened as before. Still dazed, she struggled on the gurney. Emma slid her arm around her shoulders and helped Rachel sit up.

"Hang on," Emma said, "and I'll raise this thing." She leaned down.

Rachel felt the gurney move upward to support her back. "Thanks," she rasped, touching her throat. It felt raw and hot.

Emma straightened and smiled. "How are you feeling?"

"Like I've scalded the inside of my throat," Rachel whispered.

"Here, drink some water." Emma handed her a glass.

Though her hands trembled, Rachel took it. The water tasted wonderful. The cool fluid soothed the pain. "Thanks," she said, her voice sandpapery-sounding even to her.

Taking the glass, Emma nodded. "More?"

"No." Rachel looked around to get her bearings. She'd been here at Bravo for three months. Never had she been inside the small clinic before. A number of medical people were moving and speaking quickly to one another as more injured were brought into the facility. She turned back to Emma.

"I didn't know you were here. I thought you were out flying today."

Nodding, Emma said, "I was. But I'd just landed after the Taliban attack began. Luckily, I was at the other end of the landing strip, so our helo wasn't blown away."

"God, it's awful," Rachel muttered. She pulled her legs off the gurney and allowed them to hang. Looking down, she noticed her uniform was stained with dirt and weeds. Rachel scowled. "I thought I was going to die, Emma. That damned smoke followed me like a good friend. I was in the wrong place at the wrong time...."

"You were found about a hundred feet off the revetment, Rachel. I think you knew the wind was blowing that same direction, and you were trying to crawl away from it," Emma said, her tone sympathetic.

Closing her eyes, her hands on her face, Rachel kept seeing flashes of the incident. She felt terribly vulnerable, her emotions in tatters, and her hands fell away from her face. "I have these awful images...the smells, the sounds..."

"Post-Traumatic Stress Disorder," Emma said gently. Touching her hand, she whispered, "It's going to be with you for a while, Rachel. It's important not to fight it. In time, it will go away."

Gripping her cousin's hand, she said in a wobbly voice, "Thanks for being here."

"Hey, I'm glad I was."

"Was Khalid with you?"

"No, I was flying in alone to pick up another shipment of desks and books. He's up north with his sister Kinah. We're setting up a new village today. They're up there with the teacher and introducing her around to the village elders. I got a hold of them by GPS, satellite phone, and they know we're okay."

"Good," Rachel said, feeling stronger and more alert. Though, one thing puzzled her. "You said someone brought me here?"

Emma grimaced. "Hold on to your helmet. I was already here at the clinic helping to bring in the wounded when he arrived with you in his arms. I couldn't believe it." Emma gently held Rachel's scratched and bruised hand. "You'll never guess who brought you in…. Captain Tyler Hamilton. The dude who tried to get you flunked out of flight school back at Fort Rucker."

Chapter 2

"Where do you think you're going, Captain?"

Rachel was starting to slide off the gurney when a balding physician came over. His scowl deepened. "I feel fine, Doctor. I want to get out of here."

"Hold on, you've suffered smoke inhalation."

"I'm *fine,*" Rachel insisted, remaining on the gurney. Emma had just left, and she wanted out of this crazy, busy place.

"No, you're not," the doctor said. "You've got first-degree burns in your throat from inhaling that smoke."

Coughing a little, Rachel said, "I figured that. But I want to get to my HQ. I want to make sure my copilot is all right." The fifty-something-year-old doctor rolled his eyes and then smiled.

"Captain, I've already sent an order to your CO to have you removed from the flight list for a week. You need time to let that throat of yours heal up."

"A *week* for a little smoke inhalation?" Rachel was more than a little stunned.

"Yes. Now, if you'll just sit still for about fifteen more minutes, I'll get one of my nurses over here to release you."

Shocked by the doctor's pronouncement, Rachel nodded. "I can do that, but I really don't want to not fly for seven days." That would leave her reflexes slower than usual. Rachel was used to flying every day or every other day. There were so many things to know about the Apache helicopter that it was imperative for pilots to fly often. This frequency kept them in rhythm with the multi-tasking demands made upon them.

The doctor shrugged. "Humor me, Captain. You're grounded for a week." He turned and left.

Rachel sat there gripping the sides of the gurney. Seven days was an eternity. And she felt helpless. She heard from others in the dispensary that three helicopters had been destroyed by the Taliban surprise attack. It had been a very bad day for Camp Bravo. Moving her legs back and forth out of boredom, Rachel watched the feverish pace of the dispensary. There were a lot of wounded men coming in. She was the only woman. How badly she wanted to get out of here and connect with Susan.

Her mind reverted back to what Emma had told her. How could Captain Tyler Hamilton be *here?* There were two transport squadrons at the CIA base. Apache pilots had nothing to do with them, unless used as escorts, because Chinooks lacked defenses and needed protection. Hamilton's voice was forever branded in her brain, and she would have recognized it in a heartbeat over the radio link. When did Hamilton arrive? God, she hoped his presence was temporary. Maybe he was with one of the Kandahar squadrons and had flown into the camp with some needed supplies. That meant he'd be gone by now. Back to wherever he came from. *Good riddance.*

Some relief flowed through Rachel. Her throat burned, and she reached over and picked up a glass of water sitting on a nearby stand. Of all the people in the world to rescue her! After setting the glass back on the stand, Rachel ran her fingers through her loose, dirty hair. Pieces of grass fell around her. She was filthy. All she wanted was to get the hell out of here, strip out of this smoky-smelling uniform and feel the cool water flowing across her. She could wash the dirt out of her hair, too.

A lot of old anger surfaced in her as she sat impatiently on the gurney. Hamilton had done his level best to scuttle her attempts to graduate out of Apache flight school. He was one of their top instructors. And she was the only woman in the all-male class. He'd had it in for her the moment he'd seen her at attention in the barracks. Rachel would never forget the surprise and then the raw anger that had leaped to his blue eyes as he spotted her. Her instincts told her that for some unknown reason, he'd hated her from Day One.

Rachel could never figure out why Hamilton hated her. Was it because she was a child of the Trayhern dynasty? Their family had given military service since this country had fought for its independence from England. The famous name had always preceded her. It was an honorable family tradition that most of the children of each generation would give at least six years of service to their country. Could Hamilton have hated her for that? Snorting, Rachel shook her head. Hamilton had been an enigma, always waiting for when she made a mistake to embarrass her in front of the other students. He said she couldn't fly like a man. And that is what got him in trouble.

The smell of alcohol and other antiseptics made Rachel wrinkle her nose. Couldn't she leave now? Every nurse was super busy with the wounded still coming in. Rachel pondered leaving on her own. And then she made the fatal error of looking up toward the entrance. Her lips parted in shock. Captain Tyler Hamilton walked right through the door. And he was looking for her.

Instantly, Rachel's heartbeat quickened and she gripped the gurney. Hamilton was six feet tall, lean and tightly muscled. He had military-short black hair, glacial-blue eyes, a strong chin and broad brow. He couldn't be looking for her? Impossible. How she wanted to disappear.

Anxiety and anger warred within her. Hamilton had tried to sink her career and smear her good family name. If it hadn't been for her uncle, Morgan Trayhern, Hamilton would have gotten away with it. The power that Morgan held in the military at every level had evened out the playing field. Her own father, Noah, had been in the Coast Guard for thirty years. He had flown into Fort Rucker to meet with the higher ups who had created the Apache flight program, along with her uncle Morgan. They met behind closed doors with the general. Hamilton had thought his power as an instructor pilot would bring her down and eject her from the program. He'd made a colossal mistake. No one tried to smear the Trayhern name like he had tried to do. In the end, Rachel had watched the general throw Hamilton out of the Apache program and send him to transport helicopters for the rest of his career. Further, he would never be promoted from captain. For the next twenty years he'd have no chance to climb in rank or to a better pay grade. Rachel had been told by her uncle Morgan about the behind-the-scenes change that had been made. She remembered clearly the shock written across Hamilton's face. He'd expected the general to kick her out of the program. Instead, he'd been the one jettisoned.

Lips tightening, Rachel sat back so that Hamilton couldn't see her. The bastard! She hated that he had rescued her. Five years had gone by and she'd never heard or seen him again. Until now. What kind of twisted irony was going on here? The man who hated her, who wanted her out of his training squadron had shown up again like the bad penny he was.

Rachel watched as he moved like a sinuous jungle cat through the busy dispensary. He found a nurse and talked to her. She gasped softly as the nurse turned and pointed directly at her cubicle. Damn! Hamilton turned and headed in her direction. Of all things, she didn't need this confrontation on top of all else!

Ty Hamilton approached the green-curtained cubicle where the nurse had sent him. He swallowed hard. The past was right in front of him as he walked around the desk, the other gurneys and the doctors dealing with the injured. Fear rose up in him as he drew closer to the cubicle. He couldn't see anyone, but the nurse had said Captain Trayhern was in there. He took a deep breath. With his right hand, he pulled back the curtain.

"Why the hell are you here?" Rachel snarled at him.

Taken aback, Hamilton stopped about three feet away from the gurney. The hardened look on Rachel's face made him go on the defensive. She was a beautiful woman even five years later. She'd matured and, if possible, in Ty's mind, was even lovelier than before. "I came to see if you were all right," he said in an even tone. That five years slammed back into him. She was angry. Rachel had always been a warrior. He'd seen it back in flight school. Now, sitting there, she looked like an eagle who was ready to defend over her kill. Only her gaze was directed at him.

"Get out of my life, Hamilton. I want *nothing* to do with you," she rasped.

Could he blame her for her rage? No. After all, he'd tried to deep-six her career. "Sorry, that's not going to happen."

"I don't care. Of all the people I never wanted to run into again, you're it."

He accepted her anger. In the five years since his removal by the general, who ran the Apache program, Ty had bitterly come to grips with his past. "Life is twisted, at best. You know that." He stood with his arms at his sides, his hands curving slightly. Captain Trayhern looked like she was going to leap off that gurney and attack him. His head spun with the violence of her reaction toward him. After all, he'd just saved her life. Was he expecting a thank-you? Apparently that wasn't going to happen. So why had he come looking for her? Ty didn't have an answer and that bothered him.

"No joke," Rachel snapped. She jabbed her finger in his direction. "Go back into whatever hole you crawled out of, Hamilton. I don't *ever* want to see you again. Do you understand me?"

His dark brows rose a little. Rachel's face became flushed, her gold-brown eyes narrowed on him like a hunter. He felt the full thrust of her hatred. After the secret decision by the general running the program to oust him due to his prejudice against women pilots, Ty had never seen her again. Not until now. "Five years is a long time to carry a grudge, isn't it?" he snarled back. "I just saved your friggin' life, in case you didn't realize it. If I hadn't seen you go down and the smoke covering you, you wouldn't be here right now."

Rachel squared her shoulders. "Well, let's just call it even then, shall we?"

Confused, he uttered, "What do you mean?"

"You tried to kill my career. I'll never forget what you tried to do to me. You lied to your superiors. You used every manipulation, every twist you could think of to get rid of me. I still don't know to this day why you targeted me, but that's water under the bridge. And if you saved my life, then I consider the slate between us clean. You tried to end my life back then. You saved it today."

Her raw, unfettered emotion made him step back. Apache pilots were, if nothing else, excellent killers. And the look on her face, the hoarse fury in her low voice was about killing—him. "So we're even?" he said.

"That's right, Hamilton. Now get out of my sight."

Stung, he saw Rachel point toward the opening between the curtains. Obviously, she was still reliving those events from the past. Wasn't it just like a woman to drag it into the present? In his experience, men let things like that go. They got on with life. He had. Until now. "Well, you aren't going to get your way," he warned her in a dark tone.

"What the hell are you talking about?" Anxiety sizzled through her. If Rachel had met him under any other circumstances, she'd have thought Hamilton damned handsome. Real eye candy. He appeared to be a cocky, arrogant flight jock when she'd first met him. His eyes were large and well spaced, his mouth full and certainly one that any woman would appreciate. His cheekbones were high and his black hair only accentuated his hard-jawed features.

Hamilton managed a twisted grimace with one corner of his mouth. Finally, the energy shifted to his side. "Our squadron was just assigned to Camp Bravo. We'll be stationed here for the next year." He saw the shock land across her pale features. A part of him, a tiny part, felt sorry for Rachel Trayhern. Her hair was in disarray, dirty and with bits of grass still buried in the strands. Her uniform was dusty, as well. When he'd seen her hit the asphalt and try to crawl away during the attack, he had no idea who she was. And when he'd run between the bullets and the lobbing grenades to reach her, Ty had only wanted to save a life.

Rachel felt his statement reverberate through her. She saw a bit of a savage gleam in his narrowing eyes. Realizing he was enjoying sharing that news with her made Rachel hate him even more. "You trash haulers aren't in our squadron area. That suits me fine." She'd deliberately called him a name she knew no transport helicopter pilot ever wanted to hear. The Apache pilots were the warriors of the Army helicopter fleet. Transport helos like the Chinook and their pilots were privately called "trash haulers" behind their backs. To hurl the words at him, however, was akin to throwing down the gauntlet between them once more. Rachel had no fear of this man. Her hatred of him trumped any thanks she might give him for saving her life today.

Hamilton stood there thinking through his options over her insult. The noise around them was a dull, constant roar. Doctors were yelling orders, orderlies were scrambling and nurses were hurrying at optimum speed as more injured were being brought in through the doors. Rachel was pale. She sat there coughing, her long, beautiful fingers pressed against her slender throat. Some of his anger over the insult dissolved. Without a word, he turned on his booted heel and left.

Rachel continued to cough. Relief sped through her as Hamilton exited. She watched him stalk angrily out of the dispensary, shoving the door open. It slammed against the building, he was that furious. Grabbing the glass, she poured water into it from a nearby container. She gulped the cooling liquid down her raw, burning throat and closed her eyes. She felt guilty. She shouldn't have, but she did. That bastard deserved every bit of hatred she had stored up within her. She opened her eyes and set the empty glass back on the stand.

"Captain, are you ready to leave?" A nurse with the name tag *Morayta, L.* came in. She had long, brown hair wrapped up in a knot behind her head, a stethoscope hanging around her neck. She had large, brown eyes that sparkled as she drew near.

"More than you could ever know," Rachel muttered. She had seen Lauren Morayta over at the chow hall from time to time. "You got my orders cut?"

Laughing, Lauren said, "I do." She scribbled her name on a piece of paper on her clipboard. "Dr. Henson wants to see you in three days. By then—" she turned to look around at the busy place "—we should be back to normal."

Taking the folded piece of paper, Rachel thanked her. "How many died in this attack?"

Lauren's smile disappeared. "Three so far. All burn casualties." She patted Rachel's hand. "You were the lucky one. The doctor wants you to rest for seven days."

Rachel didn't feel lucky. She slid off the gurney,

thanked the petite nurse and walked out of the chaotic dispensary. Outside, she gratefully breathed in the hot August air. Turning, Rachel walked back to her Black Jaguar Squadron headquarters. There was no way she was resting now. Black, oily smoke hung over the base like a funeral pall. Rachel could hear the roar of fire trucks over in the Ops area. She wondered if they needed help.

As she entered the busy tent, Rachel noticed how every office clerk was frantic and busy. Women were running here and there. It was an intense energy in the place as she stood just inside the door. To her relief, Rachel spotted her copilot, blond-haired Lieutenant Susan Cameron.

"Susan!" she called, hurrying over to her desk. "Are you okay?"

"Hey, Rachel. Yes, I am." She came around the desk and gave Rachel a hug of welcome. "Are you all right? I was in Ops when the attack came. I got the hell out of there and tried to find you. I never could. And then we got word from the clinic that you had suffered smoke inhalation but were going to be fine. I stayed here because they really needed me." Susan released her, relief in her gray eyes.

Rachel smiled. "It's going to take more than smoke to keep me down. Is anyone else from our squadron injured?"

"No. We're fine. Major Dallas Klein is going crazy, though."

"Why?"

"Because we've lost two Apaches."

"That sucks."

Shaking her head, Susan returned to her desk. "The major has her husband on the phone to the Pentagon right now. She's trying to find replacement Apaches for us. They aren't easy to find."

Rachel liked Major Mike Murdoch. He had joined the Army once again when his wife, Dallas, was given the BJS command in Afghanistan. "Well, if anyone can tear some Apaches loose, it's him." She rubbed her hands together. "I can hardly wait to get back in the saddle."

"Right now, we're two helos short," Susan murmured, worried. She sat down and pulled a pen from the pocket of her flight uniform. "I just hope the Pentagon doesn't screw us with wait time to get replacement Apaches. We keep our reflexes sharp because we're flying all the time."

Nodding, Rachel saw Major Klein emerge from her small office at the other end of the huge tent. She appeared grim. And when Dallas spotted her, some of that grimness fled from her expression for a moment. She seemed relieved to see her. The CO walked over.

"How are you, Rachel?" Dallas demanded.

"Fine, ma'am. Just some smoke inhalation. Nothing more."

"Good, good." Dallas looked around at the beehive of activity. "Helluva attack."

Rachel nodded. "Yes, ma'am, it was. The Taliban is really threatened by this base. It won't be the last time they try to move us out of their territory."

Dallas put her hands on her hips. She wore her usual one-piece green uniform. The BJS patch, a black jaguar snarling, was attached with Velcro on the left upper arm. The American flag was sewn on the left front of her uniform along with her last name. Embroidered yellow wings denoted she was an Apache pilot. "They screwed us royal, this time," she muttered, looking down at Susan and then over at Rachel. "They've never hit Apaches before."

"They got lucky," Susan said, lifting her head from her paperwork. "Before, they always lobbed grenades at the airstrip."

"Well," Rachel said, frowning, "they timed their attack better. We'd just landed and rolled to a stop in front of Ops. We use evasive tactics, change our flight path every day, but they got lucky this time."

"Unfortunately," Dallas agreed. "And I've got some bad news for you."

Rachel blinked. Her CO appeared grim. "Ma'am?" What on earth could this be about?

Susan looked up, surprise written on her face.

Dallas said in a low voice, "Major Murdoch just got off the phone with the Pentagon. He talked to Colonel Maya Stevens to see if we could get replacement Apaches for the two we just lost." Her thin brows fell. "We aren't getting replacements. All the new Apaches coming off Boeing's line are going directly to the Helmand Province in the south where all the action's at right now."

"But, ma'am, surely there are two somewhere," Rachel stammered, her mind spinning. If not, then she would be flying once a week. They were pilot rich right now, but with the loss of two birds, that would drastically change the pilot rotation.

"Tell me about it," Dallas griped. "What it comes down to is this—the four pilots who last flew those destroyed Apaches will be transferred out of BJS for six months. Instead, because all of you are CH-47 trained, you'll be sent to the new, incoming Chinook squadron that just arrived today. They're pilot poor and in need of more person power. They got the choppers but not enough qualified pilots. You four will fill in the ranks and help them out until we can get the two new Apaches in here."

"But…" Rachel choked out.

"But nothing," Dallas snapped. "You four are going to suck it up and do the dirty work."

"It wasn't our fault that our Apaches got targeted," Susan argued, distressed.

Of course, Dallas knew that no gunship pilot wanted to be relegated to a slow-moving, clunky transport helicopter. But it was clear she had no choice in the matter.

"You knew coming over here to our squadron that you could pull duty in the Chinooks. Now, you will." She turned to Rachel. "And you're on seven days' sick leave. That will give you plenty of time to refresh your knowledge of the Chinook and get up to speed."

Rachel felt as if the floor of the tent had fallen out from beneath her. Tyler Hamilton's squadron was the one she was speaking about. Her mouth went dry. "Ma'am, may I speak to you in private?"

Shrugging, Dallas said, "Of course. Follow me."

Once inside the small office, Dallas sat down behind her desk that was piled with work. Rachel stood at attention.

"At ease, Captain. What is it that you need to speak to me about in private?"

"Ma'am," Rachel choked out, placing her hands behind her back, "I can't be ordered over to that squadron." She launched into the details. Keeping it short, Rachel quickly explained her history.

Dallas seemed stricken by their information, but assumed a professional stance. "I can't help what happened to you in the past, Captain Trayhern. I have to run an all-woman squadron. We just lost two of our birds that we desperately needed. If you want to return to flying here when we get them, you have no other choice than to go over to that Chinook squadron."

"No question I want to remain here with BJS," Rachel said.

"What happened between you and Captain Hamilton was five years ago. Let dead dogs be buried." Dallas jabbed her finger toward Rachel. "And I don't want to hear that you're not getting along over there. You represent the United States, Captain. We're the only all-woman Apache squadron in the world, and I'll be damned if you're going to give us a black eye. Got it?"

Swallowing hard, Rachel whispered unsteadily, "Yes, ma'am. I got it."

"Dammit," Dallas growled, "make it work, Captain. I'm sorry that happened to you, but Hamilton got his just desserts. It's time to move on."

"I—I'm struggling with that," Rachel admitted hoarsely.

Dallas's eyes narrowed. "Captain, he just saved your life. That should count for something, shouldn't it? If he hadn't seen you go down and rescued you, we wouldn't be having this conversation, would we? Dismissed!"

Chapter 3

"Rachel?" Emma called as she popped into her tent in the BJS area, "I just heard what happened. Is it true?"

Rachel was at her small desk, squeezed into the corner of her tent. She turned in the chair and greeted her cousin. "Hey, I didn't expect to see you today."

"Got a minute?" Emma asked, sitting down on the end of her cot. "Is it true? Major Klein is moving the four of you over to the new transport squadron that just arrived? That she can't get her hands on two Apaches?"

Glumly, Rachel nodded and shut the manual on the Chinook she had been studying. "Yeah. Can you believe it?"

Emma reached out and touched her shoulder. "How are you? Your throat?"

"Better, thanks." Rachel gestured to the bottled water on her desk. "My throat has improved a lot since yesterday's attack. The doc ordered me to stand down for seven days because of smoke inhalation, but I'm fine."

Emma set her helmet bag on the wooden floor. "Is there anything Khalid and I can do for you?"

"Aside from Khalid buying me an Apache helo to strap my butt into, no," Rachel chuckled.

Emma nodded with a smile. "I remember when I was flying Apaches and then was ordered to fly the Chinook. I hated the slow-moving transport. Besides that, you're wide open for attack. All I had was a tail gunner at the rear of the helo. I felt like a piece of raw meat hung out in the sky with a sign that said 'shoot me.'"

"I know." Rachel liked the fact that now Emma was allowed to wear civilian clothes instead of a uniform. Her hair was growing longer and it suited her. Today she had on a dark green, one-piece flight suit with her name on it. "How are things in your neck of the woods? I was over at communications at HQ, and it seems pretty quiet out there today."

"It is," Emma agreed. "Usually, when the Taliban makes a big attack, they run and hide for a week. They don't want Apache wrath out hunting for them."

"Major Klein is like a madwoman on a wolf hunt over there," Rachel agreed. "She wants to find and blow them out of existence." And then sadly, "I wish I was in one of those Apaches. This is hell, Emma. I know I went and learned how to fly a Chinook transport, but that was years ago." She held up her hands. "This is like starting all over."

"Hmm," she agreed, "it is." Her brows drew down. "And is it true you're going into Hamilton's Chinook squadron?"

Rachel groaned. "Yes. The old squadron did its tour

of duty, and now Hamilton had been ordered in to replace it. And you know the worst of it? He's the CO!"

Emma shook her head. "I didn't know that."

"Ever since Hamilton was removed from the Apache program, he's been in CH-47s. That's five years. Plenty of time to become a CO of a squadron."

"I guess he kept his nose clean since then," Emma said with a twisted smile.

"He's a captain. He'll never rise higher in rank than that, no matter how long he stays in the Army and flies those transports," Rachel growled.

"And you're studying the CH-47 manual to bone up? When do you have to go over there?"

"Read this," Rachel told her cousin, and handed her the order she'd just received.

"Oh, God," Emma whispered, frowning. "Not only is Hamilton CO, but he's the IP? Instructor pilot?"

"It's like the universe has it in for me. Not only do I get to live with this bastard for the next six months, he has to qualify me in the CH-47. How's that for double jeopardy? I've been racking my brain trying to figure a way out of this."

"Can you get out of it?"

With a shake of her head, Rachel sighed. "Major Klein made it clear that if I want to fly the Apache when it arrives in six months, I have to sit my butt in that CH-47 and do the duty. If I refuse to fly a transport, then I'll be shipped out to another Apache squadron. You know how important it is that women fly together. You've done it. There's a camaraderie between us that no male squadron will ever have. I love it here, Emma. I don't want to give that up."

Gripping her cousin's slumped shoulder, Emma said soothingly, "Hey, I understand. I loved flying with the

Black Jaguar Squadron in Peru and then here. We're making history. We're showing everyone that a group of women can do as well as any male squadron or mixed squadron."

"That's the other problem," Rachel warned her. "Hamilton's squadron is all men. Then all of a sudden, he's getting four female Apache drivers thrown into the mix. Because he hates women and loves spreading his crap that we're not cut out for flying or war, this is going to be a nightmare for all of us."

"How are the other gals taking the assignment?"

"Better than I am. But they don't have the past history with Hamilton like I do. They were in other training outfits, not mine."

"This sucks, dude," Emma agreed, placing her hands in her lap. "Could you use some interesting news that Khalid got wind of the other day?"

Rachel perked up. "Sure. What has he heard?"

Emma leaned forward. "You have to keep this top secret."

"Oh, I will," Rachel promised, seeing the glint in her cousin's eyes. "Whatever it is, it's big!"

Laughing a little, Emma said, "Oh, it's an eye-knocker-outer."

"What? Tell me!"

Emma grinned. "There's a new Black Jaguar group forming under Colonel Maya Stevens. Khalid has been working with Maya and her husband, Dane, who were both assigned to the Pentagon. Maya was the creator of the original BJS, and she showed the boys in the Army how to use the Apache to stop the drug runners in Peru."

"Oh, she's famous for that. She's the bedrock of the

BJS," Rachel enthused, excited. "But what is this new BJS squadron?"

"Not a flight squadron." Emma's eyes glinted. "It's a U.S. Marine initiative. They've asked her and Dane to head up a group of women volunteers from the five military services who will have boots on the ground. They're specialists in language and Afghan culture. Their job is to be put in individual Marine deployment squadrons that are coming here."

Confused, Rachel said, "Women in combat?"

"Yes, with a particular mission. They're in training with the Marines right now at Camp Pendleton. Come October, they're going to arrive here, at Bravo Camp. This will be their HQ. Maya will head it up because she knows how to integrate women into all male elements. It's not flying but Maya will also be working with transport squadrons here, as well as Apache deployment."

Rachel gasped at the information. "My God, it's really happening. These women are being trained for combat roles among the Marine squadrons?"

"Yes. There will be one woman per assigned Marine squad out in the country working with villages and elders. There's a whole new effort to win hearts and minds here. And Maya was arguing this right up to the halls of Congress. She told the senators in a closed-door session that if they used women who spoke the language and worked with the wives of the elders in a given village, that more loyalty, more contact and far more information would be shared." Emma grinned. "You know how women talk to one another. These women are being trained as paramedics, too. They'll be able to give vaccinations, treat the children, wives and female elders of the village."

"What a brilliant idea!" Rachel said, amazed and excited. "Brilliant!"

"Khalid has been friends with Maya and Dane for years, so he got the inside scoop. Don't breathe a word of this. The fun part is that you will be interfacing with BJS ground troops because you'll be flying the Marine squads out with these women. Maya felt that having an all-woman BJS squadron here already would help give these ground-troop women the support they need."

"Is the Marine Corps happy about this?" Rachel wondered.

"For the most part, yes. But you know the Marines— only a man can fight. There's a lot of resentment among some of them, but Dane is working with the sergeants who command these squadrons. There's no room for prejudice out on the ground. All you care about is that the person next to you, regardless of whether they are male or female, can shoot and kill."

"And these women are volunteers?"

"Yes, all five services are represented, even the Coast Guard."

"And they're enlisted?"

"Yes. Maya and Dane chose from among all the volunteers. These are women with at least four years in the military. They are the cream of the crop. This idea was put into overdrive almost a year ago. These women had to learn an Afghan language, complete paramedic training and then go to Camp Pendleton in California to become rifle qualified. They're the whole package."

"That is incredible," Rachel whispered. She saw the happiness glowing in Emma's face. "Leave it to Maya to break down more doors. While the squad leader is dealing with the male elders, the woman soldier can be talking to the elder's wife. I'll lay you ten to one she'll get more info from that wife than the sergeant or lieutenant ever will from the man."

Nodding, Emma said with a grin, "That's exactly what Maya is counting on."

"Wow," Rachel murmured. "Does Major Klein know about this? She must. She was Maya's executive officer down in Peru."

"Oh, she sure does. Dallas is excited about it, too. She's gung ho on the whole BJS ground program."

"They'll be together again like they were in Peru. That's kismet, because we both know they were a successful team down there in stopping drug cartels from getting cocaine out of Peru. The Pentagon, the Chief of Staff know that when Maya and Dallas were a pair, things got done right."

"And their past history and record probably enabled this program to go forward."

"Absolutely," Emma said. She rubbed her hands together and added, "Kick butt, take names."

Laughing, Rachel felt some of her depression lift. Emma was always the positive one. No matter what life had thrown at her, she made mud pies out of the mud. She never let something bad, like the loss of sensation in two fingers of her left hand, stop her. The Army might have discharged her for that, but being married to Khalid had brought her right back here. Reaching out, Rachel gripped Emma's hand for a moment, "I'm so glad you're here."

"Listen, you need to get square with Hamilton." Emma released her hand, her voice lowered with concern. "When do you have to see him?"

"Today." She looked down at her watch on her right wrist. "Matter of fact, at 1400 I have to officially get inducted into his CH-47 squadron."

"Ugh. Not only is he your CO, he's your flight instructor."

"How lucky can a girl get, right?"

Emma shook her head. "Well, we know that life is never fair, but this sucks. Will you be okay, Rachel?"

"I don't know," she said, looking around the tent that had been her life with BJS. "I have such anger toward him. It just bubbles up and it surprises even me. I didn't know how much I hated him until he showed up at the dispensary yesterday. Everything, and I mean everything, came back from my flight school days. I was so surprised at how cold and angry I was."

"How are you going to deal with it? Because the Army doesn't much like it when personal stuff gets in the way of your duties."

"I'll conduct myself as an officer and work to be neutral toward him."

"You can't afford to flunk out on flying the CH-47."

"Oh, don't worry, I won't. I'm keeping my eye on the prize—in six months, I'll be rotated back to BJS and I'll strap an Apache on my ass again." Rachel gave her a twisted grin. "I have my priorities straight, believe me. I might hate him, but I'll be all business in the cockpit."

"That's going to be so hard," Emma said.

Rachel shrugged. "I'm thirty years old. I've been around the block. I guess it's my time to suck it up, see it for what it is—a test."

Emma chuckled. "Spoken like a true Trayhern."

Rachel nodded and smiled. "My parents have emailed me about it. They always have good advice about stuff like this. My dad said to just keep my eye on the future and try the best I can to remain detached about Hamilton."

Emma giggled. "I know your mom. She's a take-no-prisoners woman. What did she say?"

"Because she was one of the first women police detectives down at Miami-Dade, she said to not take anything personally. That I needed to be responsible for every action, every word I had to speak to Hamilton. And to keep a daily journal of what happened so that, in case this all goes to hell in a handbag, I have notes to rely on, not my memory."

Emma laughed fully. "Aunt Kit is a realist. I like her approach. Uncle Noah is always so philosophical about life. And she's brass tacks all the way."

"I think I got the best from both of them. I really want my position back with BJS. I'll go through this hazing with Hamilton and gut it out. But I'll also be chronicling my time with him. He sideswiped my career once. I won't let him do it again."

Emma looked toward the tent flap opening and then lowered her voice. "I had Khalid do a little inquiry into Hamilton's career since he got kicked out of Fort Rucker. He's been a good boy according to the records. But what is against him is that he's been in all-male helo squadrons since then. He's never had to interface with female pilots again. And Khalid is worried that, by you being ordered over there, this could upset his apple cart. You know that the general told Hamilton that if he ever showed one prejudicial moment against another woman, he was kicking him out of the Army." Emma straightened and she pointed toward the tent flaps. "Khalid thinks Hamilton won't try to sabotage you like he did before."

"I hope you're right," Rachel whispered fervently. "Thank Khalid for getting the dirt on Hamilton. I appreciate it."

"Well," Emma said, "if the truth be known, Uncle Morgan was already looking into it. You know he has contacts right up to the president. Khalid bumped into him at the Pentagon. When they discovered they were trying to find out more about Hamilton, they joined forces."

"The Trayherns stick together!" Rachel laughed. "It makes me feel good Uncle Morgan is in there pitching for me."

"You know he won't allow anyone to harm us in any way," Emma said. She lowered her voice. "As a matter of fact, Khalid found out something that just shocked me."

"What?"

"Your father called Uncle Morgan and told him what was going on with Hamilton trying to get you dropped out of the flight program. What no one can know is that Uncle Morgan had a direct pipeline into the general running the program. And Morgan asked the general to release Hamilton. And he did."

Rachel sighed. "I was told about it shortly after Hamilton was out of the program. I didn't realize you didn't know."

Emma smiled tightly. "No one messes with the Trayhern children. Uncle Morgan will see to that." She reached out. "So, just be aware that Uncle Morgan will be watching the reports being sent to the Pentagon by Hamilton. He'll be monitoring him like a hawk." Patting her arm, Emma said, "You have a guardian angel at your back, Cousin. You just haul your share of this load and do it right. The moment Hamilton steps out of line, Uncle Morgan is going to quietly insert himself into the equation and make damn sure he's booted out of the Army for good."

Pleasure and reassurance thrummed through Rachel. "Thank you for the pep talk. I really appreciate it. It makes going over there less nerve-racking for me."

"Well, you have to carry yourself with integrity at all times," Emma warned. "You can't lower your guard and get angry or throw a temper tantrum around him. You have to be bulletproof, Cousin. Be the officer that you are. You're a Trayhern and you have honor. If he tries anything, Hamilton will be in a world of hurt. Uncle Morgan needs you to keep your record clean."

"Got it," Rachel said. "This is incredible. My dad filled me with stories of the military and all the Trayherns that have served over the last two hundred plus years…but I never realized until this happened how powerful they really are in the military world."

"Thank Uncle Morgan. He's the head honcho. And like I said, he's got the ear of every military general in the U.S.A." She grinned and stood up. "That plus the president."

Standing up, she hugged Emma. "Thank you, Cousin."

Emma leaned down to pick up her helmet bag. "I hope Hamilton realizes by now he can't screw around with a Trayhern."

Opening the flap to her tent, Rachel said, "We're going to find out in a couple of hours."

Emma slipped through the flaps and lifted her hand. "I'll be in touch…."

Turning, Rachel allowed the flaps to fall together. The August heat made the tent stuffy. She wiped her brow and sat back down to continue reading the CH-47 flight manual. A lot of her stomach churning had settled with Emma's good news. She had even more reason to make this unholy alliance work. But would Hamilton plan on making her look bad again? Or had he really learned his lesson?

Chapter 4

Ty Hamilton dragged in a deep breath. The next woman he had to see was the one he didn't want to ever see again. His clerk had just told him that Captain Rachel Trayhern had arrived. He hit the button on the intercom.

"Tell her to come in," he ordered.

"Yes, sir."

Stomach in knots, Ty wondered if she was still pissed off at him for saving her life a week ago. Sitting behind his desk, he saw the door open. Rachel Trayhern looked a lot different today. Her brown hair was caught up in a knot at the nape of her slender neck. Her dark green flight uniform was clean instead of dirty. She wore no makeup, but she didn't have to, he thought. Willing himself to ignore her natural beauty, he watched her as she turned and shut the door. Then she came and stood at attention in front of his desk, her face unreadable. But her cheeks were red and Ty knew she was upset. Back in flight school, when Rachel was angry, her cheeks were like two red spots on her flawless face.

"Captain Trayhern reporting as ordered," she said, tight-lipped.

"At ease, Captain," Ty said. He gestured to a chair that sat near his desk, on her left. "Have a seat. We have a lot to discuss."

"Yes, sir." Rachel tried to ferret out how Hamilton really felt about meeting her again. This time, it was on equal footing rank-wise. She wasn't a newbie to flight school. Heart pounding, she kept a grip on her clipboard and sat down.

Ty flipped through a sheaf of papers and located her personnel record. As he opened it, he glanced in her direction. She sat at attention in the straight-backed chair. His heart squeezed over the hardness in her golden eyes. There wasn't a trace of an emotion on her oval face. Her lips were compressed. Okay, he deserved that reaction. Five years hadn't healed the wound. He got it.

"Your record indicates that you took CH-47 flight school training four years ago."

"Yes, sir, I did."

Nodding, Ty kept his voice neutral. "And you have forty hours in them?"

"Yes, sir."

"Well, it's obvious you need retraining, and I've set up flights with my scheduling sergeant. You will assume copilot duties from now on. We'll be flying every day." He held her hard gaze. "I'm the instructor pilot in our squadron. But you probably knew that."

"I make it a point to know," Rachel said in a low, tight tone. She searched his face. It would be easy to continue to hate him if he weren't so drop-dead good-looking. Eye candy for sure, Rachel thought. Tyler Hamilton was the perfect poster boy for an internet ad by the U.S. Army to lure young men who wanted adventure.

"Of course," he murmured, looking down at her file. He reached to his right, picked up the squadron patch and dropped it on the edge of the desk nearest to her. "You'll be wearing the Raven Squadron patch from now on. At least for the six months that you're assigned to us."

Rachel desperately wanted to keep her BJS patch on the left sleeve of her uniform. But she knew she had to relinquish it. Distastefully, she picked up the other patch. It burned in her fingers. She wanted to angrily throw it on the floor but didn't. The flicker in his eagle-like gaze revealed how carefully he watched her for any reaction. Did Hamilton still have it in for her? Rachel assumed he did. Every day in the cockpit with this bastard would be like being sent to the dungeon for torture.

"Do you have any questions?" he demanded, feeling as if he were addressing a wooden doll, beautiful but completely detached from him. Ty could have wished for a warmer response.

The other three women from BJS whom he'd also be training, had been open, smiling and enthused to be here to fly. But not Rachel. A sense of defeat flowed through him. He had hoped five years had buried the hatchet between them. Casting around for a topic, he asked, "Have you been cleared by the physician on your smoke inhalation?"

"Yes, sir, I have." She took a paper from her clipboard and dropped it on his desk. "I've been cleared to fly and ordered back to duty."

"Excellent," he said. "I'll speak to my sergeant about putting you on the flight schedule for tomorrow. In the meantime, go out to the Ops desk and get your paperwork filled out. Sergeant Johnson will give you the scoop on what you need as a copilot in our squadron. Welcome."

He rose and extended his hand to her. Stiffly, Rachel got to her feet but refused to shake his hand. "With all due respect, Captain Hamilton, I have to be here for six months, and that's it. May I be dismissed?"

The iciness in her tone shocked him. It was war, not peace between them. He withdrew his hand. "Dismissed."

The door opened and shut. Ty moved from behind his desk. The squadron had arrived just yesterday to replace the other one, which was being rotated home to the United States. He'd been here at Camp Bravo for two weeks with his transport pilots, learning the lay of the land and picking up information from the outgoing pilots. Right now, his squadron was ready to go in one of the most dangerous places in Afghanistan to fly.

Walking around the desk, hands on his hips, Ty smarted from Rachel Trayhern's demeanor. She'd refused to shake his hand. Why had he expected the white flag between them? She probably thought he was going to try and tarnish her record. Stopping, Ty raised his head, his lips pursed. She was all business. No anger in her eyes. No fear. Just that cold hardness. A real ice queen. But then he remembered back in flight school, at the beginning, how warm and open she'd been. The more he rode her during the instruction flights, the less warm and open Rachel became. He wondered if the warmth had returned in any capacity. Was she like this with everyone? Or just him?

Sighing, Ty knew he had no one but himself to blame. But dammit, he'd paid the ultimate price for his stupidity, too. In the last five years, he'd tried to reestablish his good name. And to a degree, he had. When the colonel made him squadron commander last year, Ty had drawn a sigh of relief. He thought for sure that they'd never give him a command. Now, a year into it, he'd led well. But then, there were no women pilots in his squadron, either. Now, he had four of them for six months. Damn. What a test.

From the very beginning he fought liking Rachel Trayhern. He'd found her amazingly beautiful in flight school. Everyone had responded to her like welcoming sunlight. Back then, he'd been jealous, angry. She not only was poised and confident but carried the vaunted Trayhern name. Hamilton was well aware that the Trayherns had served with honor in all of the military branches for hundreds of years. They truly were a military family dynasty. And he'd been jealous of that, too.

Running his fingers through his short, black hair, Ty circled around his desk and sat down. He had a lot of planning to do with four new pilots suddenly on board. Oh, no question he could use them. His other male pilots wouldn't have a problem with them. They didn't carry the belief that women were weak and would always be less than a man, like he had in the past.

Rachel took in a deep breath of air as she left the Ops area of the control tower. In her arms, she had more information about Raven Transport Squadron than she cared to have. The sunlight was welcome, the August morning heating up. There was plenty of activity on the tarmac. The second Apache rolled down the recently patched runway for takeoff. The first was already in the air, heavily loaded with armament. How she wished she could be there and not here!

Sadness moved through her as she walked between the tent cities that were set up on the covert base. Bravo sat on top of an eight-thousand-foot mountain. It was the nearest CIA base to the Afghanistan-Pakistan border, always a juicy target for the Taliban. The two Apaches that had been targeted and burned had been bulldozed off the runway. They sat like mangled, broken birds on the other side, and it hurt Rachel to look at them.

"Get your head screwed on straight, Trayhern," she muttered to herself as she turned down a dirt avenue to her tent. Pushing the flaps aside, she dropped all the gear, manuals and papers onto her cot.

"Hey," Emma called, opening one of the flaps, "how did it go?"

Turning, Rachel smiled a hello over to her cousin. "Flying in or out this morning?"

"Out," Emma said, tucking her flight gloves in the side pocket of her uniform. "How'd it go with Hamilton? You look pale."

Sitting down after offering Emma her other chair, Rachel said grumpily, "It went. I was so angry at him."

"And him?"

Shrugging, Rachel muttered, "He did all the right things, Emma. I couldn't see or detect that he still had it in for me."

"Did he look happy to see you?" She grinned.

"I don't know. Honestly, he had a poker face, too."

"And so did you."

"Guilty," she admitted, frowning. "It was just weird. When he tossed the squadron patch on his desk, I had this infantile reaction to grab it, throw it on the floor and stomp on it." She laughed.

"Hey, you have a right to feel like that." Emma smiled. "But like the good officer you are, you didn't allow your personal feelings to make it a messy situation."

"It was hard," she admitted, rubbing her hands down the thighs of her flight suit. "I kept trying to ferret out his hate for me. Or his anger. All I saw was officer decorum."

"Well, that might be good news then." Emma raised her brows. "Maybe he's learned his lesson, that female pilots are just as good as male pilots?"

Rachel shrugged. "I'll find out, won't I?"

"Oh, I don't think he's going to do anything but treat you right, Cousin. After all, he has everything to lose if he doesn't."

"I thought of that angle, too," Rachel said. "I can barely tolerate that he's going to be my flight instructor—again." Lifting her eyes to the tent ceiling, she said, "I wonder what I did to deserve this a second time, Emma. Talk about double jeopardy."

"Take it one day at a time," Emma counseled. She stood up and patted Rachel on her slumped shoulder. "Do the things we talked about earlier. I'm off to take a load of books, children's clothes and shoes to a village north of here."

"Be careful...."

"Oh, always!" Emma leaned over and gave Rachel a quick hug. "See you on the return. I'm due back at sunset. Maybe we can have a cup of coffee over at the chow hall then?"

"I'd like that," Rachel said. Even though Emma was now a civilian, she had access to the chow hall to eat, just like anyone in the military would. Watching her cousin leave, she felt buoyed by her presence. Emma was always positive. But then, Emma had not encountered a female-hating flight instructor, either.

Rising, she walked over to the cot. The squadron patch showed a black raven in flight. Rachel resisted putting it on and placed it on the table. She'd do it tomorrow morning. Until then, she still wanted to wear her BJS patch, a source of pride and honor to her. There was a lot to do. She had to go to BJS Ops and turn in her helmet gear. The ugly-looking transport helmet would have to be worn instead. It was all so distasteful, like she was being thrown back into hell again....

The morning air was cold at eight thousand feet. Out on the flight line, everyone's breath created white clouds when they spoke. Bundled in her flight jacket and gloves, Rachel moved slowly around the Chinook helicopter. It was the workhorse of Afghanistan. Carrying men, supplies, ammo, food and aviation fuel, the bird could do it all. She listened to Ty Hamilton as they performed the mandatory walkaround duties. Having studied the manuals, Rachel had already memorized the things she needed to check on the helicopter before ever entering the cockpit.

The sun was still below the horizon, the stars visible high in the dark sky. The crew was busy getting this helo prepped for takeoff. Today, Hamilton was flying boxes of ammunition, MREs, meals ready to eat, to an Army outpost in a valley north of the camp. As he went over their schedule for the day, Rachel tried not to like Hamilton's low voice. He was thorough and instructive but not arrogant as he had been in flight school. That was good, because Rachel would not tolerate that attitude from him now.

At the open ramp at the end of the helo, a load master, responsible for getting supplies into the huge bay, was busy. The other young, red-haired man was their gunner.

"The only protection we have is our gunner," Ty told her as they stood near the yawning ramp, which lay against the surface of the tarmac. "Once we're ready to lift off, he'll put the machine gun up in the center, there—" and he pointed to a square cut out of the platform surface "—and settle it into it and lock it. Then he'll be sitting down, legs between it, hands on the weapon. We keep the ramp down while we fly. He's our eyes and ears back here, and we'll be relying heavily on anything he sees. We'll take the ramp up shortly before we do any landing."

Nodding, Rachel knew there was little evasive protection in the Chinooks. Unlike the Apache, which could instantly know when a SAM missile or a grenade launcher was fired, this workhorse had no such protection. "It falls on the eyes and ears of the crew," she agreed. Rachel made sure she didn't have to stand any closer to Hamilton than necessary. They both wore dark green baseball caps on their heads and Nomex fire retardant gloves. It was below freezing and the Nomex warmed their hands.

"Yes," Ty murmured. "At this outpost, there's a landing area so we can set down, and our crew can get the supplies off-loaded with the help of the squad."

"Good to hear." Rachel understood that these outposts often sat on peaks high above the valley so the Army squad manning them could use their binoculars or rifle scopes to keep watch on the Afghans who farmed the valleys below. These squadrons stayed for three months and got to know the farmers. In knowing them, they could spot outsiders who were Taliban, sneaking through the area to attack American soldiers. And then they could be captured or killed.

"Let's saddle up," Hamilton told her, walking up the ramp and into the helo.

Following him, Rachel nodded to the two enlisted men in the rear. She saw no reason to be cold and standoffish with them. They had already secured the cargo with netting. She eased between the nylon seats on the side of the helo and the load. Hamilton climbed up the stairs and took the right seat, the pilot's position.

Her mind and focus were on her flying. Easing into the left-hand seat, Rachel picked up her new helmet and settled it on her head. Relieved that Hamilton was already busy, she got out her preflight cheat sheet and strapped it on her thigh. There was always a list of things to do before taking off. This was standard on any aircraft or helicopter. Plugging in the jack to the radio intercom, Rachel pulled the mike close to her lips. Hamilton had done the same.

Within ten minutes, they'd completed their preflight check. Once they had harnessed up, Rachel wondered if he would allow her to take off.

"I'll do the lifting," Hamilton told her as if reading her mind. "And once we're in the air, I'll hand the controls over to you."

"Okay," Rachel said. They were going to a dangerous area. Taliban were known to hide in the scrub brush that peppered the outpost area and wait for the helo. Other Chinooks had been fired upon earlier, so this was no familiarization flight. Already, Rachel could feel the adrenaline pouring into her bloodstream. The moment they lifted off, they were targets. She felt horribly naked without an Apache strapped to her butt.

She continued to find out what her copilot duties were as Hamilton fired up the first engine and then the second one. There was a sense of familiarity with the helo, and it made her relax to a degree. In no time, the crew was ready for takeoff.

Ty had pulled down the dark shield from his helmet in order to protect his eyes from the rising sun's rays. He noticed that Rachel had done the same. That didn't stop him from being aware that her profile was clean, her nose straight and her lips full. She was beautiful, even if half her face was hidden. Trying to ignore his male reaction to her, he said, "We're at the top end of weight limits with this cargo. And in the predawn hours, there's more humidity in the air than when the sun is up. That means it's harder for this helo to lift off. So, on days like this, I start her up by taxiing her the length of the airport runway. That way, by the time I hit the end of it, I'm applying full power, and it's easier for the bird to lift off."

"Plus," Rachel said, "it saves us fuel." She was always taxiing the Apache the same way. It saved fuel. And when they were in a hot spot, they needed to keep all the fuel so that they could protect the soldiers and Marines on the ground.

"Roger that," Hamilton agreed. "Okay, here we go."

Rachel focused entirely on the takeoff. One of the main attributes of an Apache pilot was laser-like focus and ability to multitask. Although she sat there, hands resting on her thighs, she watched the instruments, watched Hamilton's hands and absorbed it all. The Chinook groaned, and the blades thunked and whirled faster and faster. Finally, they were taxiing.

The Chinook was laborious as it trundled down the airstrip like a weighted elephant, the blades whipping at maximum. The helo shook and trembled. As they moved down the strip Rachel wondered if Hamilton would even reach takeoff speed, but he did. The end of the runway came up, and the bird lifted easily into the dawn sky. Rachel didn't want to tell Hamilton that he had done a good job. She wasn't ready to give him a compliment.

"Okay, you have the controls," he told her.

Quickly sliding her hands around the stick and collective, she repeated back to Hamilton. "I've got the controls."

"Releasing controls," he affirmed and lifted his hands away. Ty had expected the Chinook to suddenly fall a few feet, but it didn't. Rachel took over and the bird was climbing. There was no sign that one pilot had stopped flying and another had taken over. She was good. But then, he bitterly reminded himself, she was an Apache pilot. They were the cream of helicopter aviation. Deep in his heart, he was still bitter over what had happened, but he had no one to blame but himself.

"Nice job," he complimented her.

Rachel was stunned that he'd said anything. Her gloves tightened momentarily around the stick and collective. Her mouth quirked, though she kept quiet. She damn well knew how to fly a helo, even if it was this bulky, noisy bird that crawled through the sky.

Hamilton frowned. He'd expected some kind of response from her, but that icy profile was all he saw. He forced himself to stop expectations, and just continued to look out the cockpit windows for any sign of a SAM missile. They were climbing five thousand feet to avoid the grenade launchers, but a missile could blow them

out of the sky at any time. Rubbing his chin, he tried
not to feel hurt by Trayhern's cold composure. She had
smooth flight hands. Although the CH-47 shook around
them, the roar always present, it rode the air currents
without a bobble or jerk.

As he sat there in his seat, Ty tried to protect himself
and remain immune to Rachel. He saw no ring on her
finger, although to be fair about it, pilots never wore
such things. If they ever crashed and were found by
the Taliban, there had to be no identification on them.
Except for their name, rank and serial number. Still, he
wondered if she was married. And to whom?

Chapter 5

Rachel loved flying, even if it was a slow transport helo. The shaking and shuddering of the twin blades located at each end of the long, tubular helicopter soothed. It helped her relax instead of becoming tense in the cockpit with Hamilton. The day was beautiful. The sharp, brown peaks of the mountains had little foliage on them except for stubborn brush. They looked like green dots on the slopes.

"Okay, fly around that mountain and you're going to see a village. We're going to land there first. Then we'll take off and fly up to the outpost situated two thousand feet above it."

Frowning, Rachel said, "That wasn't in the orders. We're to fly the cargo to the outpost."

Ty saw her lips set in a stubborn line. "We don't put in the landing at the village because it's automatically assumed by scheduling," he explained. "There's a Special Forces team that moves up and down this narrow valley. We have some antibiotics and other medicine to drop off to their paramedic on the team."

Nodding, Rachel knew that the Chinooks were the only supply line to the Special Forces men. She had high regard for them.

"Plus," Ty said, a bit of humor in his tone, "their captain ordered up a bunch of bags of candy. It's for the kids. They love it."

She cut him a glance. He was smiling, and she'd never seen that before. Ever! Forcing herself to focus back on her flying, she felt angry. Why? Not having time to examine the feeling, she took the helo around the tall, barren peak. Up ahead, she could see a small village and an area that had been scraped free of rocks for helo landing.

Pointing, Ty told her, "Head for that flat place outside the village. We always land there."

"What about the threat of Taliban?" she demanded. Rachel always got spooked when they were near the mountains. Taliban hid in the caves and behind the huge boulders to keep from being seen. All it would take is one grenade launcher fired from the slope down on that meager landing zone to blow up the Chinook.

"Always a possibility." Ty took binoculars and began to focus on the slopes above the village. "Normally, we get an Apache escort, but with two destroyed, we go it alone."

Rachel's mouth tightened. She felt the fear leaking through her bloodstream. Her heart picked up in beat. She knew how important the Apaches were to the transport squadron. They had infrared, a television camera, and they would make routine sweeps of the area to find and locate hidden Taliban. Then they would take them out with rocket or Gatling gun fire, making it safe for the unarmed Chinook to land or drop off cargo to the outposts. "Don't remind me," she gritted out.

Surprised at the anger he heard in her low tone, Ty didn't respond. Rachel wasn't happy about being here. It was obvious she wanted no part of any of this. Scanning the slopes, he said, "So far, so good. I don't see enemy."

Snorting softly, Rachel knew that no matter how good Hamilton was at trying to spot Taliban, they could fool him by hunkering down and being invisible as they flew by the area. "You won't see them until it's too late," she said.

As they rounded the slope of the mountain, Ty put the binoculars away. He called for the gunner to remove the machine gun. Then he brought up the ramp and closed it on the Chinook. "This is the way it is," he told her. Pointing, he said, "Land it now."

Rachel did as she was ordered. It had been a long time since she'd landed this bulky helicopter. Unlike the streamlined Apache, this workhorse was like a tee-tering elephant on a small three-legged stool. As she slowly brought the helo down, the blades kicked up fierce clouds of yellow dust. It quickly turned into a sit-uation that all pilots hated. They had to land blind. She couldn't see anything and she couldn't see the ground. A ribbon of panic ate through her.

"It's okay," Hamilton soothed. "You're doing fine. Just keep going down at the same rate. You'll feel the wheels touch in a second."

Sweat popped out on Rachel's lip. Hamilton's reas-suring voice was exactly what she needed. Trusting his analysis of the blinding situation, she suddenly felt the tires anchor to the ground. Relief shot through her. Instantly, Hamilton's hands were flying over the instruments, and he shut down the helicopter's two huge whirling blades.

Sagging back into the chair, Rachel let out a sigh of relief. She began to unharness.

"I'm staying with the bird," Hamilton told her. "I want you to go in the back. Once the load master gets the boxes out from the netting, walk with him to the village. My sergeant will meet with the Spec Forces team and hand off the supplies. Then go with that captain. You need to get to know the elders. We always take these boxes of food and candy every time we fly in." He turned and grinned a little. "It's called nation building."

Nodding, Rachel pulled off her helmet. She tried to remain immune to his very male smile. He'd pushed the dark visor up off his face. His blue eyes were wide and she saw happiness in them. Hamilton obviously enjoyed doing this. She didn't. "I feel like a naked chicken on a NASCAR raceway," she growled as she got up. Making sure she didn't brush against the other pilot, Rachel added, "We're a really big target right now."

Nodding, Hamilton said, "Get used to it. We don't get Apache escort as often as we'd like. Besides, this village, just FYI, is pro-America. They know when we come, and they send people up on the slopes to make sure no Taliban are lurking around. If they did find them, they'd have come down to tell the captain. And then he'd put a call in to us because he knows the flight and our call sign. So, it's as safe as it can be."

That was good news to Rachel. She saw Hamilton pull the lever that would lower the huge ramp at the other end of the Chinook. One pilot always remained with a bird on the ground. In case of unexpected attack, the engines could be revved up, the other pilot and people could jump on board, and they would take off. "Okay, thanks for the info," she said, stepping down into the cargo hold.

Ty sat and watched from his seat. He opened the window and raised his hand to the Army captain standing near the elders. The elders waved back at him. Smiling a little, Ty felt good about what they were doing here. Every Afghan village who had seen help, food, antibiotics and support appreciated their presence. The Special Forces teams kept the Taliban out of the villages so that they could get on with their planting and harvest. They would have enough food for the winter months instead of starvation stalking them. Life out here, he felt, was tenuous at best.

He tried not to stare at Rachel but couldn't help himself as she stood out among his two crew members. The flight suit, although loose, still couldn't hide the fact that she was a woman. Her rounded hips gave her away. Ty liked the way she swayed when she walked. Rachel carried a load of boxes in her arms, even though she didn't have to carry anything. It told Hamilton she was a team player. With her helmet off, her dark brown hair glinted in the first rays of the sun edging over the peak and into the valley. He saw red and gold strands highlighted among her sable mane.

He got up and took his binoculars with him. As he strolled out of the rear of the bird, Hamilton continued to watch the slopes. No matter how good the men of this village had done their work, he never trusted the area was clear of clever Taliban. His job was to stay around the helo and keep it safe. Training his binoculars upward to the outpost, sitting on a flattened peak two thousand feet above them, Hamilton continued to hunt for enemy.

* * *

"Captain?" The Special Forces officer directed his focus to Rachel. She had just handed the paramedic in the group the medical supplies. Turning, she met the gray, narrowed gaze of the officer who commanded the team. He was easily over six feet tall, his head swathed in a dirty white-and-blue turban, his black beard scruffy. He was dressed like an Afghan man, as was the rest of his team, so they didn't stand out. His weapon hung off his broad shoulder. There was a sense of danger about this man, of a predator ready to spring.

"Captain Trayhern," she said, stopping in front of him.

"Welcome to our little slice of heaven," he said, giving her a tight grin. "I'm Captain Cain Morris."

"What can I do for you?" Rachel asked. She noticed the man's gaze was always moving across the slopes above the village. She felt safer.

"Tell Hamilton I've got the daughter of the village chief, and she needs immediate medical attention. She's only seventeen, very pregnant, and my paramedic, who's a man, can't see her, much less touch her. She's been bleeding the last three days."

Rachel saw the frustration in the captain's eyes. "That's not good. I'm not a paramedic, but even I know that."

"Yes. I've persuaded the elder to allow his daughter and his wife to fly back on your bird. You need to tell Hamilton that as soon as he drops off the cargo to the outpost above us, he has to make a beeline for the main Army base near Kabul. My paramedic says she's in real trouble, and so is the baby she's carrying. She's overdue."

Touched by the officer's concern, Rachel said, "I'll

call him and find out." She turned and walked away from the group. Hamilton had given her a radio to stay in touch with him. When he came on, she explained the situation. "What do I tell this captain?" she asked of Hamilton.

"Tell him to get the woman and the mother ready. We can't wait an hour here on the ground. They have to move pronto. The longer we're on the ground, the more we're a target. Tell Morris, ten minutes."

"Roger that." Turning, Rachel walked back to the captain. He nodded and quickly walked over to the dark, bearded man, who was in his fifties. Rachel was impressed that the captain spoke Pashto, the language of the area. The elder looked relieved and shouted orders. Immediately, two men ran down the dusty village road toward the rock homes.

Morris came back to Rachel. "I need you to stay here and wait for them. These people have never seen a helo before we came here, much less rode in one. I know the girl who's pregnant is very shy. Her mother will accompany her, but both can use your woman's touch."

"Sure, no problem," Rachel said, peering past his shoulder. A door opened and two women came out through it, dressed in black burkas, hidden from head to toe. It was obvious the shorter of the two was very pregnant.

Rachel had no time to dally. Once the women were on board, Hamilton was up front bringing the twin engines online. She smiled and patted the mother's hand. Both of them seemed frightened. Rachel just hoped the girl wouldn't deliver the baby here, in the back of the bird. She had no idea what to do to help her. Moving up front, she quickly got into the copilot's seat, pulled on her helmet and plugged the connection into the intercom system.

"Did you give those two earplugs?" Hamilton demanded, his hands flying across the instrument panel.

"Roger that," Rachel said, strapping in.

"You're taking us off. I'll direct you to the outpost and where to land."

Good, she had something to do. Gripping the cyclic and collective, she spoke to the crewmen in the back. The ramp was down, one of them manning the machine gun. Liftoff!

Flying to the outpost was a quick trip. The rotors raised thick, blinding clouds of yellow dust. Hamilton once more talked her down, and relief flooded through Rachel as she landed. In no time, the engines were shut down. This time, Hamilton leaped out of his seat.

"Stay here with the helo. And try to make these two women feel welcome. They look like they're going to bolt out of the rear."

Rachel removed her helmet. There was quick teamwork in the back. The Army soldiers from the outpost swarmed into the rear of the Chinook, helping the other three get the boxes off-loaded as quickly as possible. She stepped down and went to the two Afghan women. They looked positively frightened. Kneeling down in front of them, one hand on each of their hands, Rachel tried to soothe them. Her Pashto was rough at best, but trying to speak it made both of them appear relieved.

Within two minutes, the bird's cargo bay was cleared. Rachel divided her attention between the frightened women and the men smiling and laughing at the rear of the helo. When she saw Hamilton stride back into the chopper, she rose. Giving the women one final smile, Rachel left and went to her copilot seat.

Hamilton's body brushed against her shoulder as he came and sat down. The space between the two seats was very narrow. Her flesh tingled where he'd accidentally grazed her. Trying to ignore the sensation, Rachel did as ordered and took off once the engines were online. In no time, they were airborne. Hamilton was on the radio with Camp Bravo telling them they were detouring to Bagram Air Base outside of Kabul.

Relieved that Bravo Command gave them permission to fly the two Afghan women directly to Bagram, Rachel felt lighter. Happier. She loved change. And today, a mundane and unexciting flight had turned into something much more. As she headed the helo up to eight thousand and pointed the nose of it toward Kabul, she heard Hamilton chuckle. She turned her head toward him for a moment and saw that he was smiling. How handsome he was. Even though she couldn't see half his face, hidden by the dark visor, she definitely noticed his mouth. Nearly hypnotized by it for a moment, Rachel shook off the sudden desire that bloomed within her. What was going on? Hamilton was her enemy. He had always been that. Confused, she stuck to flying the Chinook through the early morning air.

"A good day," Hamilton told her later. They had just landed at Bravo Camp. At 10:00 a.m., the sun and air were warming up. The Ops area was busy and frantic, as always. Two Apaches had just landed and another two were trundling out to take off. Noise from the blades of two other Chinooks filled the air, making it nearly impossible to hear conversations.

Rachel had her helmet bag, her clipboard and other flight gear in her left hand. Yes, it had been a good day, but she wasn't about to let Hamilton know that. When she lifted her hand to push through the door of Ops, Hamilton beat her to it. He shoved it open and stood aside.

Shocked by his gentlemanly gesture, Rachel nodded awkwardly and shouldered past him. She was glad to be at the Ops desk since she knew the drill from there. A sergeant handed her a flight mission form. Without looking back, she chose one of the small rooms. She entered and shut the door in order to focus on the report. Only this time, Hamilton followed her inside.

Turning, Rachel placed her gear on the floor next to the picnic table that doubled as a desk. "I'm sure I can fill out a report by myself," she said.

Ty sat down opposite her. "When you're flying an Apache, your report is very different from ours," he said quietly, not wanting to face the hardness he saw in her face. Damn, she was so good-looking, and yet, that icy demeanor made him smart inwardly. Ty reminded himself he was to blame for her defensiveness. "Sit down." He opened one of his flight pockets and pulled out two pieces of folded paper. "When we fly, we have to name the outpost, village or any other items that may be important for Intelligence. This morning, we landed at a village whose name you don't know and can't spell as yet." He opened the papers and nudged one of them toward her. "I made a copy of all the villages, names of elders and outposts that we normally service. In your report, you need to not only put in the names and places but how we also transported two women to Bagram."

It made sense to Rachel. Still, she didn't like Hamilton sitting across from her. Taking the pen from her pocket, she looked down at the neatly typed list. Hamilton might be a sonofabitch, but he was thorough.

Rachel saw the names of villages, the elders' names, their wives' and children's names, the outposts. "This looks very complete," she said.

The softening in her voice made him relax a little. Giving her a slight smile, he said, "I learned a long time ago flying over here that if I didn't know the names, I couldn't connect with the people."

"No," Rachel murmured, studying the list, "you get a lot further if you know the name of a village's leader."

"Right," Ty said. He reached over and pointed to the paper. "Captain Morris supplied the name of the daughter. The wife is on this list."

Dutifully, Rachel filled out her report. She had to have help from Hamilton several times regarding the list. Her Pashto wasn't that good, and she needed to get better at it. Suddenly, a question popped out of her. "Do you know Pashto?"

Surprised, Ty sat up. "Yes, I do. Well," he added, opening his hands, "I learned it over time. I've never taken an immersion course."

Rachel cursed herself for veering into personal territory. He didn't deserve anything from her. Angry with herself, she lowered her gaze back to her report, mouth thinned.

Heartened that she was showing at least a little interest, Ty added, "You know, we have a Rosetta Stone version on Pashto here at the squadron. If you're interested, you can use it and bone up on the language a little more in your spare time."

Rachel said nothing. She signed off on the report, turned it around. "I'm assuming you'll read this, and if there are any corrections, your clerk will let me know."

Ty glanced up as she stood, grabbed her gear and got ready to leave. "Yes, I will."

"I'll find out when I fly again out at the Ops desk," she said, her voice firm as she opened the door.

Ty sat there alone in the room, the door closing once more. For a moment, the room had been warm. Alive. But now it was sterile once more. He did his best to continue with his report. His heart ached, and he had the feeling it wasn't physical. Rubbing his chest, Ty tried to figure out why things had suddenly changed. Frustrated, he tried again to focus on his report.

The more he tried to work, the more flashes of Rachel's face, her beautiful gold eyes haunted him. He'd seen the gentleness in her expression when she'd brought the two frightened women into the helo. He'd felt his heart respond when she'd smiled and patted their hands to try and relieve their fear. Like the starving wolf that he was, Ty had found himself wishing she was looking at him like that. And touching him intimately...

"Crazy, dude," he muttered darkly as he forced himself back to his paperwork. "Certifiably crazy..." Once, he'd hated her so much he was blinded by it. Now five years had passed. He'd grown and maybe matured a little. So what the hell was this emotional response to Rachel? Ty looked up, sighed and stared around the quiet room. The worst part, he was saddled with her at close quarters for the next six months.

Chapter 6

The sun had just risen as Rachel stood with the three other women from the Black Jaguar Squadron. It was freezing, and she was glad to have on her heavy green coat and gloves. Today, Hamilton would train them on cargo net hauling and delivery. He'd ordered them to meet him at the other end of the airstrip where a Chinook was standing by. What got her curious was a wooden pole about ten feet high, anchored into a bunch of sand bags. What was Hamilton up to now?

"Today," Ty told the huddled group of women pilots, "you're going to practice delivering cargo to outposts. As you know, all outposts are perched on the highest peak they can find. Those ten-man squads are cut off from normal supply routes. No one can climb those rocky mountains." He patted the thick, round pole. "So, what we do is we use two huge cargo nets. My crews will fill them with boxes of ammunition, medical supplies and MREs, meals ready to eat." He walked over to where the two cargo nets were lying on the tarmac. Picking one up, he elaborated, "These are not the normal nets you might be thinking of. They're made of steel cable that has been woven together. They are designed to carry a lot of weight. And the weight will be different on every flight. Each outpost sends in a weekly order to the Ops desk. The ground crews collect it, and then on a given day, we fly it out to them."

Rachel tried to ignore how handsome Hamilton was in front of the group. She recalled flight school and his arrogant, intimidating style of teaching. He wasn't doing it here. Instead, he was open, educational and actually nonthreatening. A far cry from five years ago. She wrapped her arms against her chest, the high-altitude cold stealing her warmth.

Ty dropped the thick, heavy cargo netting onto the tarmac and straightened. "Today we'll be practicing cargo drops and cargo pickups until you get them right and feel comfortable doing them. This pole is here for a reason. You're going to have a very small area to gently put those two huge cargo nets near the outpost. You won't be able to land. Instead, you're going to listen to your load master, who will be near the opening where they're hooked up. He'll guide you down to six feet above the ground. At six feet, they're on the ground. Then you have to hold this helo perfectly still so the load master can unhook them." He looked at each of their serious faces. Ty wanted to stare moments longer at Rachel but didn't.

"Okay," Rachel spoke up, "so we hover."

"Right," Ty said. "But you need to be aware of something. First, when those two cargo hooks are released, there are two men down under the belly of this helo."

He pointed to the CH-47. "Secondly, you can't allow mountain winds or currents to push this bird around. One small error, and you could crush these two soldiers who are under the helo. They're trying to get the cargo nets out from beneath it as fast as they can. Then once they've dragged the nets clear, four other men will quickly open them up and form a line to take the crates out of them."

Rachel withheld comment as he became deadly serious. Why did he have to have such a beautifully shaped male mouth? It would be so much easier if Hamilton were ugly, and then she could blatantly ignore him.

"Now, here's the tricky part," he told them. Using his left hand to illustrate, he said, "Here's the landing zone." He held his other hand barely above the left one. "Here you are with a heavy transport helo that is bucking local or regional mountain winds. You must hover there until they can refill these nets with empty cartridge and ammo cases, their trash and whatever else needs to go back to the base camp."

"So," Rachel said, "those men are dragging these nets back up under the helo?"

Nodding, Ty smiled a little. Rachel's cheeks were flushed, while everyone else seemed cold. "Exactly. You have two men struggling with the weight of those cargo nets. And they're risking their lives by once more, pulling them under the belly of our bird. The load master is hovering just above them, his hand stretched out to try and get one hook and then the other. This is a very delicate ballet between ground and flight personnel. The key is keeping the helo rock-solid steady during this time. Outpost drops and pickups are the hardest parts of flying out here on the frontier."

There was a murmur among the four women Apache pilots.

Ty walked over to the pole and wrapped his hand around it. "I know in an Apache, you don't do this type of flying, so none of you are really accustomed to this situation. That's why we're out here today. We're going to spend it taking the Chinook up and then hovering. You'll be working via communications with the load master. We'll hook up these two cargo nets with a lot of weight. Your job is to slowly lower the helo until this pole almost touches the belly of the helo. That is exactly how many feet you have. If you come in too fast, you'll splinter the pole. And if that had been real, that pole was a soldier waiting under the belly of your helo to get the netting released. You have just badly injured or killed him."

Rachel traded grim stares with the other women pilots.

"And then I'll have two crewmen standing by, out of range, as you bring and hover the bird just above that pole. Today, you're going to learn to trust your load master's direction and follow his orders exactly. Further, you need to learn to handle the bulk of this helo, feel the sudden loss of all that cargo weight and then the sudden addition to it. There will be a lot of bobbling up and down when that happens, and you can't allow it. You can crush the men beneath you."

"Wow, a real dance," Rachel muttered under her breath. Her brows drew down. She realized instantly that they all had a long way to go on learning this maneuver. Seeing the worry in the faces of every pilot, she knew they all got the seriousness of the training.

Ty looked over the women. "Any questions?" He saw all of them shake their heads. "Okay, then let's get going. I'm going to be sitting in the left-hand seat, and you'll each be the pilot in command. You'll have to get used to doing it from one side of the helo and the other. If you're right-handed, it's always easier to do it from the right seat. We'll build your confidence there, and then we'll transfer you to the left seat. Most pilots have a weak and strong side when they fly. You'll find out pretty quickly where that's at." He managed a slight grin.

He pointed to Rachel, "Okay, you're first, Captain Trayhern. Let's saddle up."

Great. Rachel scowled but didn't say anything. When Hamilton was her flight instructor back at Fort Rucker, he would always yell at her, curse her and tell her how bad a flyer she was. Would he do that now? God, she hoped not because she would land the damned helo and go to Ops and report him for harassment.

Joining Hamilton, she kept her distance from his shoulder. The sun felt good, the temperature only slightly higher. The rest of the base was still busy, like bees coming and going. Apaches were warming up for takeoff. Two Chinooks bearing two cargo nets beneath their bellies slowly lifted into the air, bound for outposts in the godforsaken brown mountains.

As Rachel climbed into the helo, she saw that Sergeant Tony Bail was standing near the big, square opening in the middle of the belly of the chopper. He raised his hand and smiled. Rachel nodded to him. This twenty-year-old would be giving her directions. She took her helmet out of the bag and pulled it on. Hamilton waited for her to climb the stairs. Heart pounding, Rachel quickly moved to the pilot's right-hand seat. She concentrated on their preflight list and then engaged the rear and front rotors.

"Okay," Hamilton told her, pulling his microphone close to his mouth, "let's take her up and go to five hundred feet. From there, I want you to pretend we're over an outpost. You'll have those cargo slings under you. You'll feel the load. Ready?"

"I am," Rachel said, hand around the collective and cyclic. Her boots were firm on the rudders beneath her feet. The shaking and shuddering of the helo soothed her nerves. Rachel tried to steel herself against a potential tirade from her new boss and old enemy. Lifting off, they broke connection with the earth. Instantly, as she slowly pulled the helo upward without tipping forward or back, Rachel felt the tremendous weight of the slings. She responded to it.

"Good ascent," Ty said.

Relief sped through her for a moment. Was that praise? Rachel said nothing, climbing to five hundred feet and hovering.

"Okay," Ty said, "begin to lower. Sergeant, take over?"

"Yes, sir. Okay, ma'am, I'm down on my knees near the opening. I will talk you down."

"Roger," Rachel said. She knew the other three women pilots were watching. Nerves taut, she began to ease the Chinook down.

"Your nose is high," Ty warned.

As she glanced quickly at the horizon indicator, Rachel noticed he was right. Not by much. Okay, he was going to be a stickler on a flat landing where nose and tail were exactly even. Correcting, she watched the altimeter slowly unwind. Bail's voice was high and nasal, but he was good at direction.

"Continue lowering," he told her.

Rachel lived in fear of striking that upright pole. As they got closer, sweat popped out on her upper lip.

"Twenty feet," Bail warned her. "A little slower…"

It was a delicate dance. Rachel's hands gripped the controls hard. She was constantly using her rudders to keep the helo from swinging one way or another as she continued the descent.

"Fifteen feet, keep coming…"

The winds across the base were always around. A gust hit the bird.

"Too fast!" Bail yelled.

Gulping, Rachel tried to recover from the gust. Suddenly, she heard the load master give a yelp.

"Ascend!" Hamilton ordered.

Instantly, Rachel applied power.

"Hover at one hundred feet and hold," he ordered her.

What had happened? Rachel saw Hamilton craning his neck over the seat and looking into the cargo hold.

"Ma'am," the load master said, his voice tight, "you just destroyed the pole. The bottom of the helo nearly got impaled on it."

"Roger that," Rachel said, feeling ashamed.

She looked over at Hamilton, expecting him to scream at her. Instead, to her shock, he appeared calm. "Is there another pole?"

"Yes, we have plenty of them." One corner of his mouth pulled upward. "Not to worry. We destroy plenty of them in this exercise."

Rachel winced. "If that had been a man under there…"

"He'd be dead," Hamilton finished, becoming somber.

"It was the wind."

"It's always going to be wind and air currents," he told her. "That's your biggest enemy in this exercise."

Nodding, Rachel looked out the right window. Below, she could see two crewmen taking the broken pole out from the sandbags and replacing it with another one. She gave Hamilton a quick glance, feeling on her guard. He wasn't screaming. No curses. Instead, a quiet kind of instruction. Rachel inhaled deeply. "Sergeant, tell me when that pole is up."

"Yes, ma'am. It's up and we're ready to try again."

"Okay, I'm coming in. Begin direction, Sergeant."

Ty said nothing. He saw the tension in Rachel's beautifully shaped mouth. A mouth he had a damned hard time not watching like a lovesick puppy. Why hadn't he been aware of her beauty back in flight school? Giving an internal shake of his head, Ty concentrated on her skills. She was obviously nervous and wanting to do it right. He'd learned the hard way that yelling at a student didn't bring out their best. All it did was increase tension and cause more errors in flying.

Rachel listened to the sergeant as he talked her down. This time, even though the wind was inconstant and trying to push the helo around, she held it steady. It was so different from the nimble, super-powered Apache.

"Stop and hover!" the sergeant called, his voice rising.

Instantly, Rachel held the hover. They must have been directly over the pole. She heard the load master breathing hard. It took a lot of pure muscle to get those hooks removed.

"Continue hover," Bail called.

"Roger," she murmured, praying that the wind would hit them.

And it did. One moment, Rachel was static. The next, the gust of wind hit the helo and they started to slide.

"Up! Up!" Bail yelled.

She cursed softly under her breath, her feet and hands moving at incredible speed. The Chinook was thrown sideways and started to skid. The ground was only twenty feet away, and she saw it come up fast. Instantly, she powered the helo and rose. Her heart pounded in her chest like it would jump out. Not a word from Hamilton.

As she brought the Chinook into a hover at a hundred feet, Rachel cast a quick glance in his direction. His face was unreadable, but his blue eyes were narrowed. Licking her lips, she felt shaky inside, as if she were a new pilot, not the veteran that she was.

"Nice recovery," Hamilton told her. "Take it easy. Everyone is going to do exactly what you're doing. This isn't a case of trying to look good, Captain Trayhern. It's learning the ropes. You're going to make a lot of mistakes today, so get over it."

Trembling inwardly, Rachel felt her gut twist into a literal knot. She had always wanted to do things perfectly, without messing up. But she was doing it big time this morning. What did her friends, her sister pilots, think of her screwups? Ashamed, Rachel focused even harder on the task.

"Okay," Ty said, "let's try again. You're getting better every time you do it. That's as good as it gets." He saw the pain and shame in the way her mouth twisted. The shield was down over her eyes, so he couldn't see them. Didn't matter. He knew from a lot of experience that every pilot made the same mistakes. Even he did.

* * *

The sun was setting as Rachel made her way to the Ops room to fill out her report. The other female pilots had followed her off the tarmac to their individual rooms. Once inside, Rachel closed her eyes and scrubbed her face.

"What a sucky day," she muttered, walking over to the table and sitting down. The room was quiet. A report had to be filed. Right now, all she wanted was a stiff jolt of tequila, her favorite drink when she could get it. Her gut was still tight, especially knowing that Hamilton was making his way through the four rooms. She was sure he'd be here sooner or later. Rachel ran her fingers through her loose hair and pulled the pen out of the upper-arm pocket of her flight suit.

Rachel was almost done with her report when the door opened. Hamilton stepped in, carrying two mugs of coffee. Shutting the door with his boot, he turned and said, "I figured you'd need a stiff cup of coffee about right now."

Rachel straightened. She wasn't sure how to contain her surprise. Without thinking, she took the cup from him. The instant their fingertips met, she felt the tingle. Unable to jerk her hand away, she took the cup and said, "You're right about that."

Ty walked around the table and sat down opposite her. He made sure his knees didn't touch hers. There was wariness in her face as always. "The other pilots finished their reports. I brought them coffee, too, because I know how nerve-racking this training is."

Rachel took a sip of the hot brew. "I don't know why I didn't think to get some coffee earlier. My nerves are shot."

"Understandable."

"That's some of the toughest, most demanding flying I've ever done," she admitted, signing off on the report.

"I know. And flying an Apache you have to be a multitasker, but this is different."

Rachel nodded. She wrapped her hands around the mug as he picked up her printed report and read it. Inspector pilots and flight instructors had to sign off on their students' reports. Rachel stared at Hamilton's face as he read. It gave her a moment to simply study him. Again, she wished he wasn't so damned handsome. He had a strong nose and chin, his cheekbones high. As her gaze settled on his mouth, Rachel suddenly felt heat in her lower body. She scowled. She shouldn't have any reaction to this man.

Ty looked up and caught her staring at him. Rachel suddenly glanced away. For a brief second, he'd seen something else in her golden eyes. Always, there was wariness and distrust in them when he was around. But not this time. What did he see? It was so quick, he didn't have time to register it. Rachel appeared very uncomfortable, squirming around on the bench. Why? He was doing his level best not to be a torment to her as he'd been before. He wanted her to know that he had no wish to take on the Trayherns again. Burned by past experience, Ty wanted the rest of his career to go without rancor.

"Good report," he congratulated her.

Rachel smiled uneasily as she placed the mug on the table. "Brutally frank as always."

"Well," Ty murmured, adding some sentences to the bottom of it, "you're too hard on yourself."

"I should have gotten the swing of things sooner," she muttered.

"You got it faster than the other three pilots. That should make you feel good."

Hamilton's voice was soothing and unperturbed. It was such a diametric difference from her last experience with him at flight school. "I guess," she said.

"I wish I could erase that look in your eyes," Ty said, frowning.

Rachel sat up a little more. "What look?"

Ty sighed and signed off on the report and handed it back to her. "Distrust."

Shocked, she glared at him. "Well, given our past, Captain Hamilton, do you blame me?"

Her voice was gritty. Scathing. Ty felt his shoulders tense. His heart beat a little harder over her sudden combativeness. Holding up his hands, he said, "Look, I know we have a bad past history."

"That's not the half of it," Rachel growled.

"I understand," he said, trying to speak softly so as to defuse the animosity in the room.

Rising, Rachel stared down at him, feeling all her fear and tension unwinding within her. "No, you don't. I had you screaming in my face, cursing me and threatening me for twelve weeks solid. No one would ever forget that, Captain Hamilton." She put the mug down on the table a little too roughly, some of the coffee spilling out of it. "I'll never forget what you did to me. And frankly, I'm just waiting for that mask of yours to come off and you to go after me again." Her cheeks grew hot as she hurled those words at him. He appeared positively thunderstruck.

Ty sat there for a moment, digesting the cold rage in her voice. She had her hands on her hips, leaning forward like the aggressive Apache combat pilot she was.

But there was fear in the depths of her narrowed eyes—of him. She still feared him. There was no trust.

Those realizations hit him hard. Ty tried to find the right words. But who could under the circumstances? "Look, I know I screwed up with you. I've paid a fair price for it, and I accept my demotion and the fact I'll never be let into the Apache club again. I've been trying to show you that I won't be like that now. I've learned my lesson, Captain Trayhern."

Anger roared through her bloodstream. Rachel felt herself trembling with the long-held rage. "The last place I ever want to be is in your company. I might have to put up with you for six months, but that's it. Am I dismissed, Captain Hamilton?"

Actual physical pain moved through Ty's heart. He slowly stood, staring across the table at Rachel. She was so incredibly beautiful, her brown hair shining around her and emphasizing her gold eyes. He hesitated. There was so much he wanted to say, but she wouldn't hear or believe it. Finally, he rasped, "Dismissed, Captain Trayhern. I'll see you here for a flight at 0600 tomorrow."

Turning on her heel, Rachel fairly ran out of the room. Ran and got the hell away from Hamilton. Boots thunking across the wooden floor, Rachel jerked the door open, slammed it shut and took off.

The room fell silent. Ty looked around it, the report still on the table in front of him. His conscience ate at him. Now, he was seeing what his hatred of women five years earlier had done to Rachel. Shaking his head, he scooped up the report. Her disgust of him was clearly written in her eyes. As he walked to the door and opened it, Hamilton couldn't blame her. He'd been a real bastard back then. Prejudicial, stupid, backward and letting his own childhood color his perception of women in general. Well, now he had another war to fight. With Rachel Trayhern. As he walked toward the Ops desk, the place busy as always, Ty felt depressed. He'd wounded a beautiful, smart, courageous woman who had no connection with his earlier life. And yet, he'd taken it all out on her. How could he get her to trust him?

Chapter 7

Rachel woke up in a very bad mood. On her way over to Ops to meet Hamilton, she barely acknowledged the pink sky flooding the eastern horizon before the sun peeked over the mountain range. Gripping her helmet bag, she moved through the streams of people coming and going to morning duties. How could she have dreamed of kissing Hamilton? Of all things! And it had been so real Rachel had awakened in the early morning hours feeling an ache in her lower body.

Oh, she knew that ache. Why wasn't Garrett in her dream instead? She'd loved him with her life until he'd died in an attack on the Apache base Camp Alpha in Helmand Province a year earlier. But to be kissing Hamilton? Rolling her eyes, Rachel tried to shove that heated dream down into the basement of her memory. She had to focus on the coming helo mission with Hamilton.

As she entered Ops, the familiar rush and buzz of Apache pilots was in high gear. As soon as it was light enough, the transport squadron would become active. Unlike the Apache pilots, the CH-47 had no nighttime flight capability. It was a basic, utilitarian helo that flew only during the day and in good weather conditions. Apaches had the state-of-the-art gear for flying day and night and under any conditions. How badly Rachel missed flying her gun-ship.

She went to her cubbyhole and dragged out the mission orders for the day. She didn't see Hamilton and was glad for that small blessing.

"Hey, Captain Trayhern," the Ops sergeant called, "you've got goats today." He grinned.

Walking up to the balding sergeant, Rachel set the helmet bag at her feet and opened the orders. "Goats?"

"Yes, ma'am. They just flew in a cargo hold full of goats just a few minutes ago from Bagram. You and Captain Hamilton are taking them to Samarigam, a village real close to the Pakistan border."

As she read the orders, Rachel managed a wry smile. "Goats. Of all things."

"Ever transport them?" he asked, handing her a pen.

Shaking her head, Rachel laughed and said, "No, I haven't."

"Not something an Apache pilot has to deal with," he joked.

Rachel signed off on the orders and couldn't stop herself from smiling. *Goats.*

"Your bird is to the left of the doors. Crews are moving the crates of goats into it right now. Have fun!"

Lifting her hand, Rachel said, "Right."

Pushing out the doors of Ops, she saw the CH-47 she would be flying. Sure enough, just as the Ops sergeant had promised, there was maximum activity around the opened ramp of the CH-47 that had just flown in. They had specialized equipment to lift pallets out of the helos. Only this time, as she drew near, they were lifting pallets that contained groups of goats in crates.

Rachel watched the transfer as it went smoothly from one Chinook to the other. *Goats.* Who knew? The two crewmen for her helo were busy as she walked up the ramp and made her way to the cockpit. Up ahead, Hamilton was in the left-hand seat, clipboard on his thigh, writing. Her smile disappeared.

"Goats?" she asked, stepping up into the cockpit.

Ty looked up and removed his legs from the aisle so she could sit in the left-hand seat. "Morning," he murmured. Giving her a quick look, he noted there was no anxiety or anger in her eyes. She was breathtaking. "Yes," he said as she sat down and got comfortable in the seat, "this is a special mission we've been handed."

"I'll bet," Rachel said wryly. "The Ops sergeant told me we were hauling goats. We must be blessed by the higher-ups at the Pentagon."

"Oh," Ty said, finishing off his paperwork, "not just any goats. Angora goats. And this assignment did come down from the Pentagon."

Unable to stop grinning, Rachel took her helmet out of the bag. "Angora goats? As in mohair sweaters?"

Chuckling, Hamilton warmed inwardly. It was the first time he'd seen Rachel smile. And his heart took off at a strong beat. He watched hungrily as she threaded her fingers through her shining, straight brown hair and gathered it up and tied it back with a rubber band. "Yes. The U.S. Army is working with Captain Kahlid Shaheen on this project."

"Oh?" Rachel turned, interested. "Are Emma and Kahlid going to be up at that village?"

"Actually, yes," he said. "We'll be meeting them at Samarigam."

Her whole day was turning out to be better than expected. "That's great."

"She's your cousin, right?"

"Yes." Rachel saw some anxiety in Hamilton's blue eyes. She felt as if he were trying to make up for causing her explosion yesterday in the report room. She wouldn't apologize for her sharp words. Still, a bit of guilt ate at Rachel because it was sorely obvious that Hamilton was doing his best to be friendly, attentive and engaged. And then she remembered that torrid dream last night and gulped hard.

"I talked to the captain who flew the goats in from Kabul. Apparently, the farm program of Shaheen's organization has gotten the go ahead from the Pentagon and they're bringing in Angora goats to certain villages. And then they get the women who have been widowed to create a cooperative where they shear the goats and make sweaters from the mohair. It not only improves the village on a financial line, but widows aren't starving and dying, either."

"Emma had told me that Kahlid was working to get that project off the ground. It's a great one." Rachel was all too familiar with what happened to an Afghan wife who lost her husband to the ongoing war. Poverty was so severe in Afghanistan that when the husband died, the widow was then shunned. They were supposed to be taken in by the husband's family, but that rarely happened. Each family was barely subsisting off the land or the goat and sheep herds they had. The widows then had to go house-to-house every day, begging for scraps of food to keep them and their children alive.

"Well," Ty said, gloating, "we're the first official shipment of Angora goats. Just call us the Angora Express."

Pulling on her helmet, she grinned. "Somehow, Angora goats won't impress anyone who reads my personnel jacket."

Ty chuckled and pulled on his own helmet. "I hear you." The bleating of the goats rose as more of the crates were brought in. The crew members knew how to get as many in as they could. Once the last crate arrived, he saw his load master work with the other crewmen and pull a huge, thick nylon net around all of them. That way, the crates would be strapped to the deck, and if they hit turbulence or had to take evasive action, the crates wouldn't be flying around inside the helo.

Rachel's mood lightened considerably. She would see Emma and Kahlid, an unexpected and pleasant surprise. It made the two hours they'd be flying less arduous. As she twisted around in her seat and looked at the thickly woolen Angora goats, she had to smile. In one crate stood three big rams with long, twisted horns. The rest of the crates contained ewes, who had much smaller horns. They weren't terribly big in Rachel's opinion. But what did she know about goats?

"We're getting Apache escort today," Ty said, plugging his helmet connection into the radio system. He turned and gave the signal that the ramp was coming up. The goats were secure, and the men stood away from the ramp area.

"I saw that on the orders," she said. "I'm assuming you've done the walk around?"

"Done and we're looking good," he answered.

"Roger." For whatever reason, Rachel felt calm in the cockpit. Usually, she was tense, especially with Hamilton next to her. Today was different. Was it that stupid, ridiculous dream? Rachel shook her head and pulled out the preflight information. There was a working ease between them, which hadn't happened before. Maybe yesterday's verbal explosion had cleared the air. She certainly felt better letting Hamilton know just where she stood.

The bleating of the Angora goats was drowned out as Rachel brought the first engine and then the second one online. To her left, she saw an Apache trundling up, fully loaded with weapons. How Rachel wished she was over there and not here!

"Goat One to Goat Two," she called to the Apache.

"Goat Two here..." The woman pilot gave a "baaahhhhhh" over the radio.

Rachel broke into laughter. She glanced over at Hamilton, who was laughing, too. How handsome he looked when he smiled. She couldn't ever remember seeing him laugh. Then again, she had no business noticing him. She devoted her attention to talking with her friend, Nike. "Hey, you got goats over in Greece, doncha?"

"Roger that, Goat One," Nike snickered. "Over."

"Well, good to have this goat jamboree all working together. Nice to have you along, Nike. Over."

"Roger that, Goat One. Is your cargo looking happy about all this? Over."

"Negative, Goat Two." Rachel twisted around and looked at the crates beneath the thick cargo netting. It was barely light in the hold, but she could see them. "They're looking pretty wild-eyed. Over."

"Goat One, do you think someone with a sense

of humor picked today's call sign? Over." Nike was chuckling.

Hamilton's grin widened. "Goat One to Goat Two. Roger that. I'm to blame. Over."

Rachel smiled to herself as her hands flew over the instruments with knowing ease before they were to take off. She hadn't ever seen Hamilton's sense of humor, but she liked it.

"Goat One, you are the man! Over."

Nodding, Ty glanced over at Rachel. She was still grinning. The iciness that always hovered in the cockpit between them had miraculously disappeared. He ardently absorbed the warmth between them, finally tearing his gaze from Rachel's soft features.

"Goat Two, we're ready to get this goat train airborne. You ready to take off first? Over."

"Roger that, Goat One. We're outta here. Meet you at six thousand feet," Nike said. And then she added, "Baaahhhhhhh…"

Rachel laughed uproariously. "Roger that, Goat Two. See you upstairs. Out."

Ty sat back. Happiness thrummed through him. And relief. In no time, after the Apache had rolled down the airstrip, gathering speed and finally lifting off at the end of it, it was their turn. The CH-47 shook and shuddered. The thunderous roar of the engines was muted by their helmets. Ty looked back to see how the goats were dealing with the rolling take-off. They seemed to have quieted down.

Once airborne and at flight altitude, Rachel was happy to have the Apache flying a large circle around them. She knew Nike and her copilot had on infrared to spot heat from bodies down on the rugged mountain slopes. They also had instruments to detect a SAM missile being fired. She relaxed as never before because the Apache was the big, bad guard dog in the sky.

"I was wondering if you ever have been around goats," Ty asked Rachel over the intercom.

Smiling a little as she flew, Rachel said, "No. I grew up with aquariums of fresh-water and salt-water fish. My father loves fish."

"I grew up in Cheyenne, Wyoming where my parents owned a cattle ranch."

Rachel found herself curious about Hamilton. She knew nothing of him. And the two-hour flight would go faster if they had a conversation. "So, you're a cowboy?"

Chuckling, he said, "Yeah, among many other things. When you grow up on a ranch, you do everything from digging postholes, setting new fence, to stringing barbed wire, milking cows and fixing ranching equipment."

Somehow, Rachel hadn't ever thought of Hamilton as anything but the screaming flight instructor. Now, this presented a whole new facet of him. "I wasn't around too many animals. Just the fish—and Polly, my mother's beautiful parrot. Not a very creative name, but I grew up with Polly. No cattle, though."

"We had milk goats," Ty hesitantly admitted, filing away Rachel's information. He felt starved to make a human connection with her, one that wasn't filled with anger and dredging up their past. "My mother had the goats because they provided milk for children who were lactose intolerant and couldn't drink cows' milk."

"I'll bet she had you out there milking them," Rachel said. At least his mother sounded like a nice and thoughtful person. So how had Hamilton turned out to be so…complicated?

"I don't really remember the goats too much," he admitted in a quieter tone. "My mom died of uterine cancer when I was three years old. My dad got rid of the goats shortly after that."

Her heart plummeted over that information. Glancing quickly to her left, she saw him become sad and withdrawn. She wondered how he handled growing up without a mother. She couldn't imagine losing her mother, Kit. That would have been a horrible sentence for him to bear as a three-year-old. "I'm sorry to hear that," she murmured, meaning it. When she saw him nod, his mouth pursed, Rachel realized that he still missed her. Who wouldn't miss their mother?

"How did your father cope?" Rachel asked.

Hamilton shrugged. "It wasn't pretty. Looking back on it all, I don't think many men can lose their wife and then be saddled with a three-year-old kid."

The incredible grief in his voice startled her. The visor was drawn over the upper half of his face, so she couldn't see the expression in his eyes. The corners of his mouth were drawn in, no doubt sealing in his pain. Some of her hatred of him dissolved just knowing this past history. "I'm really sorry to hear that," Rachel admitted. And she was. Abandonment could have played a huge part in his growing-up years. She could only imagine the impact her death must have had on him.

Trying to rein in her curiosity, she asked, "Did your father remarry?" If he had, Hamilton would have at least had a stepmother figure in his life.

Hamilton gave an abrupt laugh, one tinged with bitterness. "No. He was a mean son of a bitch, and all he cared about was the family name and carrying on the hundred-and-fifty-year-old ranch tradition of our family."

Rachel cringed. She heard the sudden hardness, the yearning in Hamilton's tone. "Did you have brothers? Sisters?"

"No, I was their first and only child."

Rachel moistened her lips. She continued to rubberneck and watch sky and ground, just as Hamilton was doing. More sets of eyes meant less chance of the Taliban firing at them without being seen first. "It must have been tough as an only child, then," she suggested.

"Let's just say that my father didn't like a crying little boy who had suddenly lost his mother."

"He was grieving just like you, I'm sure," Rachel said, hoping to ease the hurt she heard. "When you love someone and suddenly lose them… Well, it's hard. Really hard." She knew better than most, too.

"Let's put it this way, Captain Trayhern. My father blamed me for my mother's death. Oh, looking back on it now, he was wrong, but when you're a little kid, you believe your parent."

"That's wrong! You didn't cause her cancer," Rachel whispered fervently.

Giving her a glance, Ty heard and felt her compassion. Her soft lips were parted. In that moment, he ached to crawl into her arms and simply be held. It was such a startling thought that he sat up a little straighter. What was going on here? There was no way Rachel would ever like him. Hell, she hated him. And for good reason. Still, in that explosive moment of actually talking with one another, the need rose in him. He simply didn't know what to do with it. "Sure it was wrong," he mumbled.

"So you grew up being accused and reminded that your mom was dead because of you?" Rachel asked, disbelief in her voice.

"My father didn't accuse me of it daily. Only a couple of times…"

"What a lousy parent he was. You never saddle a child with something horrendous like that."

"My father continued to remind me that women were the weak species. They didn't have what it took to be strong and survive in this hard world of ours."

Stunned, Rachel tried to absorb that information. No wonder he had this prejudice against women. She knew she had to be careful with her words. "And you were young and believed him."

"Sure I did," Ty muttered. He lifted his hands in frustration. "I believed him body and soul until five years ago."

Wincing inwardly, Rachel suddenly wished they didn't have this mission. How badly she wanted to have time to understand the roots of Hamilton's actions. They had started with an angry, grieving father. And being the little boy he was, he'd believed his father. Women were weak because his wife had died of cancer. She'd left him with Ty, who was an innocent, grieving child. Gulping several times, Rachel fought the tears jamming into her eyes. She was grateful her visor was down and he couldn't see her face.

There was nothing she could say. His belief that women were weak had all come to a roaring halt when she'd fought back. And won. Had Hamilton really let go of his prejudice toward women? Was he really a changed man? After a week in his company, Rachel admitted that he wasn't anything like the strident flight instructor of five years earlier. Still, her heart warned her to remain on guard. Could someone who carried such an intolerance suddenly change?

"Ah, Goat Land ahead," Ty teased, trying to lighten

the atmosphere. He pointed ahead at a high mountain valley. "There's our village."

Rachel struggled for a moment before she could speak. When she did, her voice was oddly hoarse. "Goat Land? You've got a wicked sense of humor, Captain."

He glanced over and managed a smile. "Dark humor at best." Seeing her lower lip tremble, Ty felt his heart wrench in his chest. And then he saw the track of tears down her cheek. Her voice had been raspy, but he hadn't put it together until now. Crying. She was crying for *him*.

Chapter 8

Upon landing at Samarigam, Rachel was swept up in the village's excitement. To her surprise, Khalid and Emma had already flown in, their helo having landed nearby. They had transported in twenty bleating Angora goats. Some of her levity was dampened by the uneasiness that Hamilton had shared so much of himself with her. Now, she saw him differently.

"Go ahead and meet and greet," Hamilton urged her. "I'll work with the crew and the villagers to off-load these crates of goats."

Rachel nodded and quickly moved between the fuselage and crates. After placing a green scarf over her head to honor Muslim tradition, she eagerly walked down the ramp. Outside, the villagers had gathered, their faces alight with joy over receiving such an expensive gift from the United States. Threading through them, Rachel found Emma and Khalid at the corral with the elders. Before approaching them, she greeted the four old men, the elders, of the village. Protocols were important. They shook her hand and greeted her in return. Emma was smiling as Rachel came toward her.

"Hey, Cousin, look at this!" Emma threw her arms around Rachel and hugged her tightly. Releasing her, she laughed. "We did it!"

Rachel beamed at her. "You did. A dream come true." She turned to Khalid, who was still in the U.S. Army, wearing the flight uniform. His face lit up with pleasure. As Rachel moved to shake his hand, his arms went around her, and he hugged her.

"Welcome, Rachel," he said, releasing her.

"Thanks, Captain Shaheen," she said.

"Out here, call me Khalid. You're my family now. Let's drop Army protocols when we can, shall we?"

"Fine with me," Rachel said.

They led her over to the four-foot-high corral.

"This village will have forty-five Angora goats," Emma said excitedly. "Khalid and his sister Kinah have been working two years to make this dream into a reality."

Rachel saw that the rest of the villagers hung on the wooden fence, staring in disbelief at the white animals. The children were on their hands and knees, peeking between the slats, eyes wide with excitement. "This is a great day," she agreed. Khalid's arm went around Emma's shoulders and he hugged her, his face bright. "So, the widows get the wool to make sweaters?"

Emma nodded. "There are several surrounding villages to Samarigam. They're all the same clan. Khalid has a written contract agreement with the elders from six villages that the widows will receive the wool from these goats every year. Each woman will get enough to make ten sweaters."

"And then," Khalid said with a smile, "they will be sold through our nonprofit organization around the world. The widows receive seventy-five percent of the money. This will not only keep them from starvation, but it will also feed their children. No one will die. And the money the widows spend in their village on goods circulates through the local economy. It's a win-win for everyone."

Smiling, Rachel noted the joy in Khalid's expression. He was lean as a snow leopard, terribly handsome, and she was so happy for Emma. They were truly a happily married couple, who held the same vision for the people of Afghanistan. "That's incredible."

"We have Kinah to thank," Emma told her. "She's set up distribution through the U.S. for all the sweaters. And she has hired three women who will be coming here to teach the widows the patterns and how to knit them."

"You've thought of everything." Rachel looked at the goats moving around in the large, circular corral. The children had brought handfuls of green grass gathered from the hillside. The goats were settling down, anxious to eat.

"Here comes the rest of the herd," Khalid said, motioning to the village men hand carrying the crates off the Chinook.

Stepping aside, Rachel watched a long line of men struggling with each crate. The goats bleated, terrified as they were carefully carried. One by one, each crate was taken into the corral and the goats released. Upon finding their own kind already there, the animals lost their fright and eagerly crowded in to grab a few bits of grass offered by the children at the fence.

Overhead, an Apache flew in large circles around the village. It was searching for infrared signatures of human beings who could be Taliban in hiding. The enemy could lie in wait to lob a grenade at one of the two Chinooks on the ground. Craning her neck, Rachel saw the last crate leaving the ramp of her helo. Hamilton was standing by it. He was alert, looking around. It was never safe to be on the ground for long.

"How safe is Samarigam?" she asked Emma.

"Very safe. Khalid chose this village because the Taliban has not been here at all."

Khalid looked up at the Apache as it passed over them. He then glanced over at Rachel. "That doesn't mean it's safe flying here or back. It's Taliban country, big time."

"That's what I thought," Rachel said. She saw Hamilton gesturing for her to come back to the helo. "Excuse me, my boss is wanting to see me."

Hurrying through the happy crowd of villagers, who watched each release of the Angora goats, Rachel finally broke free of the people and noticed the worried expression on Hamilton's face.

"What's wrong?" she asked, coming up to him.

Hamilton looked in the cavernous hold of the helo. "Both our crewmen are sicker than dogs."

"What?" Alarmed, Rachel stepped onto the ramp. Both crewmen were sitting and looking very pale.

"They've been throwing up. A lot of nausea. I don't know why."

"Emma and Khalid are flying back to Bagram. A straight shot from here. We could ask them to take them to the hospital there."

"That's what I was thinking," Hamilton agreed. "Could be food poisoning. They both said they ate tuna sandwiches for breakfast this morning."

Rachel wrinkled her nose. "For breakfast? What a horrible thing to eat!" And there was a chow hall so everyone could get eggs and bacon. Shaking her head, she muttered, "Twenty-somethings…"

Hamilton smiled a little. "I'm going to call back to base and let Ops know. Since I'm the commander of the squadron, I can release them to Bagram and Khalid's helo."

"Good. You want me to tell Emma and Khalid? I'm sure they won't mind."

"Yes, can you?" He hesitated. "It leaves us open, though. We won't have a ramp gunner watching for the Taliban."

"I know," she said. "But they aren't going to be any good to us sick, either."

Nodding, Ty knew she was right. "Okay, you make sure it's okay with them, and I'll make the radio call to Camp Bravo."

Once she heard the situation, Emma shook her head. "These young guys are really dumb sometimes. Mayonnaise is a real lethal food-poisoning ingredient if it hasn't been chilled at the right temperature."

"Tell me about it," Rachel said.

"We'll take them to Bagram," Khalid said. "Just ask them to walk over and make themselves at home in our bird."

"Thanks," she told them. "We really appreciate this. Otherwise, we'd have to detour and fly a lot longer than we expected."

"Not to worry," Emma said, putting her hand on Rachel's shoulder. "The U.S. Army isn't going to say anything. They don't care if they're flown in a civilian Chinook or not." She grinned.

"Something nice about being a civilian, isn't there?" Rachel teased her red-haired cousin.

"Oh, yes." Emma smiled warmly up at her husband. "It's *very* nice."

Chuckling, Rachel waved goodbye to them and trotted back to their helo. Hamilton had just walked down the ramp when she approached the bird.

"Everything's in order," he told her.

Rachel said, "Good. Let's tell the guys to trade helos. They'll take them directly to the base hospital."

Ty nodded and walked inside. He told the sick crewmen what was going on. They slowly got up and walked down the ramp. He escorted them to the commercial Chinook helo that had the nonprofit name of the Shaheen's organization painted on it. The crewmen laid down on the nylon netting that served as seats on the helo.

Upon reaching his bird, he saw that Rachel had already gone up to the cockpit. She was talking on the radio.

Rachel turned and saw Hamilton coming up the stairs. She'd taken the left-hand seat to answer the radio call. He sat down, his expression curious. Finishing the call, she said, "Ops just called us. They're redirecting us to the Kabul River on the other side of the mountain and north of Peshuwar."

"Why?"

"The Kabul River is flooding due to heavy thunderstorms over the mountains. There's an anti-Taliban village that needs our help. People are trapped in the river and need to be rescued."

"Our Apache protection can't go with us. They've only got so much fuel," Hamilton said.

"I know. They have to head back and can't make that swing east to help, due to a low-fuel situation."

"Not good," Ty muttered. He looked around, thinking. "The Kabul River above Peshuwar is heavy Taliban country."

Rachel handed him the microphone. "You talk to Bagram HQ then. They're the ones ordering us to do it."

Taking the mike, Hamilton made a call into the headquarters. He argued that they shouldn't be risking their bird or lives without crewmen on board and without Apache escort, but he got no further than Rachel did. After clicking it off, Hamilton glanced over at her. She had a grim expression, too.

"This village is important to HQ. There's an imam there that hates the Taliban. Every village that fights the Taliban is one the U.S. wants to protect and help. So, we're going. Let's get this bird cranked up."

"You want me to fly right-hand seat?" Rachel wondered. She had been the AC, air commander, for the flight so far.

"No. You haven't been in that area and I have." Ty looked over at her. "You okay with that?"

"Yes, I am."

"Good, let's get the engines online and get that ramp up." He tried to keep the worry out of his tone. This wasn't a good thing and Ty knew it.

Rachel felt the tension in the cockpit. She looked at her watch. They'd scraped over the mountains and were heading down into a huge valley. Far ahead of them, she could see the Kabul River, a main water source through

Afghanistan. Farther south was Peshuwar, an Afghan outpost on the border with Pakistan. She'd never been in this area before. In August, the flat land on either side of the dark green river was lush with grass. The thunderstorms came and went regularly throughout the summer, dumping water on the desert areas. It was one of the few times places looked vibrant for a little while.

Hamilton hadn't said much at all. His mouth was tight, and she could tell he was worried. They flew at eight thousand feet, and from this vantage point, the area they were heading into appeared beautiful and peaceful. Rachel knew that was an illusion.

"This area is high Taliban traffic?"

"Yes," Hamilton muttered. "Peshuwar is thick with Taliban, spies and like Dodge City of the 1880s. A den of snakes."

"You've flown here before?"

"Yes, we've delivered food and medicine to the small village that's now being flooded out."

"I've never seen the Kabul River before today."

"It's a cold, murderous river," he warned her. "People drive their trucks through the sandy, shallow areas, and a wall of water suddenly rushes down out of the mountains and washes them away. A lot of Afghans drown. It's the thunderstorms in the mountains dumping five inches of water into a creek that flows into the river. There's a tidal wave and it comes out of nowhere. People can't see it coming until it's too late. And that water's hypothermic. It comes straight off glaciers. We routinely will get calls for flood rescue at least five or six times in the summer."

"I hope we get there in time," she said, worried.

"Me, too. Depends upon a lot of things."

Feeling for the trapped people, Rachel continued to

use the binoculars and scan for possible missiles that could be shot at them. They had no warning equipment on board. Chinooks were utterly vulnerable to attack, unlike the bristling Apache gunship.

Sitting up, she trained her binoculars on the river that was rapidly coming up. "If we can find them, that means you have to hover just above the truck so they can climb in through the belly door."

"Right. The people from that village know the routine."

"How do we know they aren't Taliban disguised as villagers?"

"We don't. But this village is right on the curve of the Kabul, and it's a fortress against Taliban. We've rescued people from there before. Their imam has a radio and he has contacted Bagram before in these situations."

"Must be a trustworthy imam," Rachel muttered.

"He is," Hamilton assured her. "Let's start descent."

"Roger."

Rachel tensed as the Chinook descended from its safer altitude toward the lower one. The closer they got, the more of a target they became.

"Do you see a white Toyota truck stuck on the sandbar in the river?" he demanded, guiding the bird down to three thousand feet.

"No…nothing…"

"Stay alert," he said. "It might have been swept off into the river and is gone. And no one will ever find it or them. That river is deep and swift."

"Roger…"

As the Chinook hit one thousand feet and began to fly over the river itself, Rachel felt fear. She always did at this altitude. They were sitting ducks.

Suddenly, she saw a flash from the slope of the mountain to her left.

"Hamilton!" she yelled, pointing.

Too late!

Rachel's eyes widened. It was a missile, aimed right at them!

"Chaff!" Hamilton roared, slamming the Chinook to the left and taking evasive action.

The bird groaned at the hard left turn. The engines screamed.

Rachel released the chaff, an aluminum countermeasure that would hopefully lead the missile to it and not the helo. Her heart surged into her throat. She saw the smoking trail of the missile. Oh, God…

It was the last thing she clearly remembered. As the Chinook was wrenched around, the missile ignored the chaff and struck the bird in the rear.

Fire erupted through the cargo hold. The helo wrenched upward, and Ty fought the controls. Screeching metal was torn out of the rear, the shrapnel flying forward. Hamilton felt a hot sensation in his left arm. His whole focus was on the helo suddenly shifting and falling. They were falling…right down into the river.

Rachel had no time to call for Mayday. The shrapnel from the explosion had sent a large, jagged piece of aluminum into the console. It instantly destroyed all their ability to communicate. Sucking in a breath, she grabbed the arms of her chair. The Chinook jerked and jumped. She heard the flailing of the rotors. Suddenly, the rear engine rotor flew apart, the long blades whirling and whipping past them like scimitars.

Choking, Rachel knew they were going to die. Smoke filled the cabin, black and thick. Hamilton was doing his best to try and make a soft landing into the water.

The Kabul River came up fast as the Chinook plummeted like a rock into the icy, furious green water. The rear of the destroyed helo struck the water first. Rachel let out a cry and was savagely jerked forward and then slammed back into the harness. Her neck snapped, and her helmet jammed into the seat for a second. The water rushed into the cargo hold.

Rachel instantly yanked off her harness, and Hamilton did the same. She pulled off her helmet and threw it behind her. Now, they had to egress this sinking helo or they would drown. Hamilton looked deathly pale, but she had no time to ask why. He'd released his harness, ridded himself of the helmet and had used his booted foot to break open the escape window. She did the same on her side. The glass shattered outward.

Within seconds, water flowed into the broken windows. It was cold and shocked Rachel as she took a huge breath. Somehow she wriggled and escaped out the window. Within seconds, she was swimming for her life. Cold water surged over her head as she flailed. The water was freezing. Her flight boots dragged her down. Striking out, Rachel kicked hard and finally broke the surface.

Gasping, water running into her eyes, she saw they were closer to the left bank of the river. Hamilton? Where was he? Unable to call him, she dodged another piece of the helo as it sank with ripping, tearing sounds, and then it gurgled beneath the foaming water. She didn't realize just how deep this river was until the Chinook completely disappeared from sight.

Rachel jerked her head around looking for Hamilton. And then…she saw him…floating, unconscious. *Oh,*

God! Without a thought for her own survival, Rachel swam straight toward his body. She grabbed his arm and managed to pull him so his head came out of the water. He was out cold. Sobbing, the current carrying them swiftly downstream, Rachel felt no confidence in their survival. In five minutes, hypothermia would set in. She'd become disoriented, her muscles would freeze up, and she would no longer be able to swim. God, no.

Chapter 9

Rachel swallowed a lot of water as she worked to bring her arm across Hamilton's chest. She went down, struggling to keep his head above water. The current was swift and icy cold. Flailing, she kicked hard, her boots tugging her downward. As she broke the surface, water exploded out of her mouth, and she gasped for air. Hamilton's head lolled against her shoulder and neck.

Adrenaline surged through her. Since they were closer to the left bank of the Kabul River, she struck out with her arm. Her efforts were impeded as she was suddenly hit from beneath the surface by a piece of the helicopter fuselage. The metal, unseen, twisted her around so that they were now looking upstream. Her eyes widened with terror. There, on the right bank, several lights flashed from the same hillside that had brought them down. The Taliban were firing at them!

Rachel gulped and allowed the current to carry them

swiftly downstream to escape the incoming artillery. The first explosion landed far above them, but the concussion blast made her ears hurt and ring. Kicking constantly, she kept them pointed toward the far shore that was thick with trees.

She heard the artillery scream and then it stopped. No! She tried to shield Hamilton with her body knowing it would land close. When the shell struck the dark green surface, it sent up a geyser twenty feet high, into the air. And when it exploded, an enormous wall of water threw Rachel and Ty ten feet farther down the river.

Rachel felt the blast pound against them. Much to her surprise, the tidal wave created by the blast beneath the water sent them closer to the bank. Choking, she continued to flail with one arm toward that shore. The river curved and they drifted around it. Rachel used the curve to actually get closer to the bank. Water kept striking her face. The cold was slowing her movements. She could no longer feel her body. Her feet felt like she had fifty-pound weights on each leg. Sobbing, Rachel knew she had to get out of the water or they were both going to sink and drown.

Within five feet of the shore, her boots struck bottom. With a cry of triumph, Rachel thrust forward, pulling Hamilton along. Her shoulder ached, and her arm had no sensation left. With each movement, she came out of the icy water. She sobbed for breath, her energy spent. She hooked her hands beneath Hamilton's armpits and dragged him out of the water and onto the shore.

Falling to her knees, she looked upstream. They had made the curve, and she knew that for the moment, they were unseen by the enemy. But that wouldn't last long.

Rachel wiped the water from her eyes with her shaking hands. There was thick brush and a grove of pine trees right in front of them. All she had to do was drag Hamilton into the area.

Looking at him, Rachel noticed a large, bloody gash on the left side of his skull. A piece of the torn Chinook had struck him and knocked him unconscious. Shakily, fear rising in her, Rachel pressed her fingers against his carotid artery at the left side of his bloody neck. She could feel a strong, solid pulse. He was alive! Just knowing that gave her the energy she needed.

If she didn't get them hidden shortly, the Taliban would find them. The enemy had radios, and even though they were on the other side of this river and unable to cross it, she knew they would call the closest Taliban unit on their side of the river. Gasping, she got to her feet. Dizziness swept over her. Staggering, Rachel shook her head. She had to think! She had to have the strength to get them to safety. They had to hide.

Groaning, Rachel gathered up his head and shoulders against her chest. She hooked her hands beneath his armpits and tugged hard. He was heavy. Grunting, she again jerked one more step backward. Every time she thrust using the heels of her boots digging into the sand, they made progress. It took a minute, but in the end, Rachel had them hidden in the thickets.

On the other side of the thickets was room to allow Hamilton to stretch out. Trembling violently from the cold and exertion, Rachel had to turn him over on his back since he probably had swallowed a lot of water. It needed to come out. Turning Hamilton so he was on his belly, she pulled his arms up above his head. She straddled his lower back, took her hands and pushed with all her might against the center of his back where his lungs were located.

A gush of water came out of his mouth. Heartened, Rachel continued to push against his torso. In five pushes, all the water was out of his lungs. It was then that he groaned.

Quickly getting off him, Rachel turned him over. She brought his arms down and knelt near his shoulder, anxiously watching his face. It had been deathly pale, but now, she could see pinkness coming back to his cheeks. When his eyes fluttered open, she sobbed.

"Ty? Ty? Are you all right? Can you hear me?" Rachel leaned over him, voice rasping. He tried to focus on her. At first, his blue eyes looked dull and murky.

Ty heard Rachel's hoarse, trembling voice. It felt like a drum reverberating inside his brain. Pain throbbed unremittingly on the left side of his head. As his vision began to clear, Hamilton belatedly realized that Rachel was leaning over him, an expression of terror on her face. Why was her hair wet and bedraggled around her shoulders? Her face was pale.

"Speak to me, Ty."

He opened his mouth. There was a brackish taste in it. He felt like he was drifting in and out of consciousness. Not only that, he was becoming aware of a deep ache in his upper, left arm. He began to shiver. Cold seeped into him. What had happened? When Rachel reached out, her hand brushing his cheek, he felt how cold her hand was. Frowning, he held her frightened gaze. What had happened?

"Talk, dammit!" Rachel whispered, inches from his face. Looking up, she quickly gazed around the area. Her ears were still ringing from the artillery explosions. She would never hear the Taliban sneaking up on them.

"Wh-what happened?" Ty rasped. He felt her hand leave his cheek. Instantly, he missed that connection with her.

As quickly as she could, Rachel said, "We got shot out of the sky by the Taliban. We crashed into the Kabul River. I just got us out, and we're now hiding in some bushes along the bank."

Suddenly, all of it came back to him. He lay there on the ground, staring up at Rachel. She was shaking, her uniform plastered against her body, her arms wrapped around herself. His own terror raced through him. When he tried to lift his left arm to touch his head, the pain was unbearable. With a grunt, he found he couldn't.

"Help me sit up," he told her.

Nodding, Rachel slid her arm beneath his neck and eased him up into a sitting position. Hamilton drew up his legs, and he placed his right hand on his brow. "You're hurt," she told him, her voice wobbly. "When the Chinook went down, you egressed out the window and into the water. A piece of the metal must have cut you and knocked you unconscious. I didn't see it happen." Rachel moved to Ty's left side so she could get a better look at the injury on his head. There was at least an inch-long gash that had laid his scalp open. It was bleeding heavily, the blood flowing down his neck, shoulder and soaking into his wet uniform.

"Where's the enemy?" Hamilton demanded, raising his head and trying to think through the haze of pain.

Rachel pointed across the river. "Over there and up on a hill, probably a mile away from us. The river carried us around a bend. We're out of sight for now." Rachel pushed the hair off her face and muttered, "I'm hoping they think they killed us with those two artillery rounds. That way, they won't start hunting for us."

"Good," he rasped. As he lifted his head, the pain almost blinded him. Biting back a groan, he asked, "Are you okay? Hurt?"

"No, I'm fine," Rachel whispered. She managed a twisted smile. "You were knocked unconscious. I didn't know that until you floated around the wreckage, and I caught sight of you." She reached out and touched his bloodied left hand. "I was so scared."

Ty moved his hand and cupped her cold, white fingers. "I don't remember anything," he said, his own voice sounding like gravel.

"You swallowed a lot of water." Rachel wanted connection with him right now. They were in enemy territory and they were alone.

Looking around, Hamilton tried to reorient. "We got hit. I remember that. The helo's rear lifted up."

"Yeah, that's where we took the hit," Rachel said. She studied the heavily bleeding head wound. Releasing his hand, she sat down and pulled the Velcro open on the deep, right-thigh pocket of her uniform. "We didn't have time to grab out egress bags," she told him.

Hamilton watched her dig around in the pocket. "What do you have in there?"

"A radio, dressings, antibiotic packs, needle, thread, aspirin," she muttered. Pulling it all out, she picked up the radio. It was wet. "I hope this works. We need to call for help."

Heartened, Ty said, "Make the call." Would it work even though it was waterlogged? His radio had been in his egress pack. Now, it was at the bottom of the Kabul River. Holding his breath, he watched as Rachel turned the small, round dial that would turn it on. When on, it would flash a small, green light on the front. Nothing happened.

"Oh, damn," Rachel muttered, twisting the dial again and again. "It's not working."

Hamilton heard the low edge of fear in her voice. "It's not designed to be dunked in water," he said, trying to make her feel better. He saw the desperation in her face, her mouth working as she turned it on and off several times. "Maybe it needs to dry out, and we can try it later?"

"We don't have later, Ty." Rachel had used his first name without even thinking about it. "We've got to get help. I know the Taliban will be looking for us."

No matter how many times she tried, the radio refused to work. Sitting there, the device in her hand, Rachel gave him a look of anxiety.

"Look, we need to take evasive action," he told her. "We didn't have time to make a Mayday call to Bravo. No one is going to miss us until we don't show up an hour from now."

"Did you call in our changed flight?" she asked.

"No, I thought you did."

Staring at him, Rachel realized it had been her duty to do that. And she'd failed. "Oh, God," she uttered. "I didn't. Bravo will think we're flying a straight line from Samarigam back to Camp Bravo." That one mistake could well cost their lives.

Hamilton felt grim. Shaking from the cold and trying to think through the blinding headache, he rasped, "There was a lot of distraction at the village."

Rachel had never expected him to say that. Blinking, she whispered, "I'm really sorry, Ty."

Hamilton gripped her hand, squeezed it once and released it. Right now, he felt raw, but he wanted to erase the fear he heard in her voice, the reality of their situation. "Let's concentrate on evasion. We need a plan. And where we're going."

Rachel knelt beside him. "We need to get this bleeding stopped." She tore open a packet. "Open your mouth, I'm giving you the antibiotics and some aspirin."

Hamilton nodded, tipped his head back, and she dropped a large, white pill into his mouth. It was hell trying to choke it down, but he did.

"I get to use all that first aid they taught us so long ago," she joked. Freezing, Rachel was grateful it was August, the temperature at seventy and it was sunny. If they were lucky, their uniforms would dry in a couple of hours. At nightfall, it dropped to the forties or even to freezing in this high mountain environment.

"Do what you have to do."

"That gash is long. I'm going to have to sew the edges together. God, I've never done anything like this before, Ty. But if I don't, it's going to keep on bleeding…."

Hearing the desperation in her voice, Ty murmured, "Take a deep breath, Rachel. It's going to be okay."

She spread out the items, steadied by his voice and the fact that he called her by her first name. He'd never done that before, but right now, she was grateful. Her hands stopped shaking so much. It was fear, she knew, but Hamilton's demeanor was one of quiet steadiness compared to how she felt inside. She marveled at his grace under pressure. "Okay, let me line up this stuff. Thank God I cram my flight pockets full of stuff."

"It's always a good habit to get into," Ty agreed. He closed his eyes. "Listen, can you do this when I'm lying down? I'm feeling dizzy."

"Sure, it will probably be easier." Rachel slid her hand beneath his neck and helped him lie down. "You're looking pale. What's going on?"

"Just exhausted," Hamilton admitted, closing his eyes. He'd nearly died, and he knew he was in shock.

Alarmed, Rachel realized she hadn't checked him from head to toe for any other injuries. "Ty, are you hurting anywhere else?"

"Yeah, my left, upper arm feels like it's on fire."

Scooting back, Rachel leaned down. She saw the arm of the garment had been slashed open. Pulling it back, she gasped. Another piece of shrapnel had cut deeply into his upper arm. "You've got another slash wound," she said.

"Bleeding bad?" he asked.

"No, not a lot. It's just very, very deep."

The concern in her husky voice flowed over him. He felt pretty light-headed. "Listen, do what you have to do. I'm feeling faint…."

Rachel watched as he lost consciousness. Stunned for a moment, she realized that there was no better time to sew up both wounds, because he wouldn't feel the pain. She grabbed a packet, ripped it open and applied the white powder of antibiotic across his scalp wound. She carefully folded up the packet and set it aside. The other half would go into his arm wound. Tearing open the next packet that said Lidocaine, she dripped part of it across his scalp. This medicine would numb the site so she could stitch it closed. Hands shaking, the hardest part was getting the thread through the needle.

Rachel was constantly dividing her attention between stitching up the two wounds and listening for enemy approach. Although they still wore their protective Kevlar vests, and each had a pistol strapped across their chest, it wasn't enough firepower against the Taliban.

The roar of the river hid other sounds. Rachel worked in silent terror as she did her best to bind Hamilton's wounds. She had used the small set of scissors to cut away some of the upper sleeve of his uniform to reach to the gash. To her relief, the scalp wound stopped bleeding once she'd stitched it closed. More than anything, Rachel was worried about infection setting in. If it did, he'd become feverish and unable to walk. And she knew they'd be doing a lot of walking very shortly.

It took an hour for her to finish. Hamilton's lashes fluttered a few times just as she got done wrapping his arm with a dressing and tying it off. When he looked toward her, she smiled.

"Welcome back to the world of the living. I just got done fixing you up. How do you feel?"

Closing his eyes, he whispered, "A little better."

"How's your head?"

Ty opened his eyes, turned his head and looked up at her. Her dark brown hair was drying around her beautiful face. Her gold eyes were dark with concealed fear. He managed a crooked, one-cornered smile of his own. "The pain has turned down ten notches. I almost feel human again, thanks."

"And your arm?" Rachel asked, relieved.

"I can't feel my hand," he said.

"Maybe that shrapnel sliced into a nerve?" she wondered. She saw him move his fingers.

"I don't know. Maybe it will go away in time," he uttered.

Sitting at his side, her hip near his left hand, she said, "An hour's gone by. I haven't heard or seen the Taliban yet."

Thirsty, Hamilton sat up with her help. As he scanned the area, he saw that she'd picked the perfect place to hide them. They were ringed with thick, tall bushes on the bank. "Did you hear a helo?" he asked.

"No..." Rachel said frowning.

Hamilton wiped his mouth. "I need to take stock of what I have. Let me dig into my flight pockets and find out."

Rachel got up and knelt nearby. "What are you thinking? Peshuwar is down farther on the other side of the river."

Ty pushed himself into a sitting position. He opened up both his Velcro flight pockets on his legs and placed his items beside Rachel's stash. "There's no way we can walk into Peshuwar. It's a den of thieves. The Taliban has a strong presence there. They see us in our uniforms, we're dead on the spot."

"You said there was an imam in Peshuwar who was pro-American. Maybe we could find him?"

"How?"

"I see your point."

Ty studied their cache. "Okay, we have ten protein bars between us. Antibiotics. Waterproof matches. A pair of scissors, a small penknife, one wet radio, two silver packs, which act as thermal blankets to keep our heat in, a compass and a map." Ty picked up the map. It had been coated, so it was waterproof. He opened it and spread it out between them.

"We're here," he said, putting his index finger down on the river, north of Peshuwar. Brow wrinkling, he squinted his eyes. "There's a very small village here, on the slope of the mountains we just flew over."

Rachel knelt, studied the area, and saw where he

was pointing. "That's a good fifteen miles inland, away from this river."

Ty looked up into her worried gaze. "There's a stream coming down off the mountains, through that village, and it flows right here into the river. We're going to need water."

"What's your ultimate goal here?" she asked.

"Survival," he said solemnly, "and reach Samarigam on the other side of that mountain range." He saw her eyes widen. "It's our only hope, Rachel. We're dead if we walk into Peshuwar asking for help. We know Samarigam is pro-American."

Nodding, she bit her lower lip and studied the map some more. "What kind of miles do we have to walk?"

"At least sixty miles, including the distance to this village on the map." Ty watched her face crumple. "Twenty miles a day. We can do it in three days. We'll have the brush and trees along that creek that leads up to this first village. We can travel in daylight."

"We'll never be able to travel at night in these mountains," she said. "And if we get to that village, there's no guarantee it isn't a Taliban stronghold, too."

"I don't think it is," Ty said, searching his memory. "The old CO of the last squadron told me that they'd flown in food and medicine to that village. Maybe they won't shoot us on sight."

Turning, Rachel straightened. She heard a dog barking across the river. She held up her hand. "Stay here. I'm going to see what or who is nearby."

Chapter 10

Rachel pulled her .45 pistol from the holster strapped across her Kevlar vest. Getting down on her belly, she moved through the thick brush to see about the barking dog. It sounded far away, as if on the other side of the wide, deep Kabul River. She prayed that was so and tucked her head down. She closed her eyes and pushed forward through the scratchy thickets.

Eventually, through the foliage from her hiding place, Rachel saw the dog. Her heart began a slow pound. There were five Taliban soldiers, all armed with AK-47s, standing on the other side of the river. A mangy, black mongrel dog, about fifty pounds, barked constantly. They were walking slowly along the other bank. Licking her lips, Rachel lay and followed them with her gaze. Were they the same group that had fired the artillery rounds at them? She didn't know. Her hand closed firmly over her .45.

It was obvious to her they were looking for something. Maybe signs of their footprints, showing that they survived the crash into the river? Eyes narrowing, Rachel watched as the group slowly moved upstream. They would bend down, look at the dirt and then straighten and move on. Yes, they were looking for signs they'd left the river and escaped.

She wriggled slowly backward through the thickets and finally got to the other side. She pushed up on her knees and looked toward Hamilton. He was sitting up, face pale, but alert. In his hand, he had his weapon, a .38. Getting up, she walked over and knelt at his side.

"There are five Taliban and a dog on the other side," she said in a low voice. "They were walking the bank of the river trying to find our tracks." Motioning toward the river, she added, "They just disappeared around the curve. Right now, we're safe."

Ty raised his brows even though it hurt. "They're going to try and make sure we're dead. The moment they know we survived, they'll bring every Taliban in the area down on our necks."

Rachel nodded, pushing the pistol back into the nylon holster across her chest. "Agreed." She gazed into his murky blue eyes. "How are you feeling?"

"The aspirin is taking hold," he told her in a roughened tone. "My head has finally stopped hurting so damn much."

"So," she teased, "you can think now?"

Just Rachel's partial smile lifted Ty's spirits. He managed a twisted grin back up at her. "Yeah, but we have a lot to think about."

Rachel sat down, drawing her knees up. "You're right, we can't go to Peshuwar. And it makes sense to follow that creek up to that tiny village on the top of the mountain. I just don't know if they will kill us or help us."

"Food and medicine has been dropped there before. We have to take a chance."

"I like the fact we can move up that stream under cover of the trees and bushes. We're less likely to be seen, and we can travel during daylight hours."

"This isn't going to be easy. When I move my head, I get dizzy. I don't even know if I can stand up and walk a straight line." Frustration settled in him over his condition. He was the helpless one. Rachel had survived the crash and was physically sound. He was not.

Reaching out, Rachel gripped his hand for a moment and gave it a squeeze. "I don't think help is coming to rescue us. Everyone at Ops will think we're on a beeline between Samarigam and Bravo. They'll be looking for us in the wrong area. And if you have to lean on me as we make it to that village, I don't mind."

The warmth of her fingers flooded his cold, chilled body. Ty continued to tremble from the cold flight suit against his goose-pimpled flesh. He saw the sincerity in her gold-and-brown eyes, and his heart opened. For one crazy moment, Hamilton wondered what it would be like to kiss Rachel. To feel the softness of her lips against his. Somehow, Ty knew she would be an incredible kisser. And then, shocked where his thoughts had gone, he sternly gave himself an internal shake. The crash must be making him think really stupid thoughts.

"If only your radio would dry out and work. That signal is set for the rescue channel on the radio at Ops…." Ty said.

"It's our only real hope," Rachel agreed, picking up the radio that she'd laid on a flat rock. "And it's only got so much battery left in it. I think we should keep it off and try it near sunset." Looking at her watch, she saw that it was 2:00 p.m. "I'm going to go reconnoiter the area. According to our map, that stream intersects the river about a quarter of a mile south of us. I want to make sure we can get there without being spotted."

"Good idea." Ty watched as she slowly rose and pulled out her .45. He managed a slight grin. "Why are you carrying that dinosaur of a pistol?" he wondered.

Looking down at him, Rachel said, "Because my father taught me if you want to stop a man in one shot, a .45 has the power to do it. I know the Army has other pistols that they prefer me to carry, but I want a big stick."

"Right now," Ty said, appreciating her logic, "that's exactly what is needed.

"Your .38 won't stop a man," she pointed out. "You'll have to fire three or four shots to stop him from charging toward you. That's a waste of bullets. We only have so many with us, and each one is going to count if we get into a firefight." Rachel pushed the drying hair off her brow. "One shot. One kill."

"Sniper speak," he said.

"My uncle Morgan was a sniper at one time when he was a Marine. When I graduated from flight school, he gave me this weapon as a gift." Rachel lifted the dull black pistol and gave it a fond look. "He knows his weapons. And carrying this pistol is like having him with me all the time. I love him very much...."

Hamilton could see it in the softened expression of her face and how her voice dropped and became suddenly husky with unseen tears. "Get going," he told her. "I'll stay here, lay down and try to rest."

"Good idea." She lifted her hand and said, "I'll be back as soon as I can...."

The pine trees were interspersed with leaf-bearing trees. Rachel walked silently in and around them. The good news was that the thickets ran almost solidly parallel to the bank of the green river. She would halt, hide behind a huge tree trunk and look around. Then Rachel would key her hearing to see if she picked up any sounds that meant a human being was near. When she could hear and see nothing, she would continue another hundred yards and do the same thing. It wouldn't get her to their objective fast, but she had no idea who or what inhabited this beautiful, green area.

Knowing that goat and sheep herders were everywhere and that they would use this river to water their herd, Rachel stayed especially watchful. Young boys were sent out to tend these herds. And she would not know if they were friend or foe. She didn't want to take a chance and remained guarded, her movements conservative. Overhead, puffy, white clouds came and went. To the north, in the mountain range, she could see dark, angry thunderclouds. Here on the flat of the valley, which was all desert except for the green ribbon of life on either side of the Kabul river, it appeared uninhabited. So far.

Rachel knew the Taliban was actively seeking proof of their death. They would be waiting for the bodies of two airmen to wash up on either side of the bank of this river. The Afghans were great trackers. As she moved silently down toward her objective, Rachel looked for brush on her way back and wiped out her tracks. There was no reason to think the Taliban wouldn't have men on this side of the river who were actively hunting for footprints right now.

Her heart never settled down as she held the gun up and ready as she walked. Every once in a while, as she stood with her back pressed to a trunk, Rachel would think about Hamilton. She'd saved his life, which struck her as ironic. He'd tried to end her career earlier in her life. And here she was saving his butt. Still, Rachel would have done the same thing all over again. Hamilton was a fellow aviator, U.S. Army and, therefore, a buddy. She would never have thought to let him drown when he was knocked unconscious.

Locating the stream, she knelt down by a pine tree and looked up. The creek was wider than she first thought. It was a good four feet wide and running strong with glacier water from high above. Rachel could see glimpses of the stream moving up the rocky slope toward the sharp peaks at least twenty miles away. Smiling a little, she closed her eyes for a moment. She opened them and slowly stood up. She broke off a pine branch and began to use it to destroy her tracks as she retraced her way back.

Ty never heard Rachel approach. He'd dragged himself over to a tree trunk and leaned against it, his weapon in hand. Startled when she seemed to appear out of nowhere, he saw her smile. Her dark hair framed her face. Her cheeks were red and it emphasized her large, intelligent gold eyes. Ty found himself wondering what the hell had possessed him to try and destroy her career. There was nothing but feminine strength and beauty, not to mention a powerful intellect, in Rachel. He began to appreciate what she brought to their collective table in this dire situation.

Rachel knelt near his left side. "How are you doing?" She had been gone a good hour. Hamilton's face had a bit of color to it now. He was no longer looking like a wan ghost.

"Better," he said. "What did you find?"

"We've got some luck on our side," Rachel said, smiling. She lifted her hand and pointed toward where the stream was located. "It's a lot wider than I thought it would be. Plenty of trees and brush to hide us for as far as I could see. I think if we get you up and walking, we'll be a lot safer." She looked up, her brows falling. "I know the Taliban has people walking the bank of this river on *our* side."

Ty nodded. "Yeah, and I'm jumpy as hell about it. It's only a matter of time before they'll be near our hiding place."

"Right." Rachel inspected his head wound. "It's stopped bleeding. Do you still have a headache?"

"It's gone," he murmured. "It's my arm."

Rachel examined the dressing she put around his upper arm. "It's a really deep gash, Ty. It's got to hurt like hell."

He shouldn't have liked the way his first name rolled from her lips, but he did. It sent an incredible, warm sensation through him. "It does. I've been trying to lift it, but I'm not doing too well. I'm just glad it was my left arm. I shoot with my right." He grimaced.

Rachel chuckled. "You need a sling for that arm. And I don't have anything to make it with." She looked around. "Maybe we'll find something along the creek."

"Don't worry about it," he said, tucking the .38 back into his chest holster. "Would you help me up?"

Rachel put her pistol away and walked around him. She held out her hand to him as he prepared to stand. "Hold on to me. I don't want you falling if you get dizzy."

Agreeing, Ty gripped her outstretched hand and was

surprised at her strength. He heaved himself to his feet. Instantly, dizziness struck him.

Rachel saw him start to fall. She stepped forward, slid her arm around his back and stabilized him. Hamilton had to lean heavily on her in order to stop from falling forward. "Easy," she whispered, keeping him in a tight embrace.

Ty didn't struggle. He was amazed she could take his full weight until he could regain his balance. She was incredibly strong. His arm had gone around her shoulders. She was five foot ten inches tall, two inches shorter than he was. Grateful that she anchored him, Ty fought the dizziness. Finally, it passed.

"Okay, I'm ready," he told her.

"Let's just walk together for a while," she counseled, glancing up at him. Rachel was once more aware of how incredibly good-looking Hamilton was. Truly, he could be the poster child on a U.S. Army ad for television. Definitely eye candy of the finest sort. And she found herself absorbing his strong body against her own, his arm around her shoulders. For a split second, Rachel wondered what it would be like to kiss him, to feel his body against hers.

Hamilton said, "Yeah, good idea. Until I know I can walk and the dizziness isn't going to nail us."

"Hold on...." Rachel leaned down and picked up her pine tree limb. "We're going to have to turn and cover our tracks as we go. Otherwise, the Taliban will find them and follow us."

Ty knew they would make a snail's pace toward their objective. "Let me try and do that." He held his hand out for the branch.

"Okay," Rachel said, keeping her arm firmly around him, her hand on his right hand. "Let's see if doing it causes you dizziness or not. If it does, I'll have to do it."

"I'll do it," Ty told her. Somehow, he had to be of help, and not utterly helpless.

"Okay, let's go…" Rachel urged in a whisper.

It was nearly 1600, 4:00 p.m., by the time they reached the fork that would lead them up the creek. Rachel saw the perspiration on Hamilton's furrowed brow. It cost him so much to continually turn, lean down and sweep their boot tracks out of the sand. Yet, he did it without complaining. His left arm didn't work well, but well enough to make the broad, sweeping movements. Rachel knew he was in a lot of pain.

"Let's sit down and rest," she counseled him. Guiding him to a thick pine tree trunk, Rachel helped him ease to the ground. She kneeled beside him. "Are you in pain?"

"Yeah, but that's all right," he muttered, feeling profoundly weakened. "I guess I'm not very good with a broom," Hamilton joked.

Smiling a little, Rachel peeked at the cut she'd made in his flight uniform arm. "Good, there's no blood showing on the dressing." She reached into her right thigh pocket and found some pain pills. "You need to take one. We've got a lot of hours of daylight left, and we've got to keep moving."

Ty didn't argue and swallowed the pill. He was thirsty. But to drink that water without purification tablets could be a disaster, too. Looking around, he spotted a plastic bottle near the stream. "Hey, go get that bottle, will you? We need something to put water in."

After spotting it, Rachel walked over and picked it

up. She laughed softly as she brought it over to him. "It's a water bottle! Just what we need."

"That village up above this creek received fresh water from the Army in their supplies. Some kid probably drank it and tossed the bottle into the creek. It eventually found its way down here."

"You're probably right." Standing, Rachel handed him the bottle and dug in her other thigh pocket. "I've got tablets that will clean the water."

"I made fun of you carrying an Army in your pockets, now I'm not," he told her with a slight grin.

"In the Apache we have an actual compartment with a bag that holds all this stuff," Rachel said. "When I found out I'd be flying Chinooks instead, I just transferred it all to my leg pockets. I'm glad I did."

"And I'll never make fun of your bulging leg pockets again," Ty swore. He saw her find a packet of water purification tablets. When he handed her the bottle, their fingers met and touched. Something good and warm flowed into Ty from that brief contact.

"I feel like a pharmacy on legs," Rachel gripped good-naturedly. "I'll be right back."

Rachel filled the quart-size bottle and dropped a tablet into it. She shook it until it dissolved. Walking back, she knelt down next to Ty and said, "Drink all you want." She handed it to him.

Ty guzzled about half of the cold, delicious water. "Here," he told her, wiping his mouth, "you take the rest."

Nodding, Rachel drank the other half of the water. Once more, she stood and refilled the bottle and put another tablet into it. "Ready to go?" she asked.

"Yeah," he muttered, pushing himself upright and using the trunk of the tree to stop him from falling.

Dizziness struck again. He closed his eyes, head resting against the solid wood. And then it passed.

"Okay?" she asked before tucking the filled bottle of water into her leg pocket.

Opening his eyes, he rasped, "Yeah. It wasn't as bad this time."

"Good. Ready?"

Ty said, "I am, but let me see if I can walk by myself."

Prepared, Rachel said, "Go for it."

"We'll make better time if I can," he panted. With an iron will engaged, Hamilton stepped away from the tree. The dizziness did not attack him. He grinned triumphantly over at her. "I can walk."

Rachel returned his grin. His blue eyes appeared less murky, especially with the pain pill taking hold. "Great." She picked up their pine broom. "You lead and I'll follow."

Feeling relief that he wasn't going to continue to be the helpless one, Ty gave her a thumbs-up sign. He pulled out his .38, and kept it in his right hand as he started slowly up the creek.

Rachel quickly covered their tracks and felt a bit happier and more relieved. She constantly looked around, her hearing keyed. They began to make good time up the gentle slope. They had survived a terrible crash. She was uninjured, and Hamilton was well enough to move on his own. Now, all they had to do was stay hidden, avoid the Taliban and make it to that tiny village on the side of the mountain.

Wiping her mouth, perspiration dotting her brow as she worked to erase their prints, Rachel realized something crucial. When night fell, they would be alone. And together. The sudden awareness of their intimacy panicked her. She had gone from hating Ty to liking him. He had been brave, courageous and a team player after the crash. She wiped her brow with the back of her sleeve. Now she understood as never before that Ty had changed. For the better. What was she going to do now?

Chapter 11

Ty fought with a vengeance the pounding headache that had come back. He attributed it to the ever steeper slope, which they quietly continued to navigate parallel to the creek. The trees would thin out here and there, and that was when they'd stop, look around, and ensure they wouldn't be seen before making it to a thicker grove of trees and brush.

Looking back, Rachel noticed Ty's face was becoming more pale. His mouth had tensed. When they got to a thick stand of pine and brush, she knelt down. He automatically knelt beside her.

"You're in pain?" she asked in a low voice.

Digging into his thigh pocket, Ty pulled out a packet of aspirin. "Yeah, it just came back. I'll pop these down and it should go away again."

"Let me check the wound," Rachel insisted. She got up and went to examine him more closely. One hand on Ty's shoulder, she gently moved his head a bit to get a good look at the wound. "It looks okay. There's no drainage. No sign of infection."

Absorbing her touch, Ty tried to keep things impersonal. "Good. It's just aftermath, is all. I'll be fine." How he wanted to reach out and grab her hand. This was all crazy, and Ty decided that the crash had made him emotionally vulnerable in a way he'd never been before.

"Here," she said, handing him their only water bottle.

"Thanks," he said, taking it from her.

"We've been climbing for forty minutes. A good hiking walk takes twenty minutes." She saw his Adam's apple bob several times as he downed the two tablets. His eyes were dull and she could tell he was in a lot of pain. Yet, he didn't complain. Rachel wasn't so sure she wouldn't have griped about it.

"We've probably gone a mile," Ty said, continuing to look around. The green strip that defined the creek quickly died and went back to the yellow grass and rocky soil. It was a barren, challenging landscape. "We're climbing and I'm slow," Ty added with a slight grimace.

"You're doing fine under the circumstances. How is your arm?"

"It would be nice to have a sling," he said. Holding it against his body kept it from really being painful. "If I drop my arm, it feels like it's on fire."

Rachel turned and craned her neck upward. "I don't see any village on that slope. Do you?"

Worry was evident in her tone. "It might be right on the creek, and we wouldn't see it from here," Ty said.

Rachel grunted. "You're probably right. Still,

we've got about two more miles to go, and it gets even steeper."

"That village is at seven thousand feet," Ty agreed. "I don't know if we should try to contact the elders in it or not."

"I know," Rachel said, worried. "They could be pro-Taliban."

"Most Afghan villages aren't," Ty said. He enjoyed simply looking at Rachel. She sat with her knees drawn up, arms around them. Her dark brown hair had dried and hung straight around her face. Cheeks red from exertion, she was a sight to behold. He wanted to kiss her. This time, he didn't overreact to the thought as he had before. Maybe because they were in a life-and-death situation, and the cards were stacked against them.

Glancing over at him, Rachel asked, "What do you want to do? Get close to it and hunker down for the night here at the creek? Contact them tomorrow morning?"

"No. It dives below freezing at night. All things being equal, I'd sure as hell like to be in a warm rock home with an elder than stuck out here."

"Mmm," Rachel agreed. Frowning, she muttered, "My ears are still ringing. I can't hear as well as I want to."

"It will go away within twenty-four hours," he said.

"I miss it. I'm afraid the Taliban will sneak up on us, and I won't hear them in time."

Reaching out, Ty briefly touched her hand. "Relax. My ears aren't ringing. We'll protect one another."

Warmth fled through her hand. Rachel was startled by his action. She could see Ty meant to give her solace. His fingers were long. *Flight hands.* Yes, he was a damn good pilot. Searching his eyes, she said, "Are you ready? Feel like going another mile?"

"Yeah," he muttered, getting to his feet. "Let's do it."

Rachel took the lead. She stayed as close to the bank of the gurgling creek as she could. The sun had moved to the other side of the peaks ahead of them, the mountains now in shadows on their side. The temperature had dropped. Rachel wished mightily for her thick, warm jacket but it had gone down in the Kabul River. Just moving kept her warm. Breath coming in gasps, she knew the altitude was getting to her.

By the time they'd gone another mile, Rachel called for a halt. Ty came and stood near her, his gaze fixed ahead.

"Do you hear that? Bells?" he asked.

"No," Rachel said. "Is that what you hear?"

"Yes," he said, focusing in on the sound. "I don't see anything but I know there's always a bell on the lead goat or sheep in a herd. Could be one nearby."

Mouth tightening, Rachel tried to see through the thick brush ahead but couldn't. "This would be a natural place for villagers to bring their livestock to eat and drink."

"Yes." Ty saw the worry in her features. "Since I can hear better than you, let me take the lead. You keep watch on our back."

Rachel nodded and moved aside. It was a good idea. Wishing she could hear better, she knew that her eyesight had to take over and make the difference. The creek had widened where they stood. As far as Rachel could see ahead around a slight curve, it continued to widen. It was perhaps ankle to knee deep here and there. Green moss floated along the bank. The grass, or what was left of it, was stubble. She was sure that the village's goats and sheep came through here regularly.

She pulled out her .45 and kept it in hand. Ty had pulled his .38. They had no idea who they might run into up above. Her heart was pounding from the relentless climb, but now, adrenaline started to flow into her bloodstream. Fear stalked her. Jittery, her nerves frayed by the near drowning after the crash, Rachel tried to focus.

As they rounded the curve of the creek, Ty suddenly went down on one knee, his pistol held up and ready.

Instantly, Rachel crouched behind him.

Ty made a signal with his hand and pointed to the other side of the creek.

Looking, Rachel saw a group of brown-and-white goats foraging up ahead. There was a young boy, about twelve years old, staff in hand, walking with them. The lead goat, a nanny with a leather collar and tinkling bell around her thin neck, took the small herd toward them. Rachel's heart began a slow pound. The boy wasn't armed and must have belonged to the unseen village above. She laid her hand on Ty's shoulder.

Twisting around, he looked at her.

"Let me get up and greet him. I know enough Pashto to speak to him. You stay hidden. If he runs or this is a trap, you can get away...."

Ty couldn't argue with her reasoning. He moved quietly into the nearby thickets, making sure he could draw a bead on the boy in case he had a hidden gun on him. Ty gave Rachel the signal to go ahead with her plan.

It was a risk but Rachel decided to put the pistol back in the holster across her Kevlar vest. If this boy was part of the unseen village, then he would know what an American helicopter pilot looked like. He'd be surprised to see her, a woman, but he would know she was American. *And, hopefully, a friend...*

The dark-haired boy was dressed in a long, blue vest, a white, long-sleeved shirt beneath it, brown trousers and, clearly, American, black hiking boots. Feeling a little more hopeful, Rachel eased from her hiding place. As she stepped to the bank of the stream, the nanny bleated and anchored.

The boy instantly looked up. His mouth dropped open.

"I come in peace," she called to the boy, giving him the customary greeting. "We need help. Can you take us to your elders?"

For a moment, the boy stared. Then his mouth clamped shut. He was frightened.

"Please," Rachel called to him in Pashto, "we are American. We need your help. Can you take us to your chief?"

Blinking, he called, "Where did you come from?"

"We were flying across your valley and we were shot down earlier today by the Taliban. We're trying to reach help."

The boy scratched his head. "Then it was *you!*"

Rachel didn't know what he was talking about. She did see the lad suddenly become excited. And then he raced to the other edge of the bank. "We saw your helicopter shot down earlier. My parents said the Americans died. But...you're here!"

Rachel smiled with some relief. "It's true. My friend, Captain Hamilton, is hurt. Can you lead us to your village? We need food and safety for the night."

"Of course, of course," the boy said. "I will bring my herd over. Wait!"

The boy sprang into action. In a blur, he quickly got

the twenty goats and herded them across the shallow stream. With his staff, he headed them up the slope. He then turned and stopped in front of her.

"I am Akmal!" He thrust his hand out to her, a big grin of welcome on his face.

Shaking his hand, Rachel said, "And I am Rachel." She turned and called to Ty, who emerged from the thickets.

Akmal became even more animated and officially introduced himself to the pilot. The boy seemed overjoyed to see them, his dark blue eyes glinting with excitement. When he noticed Ty's left arm, the bloody sleeve, he quickly took off a long cotton scarf from around his small neck.

"Here, Captain, use this to care for your arm."

Ty grinned and nodded.

Rachel took the scarf and fashioned it into a sling for his left arm. "We hit it lucky," she told him under her breath. "He's really glad to see us."

"Make that all of us," Ty murmured. His skin prickled where her fingers brushed his neck. "Thanks."

Rachel turned back to the boy. "I'd appreciate your taking us to your village. We need to talk with your chief."

"Of course," Akmal said. "Just follow me. Our leader is Hamid. He will be very surprised you lived. Allah has blessed you! Come!"

They set off at a fast pace. The goat herd trotted quickly up the mountain in front of them. Rachel walked behind Ty and kept watch on the rear. Both had put their pistols away as a show of peace. Within twenty minutes, the stone village came into view.

Rachel was amazed at how the rock homes blended into the yellow earth and rocky slope. The creek ran to the south of the village. She estimated there were twenty homes crowded together on a high bluff overlooking the valley and river below. She saw women in burkas, children playing and a couple of scrawny dogs. Though she wondered how they managed to survive in such an inhospitable land, her admiration for the Afghan people rose once more. They were tough and enduring, no question.

"Welcome to our humble village," the leader, Hamid, said to them.

Rachel and Ty sat with the gray-bearded elder in his rock home. Akmal had gone through the village proclaiming that the pilots were alive. Within moments, everyone had emptied out of their homes to stand in the street and greet them. To their relief, this village was clearly a safe place. Rachel had seen American clothing on all of the children. And each one wore shoes. In no time, they were shepherded to the end rock home where the elder of the village lived.

Rachel had been given a dark blue scarf to wear by one of the women before she entered the elder's home. "Thank you, my lord. We are so very grateful that you would take us into your home," she told Hamid. Indeed, it was warm, and finally, Rachel felt the tips of her fingers for the first time since the crash. Her uniform had dried, but she knew it wouldn't be enough against the frigid night air.

Semeen, the elder's wife, had her two daughters bring in plates of food for them. They handed each one a plate, bowed and then left.

Rachel thanked her, then noticed what was on the plates. It was American food—cheese, crackers and peanut butter.

Hamid said, "Please, eat. We know you are hungry."

Usually, their customs didn't allow this type of eating, but the leader obviously knew their plight. As Rachel and Ty dug in she asked the elder, "Do you have any way we can contact our people for help?"

Hamid shook his head grimly. "The only way to get help is to ride the trail down our mountain into the next valley and then get to the village of Samarigam."

Rachel knew there were no radios and cell phones out in this rough, wild country. "Would it be possible to send a horse and rider to that village to get us help?"

"No. The Taliban is hunting for you. They've already ridden through here twice. They've broken down the doors of my people's homes, looking for you."

Rachel interpreted for Ty. He immediately frowned.

"Will they be back?" he asked.

Rachel translated.

"No. They think that you probably died and drowned in the river," Hamid said. "But they wanted to make sure."

"I'm sorry this happened to you and your people," Rachel said to the old man. He was well into his sixties, his kind face deeply tanned and lined. There was a glint in his brown eyes that Rachel liked. He smiled often beneath his thick, long beard.

Hamid shrugged. "They know the Americans come here once a month. That is when they disappear. They know your Apache helicopters will destroy them. Once, there was an American Special Forces team here, but no longer. If they were here, they could call for help."

"I understand," Rachel said. Cheese and crackers had never tasted so good! She didn't realize just how starved she was until now. Semeen came back with warm goat's milk in cups for each of them and then quietly disappeared once more.

"I can keep you overnight," the leader told her. "You will stay with us. There is medicine for Captain Hamilton if you need it. The Americans keep us supplied and we are grateful."

Mind racing, Rachel said, "Do you have horses we can use?"

"I do. I have two very fine, part-Arabian geldings."

Rachel always kept a plastic bag that contained Afghan money. She pulled it out of her pocket. "I don't know how much they cost, but will this be enough?"

Hamid took the plastic bag, pulled out the thick wad of bills and counted them. He smiled. "More than enough," he said. "Thank you for paying for them."

Rachel knew that the money would go a long way toward making Hamid willing to help them. "You're more than welcome."

"If we get the horses," Ty said, "we need a disguise. We can't be seen riding in our flight suits or the Taliban will kill us."

Understanding his concern, Rachel asked the elder, "Is it possible that there is enough money there to buy two sets of clothing? I must appear to be a man. If the Taliban looks at us through binoculars and sees that I'm a woman, they'll attack us."

Hamid chuckled. "Indeed, they would, Captain. You will need a special turban that will not only hide who you are but allow a slit for only your eyes. That way, they will not be able to tell."

"I can handle that," Rachel promised him.

"Unfortunately, because the Taliban comes without warning, I'm going to have to take you to where we keep our herd of goats at night. There is a small room in there where you can hide." He frowned. "By Muslim law, a man and woman should not be together, but for your safety, this is best."

"I understand," Rachel murmured. "We're grateful you would help us." As she drank her warm goat's milk, her mind spun with shock. She'd be in a small room with Ty. They'd probably be sleeping together with a few blankets given by the villagers to keep them warm tonight. The sudden realization that she'd be in close quarters with him sent a frisson of fear through her. And on its heels, desire. Desire? Reeling, Rachel felt torn with indecision. That wasn't at all like her. Suddenly, her whole world had been upended.

Chapter 12

Rachel tried to keep disappointment out of her voice when Akmal showed them the small room off of the corral. The room was actually warmed by the thirty bleating goats. Most were bedded down for the night. Akmal pulled open the heavy wooden door with a leather strap.

"This will keep you safe in case the Taliban arrive at dawn. They hurt our people, steal our food and the grass we've pulled and dried for our goats to feed their horses." He wrinkled his nose in disgust.

Rachel put her hand on the young boy's thin shoulder. "This is fine. Will you come and wake us up tomorrow morning?"

"I will if the Taliban does not ride through," he promised. Moving into the narrow room, Akmal said, "Be sure to push the sacks and wooden boxes against the door. That way, if the Taliban comes in and pulls this door open, they will not realize you are hidden deeper inside the room."

Rachel shivered inwardly. "We will," she promised.

"Good night," Akmal said, lifting his hand.

The outer door to the barn closed. Rachel looked around. They had a small oil lamp that cast a very small amount of light, and she was grateful for the warmth. The smell wasn't bad because Akmal swept the floor clean every morning after the goats were let out to graze for the day.

Ty was already in the room, rummaging around, and she felt some of her terror receding. Hamid and his wife had fed them well, giving them both newfound strength. She walked into the room and set the lamp on a small shelf on the right wall.

"Need some help?" she asked.

Ty picked up a bunch of used gunnysacks that had UN painted on them. "Yes, you're going to have to get the crates out of here. I'm useless with my left arm in a sling."

She took the sacks from him and laid them near the door. "How are you feeling?"

"A helluva lot better," he told her. Straightening, Ty looked over his shoulder at her. Rachel's hair had been smashed by wearing the scarf. Still, her cheeks were rosy and her eyes sparkled. "Hot food in a safe place does wonders, doesn't it?"

"No question. We got lucky. Why don't you egress out of there, and I'll take care of those empty crates?"

Nodding, Ty backed out. With his left arm in a sling, the pain had stopped. Hot food had filled his growling belly, and the strength from eating it had been immediate. Rachel slid past him, her hips brushing against him. "I'll get the blankets and bring them in," he told her. His body tingled where she'd barely grazed him. The thought hadn't escaped Ty that they'd be lying very close to one another in a very narrow room. He pushed those feelings aside and forced himself to concentrate on getting the blankets and pillows that Semeen had given them.

In no time, their digs were in order. Rachel wiped the perspiration from her brow. "Come on in. I need you in here so I can build our wall."

Ty had brought the bedding in earlier. Stepping inside, he watched as she shut the door to the room and quickly built a wall with the empty wooden crates and grain sacks. They had been filled with food and other supplies from the United States. He knew all the crates, over time, would be broken down and used as firewood. Nothing was ever wasted out in this inhospitable area of the world. He got busy and spread the blankets across the dirt floor.

"There," Rachel said, pleased. "Does it look secure to you?" She picked up the oil lamp and brought it over to another wooden shelf jutting from the rock wall above where they would sleep.

Ty smiled. The woman had creatively used the fifty or so gunnysacks and hung them in such a way that no one could see through the wooden slats. There were two rows of crates to create a wall before anyone could get to them. "Good job," he praised.

He was sitting on the right side of their bed. Her heart beat a little harder in her chest as she went to sit by him. "This is really tight quarters," she muttered, uncomfortable.

"It is, but we'll make it work." Ty looked around. "The temperature is going to fall to near freezing." He picked up the two wool blankets that would be spread across them. "We're going to need these."

Ty had already taken off his Kevlar vest. His pistol was sitting on top of it, easy to reach. Rachel did the same. "God, it feels good to get out of this chicken plate," she griped. "I'll use it as a pillow."

"That stuff is so heavy," Ty agreed. "I'm leaving my boots on."

Rachel pushed her uncombed hair out of her face. "Yes. If something happens…"

"I think we'll be safe here tonight," Ty said, seeing the stress in her shadowed gold eyes.

Rachel didn't feel safe next to *him*. But she didn't say anything. He had taken his next set of pain pills, and he seemed relaxed but exhausted. He had more color to his face, and his blue eyes were clear. "I'm so tired," she uttered more to herself than him. Every movement took effort.

Ty laid down on his right side. He moved his injured left arm so that it was supported by his hip. "Makes two of us."

"I'm just glad Akmal has promised to stay up and watch for Taliban. I trust that if he hears them, he'll come and wake us up so we can escape before they arrive."

"The Taliban doesn't travel at night," Ty said. He watched Rachel lie down on her back. She then pulled the thick, wool blankets over them.

"Well, they do. Ask any Special Forces outpost over in Afghanistan, along the border," she muttered.

"Not on horseback, though. Remember, Hamid said the Taliban only ride in this area. They're not on foot."

Sitting up, Rachel picked up the oil lamp and blew out the flame. The room fell into a thick darkness. She carefully set it back on the shelf and lay down. The wool blankets were warm. "I know. But one thing we've learned about the Taliban is that they are creative, and you can't rely on them to do the same thing over and over again."

Closing his eyes, Ty was inches from her left shoulder. He inhaled the perfume that was only Rachel. The pillow kept his head raised, and he no longer had a headache. He hungrily absorbed the warmth radiating from her body. Not because Rachel was warm, but because he was powerfully drawn to her. When had the past disappeared and the present taken over? Ty didn't know. Like a thief and a beggar, he slowly inhaled her scent. It was like sucking life back into his numbed body. Rachel *was* life, he decided.

"You know," Ty began in a quiet tone, "you're an incredible woman."

The reverberation of his voice flowed through Rachel. She kept her eyes closed because she was exhausted. Yet, she felt wired. Her mind was wide awake. Her body was begging for sleep and rest. "Thanks," she murmured. It was a far cry from him trying to embarrass her in front of the other students at flight school. What had changed? Had they both grown up? Matured beyond their torment-filled pasts? Rachel hoped so, because she had no energy to continue to hold Ty Hamilton at bay. Their lives were on the line every second now.

Ty slowly rolled over on his back. "I can't sleep," he said, unhappy.

"Me neither. It's adrenaline."

"Yeah. Damn."

Smiling tiredly, the darkness so complete Rachel

        His Duty to Protect

couldn't see her hand an inch from her face, she said, "I feel safe here, though."

"Yes, so do I...."

Their voices were soft, so the sound didn't carry. Rachel could hear the bleat of a goat every now and then, but it sounded very far away. "I'm glad the walls are four-feet-thick rock."

"Makes two of us."

Her hand was touching his. With Ty on his back, there was no way to avoid contact. Rachel soaked up Ty's nearness. Heat rolled off his body, and she was comfortably warm. Even though the winds were blowing outside at this altitude, the rock barn kept them at bay.

"I remember when we were kids growing up that we'd take cardboard boxes and string my mom's sheets across them and make a house. My sisters and I played house for hours like that. This place kind of reminds me of that."

Ty heard the wistful tone in her voice and realized just how much he liked finding out more about her. "After my mom died," he said "play wasn't something my father had in mind for me."

"I think it's hard to be an only child," Rachel said.

"To hear my father tell it, children were good for only one thing—work."

Alarmed, Rachel said, "What?"

"It's a long story," Ty said. Yet, he felt the urge to tell her. Somehow, he knew Rachel would understand. "My father saw two things in me—football captain and worker bee."

"That's ridiculous!" Rachel said, frowning.

"I didn't mind. It kept me busy. It kept my mind off losing my mom as I grew up."

Her heart squeezed with compassion. "Do you remember your mother?"

"Vaguely," he said, closing his eyes. "I have a few photos of her. My father wasn't big on taking pictures. He said it cost money to get the pictures put on paper."

"I'm so sorry he was cruel to you," Rachel said, her mind spinning.

Ty turned his face toward her, his voice thick with regret. "I'm the one who owes you one hell of an apology, Rachel. You aren't weak. You've been the strong one here."

Rachel felt like someone had struck her in the chest with a hammer. All through flight school, he parroted the very opposite to her on a daily basis. He screamed hateful words in her face. She had to stand at attention and take it without responding. All it did was make Rachel more determined to win her wings. "No woman is weak," she said with emotion.

With a sigh, Ty whispered, "You're right...." He was remembering how he treated Rachel in flight school. Guilt washed through him.

"What changed your mind about us?" Rachel asked.

"I had five years to see women differently," Ty muttered. "After I was booted out of flight school, I was assigned to a Chinook squadron that had women and men pilots. Over time, I saw the women were just as good, sometimes better, than a man at the controls. My father was so filled with grief over the loss that he was taking it out on me."

"I remember. You were his whipping post," Rachel said, sadness in her tone. She itched to reach out and curve her hand around Ty's. She stopped herself. There was still a lot of pain from their past, so Rachel couldn't bring herself to do that.

"Yes, I guess I was. My father was lost without my mother. I realize that now. I didn't then."

"Well." Rachel snorted. "You were a child who had lost his mother, too. I would think your father had enough maturity to realize that."

"No, that didn't happen," Ty admitted. He rested his arm across his closed eyes. So many images and a gamut of feelings flowed from that time in his life. Somehow, just talking to Rachel soothed his injured heart.

"I still can't believe he wouldn't comfort you," Rachel said, disbelief in her voice. "Didn't he know you had to grieve? To cry for the loss of your mom?"

"When I cried, he'd whip me with a belt. He'd tell me to stop crying. Eventually, I choked down my grief. He hired a housekeeper by the name of Charleen Turner, who took over the cooking, cleaning and taking care of me."

Rachel sucked in a soft breath of air. "Were you able to bond with the housekeeper?" She tried to put herself in Ty's place. Knowing how much she loved her mother, she just couldn't imagine the psychic and physical damage done to Ty. No wonder he had hated women. But Rachel cautioned herself. Ty's father had beat him until he stopped his grieving for his mother. Then he'd been brainwashed by his angry father who couldn't rise above his own sorrow to help his baby son cope with the devastating loss.

"No. Charleen didn't like kids." He managed a croak of a laugh. "She was an alcoholic. My father knew it but didn't care. She was the only woman he could find who would come and live at the ranch. When she was drunk, I knew to hide and be seen, not heard. If I got underfoot, she'd complain to my father and he'd come in and beat me with a strap."

"My God," Rachel whispered in disbelief. "It's a wonder you survived. Didn't someone turn your father in for abusing you?"

"Who could?" he asked. "I lived thirty miles south of Cheyenne. Our closest neighbor was fifteen miles away, and my father never made friends. He's a bastard to this day. He's got a lot of people who fear and dislike him."

"But," Rachel sputtered, "surely your school teachers saw you were abused."

"No. My father made sure the strappings were on my back, butt and legs. No one ever knew...."

"Couldn't you have asked for help?"

"I tried to run away once when I was twelve. When my father caught up with me, he beat me within an inch of my life. He warned me to never tell anyone about the beatings. If I did, he said he'd disown me."

Rolling her eyes, Rachel growled, "Hell, you'd have been much better off with any family but him."

"I didn't know that, Rachel." Ty liked saying her name. It rolled off his lips like honey. "I was raised in a climate of fear. I wasn't about to say anything to anyone. I didn't know there was help out there." And then his voice lowered. "Look, I'd already lost my mom. I couldn't bear to lose my father, too."

In that moment, her heart broke for Ty. Rachel heard the little-boy fear in his voice even though Ty was now a grown man. "Our childhood can either support us or tear us apart," she agreed softly. She found herself wanting badly to hold him against the terrible pain he carried deep within himself.

"It took me a long time to understand what had happened," Ty said.

"Do you ever go home for a visit?" She couldn't think that anyone in their right mind would be around an abusive son of a bitch like that.

"Not anymore," Ty said, sadness evident. He took a deep breath, his heart beating hard with fear. He forced the words out. "Listen, Rachel, I need to apologize for the way I treated you back in flight school." His voice deepened with feeling. "I can't undo the past. You were right and I was wrong. You don't know how many times I picked up the phone to contact you and tell you I was sorry." His mouth thinned. "It took me three years in that Chinook squadron to come around and realize my father didn't do me any favors. I couldn't change him. What I did do is change myself, my attitudes toward women and try to rectify what I did wrong back then."

Rachel lay there, feeling his sincere words drain away her dislike of him. She reeled with all the information about his youth, his abusive father and an alcoholic housekeeper who doubled as his mother. Tears came to her eyes. She cleared her throat. "Thank you for telling me that. It helps."

Ty wanted to turn over and slide his arm beneath her neck, draw Rachel to him and simply hold her. Cautioning himself, he knew it would be too much, too soon. "I didn't have the guts to make that call," he warned her. "I was too afraid."

"I think I understand why," Rachel murmured. "Given your past, it makes sense now."

Swallowing hard, Ty wished mightily that there was light in the room. He desperately wanted to look into Rachel's eyes. To see if she really meant it. "I wanted to tell you, because if we don't get out of this fix alive, I at least want to be square with you."

Rachel fought back her tears. He was right: the chances of them getting out of this fix alive were very low. "I appreciate that."

Her soft, halting words were laced with tears. He could hear it in her husky voice. Closing his eyes, he clenched his teeth. He couldn't cry. He just couldn't. Finally, after several moments of pregnant silence, Ty rasped, "Thank you. You have no idea how good that makes me feel. I was hell on you at flight school. I didn't know it then, but I was doing the same thing my father did to me. You were a whipping post for all my grief." And then Ty did something so bold that it even surprised even him. He slid his hand beneath the blanket, sought and found Rachel's. Giving her hand a warm, firm squeeze, he added unsteadily, "Your forgiveness means everything to me, Rachel. Thank you for your courage...." He released her fingers.

Rachel was shocked by his hand around hers and felt tears flowing silently down the sides of her face. Quickly, she wiped them away. Ty's hand was not only warm but gave her a sense of security in a very insecure world. The sincerity of his voice shook loose so much old anger and hurt from those days. Rachel could literally feel the rage dissolving in her heart and flowing out of her like an unchecked flood. Relief began to fill her instead. She tried to think what to say, the right words. She wanted to cry for all the pain he'd carried for so long, unable to give it voice, to sob out his loss for his mother. His young, innocent love had been destroyed. Ty knew no other way. Until life had helped to reshape and change him. Other women had been role models to show him that women were not only strong, but intelligent. And they deserved to be in the military, flying a helicopter right alongside him.

When Ty heard nothing further from her, he added in a pained tone, "I know I don't deserve your forgiveness, and I'm okay with it, Rachel. I just…needed to get this off my chest and try to make amends before something happens."

Because she didn't trust herself, Rachel turned on her right side, facing the wall, her hands pressed against her face. The sobs tore out of her whether she wanted them to or not. And she didn't dare let Ty know that she was crying for him.

Chapter 13

"Are you ready?" Ty had just mounted his gray, part-Arab gelding that Hamid had given them. He was dressed like an Afghan soldier.

"Yes." Rachel had mounted her bay Arab gelding. Around her, the village had gathered in the dawn light to see them off. Akmal had come and awakened them an hour earlier. Despite last night's wrenching admissions from Ty, she had finally fallen into a deep, healing sleep. "Yes, I am," she said. Scared but ready. Smiling down at Hamid and his wife, who had their brown wool cloaks pulled tightly around them, she lifted her hand in farewell to them.

"If we make it to Samarigam, we'll see that you are paid for the saddles and bridles, my lord." They had only five horses total in the village, and Rachel knew they relied heavily on each of them for transportation.

"And we'll see what can be done about airlifting these two animals back to you."

Hamid nodded. "Allah be with you, Captain. It's a long, dangerous road."

"Thank you," she said. Turning her bay around, Rachel pulled the brown cloth across the lower half of her face. She wore a turban of the same color, a dark green, wool cloak over her shoulders. It felt good in the freezing morning air.

Everyone waved as they left the village and rode down the prominent trail. The sky was dark above them, stars faint along the eastern horizon. The breath of the horses as they plodded steadily down the winding, twisting path, resembled jets of steam coming out of their nostrils. There was enough room for them to ride side by side. Rachel pulled abreast of Ty. He was dressed in a brown turban, the cloth hiding his lower jaw. If the Taliban saw him without a beard, they would know he was a foreigner. Her leg brushed occasionally against his as they rode.

"Beautiful, isn't it?" she asked in a quiet tone.

Looking around, Ty kept searching for possible Taliban on this well-used trail. "If you call freezing your butt off this morning, I guess." He grinned over at her. All he could see were Rachel's eyes. The rest of her clothing, which was male, covered up the fact she was a woman. The rifle she carried was slung across her back.

Chuckling, Rachel nodded. "It's pretty cold." How badly she wanted to talk with Ty, but they had to remain alert. Hamid had warned them that this trail was used by Taliban and merchants going between the villages. He had made sure they were dressed to look like they came from his village. Each one had distinctive costumes and colors. Earlier, Akmal had put red tassels on the bridle of each horse. That would identify them as being from the village, as well. If the Taliban saw them, then there was less chance of being stopped and questioned by them.

As Ty continued to look around, the steep slope of the mountain and the rocks on the trail made the horse pick its way carefully around the objects. Overhead, the sky was beginning to lighten. Everything was silent except for an inconstant breeze that would wind through the yellow, rocky mountains surrounding them. He was glad that Hamid had loaned them two rifles with a box of ammunition. It wasn't much protection, but it was better than what little they had. He was fearful of meeting a group of Taliban on the trail but kept his thoughts to himself.

"I tried that radio again this morning," Rachel told him. "It still isn't working."

"Our luck. We're going to have to make it to Samarigam."

Nodding, Rachel enjoyed the sway of the horse between her legs. The animals were small, tough and hardy. "How far to the well? Hamid said we should reach it midday?" Fondly patting the horse on its shaggy neck, Rachel knew they would need water to keep on going. Luckily, Hamid said there were two wells on the trail. It was forty-five miles between the two villages. They couldn't trot or run their horses down the steep switchback trail. If a horse stumbled and fell, it could break a leg as well as injure the rider. This would take more time than Rachel had anticipated. She tried to quell her frustration.

"Hamid said ten miles to the first well. He said we'd

drop into the valley over there." Ty pointed to two steep mountain passes they had to ride through.

Rachel grimaced. "I don't know how these horses are going to go that far without water."

"They will," he said. "It won't be easy on them, but they've made this trip before."

"They're tougher than we are, that's for sure," Rachel said, patting her gelding again.

The trail straightened out for a bit as it headed down the rocky mountain. Ty looked over at her. "I'm glad we had that talk last night. I didn't know I'd be doing the talking, though." He searched Rachel's warm, gold eyes. "I apologized to you last night, but I wanted to do it this morning, too. You deserved to be told to your face." His heart beat a little harder in his chest, and it wasn't from the altitude. He wished that he could see Rachel's face right now.

Rachel swallowed hard. "I accept your apology, Ty. Honestly, I never expected one from you."

"When I found out you were assigned to me, I knew I had to do it." Ty managed a half smile. "It was a long time in coming. Frankly, I never thought I'd see you again."

"That makes two of us," Rachel said, chuckling. "When I found out I was assigned to your squadron, I was not a happy camper."

"I don't blame you for feeling like that."

Searching his eyes, Rachel said, "You grew up in those five years."

"Yes, I did. I never thought I'd get a chance to tell you that I was sorry for what I did to you."

Sadness moved through her. She wanted to reach out and touch his arm, but she didn't dare. Someone could be watching them, hidden in the rocks and huge boul-

ders, which were everywhere. "I felt so bad for you, Ty.
I didn't know you'd lost your mother. And your father
didn't treat you right."

"I survived."

"I can't conceive of losing either of my parents," she
whispered, brows dropping. "I tried to put myself in
your place last night, and I couldn't go there. I rely on
them so much. Even to this day, I do."

"You're lucky," Ty told her. He saw her eyes were
fraught with sadness. For him. For whatever reason,
it felt good to have Rachel think well of him for once.
He'd done so much damage to her and had tried to
obliterate her career, yet she'd forgiven him. Ty's heart
swelled with inexplicable joy over that realization.

"I am. But I worry now. I'm sure the Army has contacted my family and told them I'm missing in action.
My mom is probably crying. My dad, I'm sure, has
contacted Uncle Morgan to see what he can do to find
me."

"I'm sure my father could care less," Ty muttered.

"That's really sad."

"We split five years ago. I haven't been in contact
with him since that day."

The pain was clear in his voice. Rachel saw it in his
narrowing eyes, which became dark with obvious grief.
"The Army will tell him, though."

"I know." Ty gazed up at the sky. The stars had
disappeared, and in their place, a dark blue color remained. "I don't really care."

Rachel didn't believe him, but what could she say or
do? *Nothing.* Compressing her lips, she said, "It's hard
on everyone when we turn up missing."

Something made him ask, "Do you have a signifi-
cant other?" He hoped not, but there was no way Rachel

wouldn't be involved. She was too beautiful, poised and intelligent.

"No, thank goodness, I don't." Rachel looked over at him. "What about you?"

"No one," he said.

"You're not married? Have kids?"

Hearing the teasing in her voice, he smiled a little. "No, I haven't been very good in the relationship department. It's taken me five years and a lot of hard knocks with women to get straight about what makes a relationship run or not."

"You were sorting out your father's view on life from your own?" Rachel guessed. Why did she feel a soaring happiness when Ty said he wasn't involved with another woman? She secretly guessed that his hatred of women would cause all kinds of hell in a relationship. And until he got rid of that perspective, no woman worth her salt would put up with Ty's antics or behavior.

"Yes," he said. "I began seeing the way he treated my mother. Not that I remember much, but he was always yelling at her. Even as a young kid, I knew that was wrong."

Rachel shook her head. "He was a parent out of control. You don't yell at someone you love. You try to work it out."

"It sounds as if you know something about a good relationship," Ty said.

Pain moved through her heart. "Okay, confession time," she told him.

"Your secrets are safe with me."

Rachel smiled. "A year ago, I was engaged to be married. I met Garrett in Afghanistan. He flew with an Apache squadron out of Helmand Province."

Ty could tell by the roughness in her voice that something had happened. He remained silent.

"There was an attack on his base and he was killed," she finally admitted. Giving Ty a quick glance, she saw the worry in his exposed face. "I loved him so much. We were the best of friends."

He had to stop himself from reaching over to touch the hand that rested on the saddle. "I'm sorry. I really am. He had to be one hell of a man to get your attention."

"He was." Rachel closed her eyes for a brief moment. "Sometimes, it seems like it was just yesterday. On other days, it seems years ago, as if it was a dream, not reality."

"I remember when my mother died, I had days like that, even at three years old."

Her heart broke for Ty. She gazed over at him and thought he was as lost in the past as she was. "My parents always told me that life wasn't easy. It consisted of ups and downs. As a kid it was a concept, not a reality."

"And being here, we lose people nearly every day," Ty agreed. "Good friends…"

"Yes," she said. "This last year has made me realize I have to grab life and live. I can't think about a future. I have to be here. Now," she said, pointing her index finger at the ground.

"I've learned to hide," he admitted. "No love life."

Giving him a confused look, Rachel asked, "What do you mean by that?" Ty Hamilton was a brazen, courageous pilot. He was a man who dripped with leadership and intelligence.

"My track record with women is bad. Each one took a little bit more of my father's attitude out of me. But it was wearing on them, too. For the last year, I've been without a relationship. I didn't want another bruising round with another woman. I kept hoping for a good connection, but it never happened." *Until now,* a voice whispered to him. Ty shook his head. "I'm not exactly the type of man any woman is looking for."

Rachel disagreed but said nothing. "We're all in the learning mode, Ty. And we all make mistakes. All the time."

"Yeah," he sighed, "but not mistakes you could drive a Mack truck through." He managed a derisive laugh.

Knowing he'd been through a rough five years and was trying to turn himself around, Rachel said, "In my eyes, you're making good changes, Ty. Getting rid of your father's crap and then trying to discover who you are instead takes time."

"It's been five years," he said, smiling. "That's a lot longer than I ever wanted it to take."

Laughing, Rachel understood. As they crested the trail, they halted their horses. The next mountain looked even steeper. "If you think you're done changing, you have another think coming. My mom always said that we're a work in progress. The shaping, carving and trimming are never finished."

Ty sat up in the saddle to give his sore rear a break. He couldn't see anyone on the trail. Breathing a sigh of relief, he turned to Rachel. "A work in progress? That definitely fits me. Ready for the next mountain?"

"Let's go." She looked at her watch. "We're making good time."

"It's the company," Ty called over his shoulder as he guided his horse down the trail.

Rachel couldn't disagree. The trail was wide but not wide enough for the horses to walk side by side. "It is," she said, smiling. Just getting to talk with Ty made her feel hopeful. He'd come a long way. Her heart expanded with a quiet joy. Funny, she'd never felt like this about any other man. Not even Garrett, her fiancé. What was going on between them? Rachel didn't know, and she couldn't afford to dwell on it right now. Leaning over, she patted her horse. "I don't know about you, but I'm looking forward to that first well. My butt is killing me!"

Rachel groaned as she stepped onto the grassy area of the well, ancient and made of rock. A few scraggly trees grew around it. She had handed the reins to Ty. There was a bucket and crank. After pushing the wooden pail over the opening, she quickly lowered it. There was a splash at about twenty feet. Once she quickly wrenched the pail up with the wooden handle, they had water. The horses nickered and crowded closer. For the next ten minutes, she filled pails of water for the thirsty animals.

Ty studied the area. They'd come off the last slope, and the well sat about a mile from the actual valley between the mountains. The green looked out of place compared to the yellow, rocky dirt that surrounded them. It was 1:00 p.m., the sky a light blue with puffy white clouds dotted against it. The temperature had risen, and he was actually hot in the wool clothing.

"We're next," Rachel called, hefting the bucket down on the ground near his feet. Hamid had given them a small wooden cup, and she pulled it out of the saddlebag her horse carried. Dipping it into the water, she straightened and handed it to Ty.

"Thanks," he said before swallowing deeply.

While he was drinking water, Rachel retrieved the empty plastic bottles to refill them. The wind was inconstant, and she longed to pull the hot fabric away from her face. It was much warmer in the valley. She ached for a cool shower.

"Your turn," Ty said, handing her a mug filled with water.

Smiling, she put the bottles down by the well and accepted the welcome gift. "Thanks."

The birds were singing in the scrawny nearby trees. Far above, Ty thought he saw an eagle floating on the unseen air currents. There was nothing but natural sound. The horses were eagerly nibbling at any piece of green grass they could find. They had to be hungry. Looking back, he allowed himself the pleasure of watching Rachel drink. She was beautiful. An ache began in his lower body, but he quickly shoved the desire away. While it was true there was a white flag of surrender symbolically held between them, he didn't think she'd be interested in him as a man. Not after what he'd done to her. Sadness swept through him, and he took the horses over to a thick patch of grass.

After she finished filling the water bottles, Rachel put half of them in the saddle bags of Ty's horse and half in her own. Rubbing her wet hands on her trousers, she went over to where he was standing. The horses were famished. Hamid had advised them to let them eat for half an hour before moving on across the valley. She put a hand to her eyes, looking at the steep mountains on the other side.

"That's a lot of hard climbing ahead for us and the horses," she said.

"It is. Beautiful valley, though," he said. "A few days ago, we flew right over this area and didn't give it a second look."

Rachel chuckled. "Things change."

Didn't they? Ty forced himself to stop looking at her. Her male clothing couldn't hide those glistening gold eyes of hers. Again, he wondered what it would be like to kiss her. Would she allow him to do that? Ty didn't think so. But damn, he wanted to kiss her. Their talk last night had sprung open an old door that had been blocked deep down inside. She had released something primal within him. He tried to name it. Was it her nurturing personality? God knew, Ty wanted to be held in her arms. Somehow, she fed his thirsty, starving soul. Fed his heart that ached to be loved fully by someone. For so long, Ty had been without real love. Acknowledging that he was at fault in his past relationships, he knew he had to continue to make changes so that a woman would want him in her life.

"Ready?" Rachel asked. She saw him grow pensive. The energy around Ty shifted. He was completely immersed in his thoughts. When he lifted his head and met her gaze, he nodded.

"My butt is numb."

"So is mine," she laughed. Rachel took the reins of her horse from Ty. Mounting up, she appreciated Ty's struggle to get back on the horse. His left arm was in a sling. Yet, he made it. There was determination in every bit of his face. "How's the pain?" she wondered.

"Manageable," Ty said, picking up the reins. "I just took another pain pill."

"Good." Rachel joined him as they walked their horses together down the widening path. It felt good to be on flat land. There were trees here and there, casting shade across the grass. Looking around, she said, "I'm surprised we don't see any goat or sheep herds down here."

"Me, too." Frowning, Ty muttered, "I wonder if that

means the Taliban is around. I know villages keep their herds protected when they're in their area. The Taliban eat the animals."

"Bastards," Rachel gritted out. "Every sheep and goat is important to the people of these villages."

"It's their way of telling the villagers they're in control."

Snorting, Rachel agreed. Ty kicked his horse into a slow trot and so did she. It was ten miles across this narrow valley bracketed by steep, nine thousand foot high peaks. She noticed on the other side of the valley there were a lot of caves. This was a favorite hiding place for the Taliban. Yet, she saw no shapes or horses to suggest the enemy was nearby.

Suddenly, Rachel heard a noise behind them. To her shock, she saw at least ten horsemen coming at them at a fast gallop.

"Ty!"

Rachel's cry made him turn. His eyes widened. There, about five miles away, was a group of horsemen coming at high speed. And there was no way to tell if they were friendly or Taliban. He'd seen several small canyons near the end of the valley. "Follow me!" he yelled and clapped his heels to his horse.

Instantly, Rachel followed at a fast gallop, so fast that her eyes watered. The pounding of the horse's hooves dulled her hearing. Ty led her into the canyons at the end of the valley. Turning in her saddle, Rachel saw their weapons. And they were firing at them!

"Enemy!" she shouted.

Ty nodded. He whipped his horse and chose the center of three canyons. They were steep and filled with brush and trees. The horse grunted and leaped over some fallen logs as it scrambled high into the canyon.

Jerking a look around, he saw Rachel was right behind him. For the moment, they had made a turn and were out of sight of the enemy. Urging his mount up into the tree line, Hamilton prayed the horse wouldn't fall on the rocky ground. They had to be hidden! Breathing hard, he guided his brave horse higher and higher. Was this a box canyon? Or did it spill out onto the slopes above it? Ty didn't know. If it was a box canyon, it could mean their death. *Oh, God, let me have made the right decision....*

Winded and frightened, Rachel dismounted as Ty had. They were very high up in the canyon. They were at least a thousand feet off the valley floor. Gasping, she quickly brought her horse up beside his.

"Definitely Taliban."

Wiping his mouth after he pulled the fabric away, Ty peered down the canyon. "They can't see us up here."

"There are three canyons," Rachel breathlessly agreed. "I wonder if they'll hunt for us?"

"I'm counting on it," he growled. Looking around, he said, "I'll be damned. Look.... A cave!"

Turning and following where he was pointing, Rachel saw a sliver of an opening to a cave. It was hidden by thick brush. "Let's get in there."

"Right," Ty agreed. Leading his horse, he clambered up though the rubble another five hundred feet before reaching the opening. Without waiting, Ty plunged into the slit in the wall of the rock.

Rachel followed. They halted inside and looked around. A gray light filtered down upon them. The cave was at least ten feet high and, as her eyes adjusted, it appeared to be much larger than Rachel first thought.

"It's a dry cave," Ty uttered. Clucking to his horse, he headed deeper down into the cave. "We've got to try and hide in here until they leave. The farther down we can go, the better off we'll be."

Frantic, Rachel turned around. "Wait!"

Ty halted. He saw her go back out to the mouth of the cave and break off a branch from a cedar tree. Their tracks! *Of course.* He nodded. "Good call."

"You go ahead, I'll sweep our tracks out of here," she said.

Ty kept seeing spots of gray light here and there. He wondered if the top of the cave had holes in it. There had to be holes or he wouldn't be seeing a thing. The cave narrowed at the back. And then it had three different passages he could choose from. Ty waited for Rachel to catch up. "Which one should we try first?" he asked.

His voice echoed hollowly in the cave. She came forward and peered into all three. "Let's take the smallest one, because if they find us, they'll think we took the largest one."

"Good thinking," he praised. Rachel had pulled the fabric off her face. Her skin had a sheen of perspiration. She looked as scared as he felt. "Okay, let's go...."

Chapter 14

At a certain point in the narrowing cave, Ty asked Rachel to tie her horse's reins to the back of his horse's saddle. Though frustrated over the uselessness of his left arm, he couldn't negotiate both animals.

"It's getting narrower as we go," Rachel whispered. She choked down the panic, standing behind the last horse and looking out toward the entrance. Had the Taliban found them? There was no way to know. Her heart beat hard in her chest as she kept both hands on her pistol.

"I know," Ty said, scowling. "We don't have a choice. We're going to have to push forward."

"What if it's a dead end or it gets too narrow?"

"Then we wait it out." Ty knew the rejoinder: if the Taliban found them, they would become easy targets. They'd be dead in seconds.

Rachel wiped her mouth with the back of her hand. "Okay…keep going."

Tugging on the reins, Ty moved forward. Occasionally, a spot of light would appear. He wondered just how many holes were above them. Grateful he could see, he pushed forward as fast as he could. Where did this tunnel end? It was moving upward. Would there be another opening at the end or was it a wall?

Suddenly, Rachel heard men's voices echoing oddly down their corridor. Gasping, she realized they had been found. *Damn!*

"Hurry!" she whispered fiercely. "They've found us!"

Terror arced through him. The floor of the cave was sandy with some pebbles thrown across it. He jerked on the horse's reins and started off at an awkward run. If the Taliban had been able to figure out they were here, despite Rachel trying to cover their tracks, they'd find them in this tunnel, too. The cave floor continued to move upward. The light filtering down became brighter.

Rachel hung back. She heard more yells and cries from the Taliban. They were at the cave tunnel entrances. *Oh God, don't let them find us!* She turned on her heel and raced to catch up with Ty and their horses. Her breath came in sobs. Pressing her hand to her mouth, Rachel knew she couldn't afford to make any more noise.

Ty trotted as fast as the horses would go. They were snorting and fearful. He knew those sounds would echo back through the tunnel, but there was nothing he could do. His boots thunked hard on the surface. More light was ahead. *God, let it be an opening!*

Rachel ran up to her horse. She saw more light

ahead. The cave floor canted steeply upward. It was getting so narrow that the horse's saddles were rubbing against the confining walls. Sweat dripped into her eyes, stinging them. It was hot in the cave. Fear mixed with hope as she trotted behind her horse. She could hear the Talibans' voices. They were getting closer!

Suddenly, shots were fired.

The bullets careened and ricocheted off the walls. Rachel automatically ducked as one whined by her head. The horses bolted, the booming sound scaring them. They lurched forward, panicked.

Ty saw brush ahead. An entrance! The cave suddenly opened up, and both horses lunged past him in order to escape, their eyes rolling in panic. Gripping the reins, Ty hauled back hard on the lead horse. The animal didn't respond, and they crashed through the thick vegetation, branches snapping and leaves exploding around them. The horse was so panicked by the shots that Ty was dragged. He clung on to the reins as he was pulled swiftly through the thickets. He didn't dare let go!

Rachel leaped through the brush, saw Ty jerked off his feet by the charging and frightened lead horse. Making a leap, she managed to grab her own horse's reins. The animal slowed and turned, snorting.

"Ty!" she called.

"I'm okay," he said, clumsily getting to his feet. He cursed softly, yanked off the sling and threw it with disgust to the ground. It was making him off balance, and right now, he'd settle for pain in order to stay on his feet.

More shots shrieked and careened out of the cave.

"Mount up!" he ordered, releasing the knot of the reins from his saddle.

Rachel already had a hand on her scared horse's neck. "Right!" She leaped into the saddle.

Ty did the same. His left arm hurt like hell, but he didn't care. Seeing a small path that led up through the brush, he realized they were on top of a mountain. The path led down and then went upward. He tried to sense where they were.

After he jammed his heels into his frantic horse, Ty guided the frightened animal up through the thickets. They crashed through the underbrush.

Right behind him, Rachel was breathing hard. She held her .45 in her right hand, looking back to see if she saw the Taliban bursting out of the tunnel. *Oh, God, let us get out of this alive!* Her horse lunged, jumped and the brush exploded beneath its legs. They had to get away. Suddenly, they broke out of the thick wall of brush. *There.* She saw a thin trail, probably a goat trail, leading up and over the rise. Slapping the reins to the withers of his sweaty horse, Ty galloped upward, dirt and rock flying behind the scared animal.

Rachel guided her horse right on the rear of Ty's mount. The shooting had stopped. Anxiously looking over her shoulder, she couldn't see the opening anymore. The dense foliage wall hid it. Had the Taliban gotten through it? They must have, she reasoned, and that was why they'd stopped shooting through the tunnel. Fear curled her stomach into a tight, painful fist as she rode hard.

Ty topped the mountain. He jerked his horse to a halt. Rachel came up beside him, her animal dancing and frightened. "Look!" he cried, pointing.

Her jaw dropped. There was only one mountain between them and the village of Samarigam. Not only that, but she saw Emma and Kahlid's Chinook helicopter on the ground. They had to be dropping supplies to the village. And they were too far away for the crew to hear the rifle fire.

"Hold on," she gasped, hauling her horse to a stop. "Let me try this damn radio again!" She thrust her hand into the pocket of her flight suit. Fumbling around, her hand shaking from fear, she finally found it. She yanked it out and gave Ty a desperate look. "Pray this thing is dried out enough to work."

He held his restive horse, his gaze on the radio she held. Rachel's mouth was grim as she twisted the knob that would turn on the radio.

"It works!" she cried. The radio would have enough distance to reach Bravo Base Camp. She quickly placed the call and gave coordinates.

Ty heard a shout behind them. It was the Taliban! "Tell them we're being pursued by Taliban. We've got to make a run for the village right now!"

Nodding, Rachel heard the cries and shouts of angry men nearby. The brush was snapping and popping. They rode their horses through it to reach them. Quickly, she told Ops their position, that the Taliban was chasing them and they needed Apache intervention. Signing off, she jammed the radio back into her thigh pocket. "Let's get the hell out of here!" She clapped her heels to the horse.

They raced over the top of the mountain. The goat trail was thin and narrow. Rachel signaled for Ty to go down the steep, winding path first. She'd stay to the rear. The animals flew down the trail. The danger was in them falling as the rocks were loose and slippery. Ty's horse slid and almost fell. Rachel gulped back a scream as she saw him right the horse and keep heading downward. It was a good thing he came from a cowboy background. He knew how to ride a horse.

Just as they reached the bottom of the trail, Rachel saw the first of the Taliban appear at the top of the mountain. There were too many to count. And they all had their rifles aimed at them. They started firing down at them, the sounds echoing off the nearby mountains. Dirt spat up here and there around them. Turning, Rachel whipped her horse into a gallop. Ty was ahead of her. The mountain connected down a narrow path and then led out, once more, onto the floor of the lush, green valley. Gasping, Rachel felt her horse lose its footing.

In one moment, Rachel was on the horse. The next, the horse slipped and fell. It went head first in a flip. Rachel felt herself sailing through the air. Seconds later, she crashed, rolled into a ball and slammed into the yellow earth. Pain arced up her shoulder, but she kept rolling. She heard the grunt of her horse behind her. Would the horse land on top of her? Uncertain, when she stopped rolling, Rachel sprang to her feet. Eyes wide, she saw her horse only a few feet behind her. It had gotten back on its feet, shaking itself like a dog. She ran back, grabbed the reins and prayed that the horse wasn't injured. Leaping into the saddle, she yelled at the horse and leaned forward.

Instantly, the horse lunged ahead, galloping wildly down the trail. Relieved the horse was unhurt, Rachel found her stirrups. More bullets sang around them. She saw Ty at least half a mile ahead of her. He hadn't realized she had fallen. Rachel leaned down and pushed the horse as fast as he could go. The dust and rocks flew beneath his small, sharp hooves. The bullets kept kicking up geysers of dirt all around her. She was a target!

Rachel knew that Ty was out of rifle range. The last thing she wanted to do was die.

She and her horse burst out of the narrow, dirt path and onto the grassy valley floor. As her horse raced frantically to catch up with his partner, she heaved a sigh of relief. Ty looked back. He had a surprised expression on his face. Rachel signaled for him to keep going, but he slowed down.

It was then that Rachel knew there was more than friendship developing between them. Ty, she was sure, saw how dusty and dirty she looked and knew she had fallen. The look of care on his face touched her as nothing else could. He held his fractious mount back until she could join him.

"I fell," she shouted to him, urging her horse into a gallop. "We're okay! Let's go!"

Ty nodded. Wrenching his horse around, he noted the fifteen Taliban coming down the slope. He cursed and quickly caught up with fleeing Rachel and her mount.

"They're coming after us!" he shouted as he drew abreast of her.

"We'd better hope like hell they got an Apache to cut loose and get it over to us in time, or we're fried."

Now it was a race against death. Rachel kept low in the saddle. She looked back every few strides to see how close the Taliban were. For a while she couldn't see them. Their horses must have tired. She could feel her own mount begin to slow. His coat was covered with sweat and dirt. Up ahead, there was a goat trail that came off from the village above them, but it was a mile long. They had to try and first find it and then climb it. Looking up at the massive, rocky mountain, Rachel's hope began to die. Too much effort and their horses wouldn't last. They had to climb from five thousand to ninety-five hundred feet to Samarigam. If they stayed here, they'd be targets.

Looking up at the sky, the wind tearing past her, Rachel anxiously searched for that black speck that would mean an Apache helicopter was coming their way. But the sky was empty. Without the two Apaches that had been destroyed earlier, BJS was strapped and couldn't send a combat helicopter to every urgent call as much as they might want to. She twisted in the saddle. Her eyes widened. The Taliban had just hit the valley floor. She saw them waving their rifles. Right now, there was two miles between them. And their bullets couldn't reach that far.

"They're on the floor!" she shouted to Ty

He looked back. *Damn!* Twisting back around, he yelled, "We've gotta find that goat trail up to the village!"

Rachel rode up alongside him. Both their horses were wheezing and sucking in huge breaths of air. "I don't know where it is! Do you?"

He shook his head. "We just have to keep riding down the valley until we find it!"

Her hope was shredding as she kept looking back. Was it her imagination or were the Taliban riders getting closer? Their horses might be a lot fresher than their mounts. If that was so, they would slowly but surely close the gap between them. And then they'd start shooting at them. If a bullet hit one of their horses, that would be the nail in their coffins.

"There!" Ty shouted triumphantly. He jabbed his finger toward a trail in the distance.

Rachel noticed the goat trail that led up to the village. It was half a mile away. Her horse was slowing, breath exploding out of his distended nostrils. He was tiring to the point where he would drop from a gallop into a trot. No! Rachel dug her heels into his foaming flanks, but the horse grunted. It lurched forward, wobbling on weakening legs. Up ahead, she saw Ty's horse stagger, its head down, mouth open. They were in serious trouble.

Whipping his horse, Ty forced it back into a gallop. The animal careened drunkenly. And then freezing horror rushed through him. Another group of horsemen galloped toward them from the opposite direction. Taliban or friendly? There was no way to tell. The sky was empty. A horrible, sinking feeling moved through him.

Suddenly, his horse stumbled, and Ty flew out of the saddle.

Rachel gave a cry of terror as she saw Ty's horse collapse beneath him. It hurtled over him and then landed nearby. Yanking her horse to a stop, Rachel leaped off, reins in hand.

"Ty!" He was laying still, arms outstretched, on his belly.

No! Oh, God, no! Let him be alive!

Rachel knelt down and gripped his shoulder. "Ty! Ty, are you all right?"

She lifted her head. Two groups of horsemen came at a high gallop toward them from opposite directions. Gasping, she jerked her attention back to Ty. He was moving.

"Ty! Are you all right? Talk to me."

Groaning, Ty sat up. Blood ran down his left temple. "I'm okay...." He got to his knees and saw his horse lying nearby. The animal had heroically continued until he could go no farther.

Rachel leaped up and yelled, "Come on! We'll ride my horse!" She held out her hand to him.

Within seconds, Ty was back on his feet. He saw the Taliban approaching swiftly. But as he glanced at the southern part of the valley, he saw an equal amount of horsemen would be arriving shortly. His mind spun with what they could do. Rachel jumped into the saddle. She held her hand out, and he swiftly mounted the horse behind her.

"Make a run for the trail!" he yelled.

The echo of gunfire started. Ty knew they were within range of the Talibans' bullets.

Kicking the tired horse, Rachel felt terrible that she was asking the animal to give its all. It lurched into a wobbling trot. The trail was only a quarter of a mile away. The horsemen from the south drew closer and closer. It had to be Taliban. She knew the Taliban were always in touch by phone or cell phone. Chances were, the group chasing them into the cave had called their cohorts, who were already in the valley. Together, they were creating a pincer's movement that would crush them. In a few minutes, they would be dead. The thought scared her as nothing else ever would. The horse was wobbling badly. Suddenly, the animal grunted and collapsed.

Rachel was thrown over the horse's head. She heard the animal hit the ground. Closing her eyes, she rolled after hitting the grass. Stunned, Rachel opened her eyes after she'd stopped moving. The sky was a powdery blue above her. And empty. No Apache was coming to save them. Her heart sank as she scrambled to her feet. She saw Ty lurching up, shaken.

For a moment, they looked at one another. The rifle fire was exploding all around them. A bullet had hit her horse. That was why it had fallen. And it was dead. So were they. Gripping the .45, she yelled at Ty, "Get behind this horse! It's our only cover!"

Leaping behind the body of the horse, they flattened on their bellies, their pistols drawn. Both had taken the two extra magazines and laid them nearby. Ty lay so close he could feel Rachel against him. There wasn't much cover behind the small, dead horse. Breathing hard, he positioned his hands on the belly of the animal.

"They're within half a mile. We should wait," Ty rasped. Otherwise, their bullets could go wild. The closer the enemy, the better they could aim at them. A half a mile was too far for their pistols.

"Right," Rachel choked, breathing hard. She jerked over at Ty. "I want you to know, I forgive you for everything."

The words hit him hard. Ty managed a twisted smile. Her hair was dirty, her face sweaty, stained with dust. "Thanks. I think you're one hell of a woman. I'm proud to be here at your side."

The bullets spit up dust on either side of the horse. They watched the horsemen from the south start firing, their rifles winking red and yellow. The Taliban from the north thundered toward them at high speed.

Rachel choked and sobbed. She held on to Ty's narrowed blue gaze. "I'm sorry," she sobbed. "I'm so sorry, Ty. I like you…. I was falling in love with you…."

The words slammed into Ty, shocking him. Tears shimmered in her golden eyes, and her lower lip trembled softly. Yes, he realized, he was falling helplessly in love with this courageous warrior woman. Reaching out with his injured left arm, he gripped her shoulder for a moment. "No matter what happens, just know I love you, Rachel. I have ever since I met you again…."

Their words to one another were cut off. Several bullets whined overhead. Ty released her shoulder and wrapped his hands around his pistol. Now, they were within target range. He could see the leader, his black eyes filled with hatred, his horse flying toward them, his rifle raised.

Rachel felt her world slowing down to single frames. She had felt this same sensation when she had nearly drowned in the ocean as a child and then during her most recent brush with death. Her whole life was movie slides, and she looked at each one of them. Even though her focus was on the swiftly approaching Taliban, everything seemed to crawl. She saw the saddle leather design on the sweating, foamy horses of the their enemy. She saw each face, the hatred and felt it score her like a bullet would. Mouth tightening, Rachel felt her heart slow down into a powerful, thudding beat. She watched as the horsemen approached. She sighted on the leader. Her hand bucked. The bullet missed him, but it struck his horse. In an instant, the horse crashed to the ground, the leader flying over him. She heard firing next to her. She knew Ty was shooting now, as well. As Ty's bullet took him out and the man went flying out of his saddle, there was a surprised look on his face.

As a bullet whined by her ear, Rachel calmly sighted on another Taliban. She fired two bullets. The second one hit the man who had assumed the lead. The thunder of the horses' hooves now shook the ground. She could feel the reverberation. Every time they fired their pistols, it sounded like major explosions to Rachel. She felt out of her body, every sound amplified painfully against her ringing ears.

A bullet dug into the dead horse they lay behind. Rachel knew that trying to fire accurately from a moving horse was damn near impossible. As the Taliban rode toward them, their bullets flew wildly around them. In comparison, Rachel and Ty's shots were deadly accurate.

By the time the Taliban had arrived, six of the men and two of their horses were dead. Rachel saw the hatred toward them as the Taliban reached within a hundred feet of their position. They were aiming their rifles now, as their horses milled and panicked. She kept on firing. Her hand bucked every time the .45 barked. It felt as if she were in a shooting gallery, her focus only on the enemy she wanted to kill before they killed her.

Ty slammed another magazine into his .38. He heard the slow, systematic crack of Rachel's .45 next to him. He didn't see her, his focus on the enemy now trying to pick them off. The horse's body took so many hits he lost count. Several bullets passed close to his head. Yet, he kept his aim. His training as an Apache gunship pilot allowed him that extraordinary ability. More Taliban fell.

A third Taliban horse went down. The man leaped off, drew his sword and screamed. In a second, he was charging them. Giving a cry, Rachel aimed at the enemy. With one shot, she killed him. He fell two feet in front of their dead horse. Sobbing, she took her last magazine and slammed it into the .45. They were going to die!

Suddenly, Ty saw the Taliban firing over their heads. At what? He twisted around and his eyes rounded. The group of horsemen he'd thought were also Taliban were firing but not at them. At the enemy! Relief sang through him when he realized it must be a friendly group of horsemen, who just happened to be in the valley at the right time.

Turning, he noticed another Taliban soldier whose horse had fallen leap up. This one had an AK-47. He sprayed at them wildly, the bullets flying everywhere. Out of the corner of his eye, he saw Rachel get to her knees, holding her gun out from her body, with both hands, her face a mask of concentration. Her hand bucked once, twice. And then, to his horror, she was shot and flung backwards. With a cry, he leaped to his knees and fired again at the enemy. The AK-47 went flying out of the soldier's hands. A look of genuine surprise that Ty had shot him in the chest crossed his bearded face. The man screamed and fell forward, dead.

Ty was caught in a crossfire as he tried to reach Rachel. She was lying on her back, her eyes half open. The gun had fallen from her nerveless fingers. He couldn't help her. He had to keep firing at the Taliban, who were now making a stand. In the next instant, the horsemen from the south swept up to where he was kneeling and firing. The rest of the Taliban soldiers were killed within moments. Loose, terrified horses ran around wild-eyed and panicked.

Ty recognized the leader, a man on a white Arabian stallion. He was the warlord of the northern Nuristan Province, Rahim Khan. The man was in his forties, with a black beard, dark brown eyes. He gave Ty a triumphant smile.

Turning, Ty leaped to his feet and then fell to his knees at Rachel's side. The air erupted with cries of triumph as the horsemen swirled around the area. His heart pounded with fear as he saw where the bullet had slammed into Rachel's chest, the fabric frayed where it had entered.

"Rachel?" he rasped, leaning over her, his hand on her arm. "Are you okay?" He knew she wore the Kevlar vest. Had it stopped the bullet? Frantically, Ty searched for blood in the area of the wound. He found none. Gasping for breath, his fingers trembling, he touched her pale cheek. "Rachel, look at me."

Slowly, Rachel turned and looked up at him. Her hand moved and she touched her chest. The look in his eyes was one of a man who loved his woman. A man who was frantic with anxiety over her condition. "Damn…" she muttered, touching the bullet hole. "That hurts like hell…."

"You're all right? Any other wounds?" he demanded, looking up. He saw the leader dismount and walk toward them. "Are you okay?" Ty demanded urgently.

"I'll live. Help me up," Rachel said, holding out her hand. Within seconds, Ty's warm, strong hand wrapped around hers. He helped her sit up and then moved his body against her back so she could lean on him.

"The Kevlar stopped the bullet," he said, his lips near her ear as he kept a hand on her slumped shoulder.

Giving a slight chuckle, Rachel said, "Yes, it did."

"So," the leader boomed, "you decided to take on these miserable, flea-bitten dogs alone?"

Rachel looked up, her hand pressed to her chest. "Yes, sir, we did. Thanks for saving us."

"I'm Rahim Khan."

"Yes," Ty told him, his hand on Rachel's shoulder, "we know who you are. Thanks for saving us."

Chuckling, the leader came and knelt down on one knee and critically studied Rachel. "I would say," he murmured with a grin, "that the two of you would probably have won this fight without us."

Rachel shook her head. "No, sir, we wouldn't have." She gestured to the two empty clips near their dead horse. "We were out of ammo."

"It would have been a hand-to-hand combat situation," Ty grimly agreed.

"Still," Rahim said, looking at the bullet hole in Rachel's clothing, "you gave a good account of yourself. What were you doing out here on horseback? I received a call from Bravo Camp that you were out here. We happened to be in the area. In fact, we were coming to meet with Captain Shaheen up at Samarigam. I told your Major Klein that we could render you aid."

Rachel rubbed her chest. The bullet had been stopped by her chicken plate. She would never again curse wearing her Kevlar vest. The stinging sensation was beginning in earnest now and it hurt like hell. "That's why they didn't send an Apache to help us," she told Ty.

Rahim laughed. "No, my friends, that's not true. There were no Apaches to send. They are all assigned to other areas. The major had nothing to help you out." He grinned and thumped his chest. "And so, it came down to us. We might not fly one of those wonderful machines, but I have loyal, faithful men who would follow me to hell and back." He gestured grandly to the men on horseback, who now surrounded them. A booming cheer arose from his comrades.

Ty divided his attention between Rachel and the warlord. He refused to allow her to try and stand up just yet. "We're grateful for your assistance," he told Khan. The leader appeared very pleased.

"Without you," Rachel added, "we wouldn't be here right now."

"Maybe you would be at the gates of heaven," Khan agreed, more serious now.

"How are you feeling?" Ty demanded. Rachel looked pale, her eyes shadowed.

"My chest hurts. It was numb at first, but now it feels like it's on fire."

"No blood, though," he said, again examining her flight suit where the bullet had entered.

"No...just pain. I'll be okay." Rachel glanced up at Ty. Even though her heart was pounding with adrenaline, she felt his care and love. Her mind spun with such shock that it was impossible to deal with it all right then. "We can use my radio and call into base."

Ty nodded and opened the pocket on her left leg. "Yeah, we need to do that."

Rachel felt relief drench her. Khan had an extra mount with him. One of his soldiers brought up the sturdy black horse. It would be their transportation back to the village atop the mountain. She listened to Ty speaking with Major Klein. There was relief in her voice, too. She took a few moments to close her eyes, pushing back the tears. Their families would be notified that they were alive and safe. That would be the best news possible. Sniffing, she opened her eyes. As she looked over at Ty, she swore she saw tears in his eyes, too. But just for a moment. He handed her the radio.

"Feel like standing?"

Holding out her hand, she whispered, "Yes. Let's get to that village."

Ty gently eased her to her feet. Rachel wobbled for a moment. He slid his hand around her shoulders to steady her. She raised her hand and tried to get rid of

some of the grass and dust in her hair. So typical of a
woman, but his heart swelled with such love for her that
he almost cried. They were alive! Once at the horse,
which was held by a soldier, he boosted her up onto the
saddle. Then he climbed up behind her. In no time, the
group left the field of battle and started the steep climb
up to Samarigam.

As Ty rode, his arms around Rachel's waist, his
whole world was on a tilt. They'd said some things to
each other during the heat of battle. The admissions had
come pouring out because they thought they were going
to die. Did Rachel mean what she'd said? That she *loved*
him? The shock of that statement rolled through him.
And then he couldn't help admitting that he loved her
back. How was all of this possible? How had bitter enemies wound up loving one another? Maybe it was out
of shock. When facing death, people did funny things
they'd never do in day-to-day life.

Ty was grateful the Khan's men escorted them. Far
above, he could see people from the village gathering and watching them approach. They must have seen
the battle. Closing his eyes for a moment, he savored
Rachel's back resting against him. He could feel the
sway and rhythm of the horse beneath them. The sunlight was warm and comforting, the sky a peaceful blue
color. So much had happened so quickly. As he studied the sky above them, Ty swore that as soon as things
settled down, he had to have private time with Rachel.
He had to find out the truth…one way or another.

Chapter 15

As the group of horsemen entered the village of Samarigam, Rachel watched people crowd around them and cheer. She turned and grinned at Ty, who sat behind her. He gave her an exhausted smile and nod of his head. Emma and Kahlid were at the edge of the crowd, gesturing for them to ride over. Behind them sat their Chinook helicopter, the crew nearby.

Rachel turned their horse and edged through the crowd. The people smiled, waved and stepped aside so that they could ride toward Emma and Kahlid. When they finally arrived, Rachel dismounted first.

"Rachel!" Emma cried, running up and gripping her shoulders. "Are you all right?"

"I'm fine," she wearily assured her anxious cousin. She couldn't help looking over at Ty and, turning, she noticed how tired he appeared. A dark splotch of blood where he'd been injured before was bleeding again.

"Help me?" she asked Emma and walked over to their horse.

"Ty, let me help you down." Rachel offered her hand up to him.

"Thanks. I'm feeling a little light-headed," Ty admitted. Gripping her hand, he dismounted. If not for her arm going around his waist, he'd have fallen. As he threw his arm around Rachel's shoulders, she steadied him. Kahlid quickly came up.

"Let me help," Kahlid offered, putting his arm around him, as well. Together, they walked him into the bay of the helicopter.

They sat down on the nylon netting that served as a seat. "I'm okay," Ty told Rachel. "Just weak."

Emma said, "We have two doctors and nurses with us. They're in the village today. I'll go get one of them." She trotted out of the helo and disappeared.

Kahlid stood in front of him. "You two almost got killed down there."

"Yeah," Ty muttered, "tell me about it."

"There was nothing we could do except watch. We thought about flying the Chinook down there, but we could have been shot out of the air."

"I know," Ty told the captain. "You couldn't do anything. We needed Apache support, but there was none to be had." He saw the worry in the Afghan officer's eyes. "We got lucky with Lord Khan being in the area."

Nodding, Kahlid murmured, "Yes. I called BJS at Camp Bravo and informed the major that he was on his way here. He has some health problems and was going to meet with the docs here today."

"Good timing," Ty said. He closed his eyes. "I've

ripped open that wound on my left arm again. I'm bleeding like a stuck pig...." And that was the last thing Ty remembered.

When Ty regained consciousness, the first thing he saw was Rachel at his side. He felt her warm hand on his gowned shoulder. Slowly the room came into focus before his blurred vision. The room was surrounded by olive-green curtains. There was an IV in his right arm.

"You're okay, Ty," Rachel soothed, leaning over him and seeing if he recognized her. "You passed out from loss of blood. Kahlid and Emma flew you straight to Bagram Air Base outside of Kabul. You got a transfusion, and a surgeon fixed up your left arm. How are you feeling?" Rachel gently squeezed his shoulder. As he slowly moved his head and looked up at her, she gave him a wobbly smile of welcome.

"B-bagram?" His throat was dry, parched.

"Yes, you're safe. We're home, Ty. You're going to be okay. Are you thirsty?"

She must be a mind reader, Ty thought. Giving a slight nod, he tried to lick his dry lips without success.

Rachel took a glass that had water and a glass straw in it from the bed stand. She guided the straw between his cracked lips. "Drink..." she quietly urged.

The water tasted wonderful. He drank two glasses before he was sated. The water cleared his sluggish mind. Other sounds filtered into his consciousness. Men and women talked in quiet voices outside his curtained cubicle. The smell of anesthesia was everywhere, along with bleach and alcohol odors. Looking down at himself, he saw that he was dressed in a blue gown. His dirty flight uniform was gone. As Rachel came and sat down at his bedside, he asked, "How long have I been here? What happened?"

Rachel looked at her watch. "After you passed out, it took us an hour to fly to Bagram. Kahlid had called ahead. When we got here, there was a team waiting. You took over two pints of blood. The doctor who worked on your arm said you probably tore an artery during our firefight and said you were bleeding to death." Mouth quirking, Rachel managed a pained smile. "You went into cardiac arrest after arriving here. They had to revive you with the paddles twice before you started breathing again."

"I almost died?"

"Yes, from blood loss." Rachel leaned forward and kissed his sweaty brow. "I almost lost you, Ty, before I'd found you." Tears welled in her eyes and she seemed embarrassed. Sniffing, she wiped them away.

Nothing shattered Ty so much as a woman crying. He could barely contain his own emotional reaction to her tears. When her lips met his brow, Ty felt such life and warmth in her grazing touch. For a moment, he closed his eyes and wrestled with his own feelings. He'd nearly died. *Oh, God...* Ty opened his eyes and gazed up at her. She was still in her dirty flight uniform, her hair mussed with bits of grass and dust. Her face was smudged. She was the most beautiful sight to him.

"I didn't know...." he managed hoarsely.

"It was touch and go for a while," Rachel shakily assured him. She moved her hand gently across his broad shoulder. "But you're going to be fine now. The E.R. doc said the reason your heart cavitated was because there wasn't enough blood in the chambers. As soon as they got the transfusion into you, your heart was fine."

"And you were there and saw it?"

"Yes. They ordered me out, but I refused to go. I... wanted to be with you, Ty. We'd gone through so much together. We fought for our lives down in that valley, and we were vastly outnumbered. The least I could do was be at your side." Rachel blinked back more tears. "I—I love you, Ty. I know we said it to one another in the heat of battle, but I meant it."

Holding her tearful golden gaze, Ty saw how her lower lip trembled. How badly he wanted to hold her. Love her. Right now, he felt so weak that it was tough just to raise his good arm. His left arm was swathed in a bandage and in a sling across his chest. He moved his hand. It was painful, but he didn't care. His fingers covered her other hand resting on the side of his bed.

"Listen," he told her, his voice rough with emotion, "I meant it, too, Rachel. I don't know when or how it happened. All I know is that it did." Searching her teary gaze, Ty added, "We've just gone through hell and we've survived it. We need time to get to know one another. Time to heal up from what we just experienced together."

Rachel gently enclosed his fingers, which were cold to the touch. Ty's face was no longer pasty, but he didn't look terribly healthy, either. The doctor who had saved his life had warned her he'd be dazed for at least another twenty-four hours. "I want time with you, Ty. Our past is gone. I'm glad to release it." She smiled softly, searching his blue eyes. "There's just so much about you that is heroic and good."

His heart swelled with a fierce love for her. "I'm no hero," Ty muttered. "I was a villain of the worst kind in the past. I have a lot to make up for, Rachel. I'm grateful you'll let me try."

"You are a hero, Ty," Rachel whispered. "In *my*

eyes. My heart." Standing up, her hand still holding his, she leaned over and gently placed her lips against his. Ty's mouth was strong against hers. Drowning in the moment she'd long dreamed of, Rachel lifted her other hand and caressed his stubbled cheek. He might be feeling weak due to all his trials, but his mouth was cherishing against hers. She absorbed the warmth of his moist breath, the joy shared between them in finding one another. Slowly, regretfully, Rachel eased her lips away. She smiled into Ty's darkened blue eyes. "I need to go get cleaned up. There are shower facilities here. When I come back, Emma and Kahlid will be here."

Nodding, Ty gripped her fingers. The pain of the needle in his arm was erased by his fierce love after her wonderful kiss. "Okay, get cleaned up. I'll be waiting."

Rachel straightened and carefully unwound her fingers from his. "I'll be back in an hour," she promised.

Shortly afterward, her heated kiss lingering on his mouth, Ty dropped off into a deep, healing sleep. He had closed his eyes, simply feeling Rachel's soft lips grazing his. He had silently promised her as he spiraled downward that somehow, he'd make it all up to this heroic, courageous woman. She deserved his love, respect and admiration. And then Ty had known no more.

When Ty awakened, Emma and Kahlid were sitting on either side of his bed. He slowly sat up, feeling stronger. Emma stood and placed extra pillows behind his back.

"Welcome back to the land of the living," Kahlid told him with a grin.

"Thanks," Ty said. He looked around his enclosed cubical. "Where's Rachel?"

"She'll be here in a minute," Emma assured him, sitting back down.

Emma's red hair was shoulder length and framed her face. Ty saw that she was in her NGO, non-government organization, blue flight suit. "What time is it?" he asked.

"It's 1700," Kahlid told him. "We got here about fifteen minutes ago." He smiled over at his wife. "I had some tactics and strategies to discuss with your doctor first."

Emma grinned and touched Ty's hand. "Kahlid knows the generals," she told him. "And sometimes, that's a plus."

Confused, Ty looked at them. He was about to speak when Rachel slipped through the curtains. The change in her was shocking. Instead of her dark green flight suit, she was dressed in a pair of white slacks, a dark blue top with a white jacket over it. Her hair had been washed and dried. It hung straight and shining around her shoulders.

"How are you feeling?" Rachel asked, coming over and pressing a kiss to his brow.

"Better, now that you're here," Ty told her, managing a slight smile. Rachel's face shone and her cheeks were flushed, her gold eyes gleaming with love toward him. Ty had never felt such love before in his life. And like a beggar, he greedily lapped it up. "How are you?"

"Clean." Rachel laughed.

Emma and Kahlid joined her.

"You look beautiful in civilian clothes," Ty said. Indeed, he'd never seen Rachel in them before. Her cheeks turned a bright red, which only enhanced her natural beauty.

"Thanks," she said shyly. Standing at his bedside, Rachel placed her hand on his right shoulder. "You must have just woke up?" she guessed.

Rubbing his face, Hamilton muttered, "Yes. How long was I out?"

"An hour," she told him. Rachel looked at her cousin. "Did you tell him what Kahlid managed to wrangle from the general?"

Shaking her head, Emma said, "No, we thought you'd like to tell Ty."

Frowning, Ty looked at them. They were all grinning like cats that had some secret shared among them. "Okay," he said, looking up at Rachel, "what's going down?"

"How would you like to come with me to their home in Kabul?" Rachel asked. "It's a huge villa up on a hill, and it's guarded 24/7. Emma and Kahlid are giving us the wing that has two suites with adjoining doors. We're going to be their guests for the next three days. Kahlid managed to get the days off from the general. They're good friends. Plus, your doctor said you couldn't go back to flight duty for at least two weeks. And he's signed off on three days off base for you because of your injury."

"And," Emma said in a conspiratorial whisper, "the general authorized the two of you to stay at our home. Isn't that great?"

Rachel laid her hand on Ty's shoulder. "What do you think about this?" She didn't want him to feel pressured. Judging from the relief in his eyes, she knew Ty was fine with the decision.

"It's important you're okay with this," he said to Rachel.

"I'm fine," she murmured. Her heart opened, and she felt such an incredible rush of warmth toward Ty.

"We need the time," he agreed. Looking over at the couple, Ty said, "Thanks a lot."

Emma smiled and slid her arm around her tall, lean husband. He drew her near. "In a war zone, you don't get a lot of uninterrupted quality time just to talk."

"And that's exactly what we need," Ty said, giving Rachel a hopeful look. He didn't know where the three days would lead them, but that wasn't important.

Rachel squeezed his shoulder. "I've already called my parents and contacted my sisters. They know I'm okay."

"Good," Emma said, leaning her head against Kahlid's broad shoulder. "Because at the first opportunity, I'd called them myself."

"I know and I'm glad you did. My mom was beside herself. You saved her a couple of hours of waiting for my phone call."

"I'm sure the Army notified my father," Ty commented sourly.

Rachel patted his shoulder gently. "At least he knows you're alive." The stubbornness in his eyes gave away just how resistant he was to talking with his estranged father. She hoped that someday Ty could get past his anger for what his father had done to him. His jaw clenched. Forgiveness was a long road.

Emma said, "There's a wonderful housekeeper who will be there if you need anything. Kahlid's driver, Nabi, will take you home."

Kahlid pressed a kiss to his wife's red hair. "And

we'll be there shortly. My housekeeper doesn't speak English, but we'll be around."

"And you're welcome to join us at dinner," Emma told them. "Or if you want to take your dinner in your suites, that's fine, too. Whatever is comfortable for you."

Rachel said, "Cousin, you rock. Thank you."

Ty grinned. "I'd like to get out of this gown, get into some civilian clothes and leave all this behind." He held up his arm that had the IV taped to it.

Laughing, Rachel said, "I'll get the nurse. You've already been signed out."

"You and I are about the same height," Kahlid said, releasing his wife. "I put some of my clothes in the locker down the hall. They'll probably fit."

"Thanks. I'll make them fit." Ty gave the gown a distasteful look. "I'm not happy running around in this thing."

Chuckling, Emma took Kahlid's hand and tugged him toward the curtains. "Come on, Kahlid. We still have work to do."

"Nabi will come here to your cubicle in about twenty minutes," Kahlid said.

"I'll wait for him," Rachel said. She felt giddy inwardly, as if floating on air. She and Ty would have some quiet downtime to talk. That's what was needed now more than anything. Good, deep talks. Who knew where it would lead?

Ty couldn't believe the luxury of his suite. The driver had delivered them to the hilltop estate. It was completely surrounded by a ten-foot fence with concertina wire on top. Plus, four guards constantly patrolled the area. It was, according to chatty Nabi, one of the few homes that the Taliban had not destroyed. Ty felt safe knowing the security measures that Kahlid had taken. His arm was still in a sling. And he was grateful that Kahlid's jeans, a dark blue polo shirt and socks all fit. He was still wearing his flight boots. A fashion plate, he was not.

The suite consisted of three rooms. The first was a living room, the second a massive bathroom. On the other side of it was a room with a king-size bed with a colorful quilt thrown across. Everywhere he looked, he saw Americana. He knew Kahlid had gotten his degree at Princeton University and was steeped in American culture. As he stood looking at the overstuffed couches and chairs, Ty felt at home.

There was a light tap on his door. Turning, he called, "Come in.…"

Rachel poked her head around the door. "Hey, this is like a five-star hotel! I wanted to see your digs. Do you mind?"

Smiling, Ty said, "No, not at all." Just seeing the tension easing from Rachel's face made his heart expand with joy. "What's your place like?"

"Kahlid loves quilts," Rachel said as she entered his suite. "And my whole place is decorated with quilts, framed or otherwise. Yours reminds me more of a 1930s decor you'd find in the Midwest." She went over and touched the cherry rocker that had a small quilt hanging over the back.

"I'm not that up on decorations," Ty said, frowning. He saw that there was hot tea and two cups sitting on the coffee table. "Want some tea?" he asked.

Rachel brightened. "I'd love some!" It felt wonderful to just share time and space with Ty. She saw him struggling to do the right thing. After their past, he was trying desperately to make her feel welcome. She walked over and said, "Why don't you take a seat in that overstuffed chair. I'll pour."

Grateful, Ty sat down. "It feels good to sit," he admitted.

Rachel noted his face was pale. His eyes were shadowed. Pouring the fragrant tea into the delicate china cups, she said, "The nurse said you're going to need a solid, uninterrupted night's sleep to feel like your old self again."

Ty took the cup and saucer from her. There was nothing but grace about Rachel. Her hair was now washed, dried and shone like an ebony frame around her beautiful face. "I feel like I'm in some kind of dream," he murmured, tasting the tea.

Sitting down on the couch opposite him, Rachel sipped her tea. "It's hard going from this to a war zone not more than half a mile from your house." She appreciated his clean, brown hair, a rebellious lock fell over his brow.

"I don't know how Kahlid and Emma do it. They're out there flying to border villages every day. And they're wide open to attack. No Apache escorts for them because they're an NGO."

"My cousin is like all of the Trayherns," Rachel said, balancing the cup on her crossed legs. "We're adaptable, flexible and from the earliest time we can remember taught that life throws curveballs at us. My parents raised all of us girls to be able to shift and make the necessary changes."

Ty raised his brows. "The more I hear about your parents, the more I wish I had a set of them instead."

Losing some of her smile, Rachel felt deeply for Ty. She could see the hurt, the old anger and confusion that his father had created within him. "Your father wasn't a model parent," she quietly agreed. "But he did the best he could, Ty."

"Not damn good enough," he growled.

"You've changed despite him," Rachel coaxed in a soft tone, holding his murky stare. "And you need to give yourself credit for that, Ty. You are not your father."

"Not any longer." He absorbed the kindness in her gaze. "Rachel, I want to make up for what I did to you. You took the brunt of my misguided anger."

Her mouth lifted a little. "You're doing it right now, Ty. Don't you see that?"

"It's not enough."

"I don't want you doing anything out of guilt." There was a glint in her eyes.

"Not to worry on that point. When I first saw you at Fort Rucker, before I knew you were in pilot training, I thought I'd met an angel, died and gone to heaven." He saw the surprise in her expression. "You were as beautiful then as you are now."

Blinking, Rachel said, "I don't remember meeting you before I was assigned to your class."

"I saw you at the base hospital. There was a drive for blood, and you were standing in line."

"I had forgotten about that. Yes, I was there. Where were you?"

"I'd just given blood and was going out the other set of doors. You didn't see me." His voice lowered. "But I saw you."

"It must have been a shock for me to show up in your class."

"Yes, it was. A part of me just wanted to fall all over you like a lovesick teenager. Another part kept hearing my father's words that women were weak."

"Well," she sighed, "we know which part won out."

"Too bad the teen didn't." He gave her a hopeful look. Rachel didn't seem as upset about the past as he felt.

"Yes, I'd much rather have dealt with your attention that way." She grinned a little. "It's nice to know the rest of the story, Ty. Thank you."

His conscience eased over the words and the sincere expression in her eyes. "I didn't want to hate you, Rachel. I wanted to get to know you. I felt torn with you in the class. Later, I realized the truth about why I was so cruel."

"I was your whipping post," she agreed.

"Not anymore." Ty gave her a heated look charged with meaning. "I need to hear it again. Did you mean what you said out there in the valley? That you loved me? Or was that said in fear and knowing you were going to die soon?"

"I meant it. I wanted you to know how I really felt about you, Ty, before we died."

"When did you know?" he wondered.

"What? That I loved you?" Rachel looked up at the ceiling and then back at him. There was an incredible peace in his face now, as if some huge load had dissolved from his shoulders. He'd carried his father long enough. "When I realized you weren't going to come after me like you did at Fort Rucker. I got to see the other side of you, Ty. What I call your good side." She smiled impishly. "I felt like I was rediscovering you all over again. And I liked what I saw. I allowed myself to open up to you, Ty. You didn't know it, but I was watching you closely. I wanted to see if the 'new' Ty Hamilton was there all the time or his evil twin was going to sneak back in."

Laughing a little, Ty felt warm all over. The joy, the elfin quality dancing in Rachel's golden eyes made him feel ten times the man he was minutes ago. She made him feel good, he realized. "My evil twin is no more," he promised her in a deep voice.

"I know that now. For sure." Rachel's smile dissolved. "When we were out there in the valley and the Taliban was galloping down upon us, I knew we'd die." She moved the cup gently around in her hands, staring at the brown tea inside it. For a long moment, she didn't speak. Finally, Rachel lifted her head and tried to put how she felt into words. "I wanted you to know I'd forgiven you. And that somewhere along the line, I had fallen so deeply in love with you.…"

Chapter 16

Rachel felt like taking a dip in the hot tub. She'd just awakened from her nap after having lunch with Ty. Looking at her watch, she saw it was nearly 3:00 p.m. The sun was slanting through the floor-to-ceiling windows, brightening her suite. Emma had urged them to take advantage of the hot tub while at the villa. Rachel was still sore from the earlier helicopter crash. And she'd taken Emma's advice and used the heat to help her tightened muscles. This was their last day here at the villa. Tomorrow morning, Nabi would drive them back to Bagram Air Base and they'd fly the new Chinook assigned to them back to Bravo. Life would once more become tense and dangerous.

With a softened sigh, Rachel shimmied out of her clothes, walked into the bathroom, grabbed a bright yellow towel and wrapped it around herself. The hot tub was only about ten feet down the hall. Opening the door, she looked both ways. For a split second, she almost walked up the hall to Ty's room to invite him to join her. Rachel felt scared and hesitated. They'd talked every chance they got. Their most important conversations lasted deep into each night. Starving to explore Ty, Rachel felt her love growing for this man. She knew no human being on earth was perfect, that they had all made mistakes, large and small. Her hand tightened on the top of her towel, which hid her body. Should she go ask Ty to join her?

Nervous, Rachel decided not to do it. She was afraid of herself. Afraid that Ty might reject her, no matter how close she felt to him. He had so much to overcome. And she felt they'd come a long way in a very short amount of time. As she padded down the carpeted hall toward the spa room, she waffled. How she wanted Ty. All of him and in every way. In her nightly dreams, she made passionate love with him. Even now, the memories brought heat into her face. During their talks, she'd seen the hunger and need for her in his eyes, too. But Ty hadn't made a move, either. Maybe they were both too scared, the past hovering threateningly over them.

Yes, that was it, Rachel decided. They had such a past history of hurt that they were frightened to death of making a mistake that could destroy their fragile new relationship. They both wanted it so bad that they were afraid to make the first move. Mouth tightening, Rachel placed her hand on the brass doorknob and opened the door that led to the huge, round hot tub.

"Oh!"

Ty was sitting in the hot tub. His eyes widened considerably as Rachel entered and then froze on the spot.

"I didn't know," he began lamely, trying to make her feel at ease. He was sitting on the granite bench, the water up to his torso, his dark-haired chest exposed. Seeing the redness sweep across her cheeks, Ty realized she was embarrassed to find him so obviously naked. His muscles were aching, and the hot water helped them relax.

"I'm sorry," Rachel stumbled, her hand still on the doorknob.

"Wait. Don't go," he called. "Come on in." Suddenly, Ty's fear of rejection dissolved. He held his hand out to her. "I'd like you to come in with me, if you want…?"

Moistening her lips, Rachel hesitated. Ty's hair was wet and gleaming. His naked upper body glistened. He was so incredibly ripped. At the base camp, she'd seen him work out at least an hour a day in the gym. "Well… I…I didn't know you'd be in here." The words came out whispered and halting to her. The hope burned in his face, those large, intelligent blue eyes of his narrowing like a laser—on her. Instantly, her body responded. She felt her breasts firming, her nipples tightening. It was a hungry look, of a man wanting his woman. Even her lower body responded to Ty's heated, dangerous stare.

Her fear vanished. It was a relief, because right now, all Rachel really wanted was to be in Ty's arms. Turning, she shut the door—and then locked it. No way did she want the housekeeper accidentally coming in to surprise them. Kahlid and Emma were on a flight. They had the villa to themselves. Turning, she said, "I don't need this, do I?" She allowed the yellow towel to drop to her feet.

Ty suppressed a gasp and felt pure awe as Rachel stood naked near the door. She was statuesque, her shoulder thrown back, her chin tilted at a proud angle. "No," he rasped, standing up. "You don't. Come here...." He walked across the large, round hot tub to where the stairs were located.

She let her gaze rake his taut, muscular body. The water pooled just below his hips, and she could see that he wanted her. A slight, careless smile fled across her mouth as she walked over to him. Without a word, Rachel took his proffered hand and walked down the four steps and into the warm, swirling water. Ty released her hand, his arms sweeping about her, drawing her hard against him.

The air rushed out of her lungs as he claimed her. Rachel smiled and moved her hands upward to frame his damp face. His blue eyes burned with a hunger that intensified her own need of him. "I want you, Ty. All of you, in every way," Rachel whispered, leaning upward, her mouth claiming his. She drank in his powerful need of her.

Ty led her to the center of the bubbling water. Their bodies were locked tightly against one another. He could feel the swell of her breasts, the hard nubs of her nipples pressing into his chest. Her hips were rounded and soft compared to his angular hips. When her arms entwined around his thick neck, her fingers moving though the short strands of his black hair, Ty groaned. Yesterday he'd gotten rid of the sling. His left arm was sore, but useable. The water created a silken movement between them.

As Ty broke their heated kiss, he guided his hand upward and slid his fingers through her hair. Rachel moaned and tipped her head back, eyes closed. Her hands were busy roving slickly across his back, touching him, exploring him. Her breath came in gasps just as his did. In moments, he led her down into the warm water. It was hot because of the summer heat, but it felt embracing.

Rachel smiled up at him as he took her down into the bubbling, blue water. His return smile devastated her hungry senses. Focusing on his very male mouth, she reached out and traced his flat lower lip with her index finger. As Ty settled them on the underwater bench, she floated across his lap. Her body situated against his, she could feel his need of her. Raw desire exploded through her. Lifting her arms, she placed them around Ty's neck, and she kissed him hard.

Her mouth was wreaking fire from his lips down to his burning lower body. With each movement, Ty felt himself coming unraveled. Her mouth was wet and hot as she kissed his brow, his closed eyes, cheek, and finally, his mouth once more. Tunneling his fingers into her hair, he angled her such that he could plunder her mouth as never before as her hands drifted in exploration across his chest. And then she broke the kiss and moved away from him.

Ty knew there were several dark blue pads laying next to the hot tub. They were made of thick foam rubber and comfortable. As Rachel went toward the stairs, he held her hand. She smiled teasingly at him, which sent a bolt of powerful heat through him. There was no disguising she wanted him as much as he wanted her.

"Come here," Ty rasped, drawing her close. "Let's get out and lay on this." He pointed to it.

Rachel's smile grew. "How handy to have them."

Grinning, Ty led her out of the hot tub. "It's perfect for us…. Come on…." He led her up the stairs and onto the soft pads.

Without hesitation, Rachel laid down next to Ty. Her

hair was damp, the ends sticking against her glistening shoulders. His face was like that of a raptor: intense and focused. The air escaped her lips as Ty turned her onto her back and slid his hand beneath her neck. His head dipped and Rachel closed her eyes in anticipation. His mouth sought her hardened nipples, one after another. As he suckled her, laved his tongue across them, her entire body convulsed with pleasure. The power of the movement sent a scalding heat into her lower body. Moaning, Rachel couldn't stand the teasing any longer. Reaching up, she pulled Ty over her. Looking up into his narrowed eyes, she whispered, "Love me. Take me with you...." She thrust her hips upward to meet and meld with him.

Gritting his teeth, Ty felt her capture him. In moments, she had pulled him deep within her moist, heated confines. Her hands slid over his hips, trapping him and then moving slowly with a rhythm that shattered his mind. No longer was Ty thinking. They were reacting wildly, like the primal animals they'd suddenly shifted into and become. Leaning down, he caught and captured Rachel's parted lips, shifting her on top of him. His hands moved to either side of her head, and he groaned as they established a violent, stormy rhythm. The world dissolved into a boiling cauldron they shared between them. The movements were swift and hard. He heard Rachel's breath come in sobs, felt her fingers digging frantically into his bunched shoulders. Closing his eyes, Ty surrendered himself to her powerful, womanly core. For the first time, he allowed her love to completely envelop him.

His world slowed, burned, and Ty absorbed her fierce love for him. He felt his heart opening. It was such a strange and startling sensation, but it didn't pull him out of that cloud of euphoria. Like the starving man he was, he realized in some small, functioning part of his brain that Rachel loved him with her life. Indeed, she'd knelt at his side, firing at the charging Taliban who were intent on killing them. Rachel had shown such courage under fire. And now, she was sharing herself, her hungry body with him. Fully. No reservations. As his hands settled across her hips, he sank even more deeply into her. Ty heard her gasp with pleasure, and he plunged into a blanket of fire that roared through him. In moments, he felt himself explode within her. Simultaneously, Rachel suddenly stiffened and uttered a deep moan. His world tumbled end over end in a fire that consumed both of them. Ty felt his heart widening and love pouring through him as they collided like fiery stars into one another. Suddenly, they both froze as if paralyzed.

Rachel felt his entire body contract, his hands grip her hips as he growled and released. They were like two animals locked with one another, hungry, starving and now being sated by one another. Eyes closed, Rachel had never felt such raw pleasure as now. Ty caressed her as she lay down across him, her head nestled against the curve of his neck. All Rachel could do was sob and feel the liquid fire of her body collapsing in on itself. His fingers moved in grazing touches across her back, following the curve of her spine and caressing her silky hair.

Absorbing Rachel's relaxed body against his, Ty lay there, feeling satiated as never before. He didn't want to open his eyes yet. He simply wanted to feel the heavy warmth of Rachel upon him, the burning power of them connected with one another, her moist, ragged breath upon his shoulder. A smile pulled at his mouth as he continued to trace and memorize her shoulders, arms and back. Her hips were flared, and as his hands cupped them, he felt another powerful urge. The urge to procreate, to give her a child. Their child. In those stunning moments, Ty knew that any baby that they may have created now or in the future would be raised with love, not fear and beatings. His fingers grazed her hips, and he absorbed those powerful possibilities.

Rachel lifted her head from the crook of his shoulder. She smiled down at Ty. He had such love mirrored in his eyes for her that she felt as if the entire world had shifted. Rachel touched his cheek. "It was incredible," she whispered. "I've never felt so satisfied as right now...."

Those were the words he needed to hear. Ty realized he was still emotionally fragile with Rachel. His heart loved her with an undying fierceness, and he was playing catch-up with the stunning turn of events. Lifting his hand, he guided her so that she sat up on him. Her hair was tangled and mussed, her lips soft and pouty from their shared kisses. As her hands rested on his chest, her fingernails trailed and tangled softly in his dark hair. Ty liked the gold glimmer in her half-closed eyes, a lioness satiated. Lifting his hands, he cupped her breasts and moved his thumbs across her hardening nipples. She gave him a predatory smile.

"I'm not done with you, Ty."

Leaning up, Ty rocked her so that his knees were a support for her back. "I'm not, either," he growled, leaning over and suckling one of her nipples.

Rachel sighed and moaned, curving her arms around his broad shoulders. Everything was so right. So natural between them. The heat built in her breasts and then traveled like a line of igniting fire down through the center of her body. She felt the power of him moving suggestively within her. A sigh of pleasure whispered from her lips as he reminded her of their connection.

Rachel leaned back against his drawn up legs and savored his masculine hardness, his unmerciful teasing. His mouth traveled from one nipple to the other, inciting them, fanning the flames once more. Surprised at how quickly her body wanted Ty all over again, she opened her eyes and then gently pushed him down on the mat.

"My turn," she whispered, and she began to rock her hips forward and back with intensity.

Hands against her hips, Ty felt her power, a woman taking her man. It was something beautiful to experience, not control over one another but a sharing of that raw gift of love between them. Indeed, he saw her lips part and felt her entire body contract around him. Rachel threw her head back, exposing the beautiful curve of her neck. Her fingers dug deeply into his flesh as they once more experienced a simultaneous orgasm. The rippling heat moved against him, and he gasped with pleasure as, once more, he released into her scalding confines. For a moment, their eyes closed. Imprisoned within the heat of their passion, Ty felt his world spinning out of control.

He was in a dive that he never wanted to recover from. Never in his life had he experienced what he was sharing with Rachel right now. The world had turned over, inside out, and he was like a butterfly being born out of the imprisonment of a cocoon. It wasn't a painful sensation; it was beautiful, and life began to flow through him as never before. Now, Ty understood when someone said that love had changed them completely. Rachel's love had changed him forever and in a good way. He was finally free of his past, because she loved him enough to walk with him into an unknown future together.

Groaning, Rachel fell against Ty, spent and weak. Her head lay on his shoulder, and she relished the feel of his arms wrapped around her, simply holding her safe against his male body. She felt each breath he took, body and soul. Trailing her hand gently across Ty's left shoulder, she was always aware of his bandaged wound. She lifted her head and placed several moist kisses on that broad shoulder that had carried so many loads alone for far too long. She licked his flesh, tasted the salt of him. He groaned with pleasure as she continued her exploration across his skin. Smiling to herself, she inhaled his male scent. It was all good. She loved Ty with a fierceness that took even her by surprise. And yet, Rachel felt content as never before.

Easing off him, Rachel moved down to his side and snuggled into his awaiting arms. The humid warmth of the hot-tub room was a wonderful blanket. The late afternoon sunlight poured into the western, stained-glass windows, making it seem like the rainbow lived where they lay. She opened her eyes and caressed Ty's damp hair. Rachel drowned in his glinting blue gaze. His face had never looked so relaxed or peaceful. "I love you, Ty. With my heart, my soul. I never want to be apart from you...."

Ty heard the trembling and husky words slipping from her well-kissed mouth. He grazed her lips and whispered, "I love you with my heart, my soul, Rachel...."

For a long time, they lay in one another's arms. The bubbling sounds of the hot tub, the rainbow colors dancing around the room, all served to make their love something magical for Rachel. She was content to lay against Ty's strong, powerful body. Absorbing his tender touches, Rachel wanted to memorize every inch of him.

Finally, reality intruded upon them. Ty watched the sun leave the windows and the rainbows dissolved. The entire afternoon had been one of kisses, exploration, joy and sharing. "I don't ever want this to end," Ty admitted, his voice raspy.

Closing her eyes, Rachel murmured, "Me neither. This is so magical, Ty. Stepping into this room was like stepping into another world. A world where there is no fighting and killing. Only hope." She opened her eyes and held his tender gaze. "Here, we could love one another and not worry about the violent world around us." She touched his cheek. "And I know tomorrow morning, we're going back into that other world."

His brows fell as he saw worry shadow her golden eyes. With his index finger, Ty traced each of her brows. "Love has seen us this far," he whispered, "and it will see us the rest of the way."

Rachel nodded, her brows tingling with pleasure. "I know," she said. "But, I don't want this to end. We've just found one another, Ty."

He heard the worry in her husky voice. Drawing her deep into his arms, he simply held her. "When someone would tell me love conquers all, I always laughed and made fun of them. That was because," Ty said next to her ear, "I had never been in love before. Now, I am, and I understand what the guy was trying to share with me." He kissed her hair. "Love will see us through this year, Rachel. We'll weather whatever happens because we do love one another. Make sense?"

Rachel left his arms and sat up. Ty joined her, his

arm sliding around her shoulders and drawing her close. There was something about being naked with him that made Rachel feel safe and wanted. And he was so beautiful to look at, the dangerous gleam in his eyes, the predator who wanted to stalk her all over again. Her body responded heatedly to his intent stare. "It does make sense, Ty. We've gone through so much since we met again. We not only had to deal with our collective past with one another, but we're in a war, too."

Nodding, Ty whispered, "We have the time, sweet one." He reached out and touched her knee, then added, "There's no hurry about us. We'll be at the same base. We can see one another every time we can make it happen."

"At least I'll be with your squadron for the next five months."

Ty leaned forward and cupped her face. He wanted to erase the worry and anxiety he saw in Rachel's narrowing eyes. "Listen to me. Even though you will go back to BJS and flying the Apache, we'll find spaces and places to be with one another."

"I don't want to lose what we have," she admitted. "I fell in love before, and Garrett was killed."

Ty drew Rachel back into his arms. She rested her head against his right shoulder. "The past is the past. It's not going to repeat," Ty promised her, lips near her ear. After kissing her cheek, he made Rachel look up at him. "If we can surmount our past, don't you think there's a greater plan at work here? We didn't meet again to carry on our war with one another. We met because it was time for us to heal our wounds. And because we have, Rachel, we're going to get the reward of loving one another fully. For a long, long time."

His words made so much sense to her. Slipping her

arms around his shoulders, she whispered, "Thank you, Ty. I hadn't thought of it like that."

"We're being given a second chance with one another, Rachel." Looking deep into her sleepy gaze, he said, "And I'm grateful. We have nowhere to go but up with one another. We were as far down as two people can get five years ago."

Rallying to his optimism, she smiled. "You've come so far and grown so much, Ty. I'm in this for the long term, too. I like what we have. I love talking with you. You're an incredible man, and you inspire me in so many ways."

"I feel the same about you," Ty admitted with a grin. Looking up, he saw the sky was beginning to lose its bright, powdery blue color. "Let's take a shower together. Then we can get dressed and tell the housekeeper we're having dinner with Emma and Kahlid tonight. It's our last night here, and I'd like to thank them for their kindness."

"Good idea," Rachel said. "But one more kiss..." She leaned upward and met his smiling mouth. Ty tasted so good to her, his lips commanding against her own. And once more, she felt the fire ignite in her lower body. Breaking the kiss, Rachel laughed breathlessly. "I can't even kiss you, Ty Hamilton, without wanting to love you all over again!"

Ty got to his feet and pulled Rachel into his arms. "You don't have to look far to see what your kiss did to me."

Grinning wickedly, Rachel could see his arousal once more. "I have a feeling that we're not going to have much sleep tonight."

"Me, too," Ty gloated, picking up her towel and handing it to her.

Rachel wrapped the towel around her glowing body and watched as he put his own around his narrow hips. "I want to tell my folks about us. Are you okay with that?"

"Sure." Ty walked over and squeezed her. "The time over here isn't going to work against us, Rachel. I feel the year we share here will be good for us."

Nodding, she walked with him toward the door. "I'm thinking of getting married after we get back home." She searched his peaceful-looking features. Did he feel the same?

"I'd like that," Ty said, kissing her hair. Leaning forward, he unlocked the door. "And I love you...."

Emma was all smiles at the dinner table after Rachel had told them of their plans to marry after they finished with their tour. "That's wonderful!"

"Don't call your parents yet," Rachel warned with a laugh as she drank her after-dinner coffee. "Let me break the news."

"Of course," Emma chortled. She glanced at her husband, Kahlid, who sat at the end of the table and at her left elbow. "And Kahlid, you keep quiet, too."

"Me?" He held up his hands, feigning surprise. "Why, I'm the soul of secrets, beloved."

"Sometimes," Emma said with a wry laugh.

Ty smiled. He sat across the table from Rachel. She looked incredibly beautiful in her khaki trousers, the soft pink tee, her hair washed and shining like a frame about her face. "I think this can be all sorted out," he soothed.

Kahlid leaned forward and patted Ty's shoulder. "Listen, you two are welcome here any time you can get away. Emma and I know the joy of coming here after being out at these villages. We know we're targets. We know that the Taliban would like to kill us. But being able to come back here…" Kahlid said, gesturing around the room, "…is a slice of heaven on this war-torn earth."

Emma nodded and looked at her cousin. "All you have to do is call Nabi after you fly into Bagram, and he'll pick you up. You're welcome any time, Rachel. The suite wing is yours."

"Thanks," Rachel said, her eyes filling with tears. She sniffed and looked over at Ty. The expression in his eyes told her everything. He loved her.

"Changes are in the air," Kahlid agreed. "Getting to another topic, we had a meeting with Major Klein this morning." He got serious. "Have you heard about a ground arm of Black Jaguar Squadron being created?"

"Yes," Rachel said. "These are women military volunteers who have taken immersion courses in Pashto, gone through a year of paramedic training to be embedded in Marine squads. They're going to put a woman in each squad. She'll then make connection with the women elders of the villages they work with."

"Precisely," Kahlid said. He wiped his mouth with the white linen napkin and picked up his cup of tea. "Colonel Maya Stevenson and her husband, Dane, are flying in tomorrow. The women are already here and getting situated in the BJS tent area."

"Wow, it's moving fast." Rachel whistled.

"You'll both be invited to the meeting tomorrow at 1300."

Ty smiled. "Big changes. Women in ground combat."

"Yes," Emma said with caution, "but they're not there to fight the Taliban as much as make positive connections with the women in the villages. They'll be like a nurse, coming in to take care of the women and children. I think it's a wonderful concept."

Ty frowned. "But there's no guarantee that those Marine forces won't be attacked by Taliban. And if they are, that woman is in that squad and attacked, too."

"Everyone at the Pentagon realizes this," Kahlid agreed. "That's why they've put Colonel Maya Stevens in charge of it. She single-handedly built the all-woman BJS squadron down in Peru and choked off ninety percent of the drug flights out of that country. She's a brilliant tactician, and she's had her vision for this new breed of BJS women all along. These volunteers were also trained at Camp Pendleton, the USMC training base in California, too. They're fully combat qualified."

"Still," Rachel said, "it's a brand new trial for women in combat."

"I think they'll win the hearts and minds of the villagers," Kahlid said. "Women are able to make connections men never will." He grinned over at his red-haired wife.

Chuckling, Emma said, "Bingo!"

Rachel smiled across the table at Ty. She wanted to go to bed with him, hold him, love him until they both were too weak to move. This courageous man had surmounted so much. Tomorrow would come soon enough. They would survive this year, and she knew their love would deepen. She would marry him. And Rachel knew their love would last—forever.

* * * * *

"Tell me to stop."

Her mouth opened. He waited, praying she didn't say those words.

"Touch me," she whispered.

Joy shot through him. Before she could change her mind, he tangled one hand through her hair and tugged her towards him, kissing her hard and deep. She gasped against his mouth, then relaxed, parting her lips so he could slide his tongue inside, so he could lick and explore and drink her in.

Every muscle in his body was coiled tight. His groin throbbed, the erection straining against his zipper harder and more painful than ever. He'd been with a few women since he and Sarah had broken up, but none of them had inspired this primal reaction inside him. None of them had made his heart pound and made him hungry with desire. Sarah was the only one who did that, the only one who could satisfy his appetite, his need.

Dear Reader,

Forgiveness—so easy as a concept, but not so easy when you're the wronged party being asked for it. I'll admit, I struggle sometimes with it. It can be hard to forgive, especially when all you want to do is hold a grudge, or when you're too scared to forgive in fear that you'll be hurt again.

I decided to explore this concept with Finn and Sarah, who share a turbulent past that led to a four-year separation. As the sheriff of Serenade, Finn knows the difference between right and wrong, but the wrong he committed four years ago continues to haunt him. Asking for Sarah's forgiveness is one thing, but proving to her that he deserves it…well, that's a whole different story.

I hope you enjoy Finn and Sarah's emotional journey!

Happy reading,

Elle

THE HEARTBREAK SHERIFF

BY
ELLE KENNEDY

First published in Great Britain 2012
by Mills & Boon, an imprint of Harlequin (UK) Limited,
Eton House, 18-24 Paradise Road, Richmond, Surrey TW9 1SR

© Leeanne Kenedy 2012

ISBN: 978 0 263 89527 8
ebook ISBN: 978 1 408 97733 0

946-0512

Harlequin (UK) policy is to use papers that are natural, renewable and recyclable products and made from wood grown in sustainable forests. The logging and manufacturing processes conform to the legal environmental regulations of the country of origin.

Printed and bound in Spain
by Blackprint CPI, Barcelona

A RITA® Award-nominated author, **Elle Kennedy** grew up in the suburbs of Toronto, Ontario, and holds a BA in English from York University. From an early age, she knew she wanted to be a writer, and actively began pursuing that dream when she was a teenager. She loves strong heroines and sexy alpha heroes, and just enough heat and danger to keep things interesting.

Elle loves to hear from her readers. Visit her website, www.ellekennedy.com, for the latest news or to send her a note.

To my family, for your endless support
and encouragement.

Chapter 1

"I didn't kill her."

The quiet plea pierced into Finn's heart like a dull, serrated blade, bringing a rush of pain and helplessness. He couldn't tear his eyes from the woman sitting in front of him. He'd dreamed of being in the same room as her for so long now, but not like this. Not in this tiny, airless interrogation room, with a narrow metal table separating them, those liquid-brown eyes staring at him with anguish and resentment.

"Sarah," he began, his voice coming out gruff, "just tell me what happened the night Teresa died."

Sarah Connelly gaped at him. Even with her expression awash with anger, she was still beautiful. Her thick brown hair gleamed under the fluorescent lights on the ceiling, and her mouth, though twisted in disbelief, was as lush and sensual as ever. She was the most stunning woman he'd ever seen, and the only woman who could send a shiver of desire up his spine even when she was glaring daggers at him.

"*Nothing* happened the night Teresa died," Sarah replied in a frosty voice. "I was at home, asleep. I woke up at three to give Lucy a bottle, and then I went back to bed, where I stayed until seven in the morning."

"You didn't leave the house at all?" Finn had to ask.

"No. Not until eight-thirty, when I dropped off Lucy at day care and opened the gallery."

Finn stifled a groan. "Then how did your hair and fingerprint wind up at the crime scene? Christ, Sarah, *explain* it to me!"

"Don't yell at me, Patrick." Ice slithered into her tone. "I don't know how my hair and fingerprint ended up at the scene—but I can assure you, *I wasn't there.*"

Frustration bubbled in Finn's gut. For the hundredth time, he wished Teresa Donovan had never been killed. Not because he and Teresa had been best buds or anything, but because the woman's death had brought nothing but chaos to Finn's peaceful little town.

Exactly one month ago, Teresa had been shot in the heart, her body discovered in the living room of the majestic stone mansion her ex-husband had built for her. Cole Donovan, the ex-husband, had been Finn's prime suspect, but with the help of Special Agent Jamie Crawford—who also happened to be Finn's best friend and took a leave of absence to assist him and Cole—Cole was cleared of the crime. Now Finn was back to square one, and it was definitely a position he didn't want to be in.

Especially now, with this new evidence in his possession. Evidence that pointed right at Sarah.

"Your print was on the coffee table next to the body,"

he said quietly. "Your hair was on the floor, by the puddle of blood pouring out of Teresa's chest."

Sarah's flawless fair skin went even paler. "Then someone put it there," she whispered. "I didn't kill that woman." Her voice wobbled. "I can't believe you'd even think that."

Problem was, he *didn't* think it. From the second his deputy phoned him with the news, Finn had been in a paralyzed state of doubt. Every cell in his body, every instinct in his gut, told him that Sarah wasn't a killer. He *knew* her. He'd lived with her, kissed her, held her in his arms. She had a gentle soul, an innate need to nurture everyone around her. Even picturing Sarah with a gun in her hands, sending a bullet into someone's heart, made his mind spin like a carousel.

But he was the sheriff. He'd taken an oath to protect the citizens of Serenade. And just because he hadn't been fond of Teresa Donovan—who was?—didn't mean he could overlook this new development in her murder case.

Still, that didn't stop him from murmuring, "I don't think you killed her."

The shock in Sarah's eyes was so strong it brought a spark of irritation to his gut. "What, you're surprised?" he muttered.

She spoke in an even tone. "You showed up at my place of business at eleven in the morning on a Saturday, forced me to lock up for the day, and dragged me to the police station for questioning. Was I supposed to think you were on my side?"

I'm always on your side, he wanted to say, but bit back the words. She wouldn't believe him, anyway, and really, how could he blame her? He hadn't exactly proven to her, now or in the past, that he would stick by her.

"I'm doing my job, Sarah. I couldn't ignore the evidence." He swallowed. "And I really think you shouldn't have turned down your option of having a lawyer present."

Her eyes widened. "Do I really need one?"

"You might." Reluctance clamped over him. "This doesn't look good for you. Evidence places you at the crime scene, and there are witnesses claiming you threatened the victim."

"I didn't threaten her!"

Finn sighed. "No?"

"Well, okay, maybe a little, but I didn't actually mean it," she stammered. "She provoked me."

"Tell me how."

"I already—"

"Then tell me again," he cut in. Leaning back in the uncomfortable plastic chair, he raked both hands through his hair and fixed a tired look across the table. "Please. I need to know every last detail if I'm going to make sense of this."

"Fine." Looking very prim and proper, Sarah clasped her delicate hands together. "Teresa cornered me outside the grocery store the day after I got back to town. I had Lucy with me, and Teresa made some less-than-pleasant comments about how I had to adopt a baby because no man would ever want me. She then claimed that she'd slept with you, mocked me about how I wasn't *woman enough* to hold on to you, and finished off with a lovely threat about calling social services to take Lucy away—because a mental case like me shouldn't be raising a baby."

She recited the speech in a calm, emotionless voice,

but Finn suspected the encounter had affected her more than she was letting on. He knew firsthand how cruel Teresa could be, and being taunted by that woman would have driven anyone crazy. It drove *him* crazy, just hearing that Teresa was going around town telling people she'd slept with him.

Uh-uh, no way would that have ever happened. For him to have touched that loathsome female, the sky would need to be filled with flying pigs, there'd be a skating rink down in hell, and the Easter Bunny would be coming over for Sunday breakfasts.

But that was Teresa Donovan for you. A pathological liar. A woman intent on unleashing as much pain as she could on the world.

"Two people heard you threaten her," he pointed out.

"Not my best moment," Sarah admitted. "But she was completely out of line. And it's not like I said *I'm gonna kill you, you awful shrew.*"

He winced, acutely aware of the mini-recorder whirring away on the center of the table, recording every word being uttered. *I'm gonna kill you, you awful shrew.* Good thing Finn wasn't corrupt, or an artfully edited version of that tape could've landed in court, marked Exhibit A, Connelly's confession.

"What did you say exactly?" he prompted.

"I told her if she didn't leave me and my daughter alone, she would regret it."

The threat hung in the air, an ominous black cloud that had *motive* written all over it.

"It was just talk," Sarah insisted. "Obviously I wasn't going to hurt her. I just wanted her to go away." Her face went ashen as she realized what she'd said. "Leave the grocery store," she quickly amended. "I wanted her to *walk* away. Alive. But just go somewhere else."

Silence stretched between them. Finn valiantly tried not to stare into her bottomless brown eyes, for fear that he'd get lost in them. Just being in the same room as her, just smelling the sweet fragrance of her lilac perfume was pure torture. He'd been fantasizing about this woman for four years, dreaming of holding her in his arms again, longing to see forgiveness—the forgiveness he surely didn't deserve—etched into her classically elegant features.

As far as reunions went, this was not what he'd imagined. But what choice did he have? The mayor was breathing down his neck, demanding that Finn close this case so that the citizens of Serenade could sleep easy. *Get the murderer off our streets,* Mayor Williams had snapped during their last phone conversation.

Finn agreed with Williams—he wanted to catch this killer, too.

But he knew, without a doubt, that the killer he was searching for was *not* Sarah.

"So what's going to happen now?" Sarah's soft voice pulled him back to grim reality. "I told you what happened and you're going to let me go now, right?"

Uneasiness circled his gut like a school of sharks. "I can't let you go."

Her gasp echoed in the suddenly cold air. "What do you mean, you *can't?* Am I under arrest?"

"No." Despite the lump in his throat, he had to add, "Not yet."

Incredulity flashed across her face. "I didn't do this, Finn! Someone is obviously trying to frame me."

Yep, he'd heard those words before, hadn't he? Cole Donovan had insisted the same thing, only a week ago, when the murder weapon was discovered in the town dump. Although the gun had been wiped clean of prints, Cole had been at the dump a few days after his ex-wife's murder, which had raised Finn's suspicions. But Cole's fancy big-city lawyer had made it clear to Finn that he had no case, no leg to stand on in court, and Serenade's district attorney had been inclined to agree.

The D.A., however, did not agree with Finn regarding *this* particular suspect.

"I suggested the same thing to Gregory," Finn told her, referring to Jonas Gregory, the D.A. "But he thinks the framing angle is far-fetched."

"Far-fetched?" she grumbled. "Well, it's *true*. I'm not a killer!"

"Sarah…" His voice drifted, the growing unease plaguing his body.

Her brown eyes narrowed. "What? Just spit it out, Patrick."

She only called him Patrick when she was angry with him, and right now, he didn't blame her, especially considering the bomb he was about to drop on her. "Gregory is concerned about your, ah, history of mental instability."

Silence. Sheer deafening silence, though he could swear he heard her heart thudding against the front of her royal-blue turtleneck sweater.

"I can't believe this," she finally burst out. "God, Finn, out of anyone, *you* know what I went through. Not that you cared—" her voice cracked, and so did his heart "—but you know why it happened. I battled depression, damn it! *Four* years ago! And now, what? You're going to use that to say I'm mentally ill? That I killed Teresa because I'm insane?"

"I'm not saying anything," he said hoarsely. "I'm just telling you what Gregory said."

"Well, screw Gregory!" Her entire face collapsed. "And screw you, too, Finn." A breath shuddered out of her mouth. "I think I want that lawyer now."

With a bleak nod, Finn scraped his chair back against the linoleum floor. "I'll bring you a phone."

As he exited the room and closed the door behind him, his legs shook and his chest ached as though someone had pummeled it repeatedly. Maybe not the most macho reaction, but right now, he didn't feel big and tough. He felt completely powerless.

He strode through the bull pen toward his office, ignoring the sympathetic look his deputy Anna Holt cast his way. He loved Anna to death, but right now, he didn't want the younger woman's sympathy. He just wanted to help Sarah. He couldn't stand seeing her like this.

She hadn't killed Teresa. He refused to believe that Sarah had murdered anyone, that she'd snapped under Teresa's callous taunts and taken her life.

She snapped before.

The unwelcome thought slipped into his head like a damn cat burglar. His hands instantly curled into fists and then anger and shame jolted through him. Like she'd said, he knew better than anyone why she'd broken down. And she was right, he hadn't handled it the way he should have. But the depression and post-traumatic stress she'd battled all those years ago didn't make her a killer.

Finn entered his small, cramped office and swiped the cordless phone from the cluttered desk. Before he could leave the room and let Sarah make her call, his cell phone came to life, bursting out in a ring tone that sounded like a foghorn, which his friend Jamie continued to tease him about. But, hey, it got his attention.

His jaw tightened as he glanced at the caller ID. Mayor Williams again. That man was like a damned dog with a bone, gnawing at him, refusing to let go until Finn arrested someone for Teresa's murder.

"I can't really talk now, Mayor," Finn said, his teeth aching from the forced polite tone. "I've got Connelly in custody and she requested a lawyer."

"Lawyered up, huh?" The law enforcement slang sounded absurd coming out of the mayor's mouth. "That's a sign of guilt, isn't it, Sheriff?"

"No, just a sign of intelligence," he couldn't help but reply. "She's concerned about her rights."

"Well, I'm concerned about who she might kill next. By the way, I've got Jonas Gregory here in my office. You're on speakerphone."

Finn fought a rush of annoyance. "Mayor, I don't think we should jump to conclusions. She—"

"Did she admit to threatening the victim?" Williams boomed, ignoring Finn's attempt at defusing the precarious situation.

"Yes, but—"

"Good. Then we're all set."

A spark of wariness ignited in his gut. "All set for what, Mayor?"

"Finnegan, it's Jonas," came a second male voice. "Look, I read over the reports you faxed, and I want to move forward with this. We've got trace evidence placing Connelly at the scene, she threatened the victim two months prior to her death, and she's got a history of imbalanced and reckless behavior."

Finn swallowed. "What are you saying, sir?"

"Arrest her. We've got a good enough case here, one I can take to a grand jury."

Good enough? Finn resisted the urge to hurl the

phone into the wall and watch it shatter into a hundred
pieces. Sarah's life, her entire future, was in danger of
being taken away for *good enough?*

"Sir, with all due respect, I think this might be premature," he said, trying to keep the desperation out of
his voice. "Let me and my staff do some more investigating, make some more inquiries—"

"What more do you need?" Gregory interrupted.
"Make the arrest, and then work on tying that murder
weapon to Connelly. Right now, we have enough to
indict."

Knowing when he was beaten, Finn's shoulders
sagged, but he still made a futile attempt at getting
some leniency for Sarah. "Can I let her go after she's
charged? She's a single mother, and she—"

"We're not doing that woman any favors." This time
it was the mayor, whose words contained a twinge of
outrage that Finn would even consider such an idea.
Williams spoke again, now sounding suspicious.
"You're not still involved with her, are you, Sheriff?"

"Of course not, Mayor. Connelly and I ended our
relationship more than four years ago."

He referred to her by her last name, hoping it would
help distance himself. But it didn't. Her beautiful face
was still imprinted in his mind, the memory of her soft
laughter still wrapped around his heart. Didn't matter
what he called her. She would always be Sarah. *His*
Sarah.

"We treat her like any other criminal, Finnegan,"
Gregory agreed. "She stays in lockup until the bail
hearing."

"And when will that be?"

"Her lawyer can petition for an emergency hearing,

but Judge Rollins is in Charleston, playing a golf tournament. I doubt he'll fly back for something so trivial."

Trivial? Finn wanted shout. Taking a mother away from her child, keeping her locked up for the weekend, was *trivial?* Rage churned in his stomach. How was a damned golf tournament more important than a woman's life?

He suddenly cursed this small town, with its one D.A. and sole judge and closed-minded attitude.

"Make the arrest and we'll meet on Monday morning at the courthouse," Gregory said, his tone brooking no argument. "We really need to figure out how she got hold of that gun."

"Yes, sir."

Finn was numb as he hung up the phone. He let it drop from his fingers, and it clattered onto the desk, knocking over a small tin of paper clips. Ignoring the mess, he simply stared into nothingness, a chill climbing up his spine.

He couldn't do this. He couldn't arrest Sarah.

This is your job.

No, it isn't, he wanted to snap, but the voice of reason was right. He was the sheriff of Serenade, North Carolina, the man elected by the townsfolk to serve and protect them.

But who would protect Sarah?

Feeling as though his legs were made of lead, he trudged back across the bull pen, ignoring the curious look Anna shot him. He made his way down the hall, pausing in front of the interrogation-room door.

Sucking in a heavy breath, he opened the door and entered the room. "Sarah," he began gruffly.

She lifted her head in confusion. "Where's the phone?"

"I can't let you make the call until after—" he exhaled in a rush "—until after you've been booked and processed."

She blinked, and then horror dawned on her achingly gorgeous face. "Finn…"

"I'm sorry, Sarah, but you're under arrest."

Chapter 2

Under arrest. Sarah couldn't wrap her head around it as she silently endured the humiliation of getting her fingerprints taken and posing for a mug shot. *A mug shot.*

How was this happening?

I'm not a killer! she wanted to scream as Anna Holt inked up the pads of the fingers on her left hand.

It wasn't Anna's fault, the woman was just doing her job, but Sarah was having trouble remembering that as the deputy gently took the impression of her thumb.

"It's procedure," Anna apologized, her dark eyes swimming with compassion. "But we do already have them on file, you know, from that Proactive Crime thing you did in high school."

And, boy, didn't she regret that decision now. For her senior-year law course, she'd done an independent study on crime prevention, with the hypothesis that if citizens were required by law to submit fingerprints and DNA, crime in an area would reduce drastically. As part of the project, she'd organized a program called Proactive Crime, which involved getting all the seniors to submit prints and saliva swabs to the police. Which meant that her information was in the Serenade department database.

And for some inconceivable reason, she'd been flagged when the Donovan evidence had been logged in.

Sarah's head continued to spin as she followed Deputy Holt down the narrow staircase leading to the basement of the station. She'd never been down here before, but she knew what she would find. They were going to put her in a cell.

Because she'd been *arrested*. For a crime she hadn't committed.

Again, how was this *happening*?

Sarah felt all the color drain from her face as she got her first glimpse of what a jail cell looked like. Seeing one in a movie didn't count. This was real. And terrifying. Her pulse raced as she stared at the long row of small cells lining the lockup area. The steel bars seemed to glare at her in accusation. The clinking of keys sounded, and she turned to see Anna unlocking one of the doors.

"You'll have to wait in here until your lawyer arrives," Anna said softly.

The metal door creaked as the deputy dragged it open. Sarah's hands trembled. The cell was maybe fifteen by fifteen, boasting a narrow cot with a thin wool blanket. That was it. No toilet. No window. Nothing but this claustrophobia-inducing little space, illuminated by a single bulb dangling from the ceiling.

"I'm sorry," Anna added.

Sucking in a shaky breath, Sarah willed up some courage and forced herself to walk into the cell, head high. She only prayed that the criminal lawyer whose name she'd picked at random from the yellow pages showed up soon.

When she was on the other side of the bars, Anna dragged the door closed, and both women flinched as she locked it into place. "The sheriff will be down soon," the young woman finished in a strained voice.

Tell him not to bother.

Sarah swallowed down the bitter retort, then watched as the deputy hurried across the cement floor in the corridor. Her footsteps faded, and then Sarah was alone.

In jail.

She sat on the cot and reached up to rub away the tears pooling in her eyes. How could anyone think she'd killed Teresa? No matter what those damn DNA results said, she *hadn't* been in Teresa's house the night she died. She'd *never* been in that woman's house.

So why did the evidence indicate she was there?

It was a question she'd been asking herself ever since Finn showed up at the gallery earlier, but so far, the answer continued to elude her. Well, not quite. The answer was actually simple: someone was framing her.

But that only raised a whole slew of new questions. First and foremost—what the *hell?*

She didn't consider herself Ms. Popularity or anything, but people in town liked her. Even after her breakdown, most of the folks stood by her, offered their support during her struggle.

Not all of them, a voice laced with hostility pointed out.

That's right. One person had no problem leaving her to face it alone.

As if his ears had been burning, Finn suddenly appeared in front of the bars. When she noticed the anguish creasing his handsome features, all she could think was *too little too late*. He could look as devastated as he wanted, act as concerned as he felt like, but she didn't need his damn support. He hadn't given it to her when it actually mattered, and she had no use for it now.

"The lawyer you called just phoned," Finn said gruffly. "He'll be here in two hours."

Two hours?

She willed away a fresh batch of tears. Okay. Two hours. She could do this.

"Thanks for letting me know," she said in a clipped voice.

She expected him to walk away, but he stayed rooted in place, studying her through the narrow bars.

"What?" she snapped.

"I just…are you okay in there?"

She gawked at him. "Are you serious? Do I *look* like I'm *okay?*"

Finn shifted, looking utterly miserable. His unmistakable turmoil did nothing to soothe her. Just being in the same room as this man brought back unwelcome memories, lingering pain that she'd tried desperately to overcome. It didn't help that he was as gorgeous as ever, with those piercing blue eyes and scruffy black hair. The broad, muscular body that used to send a thrill up her spine, the roped arms that once brought her solace.

Patrick Finnegan had been the love of her life, the only man to ever have a complete and total claim on her heart.

But then he'd gone and broken that heart. Crushed

it between his big, strong fingers, leaving her to drown in sorrow. Alone.

She hadn't thought she'd ever recover from Finn's betrayal. Hadn't thought she'd ever be able to regain the capacity to love again. But she'd survived. Let go of the trauma of the past, became strong, stable, *capable*. And now she had Lucy, the beautiful baby girl she adored, who'd changed her entire life and gave her a sense of peace and fulfillment.

Oh, God, Lucy!

"What is it, Sarah?"

She'd forgotten he was still standing there, and when she lifted her head, she saw the alarm washing across his rugged face.

"Lucy," she burst out, fear wrapping around her throat like a boa constrictor. "The day care closes at four. What time is it now?"

Finn glanced at the utility-style watch on his wrist. "One-thirty."

Her lawyer wouldn't show up for two hours, and even then, he might not be able to get her out of here in time.

"I...I need to call the center," she said, urgency lining her tone. "Maybe Maggie can take Lucy home with her when the day care closes. Or maybe..."

She trailed off, her terror amplifying. What if Maggie called social services when Sarah told her where she was? The owner of the day care might be gentle and kindhearted, but she probably wouldn't be pleased to hear that the mother of her three-month-old charge was locked up. Maggie had mentioned during their initial interview that she had a legal duty to inform child welfare if the kids under her supervision weren't being taken care of.

Sarah had only adopted Lucy three months ago, and it had been an arduous two-year process. Financially, she'd been in a good position to raise a child, what with the handsome inheritance she'd received from her aunt and the prosperous art gallery she owned and ran. But her history with depression had raised a red flag at the adoption agency. Sarah had endured dozens of home interviews, therapy sessions and surprise visits from her caseworker before finally being approved for the adoption.

But if social services were called…they would take Lucy away from her. God, she couldn't let that happen. She'd waited two long years for Lucy—she refused to have her baby snatched out of her arms, not after everything she'd gone through in order to have the chance of being a mother.

She leaped off the cot and practically launched herself at the bars, wrapping both hands around the cold steel. "You need to do something for me," she whispered.

Finn's expression darkened with suspicion. "What do you need?"

"Bring Lucy here."

He balked. "What? No way, Sarah. I can't bring a baby to lockup!"

"Please," she begged. "Please do this. If I tell Maggie what's going on, she'll have to inform social services. They'll take my baby, Finn!"

Tears spilled down her cheeks, and her hands begun to shake, vibrating against the metal bars. "Just bring her here, and then we can figure out what to do with her."

Suddenly Finn's large hands were covering her

own, his warmth seeping into her cold, white knuckles. "Sarah. *Sarah*. Calm down."

She realized her breathing had become shallow, as her head spun dizzily from the panic coursing through her blood. She was also aware that this was the first time Finn had touched her in four years, and as her heart rate slowed and she regained her senses, she yanked her hands away and pressed them to her sides.

She couldn't let him touch her. Physically, or emotionally. Just being around him sent her back to that dark place, the hole she'd fallen into after he'd abandoned her.

"The mayor would have my head if he found out I brought a baby here," Finn mumbled, averting his eyes. "I can't do it, Sarah."

"Please," she said again. "I'll call Maggie and tell her that I'm giving permission for Anna to pick up Lucy from day care. I'll say I'm tied up at work. I'll find somebody to leave her with, maybe…" A thought entered her mind. "Jamie. Jamie can take her home with her until I get out of here."

"That could work," Finn said grudgingly.

"Of course it will. You know Jamie won't say no."

He scratched his head. "Let me give her a call. I know Cole was released from the hospital today, so they should be at the cabin by now…." He removed his cell phone from the black case clipped on to his belt, edging away. "There's no service down here. I'll go upstairs to make the call."

Sarah watched him go, relief flooding her body, mingled in with the gratitude over the fact that she'd befriended Jamie Crawford. A profiler with the FBI, Jamie had come to town two weeks ago to help Finn solve Teresa's murder, and Sarah had immediately hit it off with the auburn-haired federal officer. She knew that Jamie would take care of Lucy in a heartbeat, even with Cole still recovering from the gunshot wound he'd incurred while saving Jamie from one of his ex-wife's crazed lovers.

It floored her, the madness that had enveloped Serenade after Teresa's death. Not only had Cole been a suspect, but Jamie had nearly been killed by a man who believed Cole had taken Teresa from him.

Damn that woman. Sarah had never been fond of Teresa in all the years she'd known her, and now she loathed her even more. If Teresa hadn't gotten herself killed, Sarah wouldn't be in this position right now.

But Teresa was dead, and now Sarah was framed for murder, stuck in a jail cell and separated from her child. Oh, and in close quarters with the man who'd broken her heart—might as well throw that tidbit on her growing list of Why My Life Is a Total Mess.

"Oh, my sweet girl. I'm sorry Mommy can't take you home, but I promise you, Auntie Jamie will take good care of you."

Finn's heart ached as he watched Sarah cooing to her baby, as she held the child close to her breast and planted a gentle kiss atop Lucy's head. They were in Finn's office, since he hadn't been able to stomach the thought of bringing the infant into Sarah's cell. Sarah had spoken with the day care owner and arranged for Anna to pick up the child, and she hadn't said a word to him as they'd waited, not even a thank-you.

Though he didn't particularly blame her for not expressing any gratitude toward the man who'd *arrested* her.

But now she did speak, her eyes fixed on him as she asked, "When is Jamie getting here?"

"Any minute now."

Satisfied, Sarah focused on the baby again, and Finn couldn't help but notice the resemblance between mother and child. It was odd, considering that Lucy had been adopted, yet the baby had the same almond-shaped brown eyes as Sarah, the same creamy-white skin. Watching them together was almost mesmerizing, the way Sarah's features softened as she gazed down at the baby, the way Lucy's chubby little fingers wrapped around a lock of Sarah's lustrous brown hair.

Finn forced himself to turn away, unable to fight the helpless feeling rolling around in his gut. He remembered a time when Sarah had looked at *him* with that same adoration. Before he'd broken her heart and ran as far away from her as he could, coward that he was.

But he'd grown up since then, and not a day went by that he didn't regret his decision to leave Sarah. These past two weeks had opened his mind to the grave error he'd made. Watching Jamie fall in love with Cole Donovan had made him reassess his own empty life, made him realize that the only way to fill that gaping void was to win Sarah back.

Now any possibility of doing that had been squashed. Because, really, what the hell was he supposed to say to her?

Hey, I know I just arrested you, but how about getting back together?

Not likely.

"What happens when the lawyer comes?"

Sarah's quiet voice jarred him from his thoughts.

"Can he get me out of here?" she continued, her voice quaking. "Will I be able to go home tonight?"

Pain lodged in his chest. He wanted so badly to re-assure her, to tell her that she'd be holding her baby in her arms in no time, but the district attorney's words buzzed in his head like an angry hornet. "You'll need to stand in front of Judge Rollins for a bail hearing," he said carefully.

Hope brightened her face. "And he'll give me bail, right?"

"Most likely." He glanced at the baby. "You're a mother—I'm sure he'll take that into consideration when he makes his ruling. But, Sarah…"

She peered at him sharply. "But what?"

"The hearing probably won't be until Monday morning."

Her breath came out in a shocked rush. "What are you talking about?"

"Rollins is in South Carolina for some golf tournament," he admitted. "Unless your lawyer is a miracle worker, I don't think the judge is going to hurry back for a bail hearing."

The air in the small office turned as frigid as a snowy February morning. He almost winced under Sarah's cold scowl. She was looking at him as if this was his fault, like *he* was the reason the judge was off on the fairway wielding a nine iron. Before she could yell at him—which she seemed to be preparing to do—a brisk knock rapped against the door, and then Jamie Crawford poked her head inside.

"Are you okay?" Jamie asked immediately, ignoring Finn as she hurried over to Sarah.

"I'm fine, now that you're here," Sarah said, sounding relieved.

Jamie wrapped one arm around Sarah's shoulder, dwarfing the other woman with her height; at five-nine, Jamie loomed over Sarah's five-foot frame. Then she turned to Finn with a fierce look. Wonderful. Two against one, and both females seemed to blame *him* for this mess.

"What is the matter with you?" Jamie asked, disbelief dripping from her words. "You know Sarah didn't kill Teresa, Finn. I can't believe you arrested her."

"I had no choice." He resisted the urge to rip out his own hair. "You both seem to be in denial over the fact that I'm the *sheriff.* On paper, I'm not supposed to answer to anyone, but that's bull. This is politics, and the mayor and D.A. are pulling my damn strings."

"The D.A. actually thinks he's got a case?" Jamie demanded.

Finn nodded, then waited until Sarah shifted her attention to the baby before giving Jamie a pointed look. *He does have a case,* Finn communicated silently, and Jamie's lavender eyes widened slightly as she received the transmission. As a federal agent, Jamie understood law enforcement procedures, and when her expression softened, flickering with sympathy, Finn knew she understood why he'd had to arrest Sarah.

"Okay." Jamie squeezed Sarah's arm, then moved to lean against the edge of the desk. "Okay. So what's the next move? How do we get Sarah out of this?"

"All we can do is wait for the bail hearing," he said grimly. "And if this goes to trial, Sarah's attorney will build a defense for her. In the meantime, you and I will be busting our asses trying to find the real killer."

Tension hung over the room, finally broken by a tiny wail of displeasure. Finn turned his head and noticed the baby's cheeks had turned beet red. As Lucy began to cry, hiccupping between sobs, Sarah rocked her in her arms, but the gentle motions did nothing to soothe the suddenly cranky infant.

"You should take her home," Sarah whispered, glancing over at Jamie.

It was clear that the last thing Sarah wanted to do was relinquish the child, and it nearly tore out Finn's heart as he watched her hold Lucy in front of Jamie's waiting hands. The baby's cries only grew louder as she found herself in an unfamiliar pair of arms. Jamie rubbed the baby's back and murmured a few words of comfort, which only seemed to further agitate the red-faced, squirming baby.

"Go," Sarah choked out.

"Sarah—"

"Please, just go. There are diapers and bottles in the bag on Anna's desk, and if you need more formula, you can stop by my house—the spare key is under the red flowerpot beside the porch." Sarah seemed to be fighting tears. "Did you get the car seat?"

"Yeah, I stopped by the gallery like Finn asked and took it from your car."

"Then you're all set." Sarah gave a bright smile that didn't quite reach her eyes.

"Sarah…I'll take good care of her," Jamie murmured. "I promise."

"I know."

As Lucy continued to wail, Sarah moved closer to brush her lips over the baby's forehead. "Be good for Jamie," she said softly.

Holding the crying infant, Jamie walked to the door, pausing only to shoot Finn a look that said, *Fix this. Now.* She left the office, and they could hear her footsteps in the bull pen. Lucy's distressed cries grew muffled and then eventually faded as Jamie left the station with the baby.

Sarah stared at the door for an impossibly long time, before finally turning to Finn.

His stomach clenched at her lifeless expression. She looked as though someone had ripped the one thing she cared about right out of her arms, which, in fact, was what had just happened.

"Sweetheart," he started, the old endearment slipping from his mouth before he could stop it.

The dull shine to her eyes exploded into a smoldering burst of anger. "Don't you *dare* call me that."

The vehemence in her voice had him stepping back, stricken.

"And don't you dare pretend you're going to help me get out of this," she continued, her cheeks flushed with fury. "*You* got me into this. I don't care what the evidence says, or what the D.A. thinks, you know I didn't kill anyone!"

"And I'm going to help you prove that," he said hoarsely.

"Don't bother," she snapped. "You've already proven that you're incapable of standing by me when things get a little too tough for your liking. So, frankly, I don't want or need your help, Patrick." She was breathing heavily now. "Now take me back to my cell."

"Damn it, Sarah—"

"Take me. Back. To my cell."

Chapter 3

Sarah woke up the next morning feeling downright disoriented. When she stuck out her arm to fumble for the alarm clock, she felt nothing but cold air. When she instinctively turned to the right to glance over at Lucy's crib, she found herself staring at a cement wall.

She shot up into a sitting position, shoving strands of hair from her eyes as she realized she wasn't in her cozy bedroom—she was in a jail cell.

She still wore the turtleneck and jeans she'd had on yesterday, which she'd opted to sleep in because the alternative had been too humiliating to accept. The light blue prison-issued jumpsuit was still where she'd left it—on the floor next to the metal bars. The very thought of putting on that garment had brought a wave of nausea to her belly. She might be stuck in jail, but no way would she allow Finn and his deputies to dress her up like a common criminal.

Yesterday's meeting with her new lawyer, Daniel Chin, had been a total disappointment. The mild-mannered Korean man had been unable to get in touch with the judge and, in a rueful voice, he'd told her that she had no choice but to spend the weekend in lockup. After he left, Anna had taken her back to her cell. Dinner had consisted of sandwiches from the town deli, a luxury she doubted other prisoners got to experience. She'd fallen asleep at ten, though she'd spent most of the night tossing and turning on the thin, uncomfortable cot.

Rubbing her tired eyes, she rose to her feet and stretched her legs, wondering when someone would come down to take her to the washroom. Just as she thought it, a door creaked open, and then Finn strode up to the cell.

He looked exhausted, his blue eyes lined with red, and she noticed his clothes were rumpled, as if he'd slept in them. "Anna will be down in a second to take you to wash up," he started roughly. "But first I wanted a moment alone with you."

Her heart did an unwitting flip. She knew she wasn't allowed to feel anything for this man, but there was just something about him this morning that brought a rush of warmth to her stomach. Maybe it was the messy hair, or the hard glint in his eyes. He might be polite and pleasant when he was on duty, but Sarah had known him before he'd been elected sheriff, back when he'd had the whole bad-boy thing going on.

She still remembered the day they'd bumped into each other at the lake. Finn had been a few years ahead of her in high school, but their paths had never crossed until that day. She'd been twenty-two, just back from college, and she'd been walking along the lakeshore, debating if she should use part of her inheritance to buy the art gallery that had recently come up for sale in town. So lost in thought, she hadn't noticed Finn until she'd stumbled right into his hard, muscular chest. The attraction between them had been fast, primal. For a good girl like her, the pull of desire toward the rough and sensual deputy had been disconcerting. And Finn hadn't been so diplomatic back then. He spoke what was on his mind, no matter how crude, and his bold, sexy words had thrilled her. She'd fallen head over heels for him, captivated by his gruff nature and magnetic sexuality, even though she knew her feelings for him were too damn dangerous.

She caught a glimpse of that rough edge now, and those old feelings of desire rippled through her.

Ignoring her body's traitorous reaction, she met Finn's gaze and said, "Do we have to do this first thing in the morning? I just woke up."

"And I never went to sleep," he muttered back. "I was in the chair in my office all night, trying to figure out how to say this, so—"

She wrinkled her brow. "You slept in your office?"

He glanced at her as if he couldn't believe she'd even ask. "You honestly thought I could go home and get into my big comfortable bed knowing that you were spending the night in a cell? Jesus, Sarah."

Her heart lurched again. Lord, why wouldn't it quit doing that? And why did the image of Finn squished in his desk chair, as he sat awake all night, make her pulse speed up?

"Anyway, I did some thinking," he went on, awkwardly resting his hands on the bars, "and I realized the direct approach is the way to go." Frowning, he held her gaze. "I *am* going to help you, Sarah, no matter how many times you tell me you don't need my help. Because you know what? I don't give a damn what you say—you *do* need me. And you have me, whether you like it or not."

She arched both eyebrows. "You haven't changed at all, have you? Still get off on ordering people around."

A ferocious expression darkened his face. "I *have* changed. I've changed more than you know. In fact, that leads me to the other thing I wanted to say."

"I can't wait to hear it."

"Drop the damn sarcasm and listen." His tone was low, almost urgent. "You need to know something, Sarah."

"Yeah?" she said warily. "And what's that?"

"I'm sorry."

Those two words came out strained, and his chest heaved, as if the mere act of uttering them had taken a physical toll on him.

Before she could reply, he hurried on. "I'm sorry for what happened between us. For the way I ended things. But you have to know that I didn't do it out of malice." He raked one hand through his tousled black hair. "I was young, Sarah. Young and scared and the situation was too familiar. It reminded me too much of what I went through with my…"

Mother, she nearly finished. She'd heard it all before, in the parting speech he'd recited before walking—no, *running*—out of her life. Oh, he'd run, all right. As if he was being chased by the damn bogeyman, as if her depression could infect him like some airborne disease.

Resentment prickled her skin. "I understand that the situation with your mom was messed up, Finn, but you weren't the only one with parent issues."

The memory of her own parents filtered into her

mind, bringing a rush of sorrow. She'd been orphaned at the age of four, after her parents died within months of each other, her mother in a car accident, her dad from a heart attack nobody saw coming. Her mother's older sister had taken Sarah in, but Aunt Carol hadn't been the most maternal woman. More like a hermit, locked away in her isolated house and painting dismal landscapes that usually featured black, ominous swamps or mountains shrouded by dark mist. Finn might have grown up with a mentally ill mother, but at least he'd had *someone*.

"And your past doesn't excuse the choices you made," she finished.

"It doesn't," he agreed, "but I'm trying to make amends for those choices now. I want to be here for you, Sarah. The way I wasn't back then. I'm going to get you out of this mess."

A myriad of emotions spun through her body. Anger. Pain. Hope. The last one grated the most, because she didn't want to hope. Didn't want to believe Finn's promise that he'd help her. He'd already proven that he couldn't be counted on. What if she put her life in his hands, the way she'd put her heart there, only to have him let her down again?

She couldn't. But she couldn't say no, either. Not when she had Lucy to think about. As much as it pained her to admit it, she did need him.

Yesterday, when Finn had mentioned the possibility of a trial, fear had streaked through her like a bolt of lightning. She couldn't go to trial. If she did, child welfare would snatch Lucy away faster than Sarah could say *wrongfully accused*. And there was no way she was giving up her baby. She'd waited two years for Lucy, and nobody was going to take her from Sarah.

And so she managed a silent nod of acceptance, unable to look at him.

He frowned again, sensing her reluctance, then released a humorless laugh. "You might not like it but I'm going to fix this, no matter what you say—or don't say—sweetheart."

A spark of heat tickled her spine. She had to force herself to snuff it out. So what if he'd called her sweetheart. So what if those two husky syllables reminded her of all those lazy mornings in bed, when he'd used that same word to cajole her into opening the gallery late so they could indulge in another round of hot, sweaty sex.

They were over. Done. And she refused to react to this man, no matter what he called her.

"Can you just call Anna so I can use the restroom?" she said abruptly.

His shoulders stiffened at her harsh tone, but before he could reply, a tentative female voice sounded from the end of the corridor.

"Sheriff?" Anna called. "I think you need to get up here."

"What's going on?" Finn called back, eyes narrowed.

"There's an FBI agent here. He says he's taking over the case."

Sarah noticed the visible shock on Finn's face. Without another look in her direction, he stalked off, his heavy black boots thudding against the cement floor.

Wariness climbed up her chest. An FBI agent had arrived to take over the case? On a Sunday?

That didn't sound good. At all.

When Finn marched into his office, he found a tall, fair-haired man in a crisp black business suit standing by the minuscule window overlooking the brick wall of the building next door. The man turned when the door opened, offering a tight smile as he said, "Sheriff Finnegan. Pleasure to meet you."

Finn advanced on the man, wincing when he noticed the grease-covered Chinese food containers littering his desktop and the white dress shirt slung over the back of his chair. He hadn't bothered to tidy up yet, and the slept-in office definitely didn't offer a good first impression.

But the agent made no mention of the mess, simply leaning forward for a handshake that Finn reluctantly returned. "I'm Special Agent Mark Parsons," the man added. "I've been asked to assist you on the Donovan investigation."

Finn smothered a curse. He could probably take a wild guess as to who had contacted the Bureau. Or maybe two guesses, since the M.O. fit both the mayor and district attorney of Serenade. Apparently, the bastards didn't trust him to stay impartial.

"Assist, huh? Because my deputy just said you told her you were here to take over the case."

Parsons's smile didn't even falter. Finn decided, right then and there, that he didn't like the guy. There was something predatory in those pale blue eyes, something that Finn frequently glimpsed in the D.A., that power-hungry glint characteristic of a man desperate to climb all the way to the top. He wondered if Parsons was new, some rookie looking to make a name for himself. Finn made a mental note to ask Jamie if she knew the man.

"She must have misunderstood me," Parsons said smoothly. "I simply relayed the instructions given to me by my supervisor—that this investigation required a new pair of eyes."

Since Anna had a better read on people than most psychics, Finn doubted his deputy had misunderstood. Parsons was here for one reason—to stick his nose into places it didn't belong and try to punch another notch in his glory belt.

Christ, and just when he thought things couldn't get any worse.

"Mayor Williams said we've got a suspect in custody."

Finn bristled at the *we*. "Yes, I arrested the owner of the town's art gallery yesterday. Sarah Connelly. Her hair was found at the scene, along with a partial fingerprint on the table near the body."

"Yes, I was informed of that, as well."

As Parsons sat on the edge of the sheriff's desk, making himself comfortable, Finn battled a burst of anger. He had no intention of working with this man. Parsons was too cocky, too smooth in his expensive suit. He had *slime bag* written all over him.

"I was also told there's still the matter of the murder weapon," Parsons went on in a brisk, professional voice. "So our first order of business is finding out exactly where the gun came from, and how it wound up in Connelly's hands."

"Look." Finn took a breath. "With all due respect, Agent Parsons, I'm not sure what you could possibly do that my staff and I haven't already done. The gun is untraceable, wiped of any prints. And if we're being forthcoming with each other, I have to tell you, I don't think Sarah Connelly killed Teresa Donovan."

A knowing glimmer entered Parson's eyes. "Does the fact that she's your ex-girlfriend have anything to do with that conviction?"

"No," Finn snapped. "But our past association does

come into play here. I *know* Sarah. She's not a killer. She runs a gallery, she's involved in community events, and she just adopted a baby. She's a good person."

"Good people have been known to snap and commit murder." Parsons stared at him with a condescending expression that made Finn want to deck the guy. "Sarah Connelly has a history of instability. She is certainly capable of killing Teresa Don—"

"So it's true!" a female voice shrieked.

Both men spun around to gape at the raven-haired woman who'd burst into the office without knocking.

Finn tamped down an irritated sigh as Valerie Matthews barreled toward him, her gunmetal-gray eyes blazing with what could only be described as perverse satisfaction. "I *knew* that crazy bitch was up to something! The way she befriended Agent Crawford so she could squeeze information out of her…"

Valerie trailed off deliberately, which only succeeded in pissing off Finn even further. Like her younger sister, Valerie was the nastiest, most unlikable woman Finn had ever met. She and Teresa had been two peas in a despicable pod, determined to make the lives of everyone around them miserable, as if that could make up for the crappy childhood they'd endured.

When Cole Donovan had been shot, Finn had actually begun to think that Valerie might have changed, that she was starting to let go of some of her craziness. Valerie had been knocked unconscious when Teresa's ex-lover had taken Jamie hostage, and when Finn visited her in the hospital, where she was being treated for a concussion, Valerie had been…pleasant. Sweet, even.

Looked like she was back to her old self.

"I expect you to send that woman to the gas chamber," Valerie spoke up, pure loathing in her voice.

"I'm not a judge," Finn answered with a sigh. "I can't sentence Sarah to death just because you demand it."

Those silver eyes fumed. "All I'm demanding is *justice*," she snapped. "I've been sitting around for a month, waiting for you and your incompetent department to find justice for my sister, and—"

"And now you have it," Agent Parsons cut in effortlessly.

Finn's hand tingled with the urge to punch the man in the jaw. "Isn't that a little premature to say, *Agent?* Sarah hasn't even been indicted yet."

But Valerie's entire face had lit up from Parsons's reassurance, and both of them ignored Finn as she stepped closer to the other man. "And who might you be?"

Finn stifled an incredulous groan. Flirting? She was flirting? During a discussion about her sister's *murder?*

"Special Agent Mark Parsons." Finn half expected the guy to puff out his chest like a damn peacock. "And you must be Valerie. Your name came up in the case file I read on the plane."

"So you're leading the investigation now?" She held her hand up to her heart. "Thank heavens. You don't know how long I've been waiting for someone to take charge."

It irked Finn like no tomorrow how Parsons didn't correct her, even though he'd "assured" Finn just minutes ago that he had no intention of taking over. It was clear the man hadn't meant a word of it, and even clearer that along with being a pretentious jackass, Parsons had a thing for trashy women.

"Don't you worry," Parsons drawled. "I'm here to make sure Connelly pays for her crimes."

Unable to stand there a second longer without throwing up, Finn stepped toward Valerie and placed a not-so-gentle hand on her arm. "You need to leave now," he told her. "Agent Parsons and I have a lot of work to do."

She spared him a pithy glance, then turned to Parsons and smiled sweetly. "Please keep me informed about the case."

"My pleasure."

Finn's jaw was tighter than a drum as he ushered Valerie out the door. Her high heels clicked against the tiled floor and as she disappeared into the corridor off the bull pen, Finn turned on his heel and frowned at the federal agent.

He'd had enough. The mayor was driving him insane, the D.A.'s smug certainty made him want to kick something, and now those two boneheads had deposited this unprofessional ass on his doorstep. His patience was beginning to wear thin and he feared he was nearing his breaking point. The very thought of Sarah stuck in that cell downstairs brought a hot wave of agony to his gut.

Powerless wasn't an emotion he did well. He'd always been tough, capable. Even when he didn't feel it, he put on the act, *daring* people to cross him. But right now, he felt out of control. Sarah was in trouble—and he couldn't seem to do a damn thing about it.

Well, it was time to change that.

His frown deepening, he advanced on the agent and snapped, "You shouldn't be discussing the case with anyone outside this office. Especially not with the victim's sister."

Parsons shrugged. "There's no harm in keeping the lady informed." He crossed his arms over the front of his tailored suit jacket. "Now, I'd like to go down to lockup and speak to Connelly."

A protective rush seized Finn's chest like a vise. No freaking way was he allowing this jerk to get within ten feet of Sarah. She was already emotional enough as it was, stuck in jail and separated from her daughter. Even a second with this pompous ass would undoubtedly fuel her anger. And when Sarah was angry, she ranted. And when she ranted, she often said things she shouldn't, things like, oh, *If you don't leave my daughter and me alone, you'll regret it.*

His lungs burned as he inhaled. Christ, she didn't know how bad this was. That one threat, whether she meant it or not, might very well seal her fate.

Unless Finn did something to help her.

But what?

Frustration coiled around his insides like barbed wire. Now that Parsons had entered the picture, saving Sarah would be drastically tougher. Not that he even had a plan. What he did have, though, was determination. Like he'd promised her, he was going to fix this, no matter what she said. He'd move heaven and earth for her. Sacrifice anyone or anything for her.

And maybe if he did that, maybe if he managed to get her out of this, he could finally, *finally* earn her forgiveness.

Chapter 4

Finn was uncomfortable as he entered Cole Donovan's kitchen a few hours later, and not just because the room was as big as the entire main floor of the farmhouse he lived in.

Although the two of them had joined forces to rescue Jamie from the clutches of Cole's crazed assistant, they weren't exactly the best of friends. Though Finn had to admit he was warming up to the guy. Donovan might be a multimillionaire, but he wasn't the arrogant ass Finn had previously believed him to be.

Parsons, on the other hand, *was* an arrogant ass, but Finn had made sure the federal agent was occupied for the afternoon. He'd told the man that learning more about the murder weapon was the most important task at hand. Fortunately, Parsons had agreed. He'd promptly forgotten about his intention to interrogate Sarah and was now meeting with the ballistics expert who'd handled the weapon.

With Parsons out of the way, Finn had left the station shortly after and headed to the lab, determined to make some headway of his own. But the talk with the lab tech had been not only unproductive, but a total spirit killer, as well.

"Want some coffee?" Cole asked, sounding awkward as they stepped into the kitchen.

Finn noticed that the other man was moving more slowly than usual—not surprising, seeing as he'd only been released from the hospital this morning and was still recovering from a bullet wound to the abdomen.

"Coffee would be great," Finn said, lowering himself onto one of the chairs at the table. He glanced at the doorway. "Jamie's upstairs with the baby?"

"Yeah. She'll be down soon. Lucy just woke up from her nap." Cole winced as he bumped his hip against the counter. He edged back, then reached for the coffeemaker.

Silence settled between them, which Finn used to try come up with something to say. After Cole had been shot, Finn had promised himself that he'd try to be nicer to the guy, especially since Jamie was so obviously crazy about him.

She'd taken a leave of absence from the Bureau in order to be there for Cole's recovery, and you needed to be around the newly engaged couple for only ten seconds to see that they were madly in love.

"Lucy's a cute kid," Cole added as he poured hot coffee into two mugs. He turned to frown at Finn. "It's a damn shame what's happening to her mother. Did you really have to arrest her, Finnegan?"

Great, yet another name to add to the list of people who were pissed off at him.

Frowning right back, Finn took the cup Cole handed him and said, "I didn't have a choice. The evidence is pretty overwhelming."

To his surprise, Cole's dark eyes shone with sympathy. "But you don't think she did it."

"Hell, no." His throat clogged. "Sarah isn't capable of murder."

"Then prove it," came Jamie's blunt voice.

She appeared in the doorway, holding a sleepy-eyed Lucy in her arms. With her long auburn hair cascading down her back, her flawless makeup-free features and the yellow cotton dress dancing around her ankles, she made a seriously pretty picture. Finn wasn't the only one to notice, as Cole's rough face softened at the sight of her.

The couple exchanged a tender look that had Finn feeling like a damn Peeping Tom, then Jamie crossed the tiled floor and sat at the table. The baby let out a happy gurgle when she spotted Finn. His heart ached, then officially cracked when Lucy stretched out her chubby arms in his direction.

"She wants you to hold her," Jamie said with a grin, already moving the baby onto his lap.

He instinctively pulled Lucy against his chest, strands of emotion unraveling inside him as she lifted her head and stared at him with big brown eyes.

"I swear, she has the sunniest disposition," Jamie remarked, watching as the baby reached up to touch Finn's chin. "I'm already in love with her and I've only had her for a few hours."

Finn found himself going motionless as Sarah's daughter explored his face. She scrunched her tiny nose when her fingers met the stubble coating his jaw. With the curiosity that only a child could possess, she touched the sharp whiskers on his face, then gurgled in delight, as if discovering a new texture she couldn't believe existed.

Warmth spread through him. A lump rose in the back of his throat. Lord, this angelic little girl could have been his. If he hadn't abandoned Sarah, this could have been their future.

Shame exploded in his gut, making it difficult to breathe. Regrets were a side effect of life, he knew that. Everyone had something they regretted, some mistake they wished they hadn't made, but his regret…his mistake…it consumed his entire life. It moved like poison through his bloodstream, pricked his skin like tiny needles.

How could he have thrown away the woman he loved?

"How's Sarah doing?" Jamie asked, oblivious to his inner turmoil.

"Good, considering," he said. "She's eager to go home, but the bail hearing won't be until tomorrow morning."

Cole came to the table, handing Jamie a cup of coffee before joining them. "I still don't get it," the man said, shaking his head. "How did Sarah's DNA turn up at the crime scene?" He paused. "Could it have been a mistake? A lab error?"

"There was no error. I just came from the lab." His stomach clenched. "I spoke to Tom Hannigan, had him talk me through the results. The fingerprint on the coffee table is a perfect match to Sarah. So is the DNA extracted from the hair sample. She was in the house, according to the evidence."

"Evidence which could have been planted," Jamie pointed out. "If Sarah says she never stepped foot in Teresa's house, I believe her."

"Me, too," Finn admitted.

"So that means that someone took it upon themselves to put her hair there."

"And the print?"

Jamie went silent. They both knew how tricky it would be to plant someone's fingerprint. By no means impossible, but it would take a lot of careful planning to make something like that happen.

Frustration simmered in his stomach. "I just can't figure out who would want to frame her, or why. I get why someone would try and frame Cole—"

"Thanks," Cole cut in with a grimace.

"You're the ex-husband," Finn said without apologizing. "The most obvious suspect. If the killer wanted to take the heat off himself and put it on someone else, you're the best bet. Sarah had no connection to Teresa. There's no reason for someone to frame her."

"No reason we know of," Jamie said. She made an annoyed sound. "What are we missing here? We've got a list a mile long of people who didn't like Teresa. Why can't we connect anyone to her murder?"

Finn had no reply. God knows he and his deputies had been working their butts off interviewing people in town, trying to find puzzle pieces that might help them construct the bigger picture, but this case refused to move forward. All they had was an untraceable murder weapon and evidence placing Sarah at the scene.

"I still think we need to look at Teresa's lovers," Jamie added. "Look what she did to Ian Macintosh— she completely messed up his head and turned him into an enraged stalker. It's not a stretch to think she manipulated someone else."

"Well, the only other man we know she was involved with was Parker Smith," Finn answered. "And he has an airtight alibi for the night Teresa died." He glanced at Cole. "Did you manage to come up with another name? Anyone else she may have been involved with?"

Cole slowly shook his head. "No. I have my private investigator on it, but he hasn't turned anything up, either. I'll give him a call and see if he's managed to make headway, but I don't think—"

Finn's foghorn ring tone interrupted. With great reluctance, he handed Lucy back to Jamie and pulled his cell phone from his pocket. The station's number flashed on the screen.

"Finnegan," he said brusquely.

"Sheriff, it's me," came Anna's voice. "You told me to let you know what's going on with Sarah, and—"

"Is she all right?" he interrupted.

"She's fine. But she does have a visitor. Dr. Bennett. I figured you'd want to know."

Dr. Bennett?

"Oh. Okay, thanks for letting me know, Anna." He hung up, wrinkling his forehead.

"Is something wrong?" Jamie asked instantly.

"No." He paused, still confused. "Apparently Sarah has a visitor, though. It's Travis Bennett."

"The doctor who runs the clinic?" When Finn nodded, Jamie tilted her head, pensive. "He's a nice man. He treated me after the car accident. I didn't know they were friends, though."

"Yeah, me, neither."

He was helpless to stop the jolt of jealousy that pounded into his gut. Granted, he had no right feeling jealous. Sarah could be friends with whomever she pleased. He'd given up the right to have a say in her life when he'd walked out that door. But he had been keeping tabs on her all these years, and this was the first he'd heard of a connection between her and Bennett.

Were they involved?

Another hot blade of jealousy sliced into him. Travis Bennett was older, late forties at least, but he was still an attractive man, in a bland kind of way. He'd moved to Serenade three years ago from Raleigh, after losing his wife and two sons in a tragic fire. Finn had researched the guy when he had showed up in town—he always made sure to know everything about the people he served—and he'd learned that the doctor had left a booming practice to open his small clinic here. He'd been grief-stricken when he'd first arrived, barely speaking a word to anyone, but he'd eventually opened up, and the folks in town loved him.

He wondered what *Sarah* thought of the good doctor, then clamped down the inappropriate rush of anger.

Abruptly, he scraped his chair back and got to his feet. "I should get going," he muttered. "Thanks for the coffee."

Jamie and Cole both wore knowing expressions. Apparently the reason for his sudden departure was clear to all.

Ignoring the looks, he glanced at Lucy, the hardness in his body thawing as he reached to stroke the downy black hair atop her small head. "Be good for Jamie, baby girl," he murmured.

She rewarded him with a big, toothless smile.

"I'll keep you guys posted," he said to the couple at the table. "Take good care of her, Jamie. Sarah's counting on you."

Her violet eyes softened, but he strode to the door before she could respond. He didn't need her reassurance—he knew Jamie would love and care for Lucy as if she were her own daughter.

And in the meantime, he would take care of Lucy's mother.

"Are you sure there isn't anything I can do?" Travis Bennett asked in a voice laced with concern. "I still have contacts in Raleigh, some attorney friends. I can give one of them a call—"

"It's fine," Sarah cut in, forcing a smile. "I already hired a lawyer, and I'm sure he'll manage to get me out on bail tomorrow morning."

Travis didn't look appeased. His deep-set brown eyes shone with compassion, and she realized that's what probably made him such an excellent doctor. When he'd first moved to town, she'd thought him cold and unfeeling, until the day she'd caught a nasty chest infection and had been forced to visit his clinic. One minute with Dr. Travis Bennett and she'd realized he truly was a good man. Hadn't bothered looking for a new doctor, either. He'd been the first person she'd called when Lucy had come down with an ear infection last month, and like the caring person he was, Travis had made a house call and personally delivered Lucy's antibiotics.

And now he was here, trying to make everything better.

But there was nothing he or anyone else could do. Scratch that—the only person who could help her now was Judge Rollins, if he managed to step away from the damn golf course.

"I don't understand why the sheriff is keeping you locked up in the first place," Travis said.

"He's just doing his job," she said darkly.

"Well, he's got the wrong person behind bars. I want you to know I don't think you killed that woman, Sarah. And if you change your mind and need my help, all you have to do is call."

Finn's voice came from behind. "Sorry for interrupting." He strode down the corridor and stood in front of the cell, eyeing Dr. Bennett with displeasure. "What brings you here, Doc?"

Travis frowned. "I saw you leaving the lab earlier and asked Tom Hannigan what was going on. He informed me that Sarah is in police custody."

"Tom shouldn't have spoken to you about that," Finn said coldly.

"We work in the same building, Sheriff. We speak frequently." The doctor turned to Sarah. "I should probably go. Let me know if you need anything."

"I'll walk you out," Finn said, sounding anything but cordial.

Sighing, Sarah watched as the two men disappeared from sight. She hadn't missed the glitter of anger in Finn's blue eyes. It was an expression she was familiar with, yet one she hadn't seen in years. Finn had always been a possessive man, not in a creepy, violent way, but just a male making his claim. He'd donned that *back off* look whenever men in town got a little too friendly with her. Back then, she'd found it flattering.

Right now, it simply annoyed her.

"So," Finn said when he returned a few moments later. "Since when are you and Bennett so tight?"

Her nostrils flared. What right did he have getting angry over her friendship with Travis? Or even asking questions about it? He'd given up his claim on her a long time ago.

"That's not any of your business," she answered coolly.

"He's almost twice your age," Finn grumbled.

A shocked laugh escaped her lips. "So what? Travis is a friend. Who cares how old he is?"

Those dark eyebrows rose slightly. "Just a friend?"

"Yes, though I really don't need to explain myself to you." She spun on her heel and made her way to the cot, flopping down and avoiding Finn's eyes. She figured he'd just walk away, but he surprised her by unlocking the cell door and marching inside.

"Get up," he muttered. "I've got dinner in my office."

Surprise moved through her. "You're letting me go upstairs?"

Pure misery flashed in his eyes. "I'm not your warden, Sarah. No matter what you think, it kills me seeing you in here, okay?"

Her throat went tight. Sincerity rang in his voice, and there was no mistaking the pain flickering across his face. No, she supposed he didn't like this any more than she did. The only difference was—*she* was the one in this position. Not him.

Story of their lives, wasn't it? She fell apart, and he stood there, strong and stoic in the background.

She straightened her shoulders, banishing that pang of self-pity from her head. Screw that. She *was* strong. She might have fallen apart all those years ago, but this time she refused to cave under the pressure. She'd been arrested for a crime she didn't commit, and she'd be damned if she didn't keep fighting this injustice until her last breath.

Without a word, she stood and followed Finn out of the cell.

"I saw your daughter," he said as they climbed the narrow staircase.

Sarah almost tripped over her own feet at the quiet confession. Unable to stop herself, she looked directly into his vivid blue eyes. "You did? Is she all right?"

"She's fine," he said gruffly. "Jamie said Lucy is the sweetest baby in the world."

Tears stung her eyes. "I know."

She tried to rein in her emotions as they headed to Finn's office. The bull pen was empty, so fortunately she didn't have to face the curious eyes of Anna or Finn's second deputy, Max. Blinking a few times, she took a deep breath and sat down in one of the chairs in front of Finn's cluttered desk.

He'd gotten takeout from the diner—she recognized the brown paper bags with Martha's red logo printed on them. Neither of them said a word as they tackled their food, though Sarah felt Finn's eyes on her as she ate. Was he thinking about the last time they'd shared a meal together?

She was trying not to, but the excruciating memory found its way into her brain no matter how hard she tried to stop it.

You don't want to be here, do you?

She heard her own voice in her head, the lifeless words she'd uttered, the anger that followed.

Leave then. Take the coward's way out and leave!

She'd proceeded to throw his plate against the wall, staining the white wall with spaghetti sauce, sending clumps of noodles onto the hardwood floor. And then she'd sunk onto the floor herself, as hot tears poured down her cheeks, as she cried for everything they'd lost and everything he refused to give her.

"I shouldn't have left that night."

His rough voice sliced through her thoughts, and she realized as she met his tortured expression that he had indeed been thinking the same thing.

"But you did," she said flatly, pushing away her half-eaten dinner.

Finn reached for the bottle of water on the desk, unscrewed the cap and took a long swallow. After he set down the bottle, he continued to speak, his blue eyes avoiding her face.

"My mom used to do that, during her episodes. She'd curl up into a ball on the floor and sob, and I would stand there, unable to do a damn thing about it. I tried to comfort her once, but she slapped me so hard I never did it again." His voice cracked. "I didn't know what to do, when I saw you like that."

Her lungs burned so badly she could barely get out any words. "So you left."

"I left," he echoed. "And I've regretted it every day, every damn second, of these last four years."

Sarah couldn't look at him. She couldn't go down this path. It had taken two years of therapy to convince her that her reaction to everything that happened had been natural. That sometimes even the strongest of people collapsed under the strain. But it was still hard to reflect on that time in her life and not feel shame. Embarrassment.

Why hadn't she been stronger?

Why hadn't *he* been stronger?

"Sarah, look at me."

She swallowed, blinking through a shimmer of tears. *No, don't look at him.* She couldn't. This man had crushed her. He'd left her battered and broken and hadn't even looked back.

His hand was on her face.

Her head jerked in shock. She hadn't even heard him get up, yet here he was, on his knees in front of her chair, his warm, calloused hands cupping her chin. Forcing eye contact.

Breathing hard, she met his gaze and was floored by what she saw there. Regret. Anguish. Passion. Always with the passion. From the moment they'd collided into each other at the lake, the attraction between them had been impossible to control.

Even now, when she ought to despise him, when she ought to be concentrating on her own self-preservation, her body reacted to Finn. Her palms went damp, her breasts became heavy, and the tender spot between her legs began to throb.

"Sarah…"

His timber-rough voice sent a shiver along her spine. She felt the heat of his body, searing right through the thin material of her turtleneck.

His strong throat worked as he swallowed. "I miss you."

Shock filled her chest. The longing surrounding those three words stole the breath right out of her lungs. She struggled to inhale, but then Finn's head moved closer, closer, until his warm breath fanned over her mouth.

Until she knew without a doubt that he was going to kiss her.

Chapter 5

He was lost in Sarah. Drowning in the intoxicating lilac scent of her, the sight of her tousled dark hair, the way her lush lips parted in surprise. Finn's heart drummed a frenzied rhythm against his ribs. Every muscle in his body went taut, rippling with anticipation, with need so strong his vision grew cloudy. But through the haze, he still saw her. Sarah. His Sarah, with her high, regal cheekbones and satin-soft skin and that sweet, sensual mouth.

He leaned closer.

He wanted to kiss her. Just once. Just to see if that uncontrollable fire between them still burned strong.

His lips hovered over hers. He could almost taste her. Almost feel the softness of her mouth—

Her chair scraped back with a loud grating sound.

"No, Finn. *No*." Her voice contained a hint of desperation, a twinge of confusion.

Disappointment rushed through him like a flash flood. His hands shook as he staggered to his feet, the promise of reconnecting with Sarah blown away by the ragged breath that exited his mouth.

"I'm sorry," he rasped. "I didn't mean to do that."

Yes, you did.

Fine. He'd wanted to kiss her. For four very long years.

But she'd wanted it, too. He'd seen the desire swimming in her brown eyes. Heard her intake of breath. Seen her pulse throbbing in her graceful neck. He'd witnessed those same telltale signs years ago, the day they'd met at the lake, as he'd walked her to where she'd parked her car. He didn't normally make a move on women he'd just met, but something about Sarah had made him delirious with desire, desperate to feel her mouth pressed to his.

He'd kissed her, right there in the little gravel parking lot near the lakeshore, and when they'd pulled apart, she'd given a little laugh and asked him if he was always that forward. The attraction to Sarah had been daunting. She was gentle, smart, her eyes always full of laughter; he was serious, easily angered, a loner. He hadn't expected to fall in love with someone like Sarah. Hell, back then he'd gravitated toward bold, flashy women like Teresa Donovan.

But from the moment he'd heard Sarah's soft, throaty voice, from the moment he'd brushed his lips over her warm, sexy mouth, he'd been a goner.

And still was.

"Whether you meant it or not, it can't happen again," she said in a shaky voice. "I won't let it happen."

His legs felt weak, limp, so he leaned against the edge of the desk, casting a sad look in her direction.

She'd pretty much flattened herself against the wall, as if expecting him to ambush her at any second. But she didn't look scared, just wary, and that was far more disheartening.

"Would it be so bad?" he had to ask. "Starting over?"

Her eyebrows knitted in disbelief. "Starting over?" she echoed. "We can't start over, Finn."

His heart dropped to the pit of his stomach like a sinking rock. "Because I left."

"Because I don't trust you. Because I can't forget."

Her quiet admission grabbed hold of his heart and twisted it in his chest. Hard. He wasn't sure he'd ever experienced such overwhelming pain.

"And forgiveness? Can you forgive?" he found himself murmuring, practically holding his breath for her answer.

She sighed, her rigid shoulders sagging into a posture that resembled defeat. "I forgave you a long time ago, Finn."

His gaze flew to hers. "You did?"

She nodded. "But that doesn't change anything."

"It's something," he said hoarsely.

"It's nothing," she corrected, her voice equally hoarse.

Their gazes locked. She meant it, he realized, as frustration filled his gut and sorrow knotted around his insides. And she was right. Her forgiveness meant nothing, not if the trust she'd once had in him was gone.

"Okay." He cleared his throat. "Okay, then at least I know what to do now."

She glanced at him, wary again. "And what's that?"

"Make you trust me again."

The pressure weighing down on his chest lifted a little. All wasn't lost. Her lack of faith in him hurt, but it only gave him something to strive toward. She hadn't said she hated him, hadn't disregarded the chemistry they evidently still shared. If this was about trust, then he could work with that. He could fix it.

A tired laugh slipped from her lips. "You never give up, do you, Finn?"

"I did once," he said, holding her gaze. "I gave up on us. But I promise you, sweetheart, I won't do it again. I'm older. Wiser. And if it's the last thing I do in my miserable life, I'm going to win your trust back."

His declaration got to her. He could see it in her eyes. Some of the tension had even left her body. Not the wariness, but he would change that.

"I can't talk about this right now," she finally said. "I have bigger problems to deal with."

"I know, and I promise that—"

"Well, isn't this cozy."

They both looked at the door, just as Agent Mark Parsons strode into the office as if he owned the place. Finn's jaw instantly tensed, a spurt of anger erupting in his belly as Parsons studied the scene with condescending eyes. Finn knew what it looked like—remnants of their dinner on his desk, Sarah out of her cell. He didn't feel an ounce of remorse, though. Maybe he was giving her preferential treatment, but Parsons could go to hell.

With a smile that didn't quite reach his eyes, Parsons turned to Sarah. "You must be Ms. Connelly."

She stole a glance at Finn, then focused on the federal agent. "Yes…"

"I'm Special Agent Mark Parsons." He made a move to extend his hand, then stopped when he saw the look in Sarah's eyes.

Finn bit back a laugh. He knew that look. It said *touch me and I'll rip your eyes out*. He remembered being on the receiving end of it plenty of times, usually when he pissed Sarah off by forgetting to load the dishwasher or leaving his wet towels on the bathroom floor.

Parsons continued as if Sarah's rebuff hadn't affected him, but the annoyed flicker in his pale blue eyes told another story. "I must admit, I was looking forward to meeting you this morning, but the sheriff wasn't so open to the idea. I'm assuming that's why he sent me on what he believed would be a wild goose chase."

Finn didn't bother trying to look repentant. Had he wanted to keep Parsons away from Sarah? Hell yes. Had he sent him on a task that he knew would probably amount to noth—wait a second. He suddenly realized what the agent had said. *What he believed would be a wild goose chase.*

Parsons offered a pleasant smile. "That's right, Sheriff. I happened to uncover something on my assignment today."

Finn stifled a sigh. "Maybe I should take Ms. Connelly back to her cell so you and I can—"

"No need for that," Parsons interrupted. "I'd like to question her about this anyway, so we might as well do it now. Have a seat, Ms. Connelly."

With a suspicious cloud in her eyes, Sarah sat down in the visitor's chair, while Parsons took her place by the wall, his arms crossed over his lanky chest. Finn stayed by the desk, too wound up to move. He didn't like the expression on the agent's face. Parsons resembled a predator about to go in for a kill.

"As the sheriff probably told you," Parsons began, his tone implying that Finn was whispering police pillow talk in Sarah's ear, "I've been tracking the origins of the weapon that killed Mrs. Donovan. A .45 Smith & Wesson."

If Parsons had been expecting a reaction from Sarah, he didn't get it. Rather, she shot him a cool look and said, "And?"

"I still haven't been able to trace it, but I did come across some very interesting information…."

There was a long pause, which only irritated the hell out of Finn. "What did you find?" he snapped.

"Your deputies checked if any weapons matching that make and description had been reported stolen in Serenade."

"And nothing came up in the system," Finn retorted.

"No," Parsons agreed. "But I used the Bureau's database to search other precincts in the area to see if any missing weapon reports popped up." Parsons gave a smug smile. "A man in Grayden, your neighboring town, reported a .45 Smith & Wesson missing about a month ago. Four days before Mrs. Donovan was murdered, in fact."

Finn refused to let the other man see just how much the new information rattled him. "So?" he said, putting on a bored face. "What's the connection, other than the make of the gun?"

"Turns out this man, a Mr. Walter Brown, used to work at the paper mill that Cole Donovan tore down when he moved here." The federal agent smirked. "Apparently, Mr. Brown keeps in touch with some of his old friends here in town. The night his gun was stolen, he was hosting a party to celebrate a promotion at his new position in Grayden's textile factory."

Finn got a sick feeling in his stomach.

"And he claims that several Serenade citizens attended the festivities," Parsons finished, looking so damn pleased with himself that Finn wanted to clock him. The agent glanced at Sarah. "Did you happen to be in attendance, Ms. Connelly?"

Her shoulders stiffened. "No, I was not in attendance. I don't even know Walter Brown."

"Interesting." Parsons cocked his head. "Because I pulled your credit card records for the time period in question, and what do you know, you purchased gas at a station in Grayden—the same day as Brown's party."

Finn's heart dropped. From the defensive flicker in Sarah's eyes, he knew Parsons was telling the truth. She'd been in Grayden that day.

"I was visiting an artist," Sarah finally admitted. Hostility hardened her features as she stared Parsons down. "His name is Frank Bullocks, you can call him up and he'll confirm that we met that day."

"Oh, I will definitely be giving him a call, Ms. Connelly. Tell me, how long did this visit last?"

She shrugged. "An hour, maybe two. He showed me some of his new pieces, and I took a few back to the gallery. He's one of the artists I have on consignment. I can't say for sure what I did when I got home, but I know I never went back to Grayden that night—and I didn't attend some stranger's party."

"If you say so."

Finn dragged a hand through his hair, then moved from his perch on the desk. "I'm going to take Sarah back to her cell now."

"I'm not done with her, Sher—"

He silenced Parsons by raising his hand. "She answered your questions and explained why she was in Grayden that day. You can follow up with Brown and get a guest list from him. If Sarah's name happens to be on it, you'll get another chance to speak to her. But right now, I'm taking Ms. Connelly to her cell."

He didn't wait for another objection, simply took Sarah's arm and led her out of his office. In the bull pen, she opened her mouth to speak, but he used that same silencing hand. She didn't try again until they were descending the narrow staircase leading down to lockup.

"This is bad, isn't it?" she said in a hushed voice. "They're going to say I stole the gun from that man's house and used it to kill Teresa! God, Finn, you can't let that happen! I didn't steal anything!"

He heard her panic, saw the fear trembling in her shoulders, and before she could protest, he yanked her into his arms.

She went rigid for one long moment, then sank into the embrace, pressing her face against the front of his blue buttondown. Pure joy spread inside him, warming every inch of his body. She was in his arms again, and that feeling of *rightness* nearly knocked him over like a gust of wind.

Stroking her lower back with his hands, he held her, breathing in the sweet scent of her hair. "This is bad," he murmured against the top of her head. "I can't deny that, but I told you I was going to fix this. I promised you, Sarah."

She burrowed her face in the crook of his neck. Moisture coated his skin. She was crying. Lord, it tore him up, feeling her tears soak his flesh. The last time she'd cried, he'd walked out the door.

This time, he just held her tighter.

"Did you take your pain meds?"

Cole Donovan stifled a groan as his fiancée appeared in the doorway just as he'd been shoving the prescription bottle into the top drawer of their nightstand. Jamie's lavender eyes instantly zeroed in on his hand, and a frown marred her mouth. *Damn it, caught red-handed.*

"Don't you dare hide the pills again," she said, swooping into the bedroom with Sarah's daughter in her arms. "I don't get you, you know that? You just had surgery to remove a bullet from your stomach. You're in pain. Quit pretending otherwise."

Despite himself, he smiled. He couldn't remember the last time someone had fussed over him like this. His mother had always been too drunk to notice he was even around, his father was never home, and Teresa had been the furthest thing from a doting wife. He had to admit, it was kind of nice that Jamie was so concerned about him.

"Take the bottle out and swallow the damn pills," she ordered, shifting the baby onto her other hip.

Knowing when he was beaten, Cole obeyed her without argument. As he picked up the glass of water she'd brought in earlier and took the pills, he couldn't help but admire the way she skillfully held the baby. A natural mother. A rush of tenderness filled his body. He almost forgot about the pain throbbing in his wounded abdomen as he realized that one of these days he and Jamie would have a baby of their own. She wanted children. Lots of them.

And he couldn't wait to give them to her.

"There, I did it," he said after he'd taken his meds. "But you can't complain when I'm too stoned to hold a conversation with you."

"I can talk to Lucy," Jamie said with a shrug. She

tickled the baby's tummy, eliciting a delighted gurgle. "Right, sweet pea? We'll do all the talking tonight."

Cole slid down in the bed and rested his head against the pillow. Damn, those meds worked fast. His head was already beginning to feel light.

"I'm just going to warm a bottle for her," Jamie said. "I'll come up and feed her here. And remember, you're bed-bound. I made an exception when Finn was here earlier, but now you're back to following the doctor's orders."

"Yes, ma'am."

As Jamie disappeared through the doorway, Cole smiled again, wondering how he'd gotten so damn lucky. When Jamie had waltzed into town two weeks ago, he'd never dreamed that he'd fall in love with the federal agent who was supposed to profile him. Never dreamed he'd fall in love, period. After his marriage to Teresa, the thought of being in another relationship had left him in a cold sweat. But Jamie had changed all that.

He could hear her moving around downstairs, the muffled sound of her voice, broken in by Lucy's happy squeals. Lord, he felt terrible for Sarah Connelly. Sarah had always been so nice to him, even after he'd closed down the paper mill and built a hotel in its place, enraging everyone in town. But not Sarah. She'd treated him with nothing but kindness, and she didn't deserve what was happening to her.

A thud came from below.

Cole sat up, fighting a rush of dizziness. The lethargic numbness the meds provided him with made it hard to think clearly, but he still managed a quick shout. "You okay down there, sweetheart?"

He heard another crash, followed by a loud cry that hadn't come from the baby. Jamie!

Cole launched himself out of bed. The world spun for a moment, his vision assaulted by stars. He steadied himself, forced his legs to carry him to the door, as panic shuddered through him and fear coursed in his blood. He could hear Lucy wailing now, but it sounded tinny and faraway in his drugged state. He experienced another burst of vertigo at the top of the staircase. Breathed through it. Stumbled down the stairs.

"Jamie!" he shouted. "Lucy!"

He raced into the kitchen, ignoring the searing pain shooting up his abdomen. "Jamie. Ja—" His voice died in his throat as he caught sight of her.

"Oh, Jesus…" He was down on the floor, kneeling beside her motionless figure. His pulse shrieked in his ears. "Jamie, baby, wake up!"

She was on her side, and he quickly rolled her over, running his hands along her body, across her face. When he touched her hair, he felt dampness beneath his palm. He lifted his hand and saw blood. Someone had hit her in the crown of the head.

"Jamie," he pleaded. "Open your eyes, sweetheart."

She moaned. It was the sweetest sound he'd ever heard in his entire life. And then her lids fluttered open, and her violet eyes, those beautiful eyes, stared up at him in confusion.

"C-Cole?"

"I'm here, sweetheart. I'm here. Tell me what happened."

Wincing, she struggled to sit up. "I…the bottle…" She glanced in the direction of the sink. He followed her gaze, immediately spotting the broken bottle. A puddle of milk had formed on the tiled floor.

A loud bang made them jump, and they both turned to the patio door, which was wide open and being blown against the exterior wall by the wind.

An anguished cry left Jamie's mouth. "Lucy!" She sat up, shoving hair out of her eyes. "Cole, he took the baby!"

Chapter 6

The Donovan house was deathly silent when Finn hurried inside. Driving over in his Jeep with the siren blaring, he'd conjured up dozens of terrifying scenes he might find, everything from bloodstained walls to Jamie dead on the floor. What he found, however, was much worse. Four shell-shocked faces greeted him when he entered the living room, Jamie the most distraught of all.

She was on the overstuffed leather sofa closest to the bay window that overlooked the front yard, tears staining her face as she leaned against Cole for support. Finn noticed Cole looked unusually pale, but that was probably because his fiancée had just been knocked unconscious while he lay upstairs doped up on pain meds.

At least that's what Max had relayed to Finn over the phone. Finn hadn't said a word to Sarah before he'd rushed out of the station. He didn't want to worry her, especially when the only detail he'd been given was *Lucy's gone!*

His two deputies, Anna and Max, were already on the scene, and he could hear his forensics guy, Chris, puttering around in the kitchen. Five adults in the house, six including him—but no baby.

"He took her!" Jamie blurted out when she spotted Finn in the doorway. "He came up from behind… I didn't even hear him… I'm so sorry, Finn, I'm so sorry."

He bounded across the parquet floor and sat on the other side of her, stroking her arm in a soothing motion. "Jamie, calm down. Tell me what happened."

"I was preparing a bottle for Lucy." She wheezed out an unsteady breath. "I set her down in her bouncy seat and then went to get the bottle. I was checking to see that the formula wasn't too hot when I heard the back door open. I turned around, but he moved too fast. All I saw was a black ski mask. I had no time to react. He was holding something, a crowbar maybe, and he knocked me out."

Finn frowned. "He just walked through the back door? The alarm didn't go off?"

Jamie's face collapsed like a house of cards. "I forgot to set it. I was so busy today, trying to put Lucy down for her nap, and then making sure Cole took his pills. I…forgot."

A current of guilt thrashed in her lavender eyes. It was evident to everyone in the room that she blamed herself for what had happened. Both Anna and Max were staring down at their feet, waves of sympathy radiating from them. Cole looked devastated, as if he couldn't believe he'd failed to protect the two females in his house.

"Don't beat yourself up over it," Finn said quietly. "People forget to do things sometimes. Happens to the best of us."

"Not to me," Jamie said bleakly. "I'm a federal agent, Finn. I don't forget to set security systems! God, this is all my fault. Sarah… How am I going tell Sarah?"

Oh, Christ. Sarah. The sound of her name made his gut go rigid. He'd spent all evening with her in the cell, comforting her after Parsons had dropped the new information about the murder weapon in their laps. She'd been so upset, terrified that the case against her was only getting stronger. How on earth would she react when she discovered someone had kidnapped her daughter?

Finn pushed away the unsettling thought and focused on his friend, who looked as though she was struggling not to cry.

"This isn't your fault, Jamie. Whoever took Lucy knew what he was doing. He had a purpose when he came in—he wanted the baby." Finn searched her face. "Are you sure it was a man?"

She wrinkled her forehead in despair. "I don't know. Like I said, I didn't get a good look. He just sprang up on me like some kind of ninja. I guess I just assumed it was a man."

"How tall was the assailant?"

"Around my height, give or take an inch."

Finn thought it over. Jamie was five-nine, so if the intruder was male, he stood slightly below average height. And if it was a female, then she was taller than most women.

"I guess it could have been a woman," Jamie relented, looking miserable. "But I really couldn't tell. It all happened too damn fast."

"Did he or she say anything?" Anna asked.

"Nothing," Jamie said. "And if he did, I couldn't hear it. All I heard was Lucy crying."

Finn sighed. "Okay. Well, we need to get an Amber Alert out, contact the media." He glanced at Max, who was standing by the tall bookshelf across the high-ceilinged room. "I need you to canvas the neighborhood, call in our volunteer unit and comb every inch of this damn town."

"Yes, sir," Max said, already heading for the door.

He turned to Anna. "Get back to the station, start working the phones. We need to get the alert out, make sure everyone and their mother knows what Lucy looks like and that she's been abducted."

Anna responded with a nod, quickly getting up and hurrying out of the room. Thank God for his deputies, at least. At twenty-four, Anna was unbelievably efficient, always able to keep a cool head no matter the chaos around her. Max was a year younger and more of a renegade, often acting without thinking things through, but always giving one-hundred-and-ten percent in every situation. At the moment, Finn appreciated the knowledge that he had two capable people working the case.

Sarah was going to be destroyed. Hell, he felt pretty destroyed himself. He'd held Lucy in his arms only hours ago, and now she was gone.

Jamie's ravaged voice broke through his thoughts. "I messed up."

He saw the moisture gathering in her eyes and squeezed her arm. "It's okay. We'll find her, Jamie."

She simply stared down into her lap, unconvinced. Finn regarded Cole over Jamie's head, and the two men exchanged a somber look. Jamie was the toughest woman Finn knew, but she also had the biggest heart. She'd never forgive herself for letting Lucy get taken, no matter what anyone else said.

Cole gave an imperceptible nod, as if to reassure Finn that he would take care of Jamie.

Nodding back, Finn rose from the sofa. "I should call Agent Parsons. Maybe he can get things moving faster."

Jamie's head snapped up. "Wait a minute—Mark Parsons? He's in town?"

The disdain in her voice didn't go unmissed. "You know him?" Finn said warily.

A frown puckered her lips. "Yeah, I know him. Why is he here?"

"Mayor Williams called in a favor. Apparently, he thinks I need help with the case."

Jamie let out a soft curse, suddenly looking more like herself. Her cheeks took on some color, as displeasure glittered in her eyes. "I feel sorry for you, then. That guy is a total jackass."

"That's what I was afraid you'd say," he admitted. "I take it you don't like him."

"He lives in a tunnel," Jamie grumbled.

Finn shot her a blank look.

"Tunnel vision," she clarified. "He's got a reputation for it in the office. He gets his teeth into a suspect and doesn't bother examining any other avenues. It's gotten him in trouble a few times."

"So you're saying once he thinks he's got his man, he quits investigating?"

"Pretty much, yeah."

Wonderful. Sarah didn't stand a chance then.

Sarah.

For a moment there, he'd actually forgotten about

her. About the fact that someone had just *abducted* her daughter.

How the hell was he going to break the news to Sarah?

When Finn walked into her cell that night, Sarah sensed something terrible had happened. After the bomb Agent Parsons had dropped about the murder weapon earlier, Finn had spent an hour in her cell, attempting to comfort her and calm her down. As hard as she'd tried not to lean on him, she hadn't been able to control herself. She hadn't been in his arms for so long, she'd almost forgotten how strong he was. How sheltered she felt when he held her. He was so big, so masculine. She'd always felt safe in his embrace, soothed by his presence.

But it didn't soothe her now. His blue eyes were wrought with tension, his hair mussed up, as if he'd ran his fingers through it a hundred times. Unease filled her belly, congealing into a hard knot as Finn came up to her cot and sat down beside her. Not even the feel of his hard thigh pressed against her much softer one could ease her anxiety.

"What's wrong?" she asked instantly, turning her head to meet his shuttered eyes.

"Sarah…" His husky voice trailed off, which only heightened her alarm.

"Finn, what's going on?"

"I…I don't even know how to say it."

Her pulse quickened, prompting her to stumble to her feet. She stared at him, studied the deep groove in his forehead. She knew that groove. It only appeared when he was truly upset about something. Last time she'd seen it, he'd been telling her he was leaving. This time, she got the feeling the news was much, much worse.

"Tell me," she ordered, pressing her suddenly damp palms to her sides.

"Lucy's gone."

The floor beneath her feet seemed to crumble away as if the ground had split open. As her knees gave out, she staggered back to the cot before she fell over. Her ears started to ring, so loudly that she had to wonder if maybe she'd misheard him.

Hope tickled her chest. Of course she'd misheard him. She *must* have. Because no way could he have just told her that—

"She was abducted from Cole and Jamie's house an hour ago."

The world began to spin. "No," she choked out. "No, you're lying."

She felt his warm hand on her knee. "I'm sorry, sweetheart. I wish I didn't have to tell you this. I wish I could assure you that Lucy is safe and sound, in Jamie's arms. I wish…"

An incredible force of anger slammed into her body, prompting her to fling his hand off her. This couldn't be happening. It *couldn't* be. How could Lucy be gone? Why would someone have taken her? It didn't make sense.

Terror burned a path up her throat, lodging into a painful lump. She couldn't even draw in a breath. Couldn't move.

"How…" She spoke through the pressure in her chest. "How did this happen? How could you *let* this happen?"

Finn flinched as if she'd struck him, but she didn't

feel an ounce of remorse. If he hadn't arrested her and put her in this cell, she could have protected her child!

"Who took her?" she demanded, violent shudders seizing her body.

Finn's eyes clouded with despair. "I don't know. Someone came into the house, knocked Jamie unconscious and took the baby."

Air. She needed air. She couldn't breathe.

"Sarah… Lord, I'm so sorry," he whispered, each word ringing with torment. "Jamie is beyond herself—she thinks she let you down. But damn it, it wasn't her fault. The attacker gave her a nasty bump on the head…."

Sarah had already tuned him out. Her heart was beating so fast she feared her ribs might rupture. She couldn't remember the last time she'd felt this way—helpless, frightened, so completely out of control.

Someone had *taken* her baby.

The thought of Lucy at the mercy of some sadistic kidnapper brought a streak of rage to her stomach. Tears stung her eyes, then spilled over, streaming down her cheeks and soaking her chin, her neck, the front of her sweater. She heard Finn slide closer, and when he pulled her into his arms, she didn't resist, just pressed her wet face against his broad chest and cried.

"Why would someone take her?" she said between sobs. "God, Finn, she's only three months old! What if she's hungry or cold or—"

"Sarah, stop. Look at me."

His hand was on her face, cupping her chin so she had no choice but to look up at him. The agony and determination burning in his blue eyes caught her off guard. "I'm going to find her," he said in a rough voice. "I swear to you, I'll find her."

She believed him. Was she crazy for that? Everything else he'd said, his apology, his promise to help her out of this mess, his gruff declaration that he would regain her trust…she hadn't been able to bring herself to believe. But right now, she did. She *believed* he would find her daughter, even if he died trying.

Some of the terror sticking to her chest dissolved as a rush of peace floated inside of her. "Do you promise?" she whispered.

"I promise." His husky voice cracked. "I don't know who took her, or why, but I'm going to do everything in my power to get your daughter back."

The arm that had been holding her close moved up the bumps of her spine, until his hand was tangled in her hair, while his other hand drew her face to his. He bent his head, and then those lips she'd never forgotten covered hers in a kiss.

It happened so fast she didn't have time to protest, and it ended before she even could. Just the hard feel of his mouth pressed against hers, the fleeting brush of his lips, the scratch of his beard stubble against her chin.

Then he pulled back, and not giving her a chance to speak, he was on his feet and heading to the cell door. "Where are you going?" she cried after him.

His mouth was set in a straight line as he glanced over his shoulder. "I'm going to find your daughter."

She couldn't tear her eyes from the perfect, tiny creature sleeping in the crib. She'd never seen a more beautiful infant. Those impossibly long eyelashes, the cherubic cheeks and red, cupid's bow mouth. The baby's chest rose and fell at each breath she drew into her little lungs.

Emotion filled her heart, spilling over and spreading through her body.

Was this what love felt like?

The baby stirred in her sleep, sighing softly. It was physically painful to look away, but she had to make sure the changing table was stocked with all the items she'd requested. She moved across the room, smiling at the bright yellow curtains hanging on the window. She would have liked to paint the walls yellow, too, maybe put up a pretty border with clowns or balloons, but this was a log cabin, and there wasn't much she could do.

She bent down in front of the cabinet beneath the changing table, nodding in satisfaction when she saw that there were plenty of diapers, wipes, talc and anything else she might need.

A soft wail broke the peaceful silence. Lucy was awake!

She practically sprinted to the crib, eagerness soaring through her like birds taking flight. The baby had been sleeping since they'd arrived, but Lucy was up now, and she couldn't wait to hold her.

"Hi there, baby girl," she said as she reached for the drowsy-eyed infant.

Lucy blinked a couple times, then stared up at her in confusion. Another cry left her lips.

"It's okay," she whispered. "Don't cry, baby. I'm here. Mama's here."

Chapter 7

The next morning, Sarah stared absently out the window of Finn's Jeep, feeling unsettled as they drove in the direction of her house. She'd thought she'd be overjoyed to be out of that cell, that she'd throw herself on the ground and kiss the dirt, thanking God for her freedom. But the prospect of walking into her empty house and not seeing Lucy made her heart weep.

Her daughter was still missing. Despite Finn's promise that he'd bring Lucy home, he hadn't made any progress last night. She knew he'd been up all night, driving around town and knocking on doors with Max Patton and some volunteers, but they hadn't found Lucy during their search. An alert had been put out, and the media was all over the abduction—Sarah had flinched when she'd heard the radio story blare out of the speakers in Finn's Jeep.

"Woman accused of murdering Serenade resident

Teresa Donovan is in the news once again! Reports are stating her three-month-old daughter has been abducted. An Amber alert has been issued...."

The press was eating it up, and even though it killed her to hear the things they were saying about her, she would suffer through it as long as people were looking for her daughter.

The judge had been surprisingly kind to her during the bail hearing this morning. Although he'd frowned and huffed about how he didn't like granting bail in a murder case, Sarah's distress over her missing daughter must have tugged at a couple heartstrings, because eventually he'd approved her bail, under the fervent protests of the district attorney. She'd had to put up her house as bail, and the electronic bracelet strapped around her ankle was humiliating beyond belief. But Jonas Gregory had insisted on it. Called her a flight risk.

Where exactly would she flee? she'd wanted to shout. Her daughter had been *kidnapped,* for Pete's sake. Until Lucy was safe in her arms again, she had no intention of going anywhere.

"Don't forget, you need to change the batteries every twenty-four hours," Finn spoke up, sounding extremely uncomfortable. "Otherwise the thing starts beeping."

She lifted her head. "What?"

"The ankle bracelet." He heaved out a breath. "You have to change the batteries or else it beeps and alerts the D.A. Same thing if you step out of the boundaries we programmed into it. You can't leave Serenade."

Her cheeks scorched. Was this what her life had become? A woman charged with murder, forbidden to leave town, kept on an electronic leash to make sure she stayed put. Oh, and her child was missing. How could this be happening?

She drew in a breath, forcing herself not to break apart in sobs. She had to be strong. Lucy was out there somewhere. The sweet baby she'd waited so many years for had been abducted because—because what? Why on earth would someone want to take Lucy?

In spite of her resolve, tears stung her eyes. "Why would someone take her?" she whispered.

"I don't know," Finn said gruffly. "But we'll find her, Sarah."

"You sound so sure."

"That's because the alternative is too damn horrific to contemplate."

His honesty sent a cold shiver through her body. She didn't fault him for it. Finn had always been excruciatingly blunt with her. Didn't beat around the bush, or make excuses. She'd appreciated it then.

Now…well, now, the very fact that an alternative existed—*not* finding Lucy—scared the living hell out of her.

She watched the scenery whiz by, recognizing the turnoff onto her property. The house she'd inherited from her aunt was kind of isolated, tucked behind a small forest with a gurgling creek running through it. Growing up here, away from the bustle of town, had been lonely, to say the least. But she welcomed the silence now. She wasn't sure she could face anyone in town at the moment.

God, what they must think of her. Did they believe she'd murdered Teresa Donovan? Did they think that her daughter's abduction was the perfect punishment for the crime?

"What if they took her to punish me?" she blurted out, unable to keep the frightening thought to herself.

Finn slowed the Jeep, stopping right in the middle of the dirt path leading to her house. "Nobody is punishing you," he replied firmly, reaching across the seat divider to take her hand. He squeezed it, hard, his warmth seeping into her palm and heating her frozen body. "You didn't kill Teresa, and you didn't deserve to have your daughter taken away from you."

She swallowed. "But someone else might think I'm a killer. Maybe that's why they took Lucy."

"We don't know why Lucy was taken." His jaw went stiff. "But I won't rest until we find out. You have to believe me, Sarah."

"I do," she whispered.

Looking satisfied, he moved the gearshift and drove up the driveway. Her two-story farmhouse came into view, with its slate-green roof and white exterior. Sarah was startled to see several cars parked on the dirt. She recognized Jamie's SUV and the second Jeep from the Serenade Sheriff's Department, but the two unmarked sedans were unfamiliar.

"Agent Parsons is here," Finn said, following her gaze. "And several other agents flew in this morning to help with the search for Lucy." He hesitated. "Try not to antagonize Parsons, okay? The man is a loose cannon and we can't have him getting in our way."

Nodding weakly, she unbuckled her seat belt and got out of the Jeep. Outside, the weather matched her turbulent mood. The sky was overcast, gray clouds rolling in from the east, leaving the air damp and cold. She inhaled the scent of impending rain; she'd always loved a good rainstorm. Right now, though, the cloudy sky only depressed her. She'd been stuck in that basement cell for two days, eager to get out and breathe some fresh air, but she suddenly wished she could crawl back into the dark cavern and bury her head under the covers. She couldn't face all those people inside. Parsons and the federal agents. Jamie.

Finn had said Jamie blamed herself for Lucy's abduction. He'd told her the other woman was terrified of looking into Sarah's eyes and confessing her failure to protect the child. More tears pricked her eyelids. God, she didn't blame Jamie. From what Finn had told her, the assailant had been hell-bent on getting his hands on Sarah's daughter. Jamie hadn't even had a chance to protect either of them.

To her surprise, Finn took her hand as they walked to the front porch. Two days ago, she would have shrugged out of his grip, told him she didn't want anything to do with him. She didn't do that now. Every muscle in her body vibrated with fear. She felt as if she'd been beat up, kicked, punched, thrown to the ground. Finn's touch steadied her. Soothed her.

His hand was the only thing that felt real right now.

When they entered the house, she heard voices wafting out of the large living room to the left. She fought the impulse to run upstairs and avoid the imminent questions. Or at least to shower and change—she'd been wearing these jeans and this blue turtleneck for two days already. But she couldn't dodge the inevitable. Breathing deeply, she squared her shoulders and followed Finn down the hall, knowing she'd have to face everyone sooner or later. Finn said the federal agents were anxious to speak with her about Lucy and who may have taken her, and Sarah would do anything to get her baby back, even confront Parsons and his crew.

"Sarah!"

Jamie jumped off the couch and ran toward her the second she and Finn appeared in the doorway. Sarah instinctively opened her arms, expecting Jamie to embrace her, but the auburn-haired FBI agent halted abruptly, guilt flooding her violet eyes.

"Sarah," Jamie stammered. "I'm so sorry. God, you don't know how sorry I am. He came out of nowhere, hit me before I could—"

Sarah took the other woman into her arms before Jamie could even finish. After a moment of stiffness, Jamie hugged her back, her slender frame shaking. "It wasn't your fault," Sarah said, fighting another rush of tears. "I know you did everything you could to protect Lucy."

Jamie pulled away with an impassioned look in her eyes. "I'm going to get her back for you. I won't give up until we find her."

"Ms. Connelly?"

Sarah turned to the four people in black suits staring expectantly at her. Parsons was standing by the window, a slight frown on his face. The other three were on the couch, two men and a woman, each one sporting a grave expression as they introduced themselves to her. Several coffee cups sat on the long wood coffee table, all filled to the rim, obviously untouched. Finn had given Jamie the key to Sarah's house and asked her to wait with the federal agents, but apparently the Bureau's people weren't interested in coffee or pleasantries.

And they got right down to business after Sarah settled on an armchair across from the couch.

"Do you have any idea who might have kidnapped the child?"

"Do you have any enemies we need to be aware of?"

"Is the father in the picture?"

The questions flew from their mouths like shells from a shotgun. Rubbing the bridge of her nose, Sarah let out a breath, then focused on the first question, posed to her by one of the males, Agent Bradley. With a head of thick black hair and kind brown eyes, he looked far warmer than Mark Parsons.

"I have no idea who might have taken her," she said softly. She turned to the Agent Andrews, a petite blonde with freckles. "And I don't have any enemies. None that I know of, anyway."

"And the child's father?" the third, Agent Ferraro, prompted. Now *he* reminded her of Parsons—he had that same shrewd glint in his eyes.

"I don't know who the father is," she confessed. "I adopted Lucy three months ago, through an agency in Raleigh. Her original birth certificate wasn't in the file—apparently, the birth mother wanted to remain anonymous and the head of the agency said she hadn't listed a father. They issued a new certificate for me, naming me as her mother, with the father unknown."

"Do you have records of the adoption?" Parsons drawled from the window.

Her spine stiffened. What the hell did he think, that she'd kidnapped Lucy herself? "Of course I do," she replied in a frigid tone.

He offered a cheerless smile. "We'll need to see those."

"And pictures," Agent Andrews spoke up, sympathy glimmering in her eyes as she turned to Sarah. "We'll need the most recent photographs of the child."

Sarah was already standing up. "I have everything in my study. I'll go get it."

"I'll join you," came Parsons's snide voice.

She tried to hide her lack of enthusiasm. She got the feeling he was coming along to keep an eye on her, make sure she didn't try to shred the documents or something. Finn trailed after her, too, the annoyed look on his handsome face telling her he wasn't happy with Parsons, either.

The study she used was on the second floor, three doors down from her bedroom. The spacious room consisted of a walnut desk that held her desktop computer, several filing cabinets she used for her business, and a bookshelf crammed with paperbacks and art books. Moving toward the tallest filing cabinet, she bent down and opened the bottom drawer, flipping through folders until she found the one she was looking for.

She stood up and held out the folder to Parsons, who was watching her with narrowed eyes.

"It's all there," she said, cringing at the defensive note in her voice. "The records from the adoption agency, Lucy's birth certificate, her medical records." She swallowed. "Her entire life is in there."

What life? Lucy was three months old. God, her daughter hadn't even lived yet. And now…now she was gone, and who knew what the person who took her was doing to her.

Suddenly feeling weak, Sarah sagged against one of the cabinets, fighting to collect her composure.

"Sarah," came Finn's rough voice. "Maybe you should sit down."

"I…I'm fine." She took a calming breath. "I just had a moment of panic."

Parsons moved his head back and forth between them, narrowing his eyes even more.

"What?" Sarah finally snapped. "Why are you looking at me like that?"

"Just pondering, that's all." He tilted his head, a lock of blond hair falling onto his forehead. "Where's your daughter, Ms. Connelly?"

She stared at him in bewilderment. "What?"

He moved closer, a patronizing light in his eyes. "Do you know where she is?"

"Why would I—" She stopped, her spine going rigid. "You think I had something to do with this."

When he didn't answer, an eddy of anger swirled in her belly, joined by a rush of disbelief. How could anyone possibly think she'd had anything to do with her daughter's abduction?

"You son of a bitch," Finn muttered, taking a step toward the agent. "Are you accusing Sarah of kidnapping her own daughter?"

"Just looking at every angle," Parsons replied, unfazed. "In the majority of child abductions, a family member is usually the culprit."

Sarah bit back a growl. "Do I have to remind you that I was in *jail* when my baby was taken?"

He shrugged. "Perhaps you had someone on the outside helping you." He shot Finn a pointed look.

Sarah balled her hands into fists. "I cannot believe you're even suggesting this! I did *not* arrange for my child to be abducted!"

Parsons edged off to the side, as if he thought she was going to pounce on him—which she was seriously tempted to do. Taking a long breath, Sarah forced her feet to stay rooted to the floor. She could only imagine what her face looked like right now—wild eyes, tight features. She had to calm down. Parsons already thought she was a murderer. She refused to give him any more ammunition against her.

Exhaling slowly, she met the man's eyes. "I have no

idea where my daughter is, Agent Parsons, and I suggest you stop interrogating me about it and go out and do your job."

Parsons frowned. He looked ready to say something nasty, but Finn spoke up before he could open his mouth. "Sarah, can you find those pictures?"

She held Parsons's gaze for another second, then gave a brief nod. Turning away, she headed to the bookshelf and grabbed a red leather photo album from one of the shelves. Fortunately, she'd developed a ton of digital prints only three days before she'd been arrested. She flipped through the pages to find suitable photos, her heart jamming in her throat as Lucy's angelic face stared up at her.

Her hands started to tremble. Each photo sent a hot blade of agony to her chest. Lucy sleeping in her crib. Lucy lying on her back, kicking her little feet in the air as she stared at the lens. Lucy smiling her adorable toothless smile.

Battling the pain shooting through her, she selected three of the most recent pictures and silently handed them to Parsons. He tucked them into the file folder she'd given him, then exited the study without a word, leaving her and Finn alone.

Sarah looked down at the open photo album in her shaky hands, then met Finn's surprisingly gentle eyes. "She's gone, Finn. My baby's gone."

He moved toward her, his stride long and quick. A second later, she was in his arms, her face pressed against his collarbone, the album still in her hands, crushed between them. She felt his heartbeat hammering against her breasts, matching the frantic pounding of her own pulse.

Running his hands over her lower back, he held her

tight and murmured, "You're not alone, Sarah. I'm here for you."

All his words did was bring another jolt of pain to her heart. Yes, he was here, and yes, his comforting embrace was so achingly familiar she wanted to cry again. But that didn't mean she wanted to rely on him. Lean on him. This man had hurt her. He'd abandoned her. He was the last person she should be seeking comfort from.

Regaining her senses, she slowly moved out of his arms and rubbed her tired eyes. "I'd rather Lucy was here," she whispered.

A cloud of torment darkened his eyes. She knew she'd hurt him by saying that, but she couldn't stop the resentment suddenly lodged in her chest. He was here. Now. But what about before? What about when she'd needed him *then?*

"Sheriff, I'd like it if you joined us," came Parsons's voice, the sharp order drifting in from the other room.

Finn swallowed. "I…we should go back out there."

She avoided his gaze. "Can you give me a minute? I just…" Her eyes dropped to the photo album. "I just need a minute."

He nodded. "Come when you're ready."

And then he was gone, and Sarah let out a breath, walking on numb legs toward the desk chair. She sank down, still holding the album. She opened it to the last few pages, which contained the pictures she'd taken only last week by the circular fountain in the town square. Martha, the owner of the diner, had been walking by, and Sarah had asked the older woman to take a few shots of her and Lucy.

In one, Sarah had her arms up high, Lucy dangling from above, while Sarah gazed up at the child in adoration. The next one featured Lucy on her lap, her chubby hands reaching to snag a lock of Sarah's hair. Lucy loved tugging on her hair. It hurt sometimes, but she always indulged her daughter, who was so sweet, so curious and sunny and—*gone*.

God, Lucy was gone.

The sound of quiet footsteps had her lifting her head, just as Finn's deputy, Max Patton, appeared in the doorway. Apprehension lined his brown eyes and the slouch of his shoulders made him appear younger. She'd always thought Max was a cute guy, with his floppy brown hair and dimpled cheeks. And he was unfailingly nice to her when they ran into each other in town.

Right now, though, she didn't want him here. She didn't want anyone. Only Lucy.

"Ms. Connelly," Max started, shifting awkwardly, "I just wanted to tell you how sorry I am about your baby."

Her throat clogged. "I appreciate that, Max."

"I mean it," he went on. "I can't even imagine what you're going through right now, but I assure you, we're doing everything we can to get Lucy back."

"Thank you," she murmured.

He hesitated in the doorway for a few more seconds, then gave her a sad smile and disappeared, leaving her to her photographs.

The last one Martha had taken that day hurt the most to look at. Lucy was smiling. Not just smiling, but *beaming*. Looking at Sarah with sheer, unconditional love in her big, perceptive eyes.

"I can't lose you," Sarah whispered, running her thumb over Lucy's tiny face. "I can't do this again."

She tipped her head, her gaze moving to the ceiling

as agony seized her stomach and tore her insides apart. "Don't make me go through this again," she begged, hoping someone was listening to her.

Perhaps the higher power that hadn't listened before.

"Please," she whispered. "Please don't do this to me again."

After the federal agents finally cleared out of Sarah's house, Finn released a breath heavy with relief. Lord, he couldn't stand this. There was nothing worse than a child going missing. Not knowing if she was safe. If she was cold or hungry or suffering. He didn't even blame Sarah for hiding away in the study. She hadn't come out since the confrontation with Parsons, and Finn hadn't had the heart to drag her back into the midst.

There was nothing she could do, anyway. Except wait.

And pray.

"I hope one of those leads pans out," Jamie murmured as she stood in the hallway, wringing her hands together.

It took him a moment to remember what she was talking about. Right, the leads. Anna had just phoned from the station, informing him that a dozen calls had come in from people claiming to have seen Lucy, or insisting they had information about the abduction. That's why the FBI agents had hightailed it out of here, to follow-up on the incoming stream of tips.

But Finn wasn't convinced the so-called leads would amount to anything. He'd never handled a kidnapping before, but he knew from other law enforcement colleagues just how many false alarms came in during these types of cases. With the media putting a spotlight on the abduction, attention-hungry lowlifes crept from the gutters, hoping to get their fifteen minutes of fame.

Maybe this time, though… He prayed that this time one of those phone calls actually led to Lucy's safe return.

"I should get going," Jamie said, sounding reluctant. "Cole's probably pacing the house, going crazy that he can't help. He called his investigator, though, so we've got another person on board, determined to find Lucy."

"Thank Cole when you see him." Finn was about to offer to pay the P.I.'s tab, then thought twice. Cole Donovan was a millionaire, for chrissake. He probably had a whole slew of investigators on retainer.

"Give Sarah a hug for me," Jamie said as she left.

Finn closed the door after her, then turned to Max, who was leaning against the wall in the corridor. "What now, boss?" Max asked.

Finn sighed. "Now you go back to the station and help Anna field calls. I'll stay here and keep an eye on Sarah."

"You got it, Sheriff."

Once Max was gone, Finn headed upstairs, a bit fearful of what he'd find when he entered the study. He still couldn't believe Parsons had had the gall to accuse Sarah of arranging to kidnap her own child. Jamie was right—that jerk had tunnel vision, and right now, his narrow sights were set on Sarah.

But Finn knew better. He would never forget the day Sarah came back to Serenade, after spending a month in Raleigh awaiting the birth of her daughter. He'd been coming out of the diner just as she walked in with Lucy on her hip, and the joy he'd seen in her eyes had been so strong and all-consuming he was surprised it hadn't infected the rest of the town. She loved that baby. He'd been overwhelmed by the force of that love, the tenderness as she'd introduced him to Lucy.

In that moment, their rocky past had ceased to exist. Sarah had been so wrapped up in the child, swept away by a wave of maternal love, that she'd forgotten everything. She'd even smiled at him.

No way was she faking any of this. If she'd had someone take Lucy, that meant her pain, her terror, was all make-believe. And nobody was that good of an actor.

He reached the study, took a breath, and knocked. There was no answer.

"Sarah?" he said cautiously. "Can I come in?"

Silence.

Sighing, he pushed open the door, expecting to find her curled up in the corner of the room, crying over the photo album, but the study was empty. With a frown, he strode out, heading down the hall toward Sarah's bedroom. The door was ajar, and when he walked in, he found that empty, too.

His pulse sped up. Where the hell was she?

He checked the bathroom next, the guest rooms, and after he'd searched the second floor twice, he raced down the stairs, panic blowing around in his gut like street litter. Every room he peered in was deserted. No Sarah. She was gone.

"Damn it," he mumbled to himself.

She'd taken off. Must have sneaked out while everyone had been in the living room, discussing her *missing daughter*. Was Parsons right? Had Sarah somehow been involved in— He halted in the hallway. The ankle bracelet. There was a GPS in it, and both he and the D.A. had a unit that could monitor Sarah's movements.

As anger and frustration boiled inside of him, he

raced outside and flung open the back door of the Jeep, grabbing the duffel bag he'd left in the backseat. He unzipped it and rummaged around until he found the GPS locator. It was the size of a BlackBerry, with a screen that displayed a map featuring a red dot.

The dot wasn't moving.

He peered at the screen, then felt the blood drain from his face. He recognized the location on the map. It was less than a mile from here and the red blip remained static, indicating that Sarah was staying put. He knew why she'd gone there. Hell, it should have been the first place he'd thought to look.

A headache formed between his eyes. Gulping hard, he reached up to rub away the ache, then unclipped his car keys from his belt and slid into the driver's seat of the Jeep.

God, Sarah, why did you have to go there?

It was hard to drive in the condition he was in. Along with the throbbing temples, his heart thudded erratically in his chest, each beat sending a streak of grief through him. He couldn't do this, he realized as he steered the Jeep toward the turnoff. He couldn't do this. He hadn't been there in years.

Three minutes later, the wrought-iron gates came into view, and his pulse sped up even more. His mouth was totally dry. He couldn't swallow. He couldn't even park the car; his hands were shaking that badly.

Sucking in a burst of oxygen, he forced himself to calm down. Sarah was here, right beyond those gates. He might not want to walk through them, but he had no choice. Steadying his hands, he parked in the tiny gravel lot next to the gate and staggered out of the vehicle.

"You can do this," he muttered to himself.

Christ, could he?

The metal creaked as he parted the heavy gates and stepped onto the damp grass beyond the entrance. He made a conscious effort not to look around. Look straight ahead. Walk deeper into the cemetery. He was just climbing a gentle grassy slope when the rain began to fall and cool droplets stained his face. He wiped them away, reaching the top of the slope. He took a breath, then turned his head to the right, knowing exactly what he'd find.

And there she was, on her knees, huddled by a simple, blue-granite tombstone, her thick brown hair blown around by the wet breeze.

You can do this.

His legs shook with each step he took, but he soldiered on, getting closer. Closer. Until he was directly behind her. Until his suddenly moist eyes honed in on the headstone that Sarah was kneeling in front of, the headstone that had her shuddering with silent sobs.

Jason Finnegan

Beloved son of Patrick and Sarah.
Here for a short time, but forever in our hearts.

Chapter 8

Sarah whirled around as she heard footsteps from behind. She quickly swiped her sleeve over her wet eyes, then dropped her arm when she saw it was Finn. No point hiding her tears from him. He knew better than anyone what she was going through right now.

As he moved closer, the wind plastered his dark blue Windbreaker against his chest and raindrops slid down his proud forehead. He looked incredibly handsome, and incredibly sad. She suddenly remembered the day of the funeral, the way he'd looked in his black suit and tie, with the hair he'd neglected to cut for months curling under his chin and shining in the morning sunlight. That was when their relationship had begun to deteriorate.

No, that wasn't true, she realized. It happened after she'd discovered she was pregnant with Jason. *That's* when everything had changed.

"You shouldn't have run off like that without telling anyone," Finn said roughly, shoving his hands in the pockets of his jeans.

"I'm sorry," she said, and meant it. "I just... I couldn't sit there anymore. It was too quiet."

He didn't answer. From the corner of her eye, she saw that his gaze was focused on the tiny headstone. The grief slashing across his rugged features made her breathless. At the funeral he'd donned a shuttered expression, stood there in stoic silence. A part of her had wondered if he even cared about the loss of their son.

She slowly stood up, ignoring the grass stains on her denim-clad knees. Wrapping her arms around her chest, she turned to Finn, tears shimmering in her eyes and blurring her vision. "You didn't want him," she found herself whispering.

His jaw tensed for a second, then relaxed, a cloud of defeat moving across his face. "Not at first," he said hoarsely.

No, he definitely hadn't been pleased when she'd told him about the pregnancy. It hadn't been planned—she'd been twenty-three at the time, Finn only twenty-six. Neither of them had wanted a baby, not then, but although Sarah was surprised, she'd quickly adjusted to the pregnancy. Jason might have been an accident, but she'd loved him from the second she knew he existed.

Not Finn, though. She cringed as she remembered his shocked reaction. They'd been having breakfast in the kitchen of his farmhouse, where they'd lived for nearly a year. At first, he hadn't even reacted, hadn't even blinked.

And then he'd asked her if she wanted to terminate the pregnancy.

She hadn't wanted to, but in that moment, she'd re-alized that *he* did.

"I was always up-front with you about it," Finn said, his husky voice bringing her back to the present. "I never wanted children. I never wanted to be a husband or father."

She bristled. "It's not like I got pregnant on purpose."

"I know you didn't. But I still wasn't pleased about it," he confessed. "And then, when you told me you were keeping the baby, I let myself, I don't know, *hope*. I hoped that maybe everything would work out. That maybe my mother hadn't messed me up as bad as I thought and I could truly be the man you wanted me to be."

Sarah held her breath. He'd never said any of this to her before. A part of her wondered if he even realized what he was doing. His blue eyes were fixed on that little grave, his voice sounding faraway to her ears.

"Seeing you carrying him…watching your belly swell…feeling him kick against my palm." Finn let out a choked sound, his despair echoing in the air, mingling with the soft spattering of raindrops against the grass. "I *wanted* him, Sarah. I wanted him so damn badly it hurt to look at you."

As her heart pounded in her chest, she took a step toward him and reached up to touch the stubble coat-ing his jaw. "Why didn't you ever tell me this before?"

"I couldn't," he blurted out. "When we went to the doctor and saw that ultrasound…when he told us that Jason was…"

To her shock, tears filled his eyes. In all the years she'd known him, she'd never once seen him cry. He certainly hadn't cried during the doctor's visit he was describing, yet she now realized he'd been just as affected that day.

Back then, she'd believed he was relieved by the news. It was the only way to explain his lack of...lack of *everything*.

I'm sorry, but your baby's gone.

At eight-and-a-half-months pregnant, finding out her child died in utero had been like dying herself. Sarah had felt as though someone had taken a baseball bat and pounded the living hell out of her. She'd sat there, numb, paralyzed, as the doctor threw out words like stillborn and undiagnosed preeclampsia and needing to induce labor.

And the entire time, Finn hadn't said a word. He hadn't comforted her. Held her. Brushed away her tears. He'd simply shut down, leaving her to battle the grief and shock all by herself.

"I wanted to die that day," Finn said in a ravaged voice. "I kept asking myself if maybe it was my fault. If maybe God was punishing me for not wanting Jason when you first told me about him."

His heart-wrenching words brought tears to her eyes. Without stopping to think about what she was doing, she wrapped her arms around his neck and held him with everything she had. She felt his sorrow and shame vibrating from his body, his heartbeat thudding irregularly against her chest.

"God, Sarah, I blamed myself for what happened," he whispered, his breath fanning over the top of her head. "And then you fell apart, and I couldn't think straight. I'd already been through all that with my mother, all the memories just reared their ugly heads, and I couldn't be there for you. I just couldn't."

His arms tightened around her and she nearly

drowned in his strong embrace. "You never told me you blamed yourself," she said, tipping her head up to meet his tormented gaze.

"You were going through a tough time. I didn't want to drop my own issues on you and make it worse."

Her heart constricted, sending a jolt of pain through her body. Why hadn't he said this to her four years ago? Why had he let her face the depression alone, pretending he didn't give a damn about the son they'd lost? She pressed her cheek into his neck, breathing in the familiar scent of him, spicy, masculine, soothing.

She didn't know how long they stood there, holding each other as the rain gently fell over them, but when they finally pulled apart, something changed between them. Something shifted inside her.

"Come on," Finn said, reaching for her hand. "I'll take you home."

Finn felt as though he'd run a marathon followed by two triathlons as he trailed upstairs after Sarah. They'd returned to her house just as the rain became a downpour, and they'd both been drenched during the walk from the car to the porch. He was chilled to the bone, though he suspected it had more to do with his graveyard confession than the rain.

When he'd found Sarah kneeling in front of their son's grave, something had broken inside of him. For four years, he'd tried desperately to block out any thoughts of Jason, to pretend that the loss had been for the best. He hadn't wanted to be a father, hadn't wanted to settle down. That's what he'd told himself whenever the memory of his tiny son breached the shield he'd constructed around himself.

But the lies he'd clung to had unraveled like an old

sweater back at the cemetery. He'd loved his son. Loved him in a fierce, protective way that only a father could feel.

Why hadn't he been there for Sarah? She'd been suffering just as much as he was, if not more so, and instead of sharing her pain, he'd abandoned her. But it had been too much for him. Growing up with a bipolar mother had been difficult, especially since his mom refused to take her meds most of the time. He'd been a caretaker for his entire childhood and adolescence, and when his mother committed suicide when Finn was eighteen, he'd felt such overwhelming relief it still shamed him to remember it. He'd finally been free of his responsibilities, able to live his life without worrying about cleaning up other people's messes.

He hadn't lied to Sarah—he *didn't* want to settle down, or be a husband, have kids. All he'd wanted was his independence, and an unplanned pregnancy hadn't meshed with the life he'd envisioned for himself. That changed, though, when he felt Jason kick for the first time. At that moment, feeling the little flutter against his hand, he'd vowed to be the best father and husband he could be.

And then Jason had died, and Finn had not only destroyed Sarah, but himself.

"Why don't you hop in the shower and I'll throw your clothes in the dryer?" Sarah offered.

He was about to refuse, but the wet denim clinging to his legs made him reconsider. "Sure. That sounds good."

She led him to the door across from her bedroom. "You can shower here. Just leave the clothes on the bed."

His mouth went dry as he wondered whether she

planned to stick around and watch him undress. Disappointment flickered inside of him when she moved to the door, saying, "I'll give you some privacy."

Sighing, Finn sat on the bed and unlaced his boots. He kicked them off, peeled away his socks, then tackled his wet clothes. He strode naked into the bathroom, where he plucked a towel from the rack and wrapped it around his waist before going to gather up his clothing. He was just laying them on the bed when a tentative knock sounded.

"You decent?" Sarah called. "I just wanted to get those clothes."

"Yeah, come in."

She strode through the doorway, then froze when she caught sight of him. He glimpsed a brief flicker of heat, and it made him want to flex his muscles or some ridiculous crap, just to see those liquid brown eyes smolder. Her gaze swept over his bare chest, causing hot shivers to travel along his skin. His groin tightened, an erection growing beneath the towel around his hip. He shifted, hoping she wouldn't notice, but her sensual lips parted slightly, confirming she'd seen everything.

His arousal was so wrong, on so many levels. Not only had they just returned from a visit to the cemetery, but Sarah's daughter was still missing. He wasn't allowed to be turned-on right now, though in his defense, turned-on wasn't an uncommon state for him when Sarah was around.

Breaking eye contact, he took a step back, determined to control his body's response to her proximity. Hop in the shower, get dressed, offer to make her some lunch. That's what he needed to do right now.

But Sarah had other ideas.

His mouth went bone-dry as she moved closer, an

undecipherable expression in her eyes. Holding his breath, he waited to see what she would do. What she would say.

She'd changed into a tight green sweater and a pair of snug jeans before taking off to the cemetery, and the material was now soaked from the rain, clinging to her slender frame and displaying the curvy contours of her body like a damn Thanksgiving feast. Her nipples were puckered, poking against one of those paper-thin bras she'd always liked to wear. His pulse raced as he remembered those dusky-pink nubs, the way they went even more rigid when he captured them between his lips.

"Finn," she began, her voice ringing with anguish.

Before he could say a word, she had her arms twined around his neck, up on her tiptoes as she kissed him. Her mouth was desperate, moving over his in a frantic kiss, and then her tongue probed at the seam of his lips, demanding entry.

He couldn't do anything but let her in. His body went taut with anticipation, his erection thickening as she explored his mouth with her tongue and dug her fingernails into the nape of his neck.

He utilized every ounce of willpower to break the kiss. His voice came out in a ragged burst of air. "What are you doing?"

"Forgetting," she whispered, and then she kissed him again.

Somehow they moved to the bed. Somehow his hands found their way underneath her sweater, sliding up to cup her firm breasts over her lacy bra. Pure, unadulterated desire crashed into him. He squeezed her breasts, then yanked the sweater up and her bra down, and rubbed his cheek against the swollen mounds.

He covered one nipple with his mouth, suckling gently, eliciting a moan from her lips. He laved her with his tongue, nipped at her with his teeth, as wave after wave of sheer exhilaration crashed over him. Lord, he was kissing Sarah. Touching Sarah. He'd been dreaming about this for four years and as she suddenly pushed him onto his back and straddled his thighs, he realized that nothing had changed. He was harder than he'd ever been in his life, his pulse was pounding so loudly he couldn't hear a thing. She'd always done this to him, made him hot and dizzy and hungry for her. So damn hungry.

Something has *changed.*

The notion slipped into his hazy mind, pushing through the passion and arousal and uncontrollable need. With a low groan, he gripped her waist and stilled her, putting an end to the seductive roll of her lower body against his aching groin. He looked into her eyes and saw the dazed expression there, the desperation.

She didn't want him.

She just wanted to *forget.*

"Why are you stopping?" she murmured, leaning down to kiss him again.

Maybe he was the biggest idiot on the planet, but he turned his head, so that her soft lips collided with his cheek. It was physically painful to move, but he did it anyway, sliding out from under her and stumbling off the bed. Breathing heavily, he stared into her confused eyes and said, "I can't do this."

"Why not?" Biting her lip she glanced at his crotch. "I can see you want me. Don't tell me it's not true."

"I do want you," he squeezed out. "I've wanted you for four years. I've fantasized about this happening, sweetheart, so many times." His lungs burned as he inhaled deeply. "But it can't be like this. It can't be about grief, or sorrow, or you needing to forget about Jason and Lucy and this damn murder case."

Her shoulders sagged. "Maybe it's not about that."

"It is," he corrected. "It's all about forgetting."

"So?" Irritation flashed in her eyes. "Does it really matter what it's about?"

"It does to me." A lump rose in the back of his throat. "You have to want me. *Me,* Sarah. When we make love, it needs to be because you want to be with me, fully, not just to forget about everything else."

She didn't answer, and he didn't push her. She knew he was right, he could see it on her face, in that helpless, frustrated crease lining her forehead. It made his entire body ache, how damn beautiful she was. All that creamy, flawless skin, her lush cupid's bow mouth, the damp hair curling at the ends. He wanted to take back everything he'd just said, cover her body with his and lose himself inside her.

Fortunately, his phone started to ring before he could act on that foolish urge.

Turning away, he picked up the cell phone from the top of the dresser, frowning when he saw Parsons's number on the screen.

"Finnegan," he barked into the phone.

"Sheriff, it's Parsons. We may have a lead on the child."

Finn sucked in a breath. "Tell me."

"One of my agents just handled a tip from a woman who owns a baby boutique in Grayden." For once, Parsons sounded concerned rather than smug. "She heard about Lucy's abduction on the news and said she might have information. Apparently, a woman came into the boutique six days ago, looking, and I quote, 'extremely agitated.'"

Finn's instincts started buzzing. "Agitated?"

"Yeah. The owner says the customer was acting really weird and nervous. She tried making conversation with her, asking who the baby clothes were for, but the customer got even more pale. She refused to answer any questions, ended up buying a whole bunch of stuff and pretty much sprinted from the shop."

A mysterious woman purchasing baby garments and refusing to talk about it? Running out the door? Oh, yeah, for once in his sorry life, Parsons was actually on to something.

"We need to find this woman," Finn said. "Whoever she is—"

"We already found her."

He nearly dropped the phone. "What?"

"I sent Andrews and Ferraro to the boutique an hour ago. Andrews just phoned in." Parsons hesitated. "The owner showed them the security footage from the day in question. Both my agents immediately recognized the customer."

Unease washed over him. "Who was it, Parsons?"

"Anna Holt. Your deputy."

Chapter 9

"Anna wouldn't do this," Sarah said firmly, shaking her head in dismay as they entered the police station twenty minutes later.

Finn was too wired up to respond. Ever since Parsons's phone call, his head had been spinning. Like Sarah, he didn't believe that Anna was involved in Lucy's abduction, but he couldn't ignore the evidence, either. A nervous-looking Anna had been spotted buying baby clothes at a shop in the next town over.

Why hadn't she gone to the maternity store in Serenade? Why drive thirty minutes to another town? And why buy baby clothing to begin with? Anna was twenty-four years old, single, still living with her parents. What reason did she have to purchase baby stuff?

It didn't make sense to him, and as they entered the bull pen, he prayed there was another explanation for that security footage. Only problem was, Anna was out with the volunteer unit, knocking on doors and asking questions about the kidnapping. Parsons had been hell-bent on tracking her down and dragging her back to the police station, but Finn had ordered the agent not to make a single move until he got there. He had promptly thrown back on his damp clothes, forgoing the shower, then waited for Sarah to quickly change into something dry. They were out of the house in a flash, neither of them bringing up the passionate encounter in the guest room.

He would bring it up, though. Not now. Later. When they cleared up this latest mess. When they found Lucy.

Parsons and the three other federal agents were waiting in the bull pen, drinking coffee and talking among themselves. When Parsons saw Finn, he stood up and said, "Why are you all wet?"

"It's raining outside, in case you haven't noticed." Finn headed for his office, over his shoulder adding, "Give me two minutes. I need to change into some dry clothes."

In his office, he opened the metal locker near the door, ignoring the olive-green sheriff's uniform neatly hanging inside. He never wore the uniform—it was too stiff and uncomfortable. Instead, he grabbed a spare pair of jeans and a gray hooded sweatshirt, then stripped off his wet attire and got dressed. When he strode back into the bull pen a minute later, Parsons was still on his feet, arms crossed as he said, "We need to bring Deputy Holt in, Sheriff."

"We can't, not unless we want to spook her," Finn retorted. He escorted Sarah to the chair in front of Max's station, then leaned against the desk. "If she has the baby, and I'm not certain she does, then she might bolt if she thinks we're on to her."

Parsons's mouth tightened in a thin line. "What do you suggest, then?"

"We wait for her to come back." Finn glanced at the clock hanging over the coffee station. "It's three o'clock. Anna went out with the volunteer unit around noon. I'll call her and say I need her here at the station, but we're not going to turn on the sirens and go after her. If she does have Lucy and thinks we know it, she might disappear."

Parsons offered a resigned nod. "You're right. We need to play it safe. We don't want her running off."

Finn was surprised the other man gave in so easily, but even Parsons had to see the validity of Finn's point. Not that he thought Anna abducted the baby. This had to be a misunderstanding.

"Do you have a copy of the security footage from the boutique?" Finn asked.

Andrews, the pretty female agent, nodded and gestured to the laptop in front of her. "I just downloaded it. Come and take a look."

Both Finn and Sarah approached the screen, and three minutes later, they wore identical frowns. It was no mistake. Anna was the woman on the tape, and just as Parsons had described, she'd looked pale, nervous and extremely jumpy during the encounter at the baby store.

Rubbing his chin in frustration, Finn edged away from the laptop. Sarah did, too, sinking back in Max's chair as she said, "They were blue."

Everyone turned in her direction.

"The clothes," she clarified. "They were blue, like she was buying them for a boy."

"Possibly to throw off suspicion," Agent Andrews suggested. "She obviously didn't want to advertise she was planning on abducting a child. Anything pink might have raised suspicion once it came out that a baby girl had been taken."

Sarah gave a little sigh, an acknowledgment that Andrews had a point.

"Look," Finn began, "just because she was at the store doesn't mean that—"

"Uh…hi. What's going on?"

Finn swiveled his head, smothering a groan when he saw Max in the doorway. His deputy took one look around the room, picked up on the tension hanging in the air, and clumsily repeated his question. "Seriously, what's up?"

"Just discussing a new lead," Finn said vaguely.

A thought suddenly occurred to him. Max and Anna were about the same age, and Finn knew for a fact they went out for drinks together on their nights off. He wasn't sure whether they were dating—he didn't think so—but he did know they were close. If anyone might be able to help him gain insight about Anna, it was Max.

Excusing himself, Finn moved away from the group and headed toward the bewildered man across the room. He lightly touched Max's elbow. "Can I speak to you alone for a second?"

Still looking confused, Max nodded. "Sure, boss."

They headed out into the hall, where Finn got right to the point. "Listen…this might sound odd, but…you're close with Anna, right?"

Max furrowed his eyebrows. "Yeah, we're good friends."

"That's what I thought." Finn chose his next words carefully. "Is there any reason why Anna would buy baby clothes?"

The deputy seemed startled. "Baby clothes? I don't think she would, especially since—" He stopped abruptly.

Finn's hackles rose. "Since what?"

His deputy glanced at the floor. "Nothing. Forget I said anything."

"Max. What do you know?"

"Sir, this is kind of personal. I'd really rather not—"

"Max." Finn tamped down his frustration. "Why would Anna not have a need for baby clothes?"

A sigh left Max's mouth. "Because she can't have children."

Finn's stomach dropped like a lead weight. "What?"

"She was in a really bad car accident when she was fourteen," Max confessed, looking uncomfortable. "She broke her pelvis, and there was a bunch of other damage, and the doctors had to remove her…you know, do a hysterectomy."

Oh, Christ. Along with the sympathy that flooded him at the notion that Anna couldn't have kids, the knowledge also made him want to curse. Only a short while ago, he'd seen a segment on the news about a barren woman who'd abducted an infant from a hospital nursery in order to satisfy her desperate need to be a mother. What if Anna had done the same thing? What if she'd wanted a baby so badly she'd decided to steal one?

No, that was ridiculous. He'd always prided himself on being a good judge of character. Anna Holt was a first-class woman. Kind, intelligent, with a truly good heart.

"Boss, I really don't understand why—" Max's mouth fell open. "Sheriff, you don't actually think *Anna* had something to do with any of this."

"With any of what?" came a wary female voice.

Both men spun around to find Anna standing at the end of the corridor. In her green deputy's uniform, with her dark hair tied back in a low ponytail, she looked young and professional. Her strides were quick as she moved toward them, her normally astute eyes flickering with suspicion.

"What's going on?" she asked. Her voice cracked. "What's happening?"

Finn swallowed the sigh lodged in his chest. He hated that he had to do this. He'd rather cut off his own arm than cause this young woman any pain. She trusted him. Respected him. And if they were wrong here…

And if she has Lucy?

He heeded the firm reminder. Lucy was the only one that mattered right now, and if Anna knew anything about the baby's kidnapping, Finn needed to get that information out of her. If she didn't…well, maybe her trust and respect were the price he'd have to pay.

"Anna," he said gently, "I'm going to need you to come with me."

"I did *not* kidnap that baby," Anna exclaimed fifteen minutes later, her dark eyes filling with tears. She turned to Finn in accusation. "How could you even *think* that, Sheriff? How *could* you?"

Finn's heart rolled painfully in his chest. In the four years of serving as Serenade's sheriff, he'd learned how to distance himself during interrogations. It was hard to do, especially when the person sitting across the table was someone you knew well, someone you saw around town and had coffee with in the diner. But he'd always made a heroic effort to keep that distance, to treat each matter objectively and get past the fact that sometimes people he called friends might need to be punished.

But this was unbelievably difficult. This was Anna, for Pete's sake.

After he'd shown her the security tape, he'd let Parsons take over the questioning, mostly because he couldn't even look at his young deputy without wanting to clock himself in the face. As Parsons made the reason for this chat clear, Anna's confusion and wariness had transformed into outrage that palpitated in the room.

"Then why did you buy baby clothes in Grayden?" Parsons demanded.

"It…they were for my cousin," she sputtered. "Linda. She lives in Charlotte and just gave birth to a baby boy. His name is James." Anna's tears spilled over, two rivers of misery that rippled down her cheeks. "You can ask my parents. They'll tell you it's true."

Parsons looked unaffected by her obvious distress. "We've seen the tape, Deputy Holt. You look like a nervous bunny rabbit on it. The owner of the store said you refused to talk about the purchase."

"Because it hurt!"

The outburst had Finn's insides clenching. There was no mistaking the agony ringing from her voice, and in that moment, he realized that this really was a mistake. Anna's actions, now that he'd learned of her infertility from Max, made a hell of a lot more sense.

"I can't have children, okay?" she cried. "Maybe one day I'll adopt, the way Ms. Connelly did, but that doesn't mean I'm fine with it. When I see a baby, it still makes me sad. And when my cousin, who's the exact same age as me, just gives birth to a beautiful little boy…"

She let out a shaky breath. "I was buying those things for James, and the entire time I was in the store, I just wanted to run from there. I don't care if that makes me a coward, but it *hurt*."

She finished in a rush, leaving both men slightly stunned. Finn's throat was so tight he could barely speak, but he managed a quick nod at Parsons, who slowly pushed back his chair.

"We'll be right back," Finn said, unable to meet Anna's eyes.

In the hall, Parsons crossed his arms, but the look in his eyes told Finn that the federal agent was on the same page. "She didn't do it," Finn murmured.

"Yeah, I don't think so, either."

"We need to let her go."

This time Parsons disagreed. "If we do, I'm assigning Ferraro to keep an eye on her. She might have been quite convincing in there, but we can't take any chances, Finnegan. She might still lead us to that baby."

"I don't think she will."

Parsons's nostrils flared. "I don't care what you think. You might be leading the Donovan murder, but I was assigned to the abduction. If I think Holt merits more attention, you can't do a damn thing about it."

Finn tried not to sigh. So much for Parsons's transformation. The man was the same controlling jerk.

"Fine," he finally muttered. "Do whatever you want."

"Gee, thanks for the permission," Parsons said in a cutting voice. "Now I'm going to talk to Ferraro about his assignment. You can inform Deputy Holt that she's free to go."

Thanks for the permission, Finn was tempted to bite out, but he kept his mouth shut. As Parsons strode toward the bull pen, Finn leaned against the wall and raked his hands through his hair. Lord, he didn't want to go back in that interrogation room and face Anna. For the second time in less than a week, he'd questioned a woman he cared for about a crime she hadn't committed.

Such was the life of a small-town sheriff, he supposed.

But that didn't make it suck any less.

"It wasn't your fault."

Jamie glanced up as Cole entered the bedroom, but only spared him a brief look before dropping her gaze to the papers strewn across the bedspread.

Cole stifled a sigh. She'd had her head buried in those files since one of the FBI agents dropped them off earlier. They were copies of the documents Sarah had provided, and Jamie was determined to find something in those files. Anything that might lead her to Lucy.

"Did you hear me?" Cole said.

She didn't respond.

Releasing the sigh, he sat down at the edge of the bed, reached over and stilled her hand before she could pick up the next sheet of paper.

"It's not your fault," he repeated in a firm voice.

She met his eyes, her expression tortured. "I forgot to set the alarm. I turned my back on Lucy. I let someone knock me out with a crowbar. I lay on the floor unconscious while a baby was stolen." A ragged breath escaped her mouth. "How is this *not* my fault, Cole?"

"Not everything is in our control, Jamie," he said quietly. "Crappy things happen sometimes, and we can't stop them, no matter how hard we try."

His heart ached when he noticed the tears pooling

in the corners of her eyes. "Come here," he murmured, wrapping his arm around her.

She rested her head on his shoulder, trembling slightly. "I just want to find Lucy and bring her back to Sarah."

"You will. *We* will," he corrected. Tucking a strand of auburn hair behind her ears, he leaned in and brushed his lips over hers, then shifted and grabbed the nearest sheet of paper. "Come on, let's go through these together and see if anything jumps out at us."

Jamie smiled through her tears. "You're really going to help?"

"Of course. I want to get Lucy back as much as you do."

He glanced down at the paper, noticing he'd picked up the baby's medical report, which listed Lucy's eye and hair color, blood type, distinguishing birthmarks... Cole's eyes narrowed as something caught his attention.

"Huh," he muttered.

Jamie shot him a sharp look. "Huh what?"

"Did you look at this one?"

He held up the medical report and she furrowed her brow. "Yeah. It's just Lucy's basic information. Why? Do you see something I don't?"

He traced his index finger over one item in particular, watching Jamie's expression as she read the line he'd pointed out. "I don't get it," she said.

Cole didn't answer. His uneasiness grew, slowly coating his stomach until he started to feel sick. He reached up to rub his temples, forcing himself to think logically. This had to be a coincidence.

"Cole, you're scaring me." Her voice became urgent. "Tell me what you're thinking."

Letting out an unsteady breath, he met his fiancée's

worried lavender eyes, opened his mouth, and revealed the frightening suspicion wreaking havoc on his brain.

When he finished, the worry on her face dissolved into apprehension, then sheer resignation. She shook her head a few times, as if trying to comprehend what he'd just told her.

"Well?" he asked. "Do you have anything to say to that?"

She didn't answer for several long moments, and when she finally spoke, she echoed his precise thought on the subject.

"Aw, crap."

Chapter 10

Sarah watched as Finn collected the empty food containers and tossed them in the garbage bin by the back door. They'd stopped to get takeout from the diner after leaving the police station, and had spent the last half hour eating in silence in her spacious kitchen. He hadn't asked to come back to her house, and she hadn't invited, but somehow he'd ended up here and Sarah had to admit, she was grateful for his presence.

The bracelet circling her ankle was a painful reminder that her freedom had been taken away, at least to some extent. She hated that she couldn't get into her car and drive all over the damn state in search of Lucy. She was like a dog chained up in the yard, seeing a squirrel in the distance and being unable to chase after it. She hated feeling so out of control.

She'd felt that way earlier, when she'd practically assaulted Finn in the guest room. At that moment, she'd wanted nothing more than to lose herself in his powerful arms and drugging kisses. The visit to Jason's grave had torn her apart. For that one brief moment, she'd wanted so badly to forget it all. The grief, the worry, the helplessness.

But Finn had been right. It wasn't fair to use him as a means of forgetting.

"Coffee's ready," Finn said.

She glanced up to see him holding two steaming mugs in his hands. "Let's go to the living room," he said with a sigh.

"Do you need to stop by the gallery at some point?" he asked as they left the kitchen. "Anything you need to pick up there?"

The gallery? She'd totally forgotten about it, what with being jailed and then having her daughter taken away from her. She supposed she should put up a sign announcing the place would be closed indefinitely, but the thought of going into town sent dread spiraling through her.

Another thing she'd lost, the gallery she loved. Art had always been her passion. Unfortunately, her hand-eye coordination left much to be desired, and the few times she'd tried drawing or painting had resulted in embarrassment. But she had a good head for business, and she'd majored in it in college, along with a minor in art history. When the gallery had come up for sale, she'd used the money her aunt left her to purchase it, and going to work every morning used to bring her so much joy.

Now she was terrified of facing the citizens of Serenade. Terrified of the whispers and stares she knew she'd encounter.

"I don't need anything," she said softly. "Only my daughter."

She followed him into the living room, and when they were settled on the couch, each on opposite ends, Sarah held her mug between her cold fingers and sighed. "I'm sorry you had to question Anna. I know that must have been hard for you."

He grunted in response, but the pain in his eyes said it all.

"I never thought for a moment she was responsible for any of this," she added. Frustration gathered in her belly. "But who is? Where's Lucy? God, Finn, why was she taken?"

"I don't know," he said in a quiet voice.

Sarah set down her cup on the coffee table and drew up her knees to her chest. She wrapped her arms around herself, wishing it was Lucy she was clinging to instead of her own legs.

"I didn't adopt her to replace him," she whispered.

Finn looked over sharply. "What?"

"Lucy." Her throat burned. "I didn't want her as a replacement for Jason."

"I never thought that was the reason for the adoption."

"No?"

"No," he said firmly. His features creased. "But four years ago, when you…"

Shame tugged at her. "When I pressured you to try for another baby? I shouldn't have done that. It wasn't fair to you. Wasn't fair to either one of us." A heavy sigh escaped her mouth. "You were right, you know. That time, I *was* trying to find a replacement. I just wanted Jason back so badly. Having another child was the only way I thought of to make it happen, but I re-

alize now that it was a mistake. Jason couldn't be re-
placed."

"No," he said thickly. "He couldn't."

"I'm sorry, Finn."

"So am I."

They fell quiet, each lost in their own thoughts, until
the doorbell rang and squashed the first sense of peace
she'd felt in days.

"I'll get it," Finn said, standing up.

He left the room, returning a few moments later with
Jamie and Cole in tow. Sarah instantly tensed when she
caught the identical expressions on the couple's faces.
Something was up, she could sense it.

"I hope we weren't interrupting," Jamie said, fidgeting with her hands.

Sarah studied the other woman's face. Something
was up, all right. "No, it's fine. What's going on?"

"Cole and I had something we needed to discuss
with you."

"Sit down," Finn offered, gesturing to the two arm-
chairs opposite the couch. "I'll get you guys some
coffee."

"No," they said in unison.

Sarah's eyebrows rose.

"I just want to get this over with," Cole added, his
face awash with reluctance. "Let's not waste time."

As Cole and Jamie sat down, Finn joined Sarah on
the couch. This time, he sat right beside her, and her
heart did a little lurch as he took her hand in his. She
could tell he felt the same unease, picked up on the
black cloud that seemed to creep into the room and
hang over their heads like a canopy.

"What the hell is going on?" Finn burst out when

neither Cole nor Jamie said a word. "You're scaring Sarah. Hell, you're scaring me a little, too."

Jamie cleared her throat. "Okay. Well. Cole and I were going over the files Sarah gave Parsons and his team. We may have found something."

Sarah squeezed Finn's hand, unable to stop the hope that soared along her spine. "Something that might lead us to Lucy?"

Jamie and Cole exchanged troubled looks. "Maybe," Jamie said. "But first….Cole, you say it. I still don't even know if I believe it."

Cole leaned forward in his chair, clasping his hands on his lap. "Like Jamie said, we were looking at the files, and I noticed something in one of Lucy's medical records. She has a birthmark on her left shoulder, shaped like a—"

"Star," Sarah finished. She shot him a confused look. "I don't get it. Why is that important?"

"It may not be. Except…"

"Except what?" Finn barked. "Where are you going with this, Donovan?"

"Teresa had a star-shaped birthmark on her left shoulder," Cole blurted out.

Sarah gaped at him in shock. Well, she hadn't been expecting that. But what on earth was he getting at? So what if Cole's ex-wife had a similar birthmark as Lucy?

She quickly voiced her thoughts. "Lots of people have birthmarks. It's just a coincidence."

"Are you sure about that?" Jamie asked in a soft voice.

Sarah bristled. "What are you saying? That because Teresa and Lucy have star-shaped marks on their shoulders, then they're…what, related?"

Nobody said a word.

The implication settled over Sarah like a patch of thick fog. No. No, that was absolutely *ridiculous*. Strictly coincidence. Teresa had a birthmark. Lucy had a birthmark. Big deal. That didn't mean Teresa was...

"She's not Lucy's mother!" Sarah exploded, stunned that anyone could even think it. "Birthmarks aren't even hereditary. This is just a weird coincidence."

"Sarah," Cole began. He stopped, cleared his throat, and plowed on. "It's not just the birthmark. That's what caught my attention, because Teresa's mark was so damn distinct, you know? But Jamie and I were talking it over, and we realized there might be more."

"Teresa left town nine months ago," Jamie spoke up. "She told everyone she was moving to Raleigh to start a new life and put this sorry town behind her. She was gone for six months and came back to Serenade three months ago—the same time you brought Lucy home."

"That doesn't mean anything. She wasn't pregnant when she left," Sarah protested. "People would have noticed."

"She only would've been three months along. Early enough that she wouldn't be showing," Jamie said.

Sarah's mind was reeling. This was absurd. Teresa lived in Raleigh for six months. Sarah had adopted Lucy from Raleigh. This wasn't one of those dumb riddles—Bob is a lawyer, lawyers are sharks, therefore Bob is a shark. There was no proof, nothing written in bright neon announcing that Teresa Donovan had given birth to Lucy.

She suddenly grew light-headed. Letting go of Finn's hand, she rubbed her forehead, trying to clear her brain. Lucy was hers. *Hers.* She'd sat in a hotel room for two days while the birth mother was in labor. She'd held her for the first time in the nursery at Raleigh General.

She'd brought her home to Serenade—one week after Teresa changed her mind about the mysterious relocation to Raleigh.

No.

Coincidence.

Black dots moved in front of her eyes, making her sag forward.

"She's *not* Lucy's mother," she choked out. "She can't be…"

God, what if it was true?

What if Teresa Donovan had left town to conceal her pregnancy, given birth to Lucy and put her up for adoption?

What if Sarah had adopted *Teresa's* baby?

The breath drained from her lungs, while her palms went damp and started to tingle.

She heard Finn's voice saying her name, but it sounded distant, muffled. The black dots got bigger, shrouding her vision. She leaned forward, trying to breathe through a fresh wave of dizziness.

And then she fainted.

"Damn it, Jamie," Finn snapped as he held Sarah's unconscious body in his arms. "Why the hell did you two have to come here and drop this on her? It might not even be true!"

Jamie probably answered, but he didn't hear a damn word. Sarah had fallen off the couch when she'd passed out, her right temple snapping against the leg of the coffee table. She wasn't waking up, and panic rapidly entered his bloodstream, making it hard to think clearly.

"Call Bennett," he ordered as he cradled Sarah's head in his lap.

He pushed dark strands from her face, gently stroking her cheek as he said, "Wake up, sweetheart. Come on, Sarah, wake up."

He heard Cole talking on his cell phone, but all he could focus on was Sarah. Her face was completely devoid of color, save for the slight redness at her temple. She hadn't hit her head too badly, or at least it didn't look like it, but it worried him that she was still out cold.

Fighting a rush of anxiety, he pinched one of her cheeks, then cupped her chin. "Sarah...baby...open your eyes."

There was a soft moan, and she stirred in his arms, bringing an explosion of sweet relief to his body. He watched as her eyelids fluttered and then opened. Mystification swarmed her gaze as she stared up at him.

"Finn?" she mumbled.

"It's me. I'm here," he said roughly.

She shifted, slowly twisting her head. "I...passed out?"

"Yeah, you were out for a few minutes." He helped her into a sitting position, wrapping an arm around her as they sat there on the hardwood floor. Jamie and Cole were standing, each one donning a look of remorse.

Good, let them feel bad. What had they been thinking, showing up here and revealing that Teresa Donovan, the wicked witch of Serenade, could possibly be the biological mother of Sarah's adopted daughter?

His teeth clenched at the mere thought of it. Sure, he'd always thought it strange that Teresa had left town for no apparent reason, only to waltz back six months later as if she hadn't even been gone. But that was Teresa for you. Unpredictable, impulsive.

Manipulative, evil...

Hell, he didn't blame Sarah for fainting from the news.

"Bennett's on his way," Cole announced.

"Travis?" Sarah cried, her head snapping up. "No, call him and tell him not to come. I'm fine."

"You hit your head," Finn replied tersely. "I want to make sure you don't have a concussion."

She blew out a frustrated breath, wiggling from his embrace. "I don't have a concussion. I just fainted."

She tried standing, but he noticed her legs were still shaky and promptly rose to help steady her. And then it was him and Sarah, facing off with Cole and Jamie. Tension filled the air.

"It can't be true," Sarah finally said. "I know you guys think it might be, but I refuse to believe that Teresa gave birth to my daughter."

"Then you won't mind if I get my P.I. to investigate," Cole said gruffly.

From the corner of his eye, Finn saw Sarah blanch. "What?" she protested. "No."

"I know you don't want to believe it, but we need to find out if it's true," Jamie said in a gentle tone. "Sarah, if Teresa is Lucy's biological mother, then that changes everything."

"How?" Sarah whispered. "How does it change anything? Lucy is still mine. She's *my* daughter, Jamie!"

"Of course she is, honey. I just meant that it could shed new light on the abduction."

Finn's shoulders straightened. Damn. As much as he hated to even consider the possibility, the birthmark and Teresa's abrupt disappearance were hard to ignore. Jamie was right. If the unthinkable really was true, then Lucy's kidnapping could be connected to that. The Bureau had been looking into people who might hold a grudge against Sarah, people who might want to punish her by stealing her child, but if the child was *Teresa's*…

well, that could provide a different motive. A different suspect.

"The biological father," Jamie spoke up, as if reading Finn's thoughts. "That's just one example of someone who might've taken Lucy."

Finn stiffened as a nauseating thought occurred to him. "I swear to God, Donovan, if you're the father of that baby…"

Cole flinched as if he'd been struck by a fist. "What? *No.* Teresa and I had already been separated when she moved to Raleigh."

"And you didn't get together at all?" Finn asked with narrowed eyes.

"I would rather have waxed my back than touch that woman." With the contempt dripping from his tone, Cole's declaration was more than convincing.

Jamie held up her hand. "We're getting off track here. Cole is not the father. We don't even know if Teresa is the *mother.* But Sarah, we need to pursue this. We need to."

Sarah sagged against him and Finn felt her resolve begin to crumble. "Fine," she relented, glancing at Cole. "Get your investigator to look into it, but don't feel bad about wasting your money if this leads to a dead end." She stuck out her chin. "Which I think it will be."

Cole was already flipping open his cell phone and moving toward the doorway. Jamie shot Sarah an apologetic look. "I guess we'll head home, then. I'm so sorry for giving you such a shock. But Cole and I spoke about it and decided we had no choice but to tell you about our suspicions. We weren't trying to hurt you, Sarah, please believe that."

Sarah let out a sigh. "I'm sorry I freaked. I know

you weren't trying to hurt me. Like you said, it was a shock."

Although he was reluctant to let go of her arm, Finn did, so he could escort Cole and Jamie to the door. He couldn't resist frowning at the two of them as they left Sarah's house.

When he walked back to the living room, he forced Sarah to lie down, despite her insistence that she was perfectly all right. He asked her to humor him, which she did, though her lips twitched when he shoved a pillow behind her head.

He wasn't sure why he was acting like a mother hen, but he couldn't shove away the image of Sarah collapsing onto the floor, or her pale, unconscious face. At least the doctor would be here soon, though Finn tensed when he realized he'd pretty much just given Travis Bennett an invitation to come over and spend time with Sarah.

They were just friends, she'd told him the other day. He clung to those four words, determined to keep his growing jealousy at bay, but when Bennett showed up ten minutes later, Finn had trouble controlling himself.

"Sarah, are you all right?" Travis demanded when he saw her sprawled on the couch.

Friends, his ass. The way Bennett charged toward her like a damn white knight was hard to ignore. So was the way the good doctor knelt by the sofa and proceeded to put his hands all over her.

All right, one hand. And he was just examining the red spot on Sarah's temple. Nevertheless, the sight of another man touching Sarah made Finn see stars. Breathing through the sudden onslaught of protectiveness, he stood at the opposite end of the couch, keeping his hands pressed tightly to his sides.

When Bennett finally took his hand back, Finn let out a slow breath. "It's not a concussion," Bennett concluded, smiling down at Sarah. "Your pupils are fine, no nausea and you're completely coherent. I think you'll live."

Finn gritted his teeth when Sarah returned the doctor's smile. And then his jaw almost cracked when she reached to touch Bennett's arm. "Thanks, Travis. I wasn't worried, but Finn is a little overprotective."

Bennett glanced at Finn with warm brown eyes. "Well, not to worry, Sheriff. She'll be just fine."

"Then I guess you can be leaving now, doc," Finn said brusquely. "I'll take it from here."

With a tender smile, Bennett reached out to give Sarah's arm a squeeze.

Finn clenched his jaw again.

"Take it easy tonight," Bennett told his patient. "And remember, don't hesitate to call if you need anything."

"I'll take care of her," Finn practically snapped, advancing on the doctor.

Taking the hint, Bennett zipped up his black Windbreaker and allowed Finn to march him out the door. When Finn returned to the living room, Sarah was sitting up, a frown marring her mouth.

"You didn't have to be so rude to him," she said coldly.

"I didn't like the way he was touching you," he retorted, a note of anger in his voice.

"He was examining me. At *your* request." She blew a stray strand of hair out of her face, her frown deepening. "What's your problem with him, anyway? Travis is a nice man."

Finn mumbled something under his breath.

"Was that even English?" she demanded. "Seriously,

Finn, quit acting like a damn caveman. Travis is my friend, and I didn't appreciate the way you treated him."

"And I didn't appreciate him *touching* you," he grumbled back.

She shook her head, her liquid brown eyes filling with amazement. "So what if he touched me? Why do you care if—"

"Because *I* want to be the one touching you," he interrupted, frustration coursing through his blood. "Because I want to be your damn *friend*." He cursed loudly. "No, scratch that, I don't want to be your friend, Sarah. I want to be your *everything*."

She went stricken. "What…what are you saying exactly?"

"I'm saying I love you."

The baby wouldn't stop crying. She'd endured three hours of Lucy's earsplitting howls and it was beginning to seriously try her patience. She wasn't sure she blamed the baby, though. She was pretty miserable, too, holed up in this isolated cabin instead of boarding a plane that would take them to the Bahamas. But arrangements were still being made for the little beach house in Nassau, and there was no way she could show up at the airport with Lucy in her arms. No, not until the media storm died down and news of the kidnapping faded from people's minds.

She rocked Lucy in her arms, watching the rain streak the dirty windowpane. The baby's sobs were finally ebbing, much to her relief.

"I know you don't like it here," she murmured. "I don't, either. But I promise you, it's only temporary. Soon we'll be somewhere warm and sunny, and we'll walk along the sand and look at the ocean…."

Lucy's tiny eyelids started fluttering.

She experienced a burst of joy. Was the baby starting to feel comfortable with her? It was about time. She was Lucy's mother now, and these past two days of hearing Lucy cry and cry hadn't been a walk in the park.

As the baby slept in her arms, she gazed dreamily out the window, pretending she was looking at the calm turquoise ocean in the Bahamas. Soon. God, soon.

The cell phone on the little wooden table beside the rocking chair started to vibrate, yanking her from her happy thoughts. Shifting the baby, she snatched up the phone and pressed Talk before the vibrations woke Lucy.

"It's about time," she said after recognizing the caller ID. "You said you'd call four hours ago."

"I know. I'm sorry." The voice on the other end of the line sounded strained. "I had some things to take care of."

"I hope you're referring to the travel arrangements," she snapped, "because I'm getting sick of this place. So is Lucy."

"I'm doing everything I can, but we discussed this. The kidnapping is all over the news. Lucy needs to stay hidden for a while."

She frowned. "How long is a while?"

"Until people forget about her. Until you can take her out in public without someone yelling *kidnapper* and calling the police."

Valid point. She bit back the urge to argue, knowing that hiding was the smartest move at the moment.

"But you're making plans," she pressed, unable to mask the urgency in her tone.

"Of course I am." There was a pause. "Don't worry,

everything is under control. Just stay inside and take care of the baby. I'll call you tomorrow."

She hung up the phone and cuddled the baby against her breasts, happiness suffusing her body and bringing a rush of serenity.

"Soon," she whispered to the sleeping child. "We'll get out of here soon, baby girl. And then we'll disappear, far away, where nobody can ever take you away from me."

Chapter 11

Sarah was dizzy again, only this time it had nothing to do with her recent fainting spell and everything to do with the fact that Finn had just said he'd loved her.

A part of her was basking in the warmth of those three words, fighting the temptation to hurl herself into his arms and never let go. But that was the old Sarah. The one who'd been madly in love with this man and dreamed of sharing her life with him.

The new Sarah was older. Wiser. The new Sarah had put the past behind her and accepted that she and Patrick Finnegan were simply not meant to be. They'd had their shot over four years ago. And they'd failed. When a cruel twist of fate had mercilessly destroyed their lives, they'd had a choice: swim together or sink alone.

Well, Sarah had wound up at the bottom of a cold, dark abyss. She'd drowned in grief and depression, wildly flailing her arms in hopes that Finn would pull her out of that terrible place. But he hadn't been there for her.

So go ahead and call her a coward, but she had no intention of drowning again, and that's what getting involved with Finn represented to her.

"Did you hear me?" he asked gruffly, slowly sinking down on the other end of the sofa.

"I heard you," she murmured.

His blue eyes narrowed. "And you have nothing to say? No reaction?"

Sighing, she linked her fingers together and rested them on her thighs. "What is there to say? I'm sure you meant what you said, but—"

"Damn right, I meant it. I love you, Sarah. I've loved you since the day we ran into each other at the lake."

She fought the wave of nostalgia that swelled in her belly. "That was a long time ago."

"Maybe it was. But my feelings for you have never changed."

He edged closer, so that his hard thigh was inches from her socked feet. She wanted to pull her legs up, to avoid contact, but she was rooted in place, drawn to the fierce look on his handsome face.

"I'm a different man, sweetheart," he began, his voice raspy and thick with emotion. "Back then, I wasn't strong enough to handle everything that happened. I left because I didn't have the balls to fix things, and it's a choice I've regretted every day for these last few years."

Exasperation rose in her throat. "We can't keep talking about this, over and over again. You already told me all of this, and I believe you, Finn. I truly believe you regret what happened between us." She drew much-needed air into her lungs. "And I can see that you've changed. You're more mature, calmer. I see that."

He sounded as frustrated as she felt. "Then why are you holding back? Why not give us another chance?"

"Because I've changed, too."

Finn looked startled by her admission. "What do you mean?"

"I mean that I'm not the same twenty-three year old who buried her son. I had a mental breakdown, for God's sake. I spent two years in therapy trying to put my life back together piece by piece. I grew up, too."

"Then we're both in a better place. A healthier place." He let out a breath. "Let me prove to you that I can be different this time around. That I can be there for you, and take care of you."

"Take care of me? You arrested me!" A muscle in her jaw twitched. "Besides, I can take care of myself."

"I know you can. That's not what I meant." He looked frazzled. "I'm just saying I want another chance."

"And I'm saying I don't think I want to give it to you."

Pain descended on his face, but since she'd already come this far, she might as well finish.

"I don't trust you, Finn. And I don't have that same rosy outlook you suddenly seem to possess. Obstacles are always going to pop up. Even if we did get back together, there would be rough patches, arguments." She swallowed. "I don't trust that you'll stick around."

"You'll never know if you don't give me a chance."

"Maybe if I didn't have Lucy, I could do that. But I'm a mother now. I need to provide stability for my child, to give her a happy, healthy life. What if I bring you into our home and she gets attached to you, only to be abandoned if things get too tough for you again? I won't take that chance."

He recoiled as if she'd slapped him. And then his features went hard. "I won't give up, you know. I will make you trust me again, Sarah."

She almost smiled. The steely resolve in his eyes was so achingly familiar. She was reminded of that bad boy who'd been determined to win her over all those years ago. On their first date, he'd pushed for a second. On their second, a third. When she'd gotten cold feet about moving in with him, he'd seduced her with red roses and a gourmet dinner and mind-blowing sex, until she'd given in.

Not that it had been a chore. Back then she would've done anything to be with this man. Nobody knew her like Finn. They *got* each other. They both tended to be too serious, neither was quick to laugh, but together, they laughed and teased and spoke of things neither of them had told anyone else before. She'd always been scared of that deep bond, that unbreakable connection.

Well, not so unbreakable. Finn had severed it when he'd walked out the door.

And she hadn't been lying. Maybe things could have been different if Lucy weren't in her life. Maybe she could have risked her heart and allowed him back in. But she would never risk her daughter's heart. Never.

Finn's cell phone jolted her back to reality. Saved by the foghorn. She got the feeling they would've talked around in circles if not for the interruption, and though the twinge of hurt in Finn's eyes made her heart ache, she was glad she'd told him where she stood.

Finn glanced at the screen, then muttered an expletive.

Sarah's heart stopped. "Is it about Lucy?"

"No, it's the D.A." He lifted the phone to his ear and said, "Finnegan."

Sarah watched with growing anxiety as Finn spoke with Jonas Gregory. Well, Finn did most of the listening, and whatever Gregory was saying, Finn didn't look happy. He said "Yes, sir" several times, and at one point, she noticed his fingers tightening over the phone, knuckles turning white.

When he finally hung up, her anxiety was at an all-time high. "What did he say? Was it about the case?"

Finn gave a quick nod.

"What did he say?" she repeated.

After a second of visible reluctance, Finn spoke. "He wants me to send him a report and some supporting documents of the evidence against you. He's taking the case to the grand jury for an indictment."

The breath drained from her lungs. "What does that mean?"

"The grand jury will decide the charges that will officially be brought against you."

She swallowed. "But they might also dismiss the case altogether, right?"

"It's possible but unlikely. I think you're going to be indicted, Sarah."

She suddenly felt really, really cold. "When is Gregory meeting with them?"

"Monday."

Monday. That gave them five days. Five days to find Lucy and catch Teresa's real killer. Talk about pressure.

Fortunately, Finn looked shockingly calm about it. She watched as determination crept into his blue eyes, burning like a roaring bonfire. "When I told you I would get you out of this mess, I meant it," he said sternly. "I won't let you go to prison for something you didn't do."

"And if I'm indicted? If I'm *convicted?*" She couldn't keep the terror from her voice.

His jaw hardened. "You won't go to jail. Even if I have to whisk you from the damn country, you won't be going to jail."

Shock crashed into her like a tidal wave. Was she hearing him right? Had he actually just admitted he'd break the law before letting her be incarcerated?

For one long moment, she was tempted to take back everything she'd said only minutes ago. Maybe she *could* trust him again. Maybe that leap of faith he'd begged her to take didn't have such a steep drop. Finn loved his job. He was proud of his position, his service to the people of Serenade. If he could even consider throwing it away just to help her, then maybe he truly *had* changed. Enough to merit a second chance.

Her mind started spinning again. It seemed to be doing that a lot these days.

God, she couldn't think about this anymore. Not when her daughter was missing. Lucy was her main focus right now—her *only* focus.

And everything else, her conflicting feelings for Patrick Finnegan, her fear and doubts, heck, even her impending indictment…it would all take the backseat until her daughter was returned to her arms, safe and sound.

Sarah walked into the living room the next morning and found Finn sprawled on her sofa, dead to the world. Her breath caught in her throat at the sight of him. He wore nothing but a pair of black boxer-briefs that couldn't hide the impressive bulge at his groin. She swept her gaze over his bare chest and admired his defined pectorals, the dusting of dark hair that led to his waistband. Her heart thumped in a persistent drumbeat, getting faster as she stared at his muscular thighs, the long legs dangling off the end of her couch. He was the most perfect male specimen, all muscle and sinew and sleek golden skin.

She couldn't help but smile at the way he had one arm flung haphazardly over the side of the sofa. He'd always had the habit of stretching out in his sleep. She couldn't count how many times she'd woken up curled into a tiny ball at the very edge of the bed while Finn monopolized all the space.

Deciding not to wake him, she went into the kitchen to brew a pot of coffee, her smile fading when she noticed Lucy's bouncy seat on the table. Pain somersaulted inside her chest. God, why hadn't they found Lucy yet? Finn had assured her that Parsons and the other agents were doing everything they could. Apparently the Bureau's kidnapping unit had alerted all the major airports and border crossings, providing photos of Lucy and ordering officials to keep their eyes out for anyone traveling with a child matching Lucy's description. But other than the tip from the boutique owner in Grayden, none of the leads that had come in had amounted to anything.

Sarah poured herself some coffee, but the hot liquid didn't erase the chill in her body. She wanted her baby back, damn it. Her gaze dropped to her ankle monitor and she experienced a burst of anger. She couldn't even search for Lucy outside Serenade. She'd never felt so powerless before, not since she'd lost Jason.

Footsteps came from the hallway and then Finn appeared, rubbing the sleep from his eyes. He'd put on his jeans and the gray sweatshirt he'd had on yesterday. "Morning," he murmured. "Will you pour me a cup while I go wash up?"

"Sure."

He left the kitchen and she stood there, staring at the empty doorway. She wasn't sure why he'd even stayed the night, especially after the exasperating heart-to-heart they'd shared, but Finn had insisted he didn't want her to be alone. She didn't like admitting it, not even to herself, but she'd felt comforted when she slid into bed last night, knowing he was right downstairs.

Not that she'd slept. She'd tossed and turned the entire night, thinking of Lucy and Finn and Jason and everything she'd lost.

"Jamie and Cole are on their way over," Finn announced when he strode back into the room ten minutes later. He accepted the mug she handed him and took a long sip.

Sarah's heart dropped. "Why? Did Cole's P.I. find something?"

"Jamie didn't say. She only said they were coming."

Putting down her cup, she ignored the uneasy feeling in the pit of her stomach and headed for the door. "I guess I'll shower and dress, then."

She quickly hurried upstairs and showered, then slipped into a pair of black yoga pants and a stretchy green V-neck sweater, not bothering with a bra. Panic rose inside her as she dressed. Her hands wouldn't quit shaking, making it tough to roll on her black ankle socks. Why were Cole and Jamie coming over? What had they found out?

She'd been trying desperately not to think about what they'd told her yesterday, but now the frightening prospect returned in full force, causing her hand to tremble even harder as she ran a brush through her damp hair.

What if Teresa was Lucy's biological mother?

The brush dropped from her hand and fell onto the vanity table as she contemplated the outrageous thought. She'd despised Teresa Donovan. Teresa had been the cruelest woman Sarah had ever met. She slept around, went after other women's husbands, mocked people for the fun of it. Sarah had always believed that every human being possessed one redeemable quality, had *something* good about them, but not Teresa. That woman hadn't been human.

She'd been a monster.

Sarah stared at her reflection in the mirror, finally finding the courage to ask the one question she'd been avoiding since Cole and Jamie had shared their suspicions.

Would she love Lucy less if Teresa turned out to be the baby's birth mother?

The second the thought entered her brain, fury rose up her chest and clamped around her throat. No. *No.* She would love Lucy just the same, and *that* revelation grabbed the anger and transformed it into soaring liberation.

Lucy was *her* daughter. It didn't matter who gave birth to her. She was *hers.*

Squaring her shoulders, Sarah went back downstairs, picking up on the murmur of voices coming from the kitchen. Cole and Jamie were here. So was Agent Parsons, she discovered in dismay when she walked into the room. The fair-haired man was helping himself to a cup of coffee, and he greeted her with a smirk when she entered.

"Good morning, Ms. Connelly."

"Morning," she muttered before turning to the couple sitting at the table. "What did you find out?"

"I'm wondering the same thing," Parsons said. He frowned at Finn. "I see you've been running some sort of side investigation, and I don't appreciate being kept out of the loop."

"Oh, relax, Mark," Jamie grumbled with a frown of her own. "Finn had nothing to do with this. Cole and I ran this lead all by ourselves."

"And why is that?" Parsons asked, his nasty stare now directed at the auburn-haired profiler. "As I recall, you took a leave of absence. You have no business interfering with this case."

Sarah tried not to raise her eyebrows. The animosity between Jamie and Parsons was palpable. She hadn't noticed it before, when they'd both been here the morning after Lucy was taken. But now it was obvious there was no love lost between the two of them, and Jamie's hostile reaction to the man only reaffirmed Sarah's own dislike. Jamie was the most levelheaded person she'd ever met; if she didn't like Parsons, then that meant he truly was the pompous jerk Sarah had pegged him to be.

Jamie scowled. "Mark, why don't you just drink your coffee and let Cole tell everyone what we found out, okay?"

Parsons looked like he was inwardly seething, but he kept his mouth shut, gesturing for Cole to take over.

"My private investigator visited the adoption clinic yesterday evening, but as expected, they refused to divulge any records without a warrant." Cole spared a glance at the federal agent. "Perhaps you can arrange for one, if you see fit. Anyway, after my guy struck out, he visited several hospitals in the area and did some digging."

Sarah bit the inside of her cheek. "And?"

"And he found a record indicating that Teresa was admitted into St. Mary's Hospital on June 23." Cole paused in discomfort. "She gave birth to a baby girl."

Sarah gasped, leaning against the counter for support. June 23. That was the birth date the adoption clinic had provided her for Lucy. Oh, God. It was actually *true*.

"There was a birth certificate on record, listing Teresa as the mother, though she used her maiden name. The father was unknown. After that, my guy worked backward, tracking down the clinic Teresa visited during her pregnancy. She had monthly checkups and apparently took good care of herself. She put her own name on the birth certificate, but everything else she did while using the name Valerie Matthews."

"Are we sure it's Teresa then?" Finn said in a clipped tone. "Maybe Valerie is the one who gave birth."

Cole shook his head. "It's not possible. Valerie was here in town when Teresa moved to Raleigh. I ran into her several times." He scowled. "She loved to yell at me about divorcing her sister."

Finn let out a breath. "Yeah, you're right. I remember seeing her around, too, and she definitely wasn't pregnant."

"Ahem."

Everyone turned toward Parsons, who was angrily setting down his mug, his eyes flashing with irritation. "Are you saying that Teresa Donovan was the biological mother of Ms. Connelly's child?"

Jamie shot him a *duh* look. "Yes, Mark, that's what we're saying."

He went silent for a moment, then twisted around in his chair. Sarah found a pair of ice-blue eyes staring her down.

"Is that why you killed her?" he asked pleasantly.

The air swooshed from her lungs. *"What?"*

Finn was already scraping back his chair. "What the *hell*—"

Parsons stood before Finn could even finish the outraged exclamation. Crossing his arms over his chest, the agent glanced at Jamie with a cold smile. "You realize you've only succeeded in strengthening my case, right, Crawford?"

Her lavender eyes blazed. "What are you talking about?"

"Motive, Crawford." Parsons turned to bestow that same reptilian smile on Sarah. "You found out Mrs. Donovan was your child's mother, didn't you, Sarah? Was she regretting the adoption? Did she want her baby back?"

Sarah felt as if someone had slapped her. "What? No!"

"Did you kill her when she threatened to fight for her child? With your mental illness, you probably just snapped, didn't you, Sarah? She wanted her kid back, and you shot her in the—"

"Enough!"

Finn's roar reverberated in the kitchen. Before Sarah could blink, he had Parsons by the collar and was slamming the other man against her bright yellow wall. The anger rolling off Finn's big body spiked the temperature in the room by a hundred degrees, and she suddenly couldn't tear her eyes off him. Here he was, the sexy macho jerk she'd fallen for all those years ago, with that possessiveness that made her want to clobber him and at the same time melted her heart.

"Watch your mouth, you son of a bitch!" He shook Parsons hard, and Sarah's eyes widened. "She didn't kill anybody."

Parsons's face was beet red, his breaths coming in harsh pants. With his palms pushed against Finn's chest, he sidestepped his hold, his eyes wild as he glared at the man who'd just accosted him. "I'll have your damn badge for this, Finnegan! How dare you lay a hand on me!"

Finn was breathing just as hard. "You were out of line, Parsons."

"Why, because you're sleeping with her?" the other man spat out. "That's another reason I'll fight to get your badge taken away."

Finn looked ready to launch himself at the agent again, and this time Sarah refused to let him do it. It might have brought a tiny spark of pleasure, watching him defend her like that, but she wasn't going to let him throw away the career he'd worked hard to obtain because of some slimy jerk.

"Stop it," she ordered, her sharp tone snapping in the air like a whip. "I won't have you brawling in my kitchen like a bunch of damn teenagers. My daughter is *missing!*"

Both men went shamefaced, though she noticed neither one apologized. To each other, anyway. But Finn did shoot her a sheepish look and murmur, "I'm sorry." He slowly unclenched his fists. "You're right. Lucy is all that matters. The only thing we should be doing right now is finding her."

"And I think I have an idea about who may have taken her," Jamie spoke up from across the room.

Sarah spun around. "Who?" she demanded.

"Yes, Crawford," came Parsons's mocking voice. "Who took the child?"

Jamie got to her feet and approached the tense group. "You said so yourself, Mark. In child abductions, a family member is usually the perpetrator."

The agent's eyes narrowed. "Are you suggesting the child's biological father is responsible?"

"He could be, but that's not who I had in mind." Jamie gave a wry shrug. "Seeing as Teresa had more lovers than Hugh Hefner, I doubt she even knew who the father was, and if she did, I can't see her informing him that he was going to be a daddy." She slanted her head. "No, I'm thinking a different kind of family member."

Sarah gasped, the thought slicing into her brain just as Jamie voiced it.

"I think Valerie Matthews did it. Lucy's aunt."

Chapter 12

"No answer," Finn said grimly, striding up to the Jeep where Anna waited.

They were parked in front of Valerie Matthews's small townhouse, located in a residential area a few blocks from Main Street. Valerie hadn't come to the door when he'd rang the doorbell, and from the days' worth of mail piled up on her front stoop, it was clear she hadn't been home in a while. According to the law office she worked at, Valerie had taken a leave of absence one week ago. Personal time, she'd told the senior partner at the firm, claiming she planned on traveling for a couple months. But Finn didn't buy it. Not one bit.

Valerie had taken Lucy. They might not have proof of it, and hell, no evidence that Valerie had even been aware of her sister's pregnancy, but Finn's instincts rarely failed him and they were pointing all sorts of fingers at Valerie Matthews.

"She's not there, huh?" Anna said quietly.

"No, I think she's already skipped town."

"With Lucy?"

He gave a harsh nod. "I'd bet my life on it."

They both grew silent, frustration building in the air. And tension. He was suddenly aware of that, too, and guilt prickled his skin as he met his deputy's eyes.

"Anna," he started roughly, "I wanted to—"

"Apologize?" she filled in, her dark eyes twinkling.

Her playful expression caught him off guard. "I can't even begin to tell you how sorry I am that I had to question you," he said. "I never thought for a minute you had anything to do with Lucy's kidnapping."

The young woman sighed. "You were covering all your bases. I know that, boss. Can't say it didn't sting a little, though."

His guilt deepened, filling his belly. Lord, he was just alienating everyone around him, wasn't he? Arresting Sarah, interrogating Anna.

"You've definitely had a streak of bad luck," Anna said, as if reading his mind. "First Cole, then Sarah, now me."

He swallowed down a gulp of anguish, but she hurried on before he could apologize again. "Nobody thinks it's your fault, boss. A woman was murdered. A baby was abducted. I know you have a job to do, no matter where the evidence takes you."

Her gentle reassurance brought a rush of peace. He'd needed to hear that. He'd worked damn hard to get to where he was, going from a punk with a chip on his shoulder to a devoted deputy under the former sheriff. When he'd been elected to serve his townspeople, he'd never felt prouder. For years, he'd been sullen, miserable, lashing out at anyone in his path because the one person he really wanted to strike out at—his mother—was too fragile and messed up, already a victim of something completely out of her control.

But he'd battled the anger and bitterness and turned things around for himself. Being Serenade's sheriff gave him a sense of worth, a sense of belonging. Yet it didn't give him the sense of sheer *completeness* that Sarah did.

He loved his job, but Sarah…that was a whole different kind of love. She brightened his life in a way nobody ever could. She was so damn smart, so kind and patient. She could light up a room with her smile, and when she was happy, that happiness soared outward and made him feel as though he'd been touched by a ray of sunshine.

He was determined to win her back. Now that he knew the reasons holding her back, her fear that he'd abandon her and her daughter, he was determined to prove her wrong.

"So, what now?" Anna asked, interrupting the detour of his thoughts. "How do we track down Valerie?"

Finn's phone came to life then, and he quickly pulled it out of his pocket. He glanced at the caller ID and nodded in satisfaction. "Hopefully this will point us in the right direction."

"Finn, my investigator just left the adoption clinic in Raleigh," Cole barked in his ear, getting right to the point.

"And?"

"Valerie knew about Lucy."

The confirmation sent a streak of triumph through him. "You sure?"

"Oh, yeah." Cole made an unintelligible sound. "I swear, those Matthews women know how to get what they want. My P.I. flashed her picture to the employees—this time the director let him inside the clinic. Apparently she realized a missing child was more important than red tape. She claims that she never released Lucy's file to anyone, but my guy got a suspicious feeling about one of the lab techs working there.

"He talked to the kid alone, got him to admit that he'd let Valerie into the records room about a month after Teresa was killed." Cole swore in annoyance. "She seduced the poor guy, right in the damn file room. He left her alone for ten minutes, and when he came back, she was gone. He couldn't be sure she got a look at any of the files, but I'm inclined to think she did."

"Me, too," Finn said with a sigh. He mulled it over. "So somehow she figured Teresa had been pregnant, and she got her confirmation by checking the adoption files. She found out Sarah was the adoptive mother, and took it upon herself to steal the baby."

"Or she had help," Cole offered. "Jamie wasn't sure if the attacker was a man or a woman. Valerie could have arranged for someone to take Lucy."

"Maybe, but at the moment, Valerie's the only one we're certain about." Finn's lips tightened. "She has the baby, Cole. What's your investigator doing to track her down?"

"He's going over her credit card records as we speak, but we're not hopeful about it. She wouldn't be stupid enough to leave a paper trail."

"You never know. Another thing about the Matthews women—they act first, think later. We just need to pray that she slipped up."

"I'll keep you posted."

Finn hung up and tucked the phone away, turning to Anna with a hard look. "Valerie knew about Lucy."

"I got that much from your side of the conversation." She was already moving to the passenger side of the Jeep. "What do we do now?"

He slid into the driver's seat and started the engine. "I'll drop you off at the station, and then I'm heading to Sarah's. I'll call you once I hear from Cole. If we find out where Valerie's hiding, I want you and Max with me."

Anna's brown eyes shone with pleasure. "Really?"

He took his hand off the gearshift and lightly touched her arm. "I already told you once, but I'll say it again. Neither Sarah nor I thought you took that child. You're a terrific cop, Anna, and I feel better knowing you have my back."

She murmured a soft thank-you, and Finn could feel the tension leaving her body. At least one woman in his life was capable of forgiving him.

Now he just needed to win over Sarah.

"What do you mean, I have to stay here?" Sarah demanded after he'd told her where he was going.

Finn smothered a sigh as he noticed her outraged expression and the determined slash of her mouth. Damn it, he knew that stubborn look. It probably mirrored his own.

They'd received the news from Cole's investigator ten minutes after Finn strode into Sarah's house. Valerie Matthews had purchased groceries eighteen hours ago at a gas station in Holliday, a small county two towns over from Serenade. The purchase might not mean anything—could've been a pit stop on her way out of state, making her long gone by now—but they couldn't very well ignore it, either.

Holliday was a tiny township, consisting of a hand-

ful of cabins nestled deep in forested areas. It was
home to loggers and hermits, the ideal place to live
among nature and escape the world. As far as hiding
spots went, it was damn perfect. The homes were isolated enough that neighbors wouldn't hear the cries of
a three-month-old baby, and Finn knew for a fact that
several of the cabins were owned by a property agent
who handled rentals through an internet site. Use a fake
name, a bogus credit card, and you have a place to stay
for a few weeks.

According to the investigator, Valerie hadn't rented
any property using her card, but that didn't mean she
wasn't in Holliday. She'd seduced a lab tech at the adoption clinic, for chrissake. She could've easily figured
out a way to pay for a cabin without using her credit
card.

"You can't come with us," Finn said, trying to keep
the irritation from his voice.

Sarah's brown eyes flashed. "I don't believe this.
You're actually keeping me away from—"

"I mean you *can't* come," he interrupted, running
a hand through his hair. He shot a pointed look at her
ankle. "You physically can't."

Sarah's gaze dropped, her mouth trembling as she
stared at the electronic monitor clamped around her
ankle. Her entire face crumpled in disappointment,
sending a hot rush of pain to his gut.

With her lips quivering like that, he knew it was
a matter of time before she started to cry, and so he
quickly placed his hands on her slender waist and
pulled her close. After a moment of hesitation, she sank
into his embrace.

"I know you want to be there," he said, threading
one hand through her silky dark hair. "And I wish to

God I could take you with us, but if that monitor starts beeping, the D.A. will be alerted and you'll be thrown back in jail. You won't be of any use to Lucy if you're behind bars, sweetheart."

"I know," she whispered. Pulling back, she locked her gaze with his. "Do you think she's there, in Holliday?"

"I don't know," he admitted. "This could be a total dead end. Valerie's credit card might have been stolen, or if she did use it, she might have just been stopping along. But if Lucy's there, we'll find her."

Parsons would probably kill him for taking the credit away from the federal agent, but Finn had no intention of involving the FBI during this search. He'd spoken to Jamie about it, and she'd agreed, warning him that Parsons would go in guns blazing. Since he had no desire to see Lucy—or hell, even Valerie—get hurt, Finn had opted to keep this road trip from the special agent. He and Anna would be taking one car, Jamie and Max would take the other, and the four of them would do this on their own. Holliday was a minuscule county, not even on the map, and with only forty or so houses in the area, they could be in and out of there before Parsons even figured out they were gone.

Finn just prayed his gut wasn't steering him in the wrong direction. He didn't want to waste manpower looking in the wrong place, but he couldn't ignore the information from Cole's P.I., either. If Lucy was in Holliday, he damn well planned on finding her.

"Will you call me the second you know?" Sarah asked, her hurt voice making his chest squeeze.

"The second I know," he echoed, stroking her hair.

He gazed into her eyes, swallowing when he noticed

that a new emotion had joined the angst and grief on her face. He saw a flicker of heat, even a burst of pride.

"You'll get her back for me, won't you, Finn?"

"Even if I die trying, sweetheart."

She searched his face once more, and then her lips were moving against his own as she kissed him so deeply, so passionately, he couldn't take a breath. She tasted like coffee and sugar and something distinctly Sarah. Her tongue pushed its way into his mouth and he was helpless to hide his immediate reaction. She let out a soft moan when she felt the hard ridge of his arousal against her belly, kissing him even harder.

His heart was slapping against his ribs when they finally pulled apart, and he almost didn't hear her as she whispered, "Don't."

"Don't what?" he asked gruffly.

"Die trying." She gave a little sigh. "I want Lucy back, but I don't want you to get hurt. Just...promise you'll be careful, okay?"

It was hard to speak through the monstrous lump in his throat. "I'll be careful." He swept his gaze over her one last time, smiling at her red, swollen lips, her silky smooth cheeks and delicate chin. "I have to go now. I'll call you when I know something."

As he left Sarah's house and walked toward the driveway, his chest was full of emotion. His mouth still tingled from that surprise kiss, the taste of Sarah imprinted there. It drove him mad, that she was right there in front of him, yet so out of reach. It had taken him four years to realize his mistakes, to grow up and become the man Sarah had wanted him to be back then.

Now that he was ready, *she* wasn't, and he had no idea how to change her mind.

Find her daughter, then worry about the rest.

It was a sobering thought, one he held on to as he hopped into the Jeep and drove away from Sarah's house.

Anna was waiting for him in the parking lot of the police station when he pulled up ten minutes later. He'd asked her to wait there, just in case Parsons was peeking out the window. According to Max, the agent was in Finn's office, preparing a statement for the press about the status of the investigation.

"Jamie and Max already left for Holliday," Anna said as she got into the Jeep. She unfolded a square of paper and handed it to him. "Jamie said they'd check all the houses she marked in blue. We're in charge of the red ones."

Finn glanced at the map, pleased to see there were only about two dozen red circles. The clock on the dash read twelve-fifteen. It would take about forty-five minutes to get to Holliday, where they'd have the entire day and night to dig around. His gaze dropped to Anna's feet, and he gave a pleased nod when he saw she'd changed into hiking boots as he'd requested. Some of those cabins required a trek and a half through the forest, which he wasn't particularly looking forward to.

Yesterday's rain was nowhere in sight as they set off in the direction of the highway. The sun was high in the sky, bright enough that Finn grabbed his aviator sunglasses from the cup holder and slipped them on his nose. He checked the rearview mirror, spotting the baby seat he'd taken from Sarah and buckled in the backseat. Was he placing too much hope on this? Maybe. But his hunches rarely steered him wrong, and from the moment Cole told him about the grocery purchase on Valerie's card, the nape of Finn's neck had been tingling.

"Okay," Anna said, her nose buried in the map. "The first house is right after the exit ramp, so don't miss the turnoff."

They didn't say much during the long drive. Finn was too tense. Too chock-full of adrenaline. He kept thinking of Sarah's anguished face when he told her that she couldn't come with him. He wished she could be here with him. He'd been wishing it for four years.

He slowed the Jeep when the exit for Holliday County came into view. Just as Anna had instructed, he turned right at the first turnoff, steering onto a dirt path that led to a sprawling ranch house in the distance. Ten seconds later, disappointment crashed into him, as he realized they'd struck out on the first try. Five towheaded children, ranging from toddler to preteen, were playing in the front yard, shrieking with delight as they dashed through an arch of water created by the lawn sprinkler. A woman with a big straw hat sat on the porch, reading a magazine.

Anna looked equally disappointed. "I don't think we'll find anything here."

Finn concurred, but they still had to be certain. Hopping out of the Jeep, they approached the porch, where they spent five minutes chatting with the woman in the straw hat, while Anna watched the children in the yard with faint longing in her eyes. They didn't linger long, just enough for Finn's gut to tell him that this perfect family wasn't aiding and abetting a kidnapper, and then they were off to the next house. And then another. And another.

It was nearly three o'clock when Anna crossed off yet another address on their map. They'd visited thirteen houses, and no Valerie or Lucy at any of them.

Jamie and Max were striking out, too, each phone call causing Finn's spirits to sink a little bit lower.

"Maybe she really did just pass through here," Anna said, sounding glum as they drove toward their next location.

"It's starting to feel that way," Finn confessed.

"Turn left there."

He followed her directions, and they ended up on yet another dirt path, this one winding several times before abruptly ending in front of an iron gate. The two halves of the metal barrier were chained together at the middle, a *No Trespassing* sign nailed to one of the wooden posts on each end of the gate. Beyond it, the terrain was rocky, surrounded by tall trees letting in flashes of sunlight through the thick leaves.

"Looks like we're walking," Finn remarked.

Anna grumbled under her breath as they got out of the car. "Well, hopefully we don't find ourselves facing down the barrel of a shotgun again. That guy at the last house was totally scary."

He grinned. "You could have taken him."

"Is that why you hid behind me? Because you knew I could take him?"

"Naah, I just forgot to bring my bulletproof vest," he kidded.

Laughing, she followed him into the trees. Finn kept his hand on the butt of the Beretta poking out of his holster, but he knew they probably wouldn't encounter any threats. So far, the visits had been harmless, except for the shotgun man who lectured them for trespassing.

The sun shone up above, making beads of sweat pop up on his forehead. Even with the shade of the trees, it was damn hot outside. They walked at a brisk pace, sidestepping fallen logs and the occasional poison ivy bush, until the trees thinned out and Finn glimpsed a small, A-frame cabin through the branches.

His instincts hummed.

"Stay behind me," he told Anna in a low voice.

She immediately fell back and he took the lead, keeping his gaze trained on the innocuous-looking cabin a few hundred yards away. The cabin had a tin roof and a narrow wraparound porch, the weathered logs at its exterior gleaming in the afternoon sun. There was no driveway, just yellow-green grass and broken lawn furniture. The sagging porch swing creaked as the breeze hit it.

The place looked abandoned, and with no car in sight, he doubted Valerie would have chosen this as her hideout. Walking through the forest with a three-month-old infant wailing in her arms? He couldn't picture Valerie having the patience for that, and he was about to tell Anna they should turn around when she suddenly hissed out a breath.

"There's someone at the window, boss."

He followed her gaze, instantly seeing what she had. A pale face in the window, unrecognizable from this far away. They picked up the pace, staying in the trees as they advanced on the cabin. The closer they got, the more excited he felt. There was definitely someone standing in the window. A woman, judging from the long hair. Long *black* hair.

Valerie.

"Stop," Finn ordered, pausing next to one of the thick redwood trunks.

From this point on, they would no longer have the cover of the trees. They would enter the clearing in front of the cabin, completely visible to the woman in the window. Finn was debating whether to run for the door when a baby's cry sliced through the air.

"Lucy," Anna whispered.

Finn let out a soft expletive. His fingers hovered over the butt of his gun, but he couldn't bring himself to draw the weapon. What if Valerie was armed, too? What if she freaked when she saw them and hurt herself or the baby?

"What do we do?" Anna demanded in a hushed voice. "Should we break down the door?"

"She'll see us coming before we could even make it to the door." Tension knotted around his muscles. "Okay. We walk up, slowly." He unholstered his weapon and gestured for Anna to do the same. "Follow my lead."

Finn uttered a silent prayer, then stepped away from the trees, his stride cautious. There was a flurry of movement in the window. Valerie had bolted away from it.

He took a breath. "Valerie!" he shouted. "It's Finn— I'm just here to talk!"

He and Anna approached the cabin, but he signaled for her to stop before she could climb the porch steps.

"Valerie, we're putting down our weapons, okay? We're not armed."

Although Anna looked reluctant, she mimicked his actions by placing her weapon on the grass, next to his.

Finn swore he saw the tattered curtain at the window move. "Valerie!" he shouted again. "Come out here. I just want to talk."

There was no response, no face in the window, and then a baby's distressed wails came from inside the house. Finn sprang to action, leaving his weapon on the grass as he charged to the door. He was prepared to kick it in, but a try at the doorknob and he realized it was unlocked.

He burst into the musty-smelling cabin and found the main room empty, but Lucy was still crying, the high-pitched shrieks pulsing from the back of the house. Finn took off toward the corridor, his heavy boots thudding against the weathered wood floor. He heard another cry, a muffled female curse, and skidded to a stop in front of the door at the end of the hall.

His heart jammed in his throat as his gaze registered everything. Valerie Matthews stood by a white-painted crib, clutching Sarah's daughter to her chest. Her raven hair was falling into a pair of wild gray eyes, which widened in shock and anger when she spotted Finn in the doorway.

"No!" she cried, her voice sizzling with fury. "I won't let you take her away from me, Finn!"

He took a cautious step forward, then halted when Valerie clutched the baby even tighter. "Valerie," he said softly. "Val, look at me."

Those silver eyes looked out of focus as they connected with his. "You can't take her, Finn."

To his shock, tears slid down her ivory-pale cheeks. Lucy opened her mouth and belted out another shriek. Valerie looked down at the baby as if she couldn't comprehend why the child would be crying.

"She's always crying," Valerie whispered. "She's always crying. Maybe she knows..." She stared at him in misery. "Do you think she knows I'm not her mother?"

Finn had no idea what to say. From the corner of his eye, he saw Anna entering the hallway, holding the gun he'd ordered her to drop. He gave an imperceptible shake of the head, silently ordering her to stay put.

This situation was too perilous. Valerie didn't look like she was going to hurt Lucy, but she was obviously distraught. She was shaking, crying even harder now, while the baby shrieked and wiggled in her arms.

"Valerie…why don't you put Lucy in the crib so you and I can have a little chat?"

Her jaw hardened. "Do you think I'm stupid? The second I put her down, you're going to shoot me!"

"I'm not going to shoot you." He raised both arms, then did a little spin. "I'm not armed. My gun is sitting outside on the grass. I don't want anyone to get hurt here, especially you or the baby."

She blinked rapidly, her face stained with her tears. "I know you probably think I've gone insane, but I had to take her, Finn. There's so much you don't know about—"

"I know Teresa is Lucy's biological mother."

Valerie gasped. "You do?"

He nodded.

"Then you understand why I had to do this!"

She shifted the baby so that Lucy's head rested on her shoulder, but that didn't abate the child's wails. Finn's temples were beginning to throb from those shrill noises.

"Lucy belongs with me," Valerie said, gently patting the baby's back in a soothing motion. "I'm her aunt. My little sister would want me to take care of her daughter. You understand, right, Finn?"

He swallowed. "I do understand. But Val…Lucy is Sarah's daughter now. She adopted—"

"She stole her from Teresa!" Valerie roared.

Evidently picking up on the anger vibrating from the body of the woman who held her, Lucy's cries kicked up another notch, the ear-splitting volume making both Finn and Valerie flinch.

"That nutcase knew Teresa was the birth mother!" Valerie went on. "That's why she killed her! So Teresa wouldn't take the baby back!"

Her growing agitation worried him, and he took a few more steps toward her. She growled at him and he halted again, speaking above Lucy's shrieks. "Sarah didn't kill your sister. And she didn't steal Lucy. Teresa gave up her legal rights, Val. She *gave* her baby away."

Valerie hiccupped, her hand moving to cup Lucy's downy head. That only got Lucy going even more, and the frustration swimming in Valerie's gray eyes grew. "Please stop crying," she begged the screaming, red-faced infant. "Just stop crying. You're safe, little girl. I'm here, baby."

Finn took her momentary state of distraction to make his move. He bounded across the room, ignoring Valerie's shocked gasp as he plucked the baby from her arms. With Lucy tucked against his chest like a football, he stepped away, temporarily losing the function of one eardrum as Lucy howled into it.

"Give her back!"

Valerie's enraged snarl had him hurrying to the doorway where Anna was waiting. As adrenaline coursed through his blood, he deposited Lucy into his deputy's arms and snapped, "Go! Get back to the Jeep."

Anna spun around without a word, reaching the end of the hall just as Valerie launched herself at Finn, nearly knocking him off his feet. Her fists pummeled into his chest, her tears soaking her face as she pounded at him for all she was worth, sobbing and yelling incoherently.

"How could you," she choked out. "How could—" she sobbed "—you do that? She's mine."

Finn grabbed hold of her fists and locked them between his hands. Valerie's heartfelt cries were even worse than Lucy's. In that brief moment, he actually saw the real Valerie Matthews. The daughter of the town drunk, the insecure, needy woman who had never caught a single break in life, whose sister had been taken away from her, whose only living relative had just been whisked out of this sad, dismal cabin.

"How could you," she whispered, her sobs mixed with quiet, unsteady pants.

With a sigh, Finn pulled her close, wrapped his arms around her, and listened to her weep.

Chapter 13

Sarah could make out the sound of a baby crying. Even in her dream, she recognized Lucy's wail, those little hiccups and the breathy wheezing noises at the tail end of each cry. *I'm coming,* she yelled in the darkness. *I'm coming, Lucy.*

The screams only grew louder, the darkness thicker. Panic spiraled through her and then her eyelids snapped open. She gasped for air, disoriented as her gaze darted around the room. She was in her bedroom. Sunlight streamed in through the open curtains. It was nearly four o'clock, according to the alarm clock. Finn had been gone for hours, and somehow, despite the terror and anticipation wreaking havoc on her body, she'd managed to fall asleep.

"Just a dream," she murmured to herself, waiting for her raging pulse to slow.

So why did she still hear her baby crying?

Fighting back tears, she stood up, wrapping the two ends of her long shawl around her. She was so cold. So damn afraid. The muffled sound of Lucy's cries echoed in her head, driving her absolutely insane.

"Sarah?"

Finn's voice.

She went still. She hadn't even heard him come in.

And Lucy's wails were still ringing in her brain, making her—oh God, they were coming from downstairs!

The oxygen left her lungs and her legs nearly collapsed beneath her. She wasn't imagining it. She could *hear* Lucy!

Tearing out of the room, she flew toward the staircase, disbelief and pure joy spinning inside her like a tornado. When she saw Finn at the bottom of the stairs, she let out a cry, then bounded down the steps and grabbed Lucy from Finn's outstretched hands.

"Oh, my God," she said through her tears. "Oh, my God, you found her."

She clung to her child, breathing in the sweet scent of shampoo and baby powder. The warm bundle squirmed in her arms, but she didn't ease her grip. She held Lucy tight as tears poured down her cheeks and sprinkled into Lucy's face. Lucy didn't seem to mind, though. Her distress faded, as if she realized she was exactly where she belonged and had no need to voice her displeasure any longer.

"Oh, my sweet baby," Sarah whispered.

Through a sheen of moisture, she saw Finn watching the reunion with a gentle smile on his rugged face. He looked happy and triumphant and relieved, and she found herself moving into the arms he opened, letting him envelop her and Lucy in his strong embrace. The feel of his hands running over the small of her back brought a rush of warmth. Even Lucy seemed to be enjoying the hug, letting out a jubilant gurgle.

"Thank you," Sarah said, lifting her head to meet his gorgeous blue eyes. "Thank you for bringing her home."

Raw emotion moved across his face. "It was my pleasure."

Swallowing, Sarah stepped out of his arms, still holding Lucy close. "Valerie?" she asked quietly.

He nodded. "She was hiding in a cabin in Holliday. Max and Anna took her to the station. She's charged with kidnapping."

Sarah didn't feel an ounce of sympathy. Valerie Matthews had stolen her child. It didn't make a difference if the woman was technically Lucy's aunt. Sarah knew she could never forgive Valerie for what she'd put her through. All those hours of worrying, crying, wondering if she'd ever see her child again. What Valerie had done was unforgivable.

"Do you…do you think she killed Teresa, too?" Sarah asked, holding her breath. If Valerie was the killer, that would make things so much easier, but to her disappointment, Finn shook his head.

"I don't think so. She has an alibi, but more than that, I think she's truly devastated about losing her sister. Teresa was the only family she had. That's why she took Lucy, because she no longer had her sister." He sighed. "Parsons is dealing with her, since the abduction is his case, as he continually likes to remind me. But when I spoke to him on the phone to tell him the news, he reminded me, not so nicely, I might add, that you're still charged with murder."

"And in five days, Gregory will get his indictment," Sarah said dully.

"Which means I need to step up my game and find the murderer," Finn answered, steely determination in his eyes.

She couldn't help but smile. "You haven't done enough already? You brought my daughter home."

"And now I'm going to make sure she stays home. With her mother."

Their gazes locked, and Sarah experienced a burst of longing. She wanted so badly to sink into his arms again. She wanted to kiss him again.

Obviously the relief talking. Just because Finn had kept his promise and brought Lucy home didn't mean she ought to open her heart to him. Her daughter was still her first priority, and letting Finn get close to Lucy, only to have him leave again, wouldn't be good for anyone.

Lucy opened her mouth and gave the cutest little yawn, her sleepy eyes causing Sarah to focus on the present. "I need to give her a bath and put her down to sleep," she said.

"And I need to get to the station. I want to be there when Parsons talks to Valerie."

They stood there at the foot of the stairs, each of them fidgeting. Sarah got the feeling he didn't want to leave. And she didn't *want* him to leave, yet she knew it was for the best. She was so extremely grateful to him for finding Lucy, and yes, maybe she was feeling those little sparks of longing, but right now, she needed to focus on her daughter. She could sift through her conflicting feelings for Finn later.

He seemed to be waiting for her to say something, and his shoulders sagged a bit when she didn't. "All right, I'd better go. I'll let you know what happens with Valerie."

Holding Lucy against her breast, Sarah followed him to the door. As he reached for the doorknob, she was the one hesitating this time.

"Do you want to come back for dinner?" she blurted out.

His hand stilled on the knob. The lopsided smile he gave her was utterly appealing. "Do you want me to?"

She managed a nod.

"Okay. What time?"

"We'll have to make it a late dinner. Give me a few hours, and maybe show up around eight-thirty? I'll whip up some pasta. I know you like steak, but I haven't been shopping for groceries since…since everything," she finished awkwardly.

"Pasta sounds great," he said gruffly. He moved his gaze to Lucy, another smile lifting his mouth. "I'm glad she's home. Take good care of her, Sarah."

"I will."

With a quiet goodbye, he left the house. Sarah locked up after him then headed toward the stairs. Lucy had fallen asleep in her arms, and a rush of tenderness flooded Sarah's belly as she stared down at her sleeping child.

Lucy was home.

Finn had brought her home.

Gently stroking Lucy's unbelievably soft cheek, Sarah walked upstairs, holding her beautiful daughter.

Finn stopped off at his house to shower and change after he left the police station, but didn't bother with a shave. He knew Sarah had a thing for his scruffy look, and right now, he needed every weapon in his arsenal to win her over. She was warming up to the idea. He'd seen it in her eyes earlier, when she'd invited him to dinner. He knew she was scared—he'd seen that on her face, too, but he planned on proving to her that she had no reason to be afraid.

He'd grown up these past few years, acknowledged the grave mistake he'd made when he'd walked out of Sarah's life. All he needed now was a chance. A chance to show her that everything could be different this time around.

He'd probably have a better shot at it if he found out who the hell had killed Teresa Donovan. As long as Sarah had this murder charge hanging over her head, she would be less open to the idea of accepting him back in her life. Why would she, if she would only be hauled off to jail?

He'd hoped that Valerie would help shed some light on that topic, but to his extreme frustration, she was refusing to talk. He and Parsons had attempted to question her, but gone was the woman who'd cried in Finn's ly hours ago. The old Valerie had returned, with sense of self-importance and that nasty r failed to annoy him. She'd coldly r lawyer would at the point where he'd take all the assistance he could get, even if it came from Valerie Matthews.

He could think about all that tomorrow, though. Tonight he simply wanted to convince Sarah to give him a second chance.

After slipping into a clean pair of jeans and a black cable-knit sweater Sarah had given him years ago, he left his bedroom and headed downstairs, acutely aware of the complete lack of furniture or decoration in the main floor of his farmhouse. He hadn't grown up here—the house he'd shared with his mother had been sold years ago—but this farmhouse gave him the same sense of loneliness his childhood home had evoked. He'd bought this place hoping to build a life with Sarah. After she'd moved in, they had so many ideas about what to do with the place, how to renovate it, but within two months, Sarah got pregnant, and the only room they'd focused on was the nursery.

The nursery was still up there, across from the master bedroom on the second floor. He hadn't even cleaned it out, simply locked the door and for— self to forget about what lay inside. Ja— sky-blue wallpaper and shelves of — in four years when he climbed the porch and knocked on the door, she didn't answer. He considered using the doorbell, but didn't want to wake Lucy if Sarah had just put her down. Instead, he let himself in and quietly called her name.

Again, no answer, but he knew she was home. Her purse was on the little credenza in the hall, as were her car keys. He almost raised his voice and called out again, then realized he knew exactly where she was.

Taking the stairs two at a time, he made his way to Lucy's nursery, pausing in front of the doorway. The room was dark, save for a Winnie the Pooh night-light plugged into the wall by the door. In the dim glow, he saw Sarah standing by Lucy's crib, her long hair falling over like a silky curtain as she gazed down at her child.

"Sarah," he murmured.

She jumped, spun around, then relaxed. "Hey," she whispered. "Talk quietly. She's sleeping."

Moving slowly so his boots wouldn't thud against the floor, he approached the crib and peered down, his chest becoming hot. Lucy was on her back, looking sweet and clean in a pink sleeper, her eyelids closed in slumber. A smile tugged at his mouth when he noticed that her bottom lip was sticking out in a little pout.

"She's beautiful," he said.

Sarah gave him a sidelong look. "I know, isn't she? I haven't been able to stop looking at her. I swear, I've been standing here for the past two hours, just watching her sleep." She suddenly gave a little gasp. "Shoot, dinner!"

The baby stirred at her mother's outburst, and Sarah quickly lowered her voice before continuing. "Finn, I didn't even start dinner yet. I was—"

"Watching your daughter sleep," he finished with a faint smile. "No worries. We'll fix something together."

Not that he was even hungry. His stomach had been in a state of clenched anxiety since the dinner invitation. Probably not the most masculine reaction, but he couldn't get rid of those damned butterflies fluttering around in his gut. This was the closest he'd come in years to getting Sarah back, and a part of him desperately feared he'd blow it.

Sarah reached down to stroke her daughter's cheek, then tucked the thin blanket up to Lucy's chin. "Okay, let's go downstairs and—"

A loud beep broke the peaceful silence, followed by three more sharp chimes that had Finn ushering Sarah out of the nursery. He closed the door behind them, then peered down at her ankle with a frown. The bracelet displayed a red light, which blinked in time with the beeps.

Sarah's lips tightened. "I forgot to change the batteries."

The electronic monitor was a reminder of yet another obstacle that stood in his path, and Finn resisted the urge to put his fist through the wall. Lord, she didn't deserve this, being kept on a damn leash while the real murderer roamed the streets, free to do whatever the hell he wanted.

Trying to hide his anger, Finn took her arm and led her to the bedroom. "Do you still keep batteries in your nightstand?" he asked.

She laughed. "You remember that?"

He was already yanking open the top drawer. "You used to keep everything in there. Batteries, spare keys, pencils, Band-Aids—I never understood why you needed all that stuff so close at hand. That's what hall closets are for."

"A nightstand is as good a place as any," she protested.

"Whatever you say, sweetheart." He rummaged around in the drawer, which was filled to the gills, until he finally found an unopened pack of batteries. "Sit down, I'll do it for you," he said over his shoulder.

He heard the bedspread rustle as she lowered herself on the mattress. Tearing open the cardboard, he took out two fresh batteries and knelt on the floor in front of Sarah. She seemed to hesitate, then raised her foot. She'd changed into a pair of knee-length black leggings and an oversize green sweater that hung down to her knees. She wasn't wearing any socks, and her pale pink toenails made his mouth go dry. So did the sight of her sleek calves and delicate feet.

When he placed her foot in his lap, her breath hitched. "Are my hands too cold?" he asked gruffly.

She slowly shook her head. "No."

Finn swallowed in order to clear the sawdust from his mouth. Then he popped open the small compartment on the ankle bracelet, removed the dead batteries and slid in the new ones. The second he snapped them in place, the beeping stopped and the red light went off, but for the life of him, he couldn't let go of her foot.

Her skin was hot to the touch. When he moved his gaze up her body, he noticed her nipples poking against the front of her sweater. The material was so thin, he could tell she wasn't wearing a bra, and his mouth promptly turned into a desert once more.

Unable to stop himself, he caressed the arch of her foot.

"Finn," she breathed. "What…what are you doing?"

He didn't answer. Wrapping his fingers around her other ankle, he caressed her smooth skin, then dragged both hands up to her knees, her thighs, her waist, her flat belly. He could see her pulse throbbing in her graceful neck, but the expression on her beautiful face was encouraging. He saw anticipation, heat.

He moved his hands higher, resting them just below the swell of her breasts. He waited, met her eyes again, and glimpsed only desire. Emboldened, he cupped her breasts over her sweater, squeezing the full mounds and eliciting a shaky sigh from her lush mouth.

"Finn," she murmured again.

"Tell me to stop," he murmured back. "Say it, and I'll walk out of this room."

Her mouth opened. He waited, praying she didn't say those words.

"Touch me," she whispered.

Joy shot through him. Before she could change her mind, he tangled one hand through her hair and tugged her toward him, kissing her hard and deep. She gasped against his mouth, then relaxed, parting her lips so he could slide his tongue inside, so he could lick and explore and drink her in.

Every muscle in his body was coiled tight. His groin throbbed, the erection straining against his zipper harder and more painful than ever. He'd been with a few women since he and Sarah broke up, but none of them had inspired this primal reaction inside of him. None of them had made his heart pound and made him hungry with desire. Sarah was the only one who did that, the only one who could satisfy his appetite, his need.

As their tongues danced and dueled, he bunched up the hem of her sweater and pulled the material over her head. Her bare breasts gleamed in the patch of moonlight shining through the open window. He went dizzy for a second, lost in the incredible vision of those mouthwatering mounds and the tight pink nipples begging for his attention.

When he lowered his mouth and sucked one rigid bud deep in his mouth, Sarah moaned, then cupped his head and brought him closer, welcoming him, trapping him. He circled each bud with his tongue. Sucking, licking, while his hand moved between her legs to rub her over her leggings.

She gasped, arching off the bed, and when her thighs parted slightly, he cupped her fully, grinding his palm over her hot core.

"Let's get these clothes off," he rasped, already moving to his waistband.

Sarah looked as anxious as he felt, and soon their clothes were being peeled off and thrown aside, until they were both naked and stumbling onto the bed. He covered her body with his, groaning at the feel of her soft curves beneath him, her peaked nipples rubbing against his chest.

Burying his face in the crook of her neck, he kissed the soft flesh there, gliding his mouth down to her collarbone then resuming his ministrations on her breasts. Her fingernails dug into his shoulders, her legs scissoring relentlessly as she moaned in pleasure.

"I've missed this," she whispered.

"Me, too," he said hoarsely.

He sucked her nipple deep in his mouth, then blew a stream of air over it, enjoying the way it hardened, the way she sighed. Turning his attention to the other breast, he slid his hand between their bodies and teased her core, finding her damp and swollen and drenched with desire. He stroked, explored, then pushed his finger inside of her, nearly losing control when her inner muscles clamped around it.

Lord, he could touch her for hours. Days. And never grow tired. He dipped his head and kissed her again, and when she swept her tongue over his bottom lip, he groaned. Knew without a doubt that this was where he belonged. This was who he belonged with. No, who he belonged *to*. He was Sarah's, always had been, always would be.

"You're teasing me," she choked out as he drew another finger into the fold.

He shot her a heavy-lidded look. "Are you complaining?"

"No, just contemplating payback."

"Payba—"

Before he could finish, she had her palms on his chest and was pushing him off her. He rolled onto his back, his pulse kicking up a notch when Sarah straddled him. She leaned forward, her thick dark hair cascading over one shoulder and tickling the hair on his chest. When her warm mouth pressed a kiss on his scorching skin, he almost lost it again. Breathing through his nose, he clenched his fists at his sides, forcing himself not to move.

Sarah's eager hands and wicked tongue had him seeing through a red haze of arousal. She placed open-mouthed kisses on his chest, her tongue darting out to taste one flat nipple. His world began to spin, potent desire sizzling his nerve endings. He forgot how to breathe as she moved down his body, getting perilously close to the erection threatening to turn this mind-blowing encounter into total embarrassment.

Gritting his teeth, he allowed her mouth to close over

his tip. Her tongue to trace a path along his shaft. One soft lick, two—and then he gently grabbed hold of her hair and yanked her up.

"I'm too close," he murmured.

A playful smile lifted the corners of her lush mouth. "What happened to the famous Finnegan endurance?"

He choked on a laugh. "It took one look at your sexy naked body and ran out the door."

Her responding laughter only made him harder. He loved the way she laughed, that melodic, throaty lilt. It had been far too long since he'd seen the amusement dancing in her eyes.

Sarah climbed off him, eliciting a jolt of disappointment. But then he realized she was turning to her trusty nightstand, and anticipation kicked in. She found a condom and handed it to him, and his damn hands shook as he put the thing on. He felt like a teenager again, out of control, nervous that he might screw this up.

But Sarah wasn't complaining as he covered her body again and slid into her in one powerful thrust. Moaning, she hooked her legs around his waist, the heels of her feet digging into his buttocks as he moved inside of her. The feel of her tight heat surrounding him made him groan in sheer desperation. It wasn't enough. He needed more. Needed to be deeper.

Their mouths fused together, tongues swirling in a hot, reckless kiss as he quickened his pace. He thrust into her, over and over, harder, faster, until a wild cry escaped her lips and she shouted his name. When she moaned a fervent *Yes* and shuddered beneath him, he toppled right over the edge.

Shards of pleasure assaulted his body, sizzling down his spine and filling his groin. With a hoarse groan, he let go, letting release take over, his body shaking and throbbing from the unbelievable sensations.

When he finally crashed back to earth, he heard Sarah laughing again, the beautiful sound tickling his chest. Cranking open his eyes, he peered down at her and muttered, "Something funny?"

She wrapped her arms around his damp back and pressed a kiss to his shoulder. "Nope. Not funny, just amazing."

Unable to let her go, he rolled them over so that he was on his back, Sarah's head resting against his chest. His heart continued to pound, every muscle in his body contracting and throbbing with lingering pleasure.

As he lay there holding Sarah, sated beyond belief, warmed by love and emotion, he couldn't stop his next words from slipping out of his mouth.

"Will you give me another chance?"

Chapter 14

Leave it to Finn to take the most incredible sexual afterglow and turn it into thick, throat-clogging tension. Sarah slid up and leaned against the headboard, the pleasure coursing through her body transforming into a dull ache of pain. Why did he have to push this? She'd thought that sex would be enough for him, but Finn was never satisfied with halfway. He always wanted it all.

Not that she'd slept with him to make him forget his desire to get back together. She'd wanted him. *Craved* him, and she couldn't deny that this man still had incredible power over her. He made her body sing, he made her feel alive.

But he also had the power to destroy her.

"Did you hear me?" he asked in a rough voice.

She sighed. "Yeah, I did. I just don't know what to say to that, Finn."

Fully naked, he got up and picked his boxers off

the floor, quickly slipping them up to his trim waist. She couldn't wrench her gaze away from his spectacular body, his muscular thighs, washboard stomach, the dusting of dark hair on his sleek chest. With his black hair messed up from their lovemaking and the stubble dotting his strong jaw, he looked rugged and sexy and unbelievably appealing. She'd always been a sucker for his scruffy look.

The expression in his eyes made him appear more dangerous than usual, a glimmer of anger and disbelief, directed at her. "You could say yes," he finally replied. "You could agree to give us a second chance."

Frustration crept up her throat. "I already told you before, this isn't just about us anymore. I have Lucy to think about now."

He looked wounded. "Do you think I would ever hurt her?"

"Not intentionally," she murmured. "But...I just don't want her depending on you, or falling in love with you, only to have you walk out if things don't work out between us."

He moved to the foot of the bed, curling his fingers over the wooden bed frame. "Who says it won't work out?" His features creased. "I don't remember you being a pessimist."

"I'm realistic," she snapped, suddenly growing annoyed with all of this. She hopped off the bed and searched for her underwear, finding her panties under the bed and her sweater hanging over an open dresser drawer. In their passion, they'd thrown items of clothing all over the place, and it only irritated her more as she gathered up the garments and got dressed. She always seemed to lose control when Finn was around.

"You're scared," he corrected, bending down to pick up his jeans.

The anger in the air hissed and crackled as they each dressed in a rush, as if the cotton and denim and other materials could protect them from the tension brewing between them.

"I understand why," he went on, looking shamefaced. "I broke your trust when I walked out on you, but the only way I can prove to you that I've changed is if you give me another chance. If you take a leap of faith and open your heart to me again."

She swallowed. "I don't know if I can."

"Then why am I even here?" he shot back.

She stared into his eyes and saw the dissatisfaction boiling there. He was right. Why *was* he here? Why had she allowed him to make love to her, why was she willing to give him her body, but not her heart?

Because he already broke it once.

"I love you, Sarah."

His quiet voice pierced right into her heart and made it ache.

"I want to be with you," he went on, his voice hoarse. "But not as an occasional lover, someone you sleep with whenever it tickles your fancy. I want a relationship with you."

Tears stung her eyes. A part of her wanted to throw herself into his arms and tell him that she loved him too, but those three frightening words got stuck in her throat like a wad of gum. She couldn't stop thinking about the last time she'd said those words, when she'd been curled up on their kitchen floor, pleading with him to stay.

"I don't know if I can give you what you want," she

whispered. "I can't make a decision like this on the spot. I need…time."

His jaw stiffened. "So you can think in circles and come up with reasons why we shouldn't be together? I can't sit around while you decide if I'm worth loving again. Either you love me, or you don't. Either you want to try again, or you don't."

"You're not being fair," she protested. "Why does everything have to be so black and white with you?"

"Because in this case, there's no gray. I'm in love with you, sweetheart. I want to be with you and show you I've changed. So either you're willing to take the chance, or you're not."

Silence stretched between them, an impassable chasm Sarah couldn't bridge. Everything he said made sense. If things were to work out between them, she *had* to take that chance. But fear was holding her back. No matter how hard she tried, she couldn't swallow down the terror coating her throat.

"Move back in with me," Finn said suddenly.

Her eyes went wide. "What?"

"Let's start over, Sarah. Live together again. There's even a nursery for Lucy."

Panic shuddered through her. "I…I can't. This is too fast for me, Finn. I can't make any of these decisions right now."

His expression clouded. "No, you're just too scared to make them."

She clenched her teeth, so hard her jaw started to hurt. "And you think dropping ultimatums is going to make me less afraid? God, Finn, I'm only asking for time. Why does everything have to be done your way, when *you* want it?"

"Because we've wasted enough time already," he

said hoarsely. "Because I love you and want to be with you." He met her eyes. "The question is—do *you* want to be with *me?*"

That same rope of fear wrapped around her throat. "I…"

Her voice trailed, and Finn sucked in a harsh breath. "I'll take that as a no then."

She made one final attempt to make him see reason. "Finn, come on, don't be like this."

His shoulders were stiff as he headed for the door. "I'm sorry, Sarah, but I won't wait around for you to decide if you love me or not."

She gaped at him. Why was he being so damn difficult? This had nothing to do with love, and he knew it. It was about trust. Faith. And yes, fear. But how could he blame her for being afraid after what happened the last time?

Her body tightened with irritation. Fine, if he was going to be a total jerk about this, she wasn't about to indulge him.

"Then go," she said coolly. "Because there's no point in you sticking around, right?"

His blue eyes flickered with hesitation, then hardened in resolve. "No, I guess there isn't."

And then he walked out the door.

It wasn't until eleven o'clock the next morning that Finn managed to get Valerie Matthews alone. She'd been with her lawyer for the past two hours, a man from the firm where Valerie worked as the office manager. Finn had loitered in the hall the entire time, waiting for his chance, which finally came when Valerie's attorney left to get himself and his client some lunch. Finn ducked into the neighboring interrogation room, waited until the man's footsteps retreated, then slid out and entered Valerie's room.

She scowled when he came in. "I have nothing to say to you, Finnegan."

"I don't suppose you do," he said pleasantly. "But I've got a lot to say to you."

He sat across from her, and for a moment, he didn't see Valerie, but Sarah. He remembered how distraught Sarah had been when he'd questioned her, how hurt. It almost thawed the icy band around his heart, the pain that had plagued him since he'd left Sarah's house last night.

He probably shouldn't have given her an ultimatum. He regretted it now, but at the time, he'd been too annoyed to think straight. Not even the incredible sex they'd shared had managed to convince her to let him back in. He'd already saved her child, and now he was racing to find the killer in order to clear her name. He wasn't sure what else he could do to prove to her that he truly loved her, that he'd genuinely changed.

Shoving away the bitterness, he focused on Valerie, deciding to go for the blunt approach. "You're going to jail, Val. Whatever your lawyer has been telling you, there's no way you're walking away from this without jail time."

Her gray eyes flashed. "You're a small-town sheriff. What do you know?"

"I know that no jury is going to buy a temporary insanity plea, or whatever your lawyer will have you say." He clasped his hands together. "You planned the kidnapping. You had a cabin ready—my deputies have been going through the place and informed me that you stocked up on supplies. This has premeditation written all over it. You're going to jail."

Some of her confidence chipped away. "I won't."

"Sure you will." He leaned back in his chair, as if he had all the time in the world, when in reality, a ticking clock was going off in his head. Four days. Gregory was taking Sarah's case to the grand jury in four days, unless Finn found a way to stop him.

"But your sentence might be reduced—if you're willing to cooperate."

She raised a brow. "Cooperate how? What information could I possibly have that will help you?"

"You can tell me who killed your sister, for starters."

Pain exploded in her eyes. "Why on earth would I know who killed Teresa?"

Damn. Finn hid his disappointment as he stared into her shocked face. Just as he'd suspected, Valerie obviously had no idea who killed Teresa. But maybe she could still offer something of use to him.

"You two were close," he pressed. "She must have told you she was sleeping around on Cole. So tell me, who else was she involved with? We know about Ian Macintosh and Parker Smith, but there were more men."

Valerie's expression went shuttered and a spark of triumph lit Finn's body. Bingo. She definitely knew something about *that* particular subject.

"My sister was misunderstood," Valerie finally replied, her voice cool. "She only cheated on Cole because he neglected her. He was never here."

Finn waved a dismissive hand. "I'm not interested in her motives. Just names." When Valerie didn't answer, he hardened his tone. "Give me a name."

Her throat dipped as she swallowed. "I don't know who she was involved with."

"That's bull. Teresa told you everything."

"Not everything," Valerie muttered.

Sensing he'd hit a nerve, he instantly pounced on the opening she'd given him. "You must have been furious when you found out she had a kid and gave it up for adoption. When did she tell you about it?"

"She didn't," Valerie corrected, then snapped her mouth shut as she realized what she'd said.

Finn raised his eyebrows. "If she didn't tell you, how did you learn about Lucy?"

The resolve in Valerie's eyes crumbled. "A medical bill came in the mail," she admitted. "It was under my name, charging me for a few tests that weren't covered by my insurance. Only problem was, I never underwent any tests, especially from a hospital in Raleigh. So I called them, and was informed that I gave birth to a baby girl." She shook her head, incredulous. "I immediately put two and two together and realized what she'd done."

"So you seduced some poor guy at the adoption clinic to see who adopted your sister's baby," Finn finished. He cocked his head. "What else did you figure out?"

"What do you mean?" she mumbled.

"Do you know who the father is?" Valerie went quiet, triggering Finn's inner alarm system. "You do, don't you? Who is it, Val? Who did Teresa conceive that baby with?"

Her lips were set in a tight line. "I have no idea what you're talking about."

Anger simmered in his stomach. "Don't play games, Valerie. I promise you, if you give me the information I'm asking for, I will personally go to the judge and plead for a lighter sentence on your behalf."

Valerie's reluctance was palpable, but he also witnessed a glimmer of optimism. She knew he was a man of his word. He'd proven that to her by working furiously to solve her sister's murder, no matter how much he'd despised Teresa. He followed every lead, every shred of evidence, even when it led to people he cared about, people he longed to protect.

"I'll discuss it with my lawyer," Valerie finally said.

He ignored the crushing disappointment. "Get back to me after you've done that, then. But time is of the essence, Val. I can't solve your sister's murder unless I have every detail available to me."

"You already solved it," she shot back. "Sarah Connelly did it, and I hope she rots in hell."

"Sarah didn't kill anyone," he said coldly. "Which means there's still a killer on the loose. If you want vengeance for Teresa, I suggest you help this investigation rather than hinder it."

He decided to leave that as his parting words. Scraping back his chair, he got to his feet, just as a knock rapped against the door and Max poked his head into the room. Shifting awkwardly, the deputy lifted the bright yellow mug in his hand and said, "I brought Ms. Matthews the coffee she asked for."

Finn stifled a sigh. He shouldn't be surprised that Valerie was sending his deputy out to fill her drink orders. That woman had more nerve than most people.

As Max walked to the table and handed Valerie the cup, Finn gave her one last pointed look, then left the room and headed for his office. He was annoyed to find Parsons behind his desk, reading over the report Anna had typed up about yesterday's rescue.

Parsons lifted his head when Finn came in. "I thought I made myself clear about keeping me updated on all leads relating to the abduction."

"There was no time," Finn lied. "Cole Donovan's P.I.

called me about the gas station receipt from Holliday while you and Agent Bradley were interviewing Valerie's coworkers. I didn't want to interrupt you, I figured it would be a false alarm anyway, so I decided to take my deputies."

Parsons saw right through the fabrication. "You decided to take the credit, you mean." The agent glared at him. "I'm sick and tired of your unprofessional attitude, Finnegan. And just so you know, I've been in constant contact with Mayor Williams and I've made it clear to him where I stand in regard to your badge."

"Whisper whatever you want into the mayor's ear. The people of Serenade know who they voted for." Finn stepped forward. "Now if you'll excuse me, I need to go over some files, and I believe you're in my chair."

Although he didn't look at all pleased, Parsons relinquished the seat, tucking a file folder under his arm. "I'll be working at Deputy Patton's desk. I'm writing up a report for my supervisor about the abduction."

"Make sure you mention the part about me finding the baby," Finn couldn't help but bite out.

Parsons stalked out without another word, as Finn grinned to himself. Totally juvenile, maybe, but he liked ruffling Parsons's feathers. The guy was a narrow-minded ass.

Settling in his chair, Finn unlocked the top drawer of the desk and pulled out the folder containing the interviews he and his deputies had conducted after Teresa was killed. He retrieved the first sheet, the statement from Parker Smith. Smith was the young bartender Teresa had slept with, the only one whose name she'd revealed to Cole. Five minutes later, Finn reached for the next interview. He read each one carefully, trying to see if he'd missed something, but by the time he closed the folder, he hadn't learned anything new. Everyone they'd spoken to claimed to have heard Teresa bragging about her lovers, but not one person had a name to back it up with.

But Finn was certain one of those mysterious men was the key to everything. He was particularly interested in Lucy's biological father, but unless Teresa rose from the dead and spilled her carnal secrets, he had no clue how to uncover the identities of her lovers.

Glancing at the clock on his screen saver, he noticed it was past noon. He'd been reading for almost an hour, and now his stomach growled, reminding him he hadn't eaten all day. When he'd woken up this morning, his appetite had been nonexistent. There had been a painful rock in his stomach since he'd left Sarah's last night.

Four years ago, she'd begged him to stay.

Last night, she'd told him to leave.

And like the idiot he was, he'd walked out that door for a second time. Why hadn't he stayed and tried to make her see how sincere he was?

She's too scared to see it.

He released a breath, knowing it was the truth. Sarah was afraid of getting hurt again. And worse, having Lucy get hurt in the process. He knew her resistance to a relationship with him had a lot to do with the fact that she was a mother now, but he had no idea how to convince her that he would never leave her—or Lucy. He was already madly in love with that baby girl. And he was madly in love with her mother, too.

He just wished Sarah could trust him enough to believe it.

"We need an ambulance!"

The shrill shout jolted Finn from his thoughts.

What the hell?

Scrambling to his feet, he raced out of the office, slamming into Parsons in the bull pen. Both men exchanged a puzzled look, as Parsons said, "What is going on?"

The two men hurried toward the commotion, flying into the corridor at the same time Anna and Max skidded to a stop. Both deputies looked shocked and confused, and all eyes turned to the open door of the interrogation room Finn had left Valerie in.

He rushed to the doorway, his body going cold when he saw Robert McNeil, Valerie's attorney, down on the floor, bending over his client. McNeil looked up with frantic eyes. "Call the paramedics!" he exclaimed. "She's not breathing. I came back with lunch and found her on the floor—Jesus Christ, why weren't any of you people watching her?"

Sucking in a gulp of oxygen, Finn burst into the room and joined McNeil on the floor, where Valerie lay motionless. Her eyes were closed and her face was paler than snow, contrasting with the black hair fanned out beneath her. It was like Teresa Donovan all over again, except this time there was no blood, no sign to indicate what had happened to Valerie.

Finn shrugged off the attorney's shaking hands and lowered his head over Valerie, listening carefully. McNeil was right, she wasn't breathing. As dread snaked up his spine and chilled his chest, he placed two fingers on her neck and checked for a pulse.

Nothing.

No pulse.

Valerie was dead.

Chapter 15

Finn was stunned speechless as he staggered to his feet. He couldn't bring himself to look at Valerie's lifeless body. She was dead. But how? Why? He'd spoken to her only an hour ago, and she hadn't exhibited any signs of...well, of *going to die soon*. Was it a heart attack? A seizure?

His brain was running a million miles a second as he stepped into the hallway, where Parsons, Max and Anna waited, staring at him in shock.

"What's going on?" Anna asked in bewilderment.

"Valerie's dead."

Both Anna and Max gasped, while Parsons gave him his trademark scowl. "What the hell are you talking about, Finnegan? I spoke to her an hour ago."

"So did I." He raked his fingers through his hair. "And now she's dead. Anna, call the coroner, tell him to get over here ASAP. We need to find out what happened to her."

Anna rushed off with a word, nearly colliding with Parsons's colleague, Agent Andrews, in the doorway. The blonde federal agent apologized to the deputy, then hurried toward the three men, a sheet of paper clutched in her hand.

"Sir," she said to Parsons, her tone urgent. "I just—"

"Not now, Charlene," he snapped. "We have a situation here."

The woman protested, but Parsons was already turning to glare at Finn. "Who saw Matthews?" he demanded. "Who went in to talk to her today?"

Finn frowned. "Do you think she was killed?"

"I'm not ruling anything out." Parsons swore loudly. "I find it mighty suspicious that she dropped dead an hour after I accused her of having an accomplice."

Finn faltered. Parsons had accused her of that? He suddenly recalled his own chat with Valerie, his demand that she give up the names of Teresa's lovers. Parsons's accomplice theory wasn't that far from his own. For all Finn knew, Valerie *had* been working with someone—her sister's lover, perhaps.

He glanced through the open doorway, flinching at the sight of McNeil doing chest compressions on Valerie. The thin man looked shell-shocked as he counted softly to himself. It wasn't every day a lawyer found his client dead on the floor, and Finn suspected McNeil was in shock, judging from his glazed eyes.

He was also potentially destroying evidence. Jumping to action, Finn strode back into the room and laid a gentle hand on McNeil's shoulder. "She's gone," he said in a low voice. "You need to step away now, Mr. McNeil. The coroner works right across the street and will be here any second."

When the lawyer seemed reluctant, Finn added, "This is a possible crime scene. You need to step away."

Removing his hands from Valerie Matthews's chest, McNeil allowed Finn to help him to his feet. "Why don't you fix yourself a cup of coffee and sit down in the bull pen?" Finn suggested. "Someone will come and talk to you soon."

The lawyer walked away, looking numb.

Finn turned back to Parsons, picking up where they left off. "Okay, you and I were both in to see her. McNeil. Anna brought her a glass of water this morning."

"I brought her coffee after you spoke to her," Max piped up.

"Anyone else?" Parsons barked.

"Sir," Agent Andrews began, still clutching her paper. "I have—"

"Not now, Andrews," he cut in. "Who else was in that room?"

"Nobody," Finn said flatly.

"I guess Dr. Bennett could have seen her on his way to your office," Max offered. "Maybe he went in and—"

"Bennett?" Finn said sharply. "What are you talking about?"

Max looked confused. "I saw him in the lobby. He said he was coming to speak to you, so I told him to go on back to your office."

Finn's body stiffened. "The doc never came to see me, Max."

"What? But he said—"

"Can you people just listen to me?" came a piercing female voice.

Finn gaped at the petite blonde who'd yelled at them,

noticing for the first time just how panic-stricken she looked. And she was holding on to that piece of paper as if it contained state secrets or something.

"If you'd all just quit ignoring me, I might be able to shed some light on this situation," Agent Andrews said stiffly.

Parsons had the decency to look repentant. "What is it?"

"I followed up with Walter Brown like you asked me to." She turned to Finn, adding, "The man who hosted the party in Grayden, his gun was stolen? Anyway, he gave me a list of the people at the party, the ones from Serenade."

She shoved the paper in Finn's hands. "Most of them were older men who worked at the paper mill with Brown and didn't have any connection to Teresa. But look at the second-to-last name."

Finn stared at the neatly handwritten list, his eyes narrowing when he saw what she indicated. Dr. Travis Bennett.

"He was at that party the night the murder weapon was stolen?" Finn demanded.

Andrews nodded. "And get this, Brown remembers giving Bennett a tour of the house, a tour that included the study, where Brown showed Bennett the gun. Bennett even admired it, said he wished he had one of his own."

"Son of a bitch," Finn muttered.

Travis Bennett had attended Brown's party, the same night Brown's gun was stolen. And Bennett had been here just now, claiming he'd come to see the sheriff— yet he never found his way to Finn's office.

"Who's this Bennett?" Parsons demanded, furrowing his pale eyebrows. "The name never came up in the case files."

"Because there was no reason to connect him to any of this," Finn replied. "Travis runs the clinic, you probably walked by it when you were at the lab—it's in the same build—" Finn spit out a curse.

Bennett's clinic was in the same building as the lab. The lab where the trace evidence from the Donovan crime scene had been stored. The hair found next to Teresa's body, the fingerprint on the coffee table. When the tech had run the evidence, Sarah's DNA and fingerprint had been flagged.

"He framed her," Finn mumbled. "He switched the results. He must have gotten into Tom's computer and somehow changed the real results, so that Sarah's DNA, which was already in the system from that stupid high school project, would pop up."

"What are you muttering about?" Parsons grumbled.

"Or...or he could have switched the samples," Finn realized, growing sicker by the second. "He's her doctor—he could easily get her DNA, a fingerprint, and pin the murder on her."

"Finnegan," Parsons said sharply. "Fill us in here."

Finn rubbed the sudden ache in his temples. "I think Bennett framed Sarah for Teresa's murder. He must have been one of Teresa's lovers."

"That's a pretty big assumption," Parsons retorted.

"It makes sense. Bennett had access to the crime scene evidence, he could have easily tampered with the results. And he had opportunity to steal the murder weapon from Brown's house." He cursed. "And I think you were right—Valerie had an accomplice. It must have been Bennett, and he killed her to shut her up."

"Unless she died of natural causes," Parsons pointed out.

"She didn't," came a grim voice.

Len Kirsch, the coroner, briskly exited the interrogation room, unsnapping a pair of white gloves from his hands. Finn hadn't even seen the man arrive, but then again, his mind had been somewhere else.

"I believe Ms. Matthews suffocated to death," Kirsch announced, tucking the gloves in his medical bag. "I found petechial hemorrhages in her eyes, which is a sign of—"

"Petechial what?" Finn interrupted.

"Hemorrhages," the coroner repeated. "They're tiny red spots caused by areas of bleeding. It's usually indicative of suffocation."

Finn wrinkled his brow. "So she was smothered to death?"

Kirsch shook his head. "I'll run tests at the lab, but I don't think so. It looks like an internal suffocation, maybe induced by a drug. I found a small pinprick on the right side of her neck. I think she may have been injected with something." He clicked his tongue. "Most likely phenobarbital—it's used in physician-assisted euthanasia, stops the breathing reflex and causes death by suffocation."

The word *physician* stayed in Finn's mind. Bennett would have access to drugs like that. And Bennett had been here, less than an hour ago, without visiting Finn's office like he'd told Max.

"Damn, Finnegan, I think you're right," Parsons said in a grudging tone. He turned to Andrews. "Take Bradley and go to Bennett's office, try to bring him in without a fight. Say we just need to ask him a few questions and—"

"He won't be there," Finn interrupted, a sick feeling creeping up his chest.

Parsons frowned. "You think he skipped town already?"

"No." He swallowed down the bile lining his throat. "I think he's going to tie up loose ends. He's going after Sarah."

When the doorbell rang, Sarah experienced both a burst of joy and a pang of dread. She knew it must be Finn, here to deliver news about Valerie's questioning, but a part of her was terrified to look into his eyes and see that dull expression he'd donned yesterday. She knew she'd hurt him by refusing to jump headfirst into a relationship with him, but she wished he could see where she was coming from. They had so much baggage, she and Finn, a rocky history punctuated by him abandoning her in her darkest hour.

He'd accused her of being scared—well, of course she was scared! Not only of getting her heart broken again, but of letting her daughter grow used to Finn as a father figure. If he could have just offered to take things slow, really slow, she might have given him that chance he'd asked for. But with Finn, it was always all or nothing.

And so he'd forced her hand, pushed her into a decision she wasn't ready to make, and as a result, got the answer he hadn't been looking for.

With a sigh, she picked the baby monitor off the kitchen counter and headed to the front door. Lucy was sound asleep upstairs, after the busy morning they'd had in the backyard. They'd enjoyed the sunshine, Lucy wiggling around on a flannel blanket while Sarah just lay there, staring at her daughter, afraid to take her eyes off her for even a second.

The doorbell chimed once more, and when she opened the front door, she was startled to see Travis Bennett on her porch. "Travis? What are you doing here?"

"Can I come in?" he asked.

She hesitated for a moment, bothered by his appearance. He was normally perfectly kempt, his suits starched and pressed, not a hair on his head out of place. Right now, though, he looked extremely agitated. His tie was off-kilter, his sleeves rolled up haphazardly, and nervous sparks flickered in his dark eyes.

"Are you okay?" she asked cautiously.

He shifted in his feet. "Not really."

Never one to turn away a friend in need, she opened the door wider and gestured for him to come in. It wasn't until he stepped inside that she noticed he was holding something at his side. A large metal can.

She furrowed her brow. "What is that?" Her eyes narrowed as she stared at his hand. "Is that a *gas* can? What's going on, Travis? Why did you come here?"

"I'm here for my daughter."

Sarah's mouth fell open. "What?"

His eyes were wild as he repeated his statement. "I'm here for my daughter. Lucy."

She gasped, overcome by a surge of shock. What on earth was he saying? And why had he brought a gas can into her house?

Before she could speak, Travis lunged at her. He pushed her against the wall, his wrist pressed against her throat, making her gag. "I don't have a lot of time here, Sarah, so please, don't make this harder for either one of us." His voice came in ragged pants. "I just want my daughter."

"Your daughter?" she choked out. "Lucy's mine, Travis. I adopted her—"

"Because that whore gave her away!" he boomed. "She never even told me that I had a child! If I'd known, I never would have approved a damn adoption!"

Sarah tried to squirm out of his grip, but he held her against the wall, his face hard. "Teresa never gave me a choice," he hissed. "But I have a choice now, and I choose to be a father to my child."

She couldn't believe she was hearing this. Travis had been involved with Teresa? *Travis* was Lucy's father?

And then an even more terrifying thought occurred to her.

"You killed her," she gasped.

Regret flickered in his gaze. "That was a mistake."

Sarah gaped at him. "You *mistakenly* shot her in the heart?"

"I only brought the gun to show her that I meant business, to scare her into telling me what she did with our daughter. I gave her a chance to make amends, to tell me where Lucy was, but she just stood there and gloated about giving our child away. So I shot her."

The Travis she knew no longer seemed to exist. The grief and rage ravaging his normally pleasant face had transformed him into a stranger. She could picture the encounter he had described, perfectly envision Teresa taunting this man, the way she'd taunted everyone else. Despite the fear coursing through her body, Sarah actually experienced a spark of sympathy. Travis had lost his wife and two young sons a year before he moved to Serenade. Finding out he had a daughter, only to discover that the child had been given away without his consent…it must have crushed him, as badly as he'd been crushed when he lost his family in that fire.

Fire.

Her gaze dropped to the gas can. Oh, God. Was he planning on setting her house on fire? With her and Lucy inside it?

No, he wanted Lucy. He'd said so himself.

As if her ears were burning, Lucy's soft cry crackled from the baby monitor, causing both Sarah and Travis to look at it.

"Is that her?" His voice caught in his throat. "Is that my daughter?"

"She's *my* daughter," Sarah said softly.

His eyes blazed. "No! Nobody else is going to take her away from me, not even you, Sarah. Valerie and I had an arrangement, we would raise the baby together, but now that Valerie is out of the picture—"

Sarah gasped in interruption. "What?"

"She was going to tell the cops about my involvement in the kidnapping," Travis said defensively. "I couldn't let that happen."

"You were working together?" Sarah shook the cobwebs from her head. "Valerie joined forces with you even knowing you killed her sister?"

"She didn't know. Nobody knew. But now you do, and I'm sure the good sheriff has figured it out, too." He grabbed her by the collar and yanked her away from the wall. To her terror, he sloshed the gas can from side to side, dousing the walls and floor with gasoline as he pushed her toward the stairs.

Adrenaline spiked in her blood. He wasn't even armed, save for that metal can. She sidestepped, heart pounding. She had to make a run for it, race upstairs to get her baby before—

Pain crashed into the side of her face, making stars dance in front of her eyes.

"Don't even think about it," Travis snapped. "I'll knock you out and leave you in a puddle of gasoline if you try to escape. Now go up the stairs."

She should still fight. Kick him in the crotch, try to get to Lucy. But Travis was a tall man, stronger than her, and his threat of knocking her unconscious refused to leave her head. As long as she cooperated, he wouldn't hurt her. Not until he had Lucy, anyway. She didn't think he'd set fire to the place until he was out of the house, but she was scared he might panic if she fought him, and kill them all.

Taking a breath, Sarah slowly ascended the stairs, shooting Travis a sidelong look. "You framed me for the murder."

His voice was thick with remorse. "I had to. I tried pinning it on Donovan, but it didn't work. When you told me about the threat you made to Teresa, I figured I could use that."

"To cover up the fact that you're a killer?" she said darkly.

"I'm a *father*," he snapped back. "*I'm* the victim here. That bitch thought she could rob me of my child, even after I told her about the agony of losing my family. She deserved to die for what she did."

"And what about me?" she whispered. "Do I deserve to die?"

They reached the top of the stairs.

"No, you don't," he admitted. "But it's the only way."

"It doesn't have to be," she protested. "What if I let you see her? We could work out a visitation sched—"

"*Let* me see her?" he echoed in anger. "She's mine,

Sarah. Not yours. She was never yours. Now where is the nursery?"

She was going to lie, point in the other direction of the hall, but then Lucy started to wail, pretty much announcing her location. Travis gripped Sarah's arm and dragged her down the hall. She thought he would take her to the nursery, but then there was a blur of movement, and the next thing she knew, he was shoving her into the small bathroom across from the baby's room. Her butt landed on the tiled floor with a thump. She registered what had happened just as the door slammed.

Sarah launched herself at it, twisting the knob, but it didn't budge. There was a scraping noise, as if someone was dragging something across the floor. He was barricading the door, trapping her inside.

"Travis!" she screamed, pounding her fists on the door. "Let me out! Please, don't do this!"

There was no reply, only the muffled sound of Lucy's screams. Sarah darted to the bathtub, inhaled deeply, then took off at the door and slammed her shoulder into it. Pain streaked up and down her arm, but the door didn't move.

She couldn't hear Lucy crying anymore.

She kept throwing herself at the door, trying to break it open, but Travis had effectively locked her in. Fear pummeled at her, slapping her skin and bringing tears to her eyes.

"Travis! Don't *do* this!"

Her pleas went unanswered. She couldn't hear a damn thing behind the door. Not footsteps. Not Lucy. Nothing.

And then she smelled the smoke.

Chapter 16

Finn couldn't believe his eyes when the Jeep skidded to a stop in Sarah's driveway.

The house was on fire.

Feeling as though he'd been punched in the gut, he stared in horror at the orange flames licking at the curtains on the second floor. Smoke curled through the open windows, thick gray plumes rising up and getting carried away by the afternoon breeze. The smell of scorched wood drifted toward him, burning his nostrils as his passenger let out a piercing expletive.

"What the hell is going on?" Parsons demanded, opening the door handle and jumping from the vehicle.

Finn dove after him, stunned by what he was seeing. His shock reached a new high when he spotted the silver Lexus parked a few yards away on the dirt. He'd been so focused on the smoke and flames that he'd failed to notice the car. It wasn't Sarah's—she kept her station wagon in the garage.

Bennett.

"He's here," Finn burst out, already pulling his cell phone from his pocket. He tossed it to Parsons, who caught it in surprise. "Speed dial six," he barked. "Volunteer fire chief. Get him over here now!"

As his pulse drummed in his ears, he tore toward the porch, reaching the front door just as it swung open.

Travis Bennett stood in the doorway, his brown eyes wild, his arms clutching a confused Lucy, who let out a cry when she noticed Finn standing there.

Bennett blinked like a deer caught in headlights, then whirled around and ran back into the house. Finn lunged at the door but Bennett had locked it.

"Travis!" he shouted. "Open the door!"

He heard a muffled sound from inside, followed by Lucy's hearty wails. As adrenaline sizzled in his blood, Finn glanced over at Parsons, who had just hung up the phone. "Back door!" he ordered. "He might make a run for it!"

Parsons sprinted off without a word, removing his Glock from his holster as he disappeared around the side of the house. As the odor of smoke grew stronger, thicker, Finn went to work on the door, slamming his shoulders into it. He felt the lock give away and kicked open the door, bursting into the front hall. Smoke instantly filled his nostrils, making his eyes water like a leaky faucet. He coughed, covered his nose with his sleeve, then rushed down the hallway, following the sound of Lucy's cries.

The kitchen. Bennett was in the kitchen. But where was Sarah? He called her name, but there was no answer. The main floor of the house didn't seem to be ablaze. There was a canopy of smoke gathering on the ceiling, but he realized the fire must have been ignited upstairs. He registered the sharp scent of gasoline, noticing that the throw rug near the stairs was soaked. Christ, once the flames from above found their way downstairs, the whole place would turn into a raging inferno.

After a second of indecision, he raced to the kitchen, sliding into the room just as Bennett was stumbling to the patio door.

"Travis!" Finn barked. "Don't move."

Bennett ignored him, holding the baby in one arm as he fumbled for the doorknob. He'd just thrown open the door when Parsons appeared on the back lawn, his gun raised in an ominous pose.

Bennett spun around, only to find himself staring at the barrel of another weapon. Finn saw the panic enter the other man's eyes, the way his gaze dropped to the red-faced baby in his arms.

"Travis, there's no way out," Finn said quietly. "Give me the baby."

Bennett's face turned bright scarlet. "This is my daughter, Finnegan! I'm not giving her to you, or anybody else."

Smoke billowed in through the open doorway. Finn blinked rapidly, trying to ease the sting in his eyes, doing his best not to breathe too deeply. The fire upstairs was getting worse. He could feel the temperature rising, the heat bringing beads of sweat to his forehead. Bennett, too, was sweating, profusely, the acrid scent of his fear and desperation mingling with the smoky haze thickening the air.

"If you cared about your daughter, you would give her to Agent Parsons," Finn told the doctor. "The smoke can't be good for the baby. You're a doctor, Travis, you know this."

Bennett's flushed face became ash-white. As a physician, he was more than aware of the risks of smoke inhalation. And the way Lucy was gulping between sobs insured that smoke was finding its way into her tiny lungs.

"Oh, God," Bennett choked out. "Oh, my God, what am I doing?"

Finn didn't want to feel sympathy for this man. He didn't want to empathize with the agony swimming in Bennett's eyes. But he did. In that moment, he realized that Bennett wasn't an evil man. He was just broken.

"What's happening to me?" Bennett whispered. "I'm a doctor. I took an oath to *save* lives, not take them."

Finn stepped closer. "We need to get Lucy out of this house, Travis."

He glanced past Bennett's shoulders and noticed that the cavalry had arrived. Anna, Max and Jamie all stood behind the glass door. Jamie's violet eyes were lined with worry. Finn saw her look up, probably at the flames ravaging the second floor. Her expression went pale. The fire was bad. He could see it on her face.

"I want you to turn around and look outside," Finn said softly. "There's a woman standing there. Jamie Crawford. You knocked her unconscious when you broke into her house and took Lucy."

Tears streamed down the other man's cheeks, though Finn wasn't certain if due to the smoke filling the room, or from sorrow. Slowly, Travis turned and followed Finn's gaze.

"Give Lucy to Jamie," Finn said with patience he didn't feel. God, where the hell was Sarah? Her absence caused foreboding to climb up his spine, but he forced himself to focus on Bennett. "She'll take good care of Lucy, I promise you."

Bennett's large hand covered Lucy's head, as if he were trying to shield the child from the smoke. Glancing back at Finn, he began to cry in earnest. "I didn't want any of this to happen," the man stammered. "I didn't mean to kill her. I just couldn't lose another child. I couldn't do it again."

Finn's throat tightened. "I know. And believe me, I understand. Sarah and I lost a baby, four years ago. It was—" he took a breath, then coughed when he ended up drawing smoke into his chest "—the worst thing that's ever happened to me. I used the tragedy as an excuse to push the one person I cared about away, and I regret that now."

"There's no excuse for what I've done," Travis whispered. "I deserve to be punished. I deserve to be in prison."

"Get your daughter out of the house first. You can worry about everything else later."

Finn was convinced he had him. He saw Bennett's hand move to the doorknob, saw him start to turn it, but then the other man spun around, his eyes wide. "Sarah!" Bennett blurted out. "I locked her upstairs."

A sledgehammer of horror collided with Finn's chest. "You did *what?*"

"I…I j-just wanted my daughter." Moisture stained Bennett's face. "I have to go and save her!"

The man charged forward, but Finn blocked his path, gesturing to the group outside to approach the door. "You take care of Lucy. I'll get Sarah."

As Jamie and Agent Parsons entered the smoke-filled kitchen, Finn hurried off, hearing Jamie's soft encouragement as she gently took the baby from Travis Bennett. He didn't stick around to watch Parsons arrest the doctor—he just thundered out of the room, reaching the bottom of the stairs right as an enormous fiery beam broke apart from the ceiling and crashed onto the floor. Directly obstructing his path.

Sweat dripped down his face, the heat of the flames unbearable. As little orange wisps licked at his shoes, Finn stared in growing terror at the wall of fire between him and his only way to Sarah.

Sarah bent over as another coughing fit racked her body. She couldn't breathe. Couldn't draw a single puff of air into her aching lungs. The sting from the smoke made moisture pour from her eyes like water from a dam. After spending five minutes banging into the door, she'd finally given up, and the only fruits of her labor were bruises and an incredibly sore arm.

She refused to succumb to the panic, but she was starting to think she might actually die in this tiny bathroom. The crack beneath the door seemed to be glowing. It terrified her to think what lay behind the door. Yellow-orange flames, a black tunnel of smoke. At least she could die knowing that Lucy was safe. She was certain Travis had already whisked her daughter out of the house.

Burying her face in her sleeve, she took a breath, then held it. She couldn't decide what would be worse—burning to death, or dying from the smoke inhalation.

Probably the burning to death part. At least with the smoke she would pass out first.

You are not going to die. Think, Sarah!

She peered through the smoke, studying the window over the toilet. It wasn't very big, probably too tight a fit for her, but hell, she had to try *something*.

She stood on the toilet seat, fighting a wave of dizziness. God, she felt like she was going to faint. She could hardly breathe anymore. Had she ever even opened this window before? For all she knew it was welded shut.

She flicked the lock to the side and pushed against the pane, relief soaring through her when the window creaked open. She stuck her head out and gulped fervently, her chest heaving as the fresh air slid into her body. Dizzy again, this time from the rush of oxygen, but then her head began to clear, and she realized in disappointment that the ground below was scarily far away. It was a twenty-foot drop, at least. She'd break her neck if she tried to jump.

Or you might survive...

Sarah looked at the door, swallowing when she spotted the wisps of smoke curling beneath the doorway. And the wood seemed to be...splintering. Oh, God. The white paint was turning black!

Fighting a jolt of panic, she stuck her head out the window again. She couldn't believe how bright it was. The sun was shining and she could even hear the damn birds chirping. Another glance at the door showed the wood was beginning to crack. Taking a breath, she peered outside and shouted, "Help!" at the top of her lungs.

She expected nothing but silence in response, but to her shock, she suddenly heard Finn's voice.

"Sarah?"

And then he was racing around the side of the house, his blue eyes staring at her in terror. "Sarah!" he yelled. "Christ, you don't know how happy I am to see you!"

Relief flooded her body. "Finn! You have to get me out of here!"

"The fire department volunteers will be here in less than ten minutes. Are you all right up there? How bad is the smoke?"

She glanced behind her, fear clamping around her throat when she saw the hungry flames eating at the charred skeleton of the door. The fire crackled, snaking into the bathroom, then licked at the white shower curtains.

"The room is on fire!" she called down to Finn, her heart pounding.

Even from high above, she could see the unhappiness creasing his handsome features. "Then we don't have any time, sweetheart. You're going to have to jump."

Her stomach clenched with fear. "I can't! It's too high."

"Sarah, listen to me. I want you to lower yourself out the window."

"I can't!"

"Yes, you can." Assurance rang from his tone. "You can do it. Just climb out and let yourself hang. When I say the word, let go."

The flames crept closer, causing the flowered wallpaper to peel and burn. Finn was right. She had no choice but to get out of here. Not unless she wanted to kiss her life goodbye.

Ignoring the panicked butterflies taking flight in her stomach, she pulled herself up onto the window ledge, then lowered herself through the tight space, backward. Letting her legs dangle, just as Finn told her to. She refused to look down. Heights had always been her biggest weakness. She didn't even own a ladder, damn it. That's how scared she was of not having her feet touch the ground.

"Now let go," Finn shouted from below.

Let go?

"I'm here," he added. "I'll catch you."

She sucked in a burst of air, feeling light-headed again. Oh, God. What if he missed? What if she tumbled to the ground and smashed her head in? Her chest heaved, tight with fear, and she couldn't help but twist her head so she could look down at Finn.

To her astonishment, his blue eyes shone with calm determination. "Don't be scared." His husky voice drifted up and wrapped around her heart like a warm embrace. "Take that leap of faith, baby. I promise, I'll catch you."

He was talking about more than just this moment. About more than this jump. Sarah's heart pounded. This was it. Crunch time. Decide once and for all whether she was willing to love Finn again.

When did you stop?

The thought flew into her head, making her swallow hard. She hadn't. She *hadn't* stopped loving him. Not for one single second.

Take that leap of faith.

Sarah couldn't help herself. She began to laugh. There she was dangling twenty feet off the ground, while fire ravaged her home, and yet her heart felt so full she feared it might burst. She *loved* Patrick Finnegan.

"Finn…I'm letting go now."

And then she was soaring through the air, sinking, falling. True to his word, Finn caught her. She landed in his strong arms with a thump, her entire body shaking as it came down from the adrenaline high. Rather than set her on her feet, Finn just supported her bottom and shoulders, and pulled her close, his relief trembling through him. As tears slid down her soot-covered face, Sarah wrapped her arms around his neck and clung to him.

"You caught me," she whispered.

He bent down to look in her eyes, and she saw love shining on his face. "Of course I did," he said thickly. "I told you I would."

Disappointment shuddered inside her when he finally put her down, but then his palms were cupping her chin and his mouth came down over hers in a kiss. "I love you, Sarah," he murmured. "I love you so damn much."

She opened her mouth but he placed his index finger against it, his features taut as he rushed on. "And I'm going to give you all the time you need. I should have never pushed you to make a decision. I was just being my usual, bullheaded self, but I see now that it wasn't fair to either one of us. If you want to be with me, it should be your decision, not the result of an ultimatum that I—"

"I love you."

He faltered, his blue eyes filling with shock. "What?"

This time she was the one putting a finger against his lips. "I love you, Finn. I'm not scared to say it anymore."

His throat bobbed as he visibly swallowed. "What are you saying?"

"I'm saying I don't need time." Joy soared up her chest and surrounded her heart. "I'm saying I want to be with you. I want you and me and Lucy to be a family and—Lucy!" she suddenly cried. "Travis—"

"Jamie took her to the hospital in Grayden, to make sure she didn't inhale too much smoke," Finn cut in, a smile lifting his mouth. "Travis gave himself up. Parsons already took him back to the station."

She couldn't bring herself to voice her next words, but she forced them out. "Then...it's over?"

Finn stroked her cheek so tenderly that tears sprung to her eyes. "It's over, sweetheart. Bennett confessed to killing Teresa—the D.A. will have no choice but to drop the charges against you."

With a happy shout, Sarah threw herself into his arms again, basking in the warmth of his embrace, the feel of his lips pressing against the top of her head. She could've stayed there forever, but then the sound of sirens blared in the air and they both turned to see the town's fire truck racing up her driveway. The reminder had her looking at the house, disbelief flooding her body as she stared at the flames engulfing the entire second floor of her home.

"I..." She tipped her head to meet Finn's eyes. "I guess I'll be moving in with you after all."

Regret lined his forehead. "There's no pressure, Sarah. You don't have to do anything you don't feel comfortable with."

"I don't have to," she agreed. "But I *want* to."

Finn's smile lit up his entire face. "Are you sure?"

"I'm more than sure."

Taking his hand, she led him away from the house. Serenade's volunteer firefighters were already springing to action, aiming hoses at the flames and working to control the blazing conflagration. Sarah and Finn kept walking, neither one looking back. When they reached Finn's Jeep, Sarah pressed her body to his and yanked his head down for a soft kiss. There was a fleeting brush of her lips against his, and then she pulled back and said, "Come on, Patrick. Let's go to the hospital and see our daughter."

Raw, all-consuming emotion flooded his gorgeous

blue eyes. He dipped his head to kiss her once more, then took her hand and murmured, "I can't think of anything else I want to do more."

Epilogue

Two Weeks Later

"Are you really okay with Lucy coming along on our honeymoon?"

Sarah fought a pang of distress as she waited for her husband's answer, but when she looked into his eyes, she saw only warmth and sincerity reflecting back at her. "Lucy is part of our family," Finn said thickly. "Of course I want her with us."

She couldn't control the rush of happiness that filled every inch of her body. Shifting her head, she gazed at Cole and Jamie, who were sitting on the wooden steps of Finn's deck, fussing over Lucy. The couple looked absolutely smitten, Jamie fixing the hem of Lucy's filmy white dress, while Cole tickled the baby's tummy and said something that made his fiancée laugh.

"Jamie will be disappointed," she said with a grin.

"She and Cole were hoping to practice being parents. They're planning on having like a hundred babies."

"So am I," Finn said with a grin.

Her heart jammed in her throat as she wondered how she'd gotten so lucky. Finn had been so damn wonderful these past two weeks. With Travis Bennett arrested for the murder of Teresa Donovan, Serenade had returned to its peaceful, crime-free state, leaving Finn plenty of time to lavish Sarah and Lucy with love and attention during the days. And at night… Her cheeks went hot as she thought of all the passionate nights they'd been sharing. The bad boy she'd fallen in love with always made a reappearance in bed.

Her gaze dropped to the simple silver band around the finger of her left hand. Her husband. It had taken them four years to find their way back to each other. She almost wept when she thought of all the wasted time, all the senseless heartache.

Sarah quickly pushed away thoughts of the past. She and Finn were married now, having just exchanged their vows in a quiet, private ceremony in the backyard of their farmhouse. They had the rest of their lives to make up for all the time they'd lost.

"Well, if you want more babies, then we should definitely get a head start in Aruba." Sarah arched a brow. "Making babies is hard work, you know."

Heat flickered in his eyes. "Guess we'll just have to suck it up and muddle through all the…ugh…sex."

Sarah burst out laughing. "Poor Finn. Don't worry, I'll make it painless for you." She swept her gaze over him. "By the way, did I tell you how sexy you look in that suit?"

"Not half as sexy as you look in that dress."

She glanced down at her white empire-waist dress

with the slender black ribbon wrapped around the bodice. She and Jamie had found it in a boutique in the city, and from the appreciation glittering in Finn's blue eyes, she decided the huge price tag had been worth it. She loved the way Finn looked at her. Like she was the most beautiful creature on this planet.

"Seriously, I'm digging the dress," he went on. "It looks good on you." He lifted an eyebrow. "It would look even better on the bedroom floor, though."

Another laugh pealed out of her chest. "That might be the worst pickup line I've ever heard."

"Did it work?"

Hot streaks of awareness sizzled between them. She stared at her husband, at the black jacket stretched over his broad shoulders, the trim fit of his trousers, and a healthy dose of desire found its way into her bloodstream.

Sarah slanted her head. "Right now? No. But say it again in Aruba, after Lucy's fallen asleep, and you might get a different answer," she said with a faint smile.

"I'm counting on it." Flashing her a grin, he took her hand. "Come on, Mrs. Finnegan. Let's say goodbye to our guests."

"What's the rush?" she teased.

His voice was husky as he said, "Just eager to start our life together. Got a problem with that?"

She leaned on her tiptoes and brushed a kiss over his mouth. "Nope, I don't have a single problem with that."

"Good."

Still grinning, he led her across the yard, where their daughter—and their future—awaited.

* * * * *

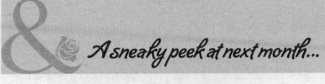

A sneaky peek at next month...

INTRIGUE...

BREATHTAKING ROMANTIC SUSPENSE

My wish list for next month's titles...

In stores from 18th May 2012:

❏ A Daughter's Perfect Secret – Kimberly Van Meter

& Lawman Lover – Lisa Childs

❏ Operation Midnight – Justine Davis

& A Wanted Man – Alana Matthews

❏ High-Stakes Affair – Gail Barrett

& Deadly Reckoning – Elle James

❏ Cowboy's Triplet Trouble – Carla Cassidy

Available at WHSmith, Tesco, Asda, Eason, Amazon and Apple

Just can't wait?

0512/46

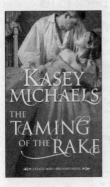
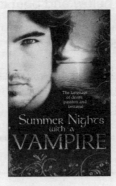
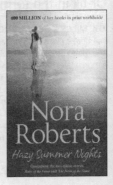

The World of Mills & Boon®

There's a Mills & Boon® series that's perfect for you. We publish ten series and with new titles every month, you never have to wait long for your favourite to come along.

Blaze.
Scorching hot, sexy reads

By Request
Relive the romance with the best of the best

Cherish
Romance to melt the heart every time

Desire
Passionate and dramatic love stories

Visit us Online
Browse our books before you buy online at
www.millsandboon.co.uk